CW01430506

HEARTTHEFT

APOCRYPHA

RUKIS

HeartTheft Book 2: Apocrypha

Production copyright FurPlanet Productions © 2024

Copyright © Rukis 2024

Cover Artwork and illustrations © Rukis 2024

Published by FurPlanet Productions
Dallas, Texas
www.FurPlanet.com

eBook ISBN 978-1-61450-624-9
Paperback ISBN 978-1-61450-623-2

First Edition Trade Paperback 2024

All rights reserved. No portion of this work may be reproduced in any form, in any medium, without the expressed permission of the author.

This is a work of fiction. All characters and events portrayed within are fictitious.

CONTENTS

A FOREWORD FROM THE AUTHOR

HeartTheft is part of a collection of novels in the *Red Lantern* universe, a Historical Fiction setting that is not intended to be analogous for the real world, at any set point in time. The characters, places, events, religious practices, and cultures in this world are also not intended to be compared to reality, either past or present. It is a fictional setting, and the opinions and thoughts of its characters are similarly fictional. These animal people are not role models. They are flawed and messy, as is their world.

While my writing is inspired heavily by history, my own lived experience, and the lived experiences of others, I did not create *Red Lantern* as an analogy for our human world. *Red Lantern* is meant first and foremost as entertainment and to inspire creativity, open-mindedness, and empathy for those around you.

This book contains themes some may find uncomfortable or hard to read, including:
Violence, Sexual Content, Religious and Familial Abuse, Self Harm, Substance Abuse, and Suicide.

If you or anyone you know or love is considering suicide, or would like emotional support, the 988 Lifeline network is available 24/7 across the United States.

OH FATHER, DELIVER US
FROM SIN

I had gotten so accustomed to breaching personal space during my time with Darcy, not to mention many other improprieties, that I very nearly collided with my Father Helstrom in the same way Malachi had done so with me when we finally laid eyes upon one another.

He saw us from across the yard at the Ministry Office, no doubt freshly-awakened by the chiming of the arrival bells from the gate. His fur was as unkempt as it got for a man as neat and tidy as he, but moreover, his ears and eyes were still wet from where he'd splashed water on them hurriedly. Bloodhounds, I was given to believe—and *especially* Father Helstrom—were near regimental about face-washing, given the wrinkles and the tendency their ears had to dip into and brush over everything. It had always been a bit of a game at the dining table amongst the kids to try to keep ourselves from alerting him to the fact when Father had gotten soup on his ears, or pudding, or any number of other things. Nicholas was usually the one who gave it away by snickering first.

I had never been so happy to see my Father and his wet ears. I strode across the courtyard as quickly as I could without breaking into a run, and he did the same, and we only just barely managed to catch ourselves when we were but a few feet apart before we embarrassed ourselves.

"Father," I greeted him, panting and smiling, instead.

"Son," he said, keeping his tone repressed, but relieved.

"Oh, come on, you two," Malachi piped up from over my shoulder. "You can do better than that. To hell with decorum, Isidor, this man thought you were dead. God wants you both to rejoice in this moment. Trust me."

I don't know why, but even as an outsider, Malachi's affirmation seemed to be all it took. I looked once more to my father to be sure, but when his jowls turned up in a rare smile, I knew I had my go-ahead.

I leaned in and loosely wrapped an arm around his shoulder as he did the same to me on the opposite side. It was polite, gentle, and exactly right for the two of us. It reminded me of how he'd handled me when I was younger. The nights he'd come and feed me broth when I was having stomach pains, sitting beside me on my bunk and rubbing my back until I fell asleep.

"I suppose there are instances that warrant eschewing the five-paw distance," he relented, his hand holding tight to my shoulder despite the rectitude he was holding fast to with his overall countenance.

"I missed you, Father," I said.

He chuckled, his voice a little rough around the edges. He sounded tired, and I wondered how much sleep he'd really gotten. "How saccharine," he tutted at me. "You always *were* my most sensitive whelp."

I laughed back breathlessly in response. "Perhaps I got it from my Father, then. Malachi said you took *every* swift carriage in the land you could find, back-to-back, to make it out here as fast as you did."

"I'd prepared to come here to assist in the Investigation in

2

Redcoven *before* I was informed that you'd been harmed in an attempted arrest," he said, his sunken eyes becoming a bit sharper, a bit fiercer, when he said as much. "I only sped up my trip because you went and did something foolish, child. But you are hardly alone in your trespasses. Your superiors here did nothing to dissuade you—" he said with a flick of a glare at Malachi, "-and in fact *further* bent away from reason by ignoring Ministry protocol. Protocol you know far better than my young trainee, Inquisitor Malachi."

Malachi dropped his eyes from Father Helstrom's wilting glare just as quickly as I did and mimicked the subservient position I found myself taking up by instinct, stood at attention with our hands at our sides, heads bowed. We both knew how to get through a talking-to by our Fathers.

"I'm still endeavoring to catch up on how many breaches in conduct I will need to report for the both of you, by the way," Father sighed long-sufferingly. "Suffice it to say, your debriefing later will be long, and unpleasant. It cannot be helped."

"Later?" Malachi asked, lifting his head a moment. "I'd thought we'd be getting to that right-off."

"First is a cleansing and physical inspection for my son," my Father said with a shake of his head. "Most important, given," and here he looked to me with the faintest trace of fear in the recesses of his eyes, "what I can only assume was... an arduous week spent as a prisoner or a hostage of this criminal."

Oh, God. I had to lie to my Father's face, right now, because Malachi stood at my side. I couldn't tell him the whole truth. Not *yet*. I considered how I'd pick my way around the words. On the road, I'd given Malachi the broad strokes of our practiced story, and he'd believed it as far as I could tell. But I couldn't even lie to my Father about taking an extra apple at dinner without being seen through. How was I going to do this?

"Oh, of course," Malachi said in response to Helstrom. "Get

3

him cleaned up and looked over, yeah. Can't give a report faithfully if you're run-down and dirty. Been there."

"Was my guess correct, then?" Father said, his eyes locked on mine—they had been this entire time—intense beyond his usual severe expression, which was saying something because he was *always* intense. His eyes said he wanted something from me. I could only pray I knew what it was. "Given we received no demands or a ransom letter, it was captivity or death, and you stand before me, so..." he continued, trailing off and giving me space to speak. *Compelling* me to speak.

"Yes," I said, trying not to squawk out the word. "I was not taken from the city though, I was even more foolish than you likely realize, Father. I went out there to Dyre Point on my own, intentionally. I was convinced I could scout the area and report back, but—"

"It's ten miles away," Malachi filled in for me. "In good country, that'd be nothing. A jaunt. On a swift horse, if you know the countryside? Two hours, maybe. The roads are overgrown, but it seems like there's still a clear enough path. *If* you know where you're going. Brother Dolus and I had trouble finding the old road. And this one," he jerked a thumb back at me, "went out in a bleeding snowstorm, while he was still ailing from the last bit of bad weather he'd been caught out in."

Now *I* was on the receiving end of Father Helstrom's infamous glare. I felt his eyes boring into my soul, and I shrunk back like I was a child again.

"And I can only assume based on how long it took them to deduce where you'd gone," Father said, "that you acted while knowing full well you were superseding your authority, because you did not tell anyone where you were scouting. Did you?"

I hung my head again. "No, sir. I mean... yes. You are correct. I did not inform anyone where I was headed because I couldn't have explained where I got the information."

Malachi was swinging the now unlocked manacles he'd

taken off me on the ride over on one of his large, clawed fingers, snuffing at me. "I wouldn't have cared, Brother. Wouldn't have told anyone, either. I should have thought of it myself, ashamed I didn't, really. We could've just claimed I was half as clever as you. We need to get your young lad here through his Ministry training so we can get him documented and ready to work, Father. He's got a *gift* for this. I'd be happy to work under him as his Enforcer when he's ready for it. I haven't had a partner in years, but we ran this one down quick. I think we'd get on well. Complement each other well."

I looked back at him, shocked. Malachi was eight years my senior and an experienced Inquisitor to boot, yet what he was offering was very clearly to work beneath me once I was—and this was assuming quite a lot—appointed as an Investigator by the Ministry. Enforcers were exactly what they sounded like, and while it wasn't necessarily a lesser rank in rights and privileges, they generally didn't take the lead in investigations. They enforced orders, thus the name. I'd long suspected Brother Dolus was an Enforcer. He rarely seemed to research his tasks; he was usually dispatched via a messenger from up on high.

"*You*, young man," Father said to Malachi, "need watch your tongue. Especially where it concerns my son. You just confessed to yet another trespass I would need report on if I was your handler. If my son here was accessing information he wasn't privy to, you shouldn't be *enabling* him or excusing the behavior."

Malachi shut his mouth quickly.

"I would need to report it, as I said... If I was your handler," the bloodhound said, arching an eyebrow. "Speaking of, your own Father is as eager to hear back from your venture today as I have been. You're not hurt, are you? Do you need to see the Cloistered Physician as well?"

"No, the thief ran," Malachi sighed. "As far as we know. Isidor seemed certain anyway, and I trust he knows them better at this point than we do. Your Brother Dolus is up there trying to run them down though, for all the good that will do. I think we were just a bit too late. As ever."

"So long as it gave my son a chance to escape, we've still done God's work this day," Father said, tugging at the beads of his rosary where they were wrapped—tightly, I realized—around his wrist. A habit I'd had myself in the past when I was younger, whenever I got nervous. It was odd to think my father figure may have picked it up from *me*, although more likely, I realized, that I'd gotten it from him. Oddly endearing, too.

"I honestly can't believe it took you as long as it did," Malachi said, patting me on the back a bit too hard, as he was wont to. "Did you have your kit on you? You got the one cuff off. They couldn't have had eyes on you every waking moment."

"They kept me manacled to a bed for a while," I answered truthfully. "Too far from my things."

"What in Ciraberos's name did you *do* for a week up there?" Malachi wondered aloud.

I froze.

"I've done my own time in repentance and lock-down at a camp," he said casually, referencing a place of reformation I only knew the fringe horrors of. It was like talk of Hell, used to frighten children away from immoral behavior. 'Don't go breaking your Father's heart or they'll be sending you to a Reformation Camp'. I knew little of what happened at them, truth be told. "...but they tend to keep you busy there," he said, eyes going distant for a moment, before he shook his head and plastered that big wolfish smile back on to his muzzle. "I've done a lot and seen much of the world, but I can't say I've spent time in solitary confinement or prison yet. Wouldn't want that much time with my own thoughts though, I'll tell you that much."

"It was very difficult," I agreed softly.

"Isidor," Father Helstrom's voice came back into the

conversation, grounding me with his uncanny, deep baritone pushed down low but always somewhat evident. Bloodhounds had the most powerful voices of all canine kin when they wanted to exercise that gift. I had rarely heard my father bay or yell, but even the few times he'd gotten close, it was blood-curdling. The timbre of that distinctive voice was like the singing of a seasoned blade as it was pulled from its sheath, promising that if used, it could become the battle cry it once had been.

All of this, I felt in my Father's voice, most particularly in that moment. Deadly seriousness and command. It was like when he'd stared at me just minutes ago. Telling me to comply without telling me.

"I know my son," he said, "and I know your mind. You stayed willingly, didn't you?"

My throat went dry. I searched his eyes, trying to discern what he wanted from me. The cryptic message in that letter, the fact that he'd rushed out here before he'd even known I'd been captured, and the way he was speaking to me right now. Not like a child. Not even like a young man under his care.

This was the Inquisitor inside my father's skin that I had never seen. The being who had retired from service before I'd even known him. I'd seen shades of who he'd once been, throughout the years—every child at Ebon Gables had—but only hints. Wielded for intimidation, revealed carefully to keep us in line, to make sure we knew we could not deceive our Father. The shadows of his time in service were little more than a cudgel slapped in a palm, to keep us all on the upright path. That's all I had ever seen of it.

Until now. This… this was Germain Helstrom the Inquisitor.

He couldn't have possibly trusted Malachi more than I did, he hardly knew him and my father's trust was *not* easily won. So why, then, did he want me to talk about this in front of him?

"You were trying to flip him," he said coolly. Calmly. And

with a certainty that was either genuine or a *very* convincing lie. I began to see…

Malachi seemed surprised. "Is that true?"

"Isidor is fresh from academic training and new to fieldwork," Father explained. "He has a more optimistic, clean outlook on what he thinks this work will be like, Brother Malachi. I know because I raised him, and I know precisely how fervently he believes in the importance of redemption. You were particularly keen on the transformation of criminals to Ministry assets, if I remember correctly. The Gilbriar case comes to mind. We had many debates on that trial while it was ongoing."

"That sodding ferret," Malachi growled, irritably. "Murders a city patrolman and thinks the world owes him to slip the noose just because he's got dirt on a Pedigree or two."

"Gilbriar owned a printing press that was being used to spread anti-theistic propaganda funded by a corrupt Burgher," I said, standing up for that very case, as I had in fierce debates with my Father and the monks nearly a year ago when it had happened. "Flipping him meant unearthing the whole network spreading those leaflets across the countryside, and that *mattered*. I saw one of the leaflets. Heresy like that does not need to be whispered about in public houses by the common folk."

"Most of them can't read it, anyway," Malachi muttered.

"Atheism is a passing folly for the young and privileged," Father asserted. "And to those fool enough to deny God when they should be wiser by the world, I say the Word is already lost on their ears. Let them embrace hopeless, fearful lives if that is their predilection; our efforts should be for those deserving of His Grace. And murderers should be punished, no matter what."

"The Heart Thief isn't a murderer," I blurted out.

Both men stopped and stared at me, Malachi in shock, Father Helstrom with a piercing glare. I shrunk from it less than I had in the past.

"Oh, hell," Malachi uttered. "You *did* get information out of him, didn't you? We dealing with collaborators, then? An organization?"

"So, I've guessed correctly, then," Father Helstrom said, getting us back on point. "You were trying to turn her—"

"Him," Malachi said.

"-it hardly matters, does it?"

"I couldn't agree more," I murmured.

"-turn *them*," Father said impatiently, "into some kind of asset with promises of salvation?"

It wasn't entirely an incorrect statement. So, I just nodded.

"I'm assuming there's more of a network of thieves at work here," the bloodhound said. "We've always assumed that. But, lad, this isn't mere theft. It's heresy. Your heart may have been in the right place, but..." he sighed, taking a few moments to compose himself. "Alright, well. You doubtless got useful information out of them over the course of a week. You've a clever tongue in that head. Let's hear it all once you're cleaned up and ready."

He extended an arm to me, waving me onwards ahead of him, towards the Ministry building.

"Keep the cloak," Malachi called, as he began to head for the gate and to his own keeper. "You don't seem to have an all-weather cloak of any quality of your own, Brother. Please, consider it a gift."

"Malachi, I can't—"

"Enough, let him," my father urged, dropping his voice. "The young man's fond of you, clearly. It's a kind gift, and one you could use. Don't be rude."

I nodded and turned over my shoulder to loudly thank Malachi as he left. He gave me a last smile and a hand up as he jogged off, making his way down the road towards the Church.

"I can bathe outside," I began when I turned back towards

my father. "There's a communal area at the Church actually, if you'd rather—"

"You are going exactly nowhere within scent range of anyone else in the Ministry until I scrub you raw," my father snapped suddenly.

I was taken aback. His tone had changed very swiftly after Malachi had left.

"You are following me to my quarters; there's a small tub in the adjoining room," he said, glancing through the window of the side door into the residences at the Ministry building. Once he confirmed it was clear, he opened it and ushered me inside. "You are keeping that cloak on, and once we've got you cleaned up, then you can explain to me why you reek of feline and mead."

I was caught. I hardly knew what to say except, "It's that strong?"

"I cannot say." He scrunched up his nose a moment. "My sense of smell is better than most canines'. If Brother Malachi noticed, he was good enough not to say anything, or he didn't require an explanation because he is simple. I don't know the man well."

"He's not..." I trailed off. 'Simple' wasn't the term I'd use for the malamute. For some reason, my mind kept going to 'pure'. I'd seen a dark streak in him, but it was clear it was exactly what they'd tried to foster in all of us—our predatory instinct, plus training on how exactly to employ it as an intimidation factor. I wasn't certain how much of it was real.

"He seemed to believe the story about converting the thief to an asset, at least," he muttered, all but pushing me down the hallway towards whatever one of these doors was his.

"It's true, from a certain perspective."

"Enough, boy," he hurried me forward. "I always worried you were too earnest for this work. Not until we're *alone*."

We walked into the banal stone building the Ministry

headquartered in here in Redcoven. Other than the red symbol of the Templar Order emblazoned on the front door, you could have easily overlooked this building. I remembered thinking the same when I'd first glimpsed it during my arrival in Redcoven. I'd always preferred the near-ascetic lifestyle of Templar to the idea to chasing any thoughts of grandeur, wealth, or prestige. All that talk Father Helstrom and Brother Dolus and the elder monks made about the temptations of the world and how men faltered in their devotion to the Order for such pursuits... I'd never thought any of it would apply to me. I didn't need a fine house, servants, silk clothing, or exotic luxuries. I didn't want power in the military or the navy, and I shuddered at the thought of Court. I wasn't looking to become a Knight.

I'd overlooked companionship as a want that might unravel me. But now, here, I found myself earnestly asking whether I'd give this all up—my life's passion, the only vocation I'd ever considered, and the connections to my adoptive family—all of it. Over one person.

One person I very much wanted to help. And know. And...

I was about to get naked in the same room with my Father. Now was emphatically *not* the time.

There was just never a good time to think of Darcy.

"I..." I stopped when we reached the door and watched as Father leaned a bit more heavily on his cane so that he could drop down to briefly glance under the crack in the door. A habit of his I was beginning to understand. I saw the velvety tips of his ears twitch as he 'perked' them to listen and gave him silence while he did so. After he seemed satisfied, I continued, "I really was trying to understand them, Father. And I truly am hoping for a path towards redemption."

"For this thief?" he asked, turning to regard me with hard eyes. "Or yourself?"

He opened the door, and while I was stammering, said, "Do not answer that. Not yet."

"Yes, Sir," I said quietly.

He led me inside, then shut the door, and stood there a moment, rubbing a wrinkled palm over his even more wrinkled face. When he finally scrubbed the folds over his eyes for the last time and regarded me, he looked less fierce, but no less exhausted.

"Son," he whispered, "what have you gotten yourself into?"

Father Helstrom took me into the adjoining wash room, which was for use by three separate rooms all connected to it with a doorway of their own. He left the room while I undressed, insistent upon checking to ensure the other two rooms were unoccupied. Then, when he returned, he tested and locked each of the doors into the wash room all the same.

By that point, I'd done us both a favor and gotten undressed and wrapped in a bathing robe. The tub already had water in it. It looked like he'd had it filled the night before to wash the road off, but wasting more water than necessary during the winter out here was not advisable. They refilled the tubs once a day, he explained. In the evenings. No chance we were walked in on.

The water was cold, but he set to boiling a pot to render the whole of it lukewarm once we dumped it in. And while we waited, he pulled up two small bath stools, hunkered down in front of me in the tiny, humid room with one small candle flickering away and no window, only a pipe from the small stove used to heat the water out, and a second to vent the steam... and held his hands out to me.

I had given Confession under a number of circumstances over the last few months that I never would have expected. Nearly nude—sitting on a bath stool while I waited to get the cat and booze scrubbed out of my fur by my Father—was not one I would normally have relished, I think.

And yet, I was so, *so* relieved to talk to him. To a man I

trusted, whom I knew would keep this conversation between us and God. I didn't care. I reached back out for his hands all but immediately, the story and the questions and the *fears* all vying for my attention to come first.

He took a long, steadying breath, and so did I.

"When last we spoke," he said measuredly, "I had concerns about this case. But not *you*, Isidor." He almost sounded hurt when he said that. "Never you. You've always been such a *good* boy. Not one of my children I ever thought I'd have to protect from his own worst inclinations. The world, perhaps. You've always been curious, thoughtful, even to your detriment, your head always lost in a book or a cloud. I worried you'd be taken advantage of. By your Patron Lord someday, or in marriage, even by the Ministry itself."

"Perhaps I have been," I said. "Perhaps we *all* have been. Even you said you had concerns about this case, Father. I… we need to talk about that…"

"First, you will tell me what the Hell has been happening to *you*," he said, narrowing his eyes. "*You* are my first priority here, Isidor. The case can wait."

I was touched briefly until he began to recite the Confessional prayer. My hands quaked. I closed my eyes and tried to center myself. Tried to reach out for even a small thread of that certainty I'd felt the night before. My inner voice, assuring me I was in fact, despite all appearances, pursuing a path that God would approve of. I hesitate to say He'd 'chosen' it for me because it was impossible to deny I'd made a lot of my own decisions to come this far. But God was a shepherd King, not a tyrant King. He'd led me towards Darcy, again and again. I needed to feel now, as I had then, how right this was. Despite my sin, despite my yearnings, we had been meant to find one another in our own separate ways.

There it was. There was that certainty, that lifeline. I held fast to it.

I brought in a deep breath, opened my eyes, and then I told my Father…

Everything.

I spoke with Redcoven's Cloistered Physician after my long Confessional and scathing scrub-down and hoped the whole while that he would not somehow detect any remaining traces of Darcy or the mead in my fur. We'd rinsed and scrubbed and rinsed and scrubbed until even Father Helstrom could no longer smell it, so I was assured.

The man said very little to me during the exam, except to look over the health report Father had brought from Ebon Gables and commend me on losing weight since my last. I didn't want to tell him that it was because I'd been ill, traveling with no food, and eating some of the rations that had been meant for one, far smaller person, while I'd been at the Lodge.

He seemed content with my health, and I suppose that's all that mattered. Afterwards, Father and I shut ourselves back in his room, awaiting the Inquisitor who would take my debriefing for the Ministry. As Father wasn't acting any more, it couldn't be him.

I knew I'd horrified the man. He was holding an even temper and focusing on preparing me for speaking to the Ministry agent for now. But I could not even imagine the torment I was putting him through, knowing how far one of his sons had fallen.

He seemed uncomfortable through at least half of it, but the bloodhound was silent *nearly* the whole way through, offering neither censure nor suggestions for penance I might pay. Which was worrisome. He had *always* given me some means to make myself right with God when I gave Confession. I'd honestly been relying on it, hoping for it, when I'd begun this. I wanted— needed—to feel better. Feel as though I finally had a clear path towards cleansing myself. Or at least knowing which failings I *could* still be cleansed for.

The only part of my Confession that evoked a strong enough reaction from him—where he offered a glimpse into his distress—was when I mentioned the self-flagellation. He stared at me in dumb shock for the whole of the while I explained how I'd come to the idea, how I'd inflicted it, and how it made me feel.

And now, sitting here with him, awaiting being released by the Physician, he chose his moment to speak on it.

"Isidor," he said, hands pursed at the front of his muzzle. "Before you are debriefed, I must say…"

I waited silently. There could be so many things he wanted to say to me right now. Heaven knew.

"I must plead with you personally," he said, softly. "As your Father. The welts were… hard to see. And I find I cannot be silent on this subject, regardless of my staunch belief that it is a matter of personal choice in worship. Self-flagellation is a *ritual*. An ancient and…" he struggled for his words for a few moments. Unbelievably uncommon for him.

"Becoming a flagellant was a practice of more barbaric times, reserved now for only the most *extreme* disciplinary cases, and even then, there are ways it can be done *safely*. Brother Malachi may feel he needs it, or you," and here he brought in a long breath, "you may feel you need it. But for the love of all that is Holy, please *come* to me before you consider harming yourself with a bloody horse crop again. There are better implements, salves to prevent infection, and…"

His words bled off, and it was clear speaking on the subject pained him. So, instead of allowing it to continue, I merely squeezed his hands and said, "I won't do it again."

"You had better not," he said tiredly. "I want to respect your path through the Faith, son. But it wounds me deeply to see you take this tack. If my teachings somehow lead my son to believe he deserves such pain, then I have failed you."

I stumbled over a few versions of what I wanted to say in my head before ultimately deciding that blunt truth was—and had always been—the best choice with my Father.

"Even after all I told you today in Confession," I said, "you *still* don't believe I deserve that kind of punishment?"

He looked me in the eyes, red-rimmed and tired, but firm. "No, son," he whispered. "Your sins are no greater than any youth struggling with a confusing and unfair world. You have stumbled, you have been immoral, you have *certainly* been wanton with your desires both carnal and, far more importantly, in your pursuit of knowledge. But you are *so* much farther above the water line than you realize. It can be easy to catastrophize impure thoughts and transgressions of duty, especially when you are young, but I assure you that the depths of what cruelty or callous action you are capable of, what brutal violence and pain you can inflict have not yet been tested."

He brought in a long breath, then let it out slowly, dropping his eyes from mine to the simple patterned tile floor of the room we waited in. "I came here, worried over your involvement in this case, because I do not *want* you to discover what real sin feels like, when its rotten blossoms grow inside you. That is not something I ever wanted for any of my children."

It was then that the Cloistered Physician returned, gesturing for me to stand. "The Inquisitor is ready for you."

I looked to my Father and then to the doorway. Then, to my father again. He nodded at me, calm in all ways externally. But I knew better, now.

I tried to channel my Father's steadiness, his confidence, as I walked the halls behind the Physician towards what would be my first Ministry Debriefing. Not long ago, I would have been nervously excited to report on what I'd learned about this case. It would be a chance to have all my hard work recognized and bring my superiors into the fold, to share the information I'd so laboriously dredged up and pursued.

Now, I was nervous for entirely different reasons.

Those feelings only amplified when the man I found waiting for me in the small, windowless room, was the very man I'd feared.

"Brother Dolus," I greeted him, unsurprised but fighting back the sinking sensation in my chest all the same. *Calm. Steady.* Father Helstrom and I had gone over what I was going to say, repeatedly. I had literally rehearsed this, but I needed to make it sound unrehearsed.

I was a poor liar and an even worse actor. But I had to do this not only for my own sake. It was also for my Father. For Darcy. That strengthened my resolve.

The lean older monk stood on the other side of the small table in the room. He did not bother to sit when I pulled my own chair out and did so. He only greeted me with an upturned gesture of his chin and a low hum.

And then, without any further preamble, he said, "Let's begin."

I took stock of his state. He looked fresh from the road, fresh from a whole night spent out on the roads, in fact. There was still moisture in his fur, still dirt and the crust from dried snow and ice up the legs of his simple trousers. He'd not bothered changing, washing his face, or, by the look of it, resting even long enough to catch his breath. His posture was weary, his demeanor somewhat frayed for him. He'd *just* gotten in off the road. Obviously without any success, judging by his poor spirits.

The man was aged, outside his Parish, and there *had* to be another Inquisitor here in the city. Why did it have to be him? I'd almost hoped it would be Malachi, but given his involvement with the Archives Office, they probably had him writing reports now rather than taking them. Dolus made sense. But still.

Bad luck.

"By the Grace of God this day, I compel thee—speak the truth, answer all questions asked in as detailed a recounting as your faculties are capable of, make no excuses for sin or misbehavior, and know that deception of any kind under His eyes is grounds for retribution upon the flesh in this mortal world and descension of your soul in the next."

"So, He has said, and so I swear upon His name," I answered the opening prayer, closing my eyes and casting my own silent prayer in the silence following.

Look upon me, Oh Lord, and know that I am an instrument of your great works. And if during the course of those works, for the sake of the Ministry and Canine kind, for Amuresca itself, I need deceive anyone... even my superiors... if I feel I must to uproot corruption, to unearth sin...

... then deceive, I shall.

"How did you end up in the Heart Thief's hidden abode?" Dolus asked. "I know you've a nose for solving puzzles and mysteries my boy, but I think I may have underestimated your ability to translate that cleverness into actual fieldwork."

I opened my eyes. That wasn't how I'd expected this would begin. The question felt almost informal. Like a conversation. Not an interrogation. What's more, I knew Brother Dolus well enough by now to know when he was softening his tone, using his congeniality, to lull you into a sense of false security.

This was not how I'd thought the man conducted his Inquisitions. But to be fair, I'd never been present for one. And I could see how this might work.

But I knew better.

I rubbed my finger pads over the bone just under the surface of my pinched skin and fur, where I was missing my finger. And I focused on that. For once, focused on the memory. The phantom pains. And I reminded myself who this man was.

I told him the story of how I'd come across the Physician's

files, how I'd followed him, and then dug through his records. The Lodge had stood out to me, because we'd been looking for some kind of safehouse that wouldn't be easily known. An abandoned property from over a decade ago that at least one of our suspects had a connection to? I couldn't deny or obscure the link between Rathborne and Darcy. The fact that they'd stayed at the Lodge all but confirmed it, and I had to choose my lies carefully. But herein is where I diverged.

No mention of Cillian's visits. No mention of any further ties between the two of them. Only that Darcy had said at some point during my stay that they'd once been in Cillian's employ. That they'd worked at the Lodge, long ago. That there seemed to be contention—perhaps even hatred—between them now, at least on the Heart Thief's part.

… honestly, the grain of truth therein helped me sell the story, I think.

I went with a modified version of the truth, bolstered by my Father's instruction on how to sell the tale. My original intention to scout the property, which boiled away into a desperation ploy to stay alive and plumb information from the Heart Thief, after I was 'captured'. My illness and the rather well-made manacles, as well as my own incompetence at picking them, which kept me trapped in the unfortunate situation.

And lastly, the Heart Thief's own motives… elusive to me in this story as they were in real life. Why they'd kept me without killing me for so long, I could not say. But I suspected they'd been trying to hold me until some point at which they'd use me as a distraction to make their escape. Which is precisely what they'd done in the end.

It had the added benefit of turning me into a liability, an incompetent young Templar who'd been gotten the better of, and accidentally facilitated the thief's escape. Better to appear a fool than be the hero in my own story. It was more believable.

I certainly *did* feel like a fool. Those feelings would be evident in my telling and render it more convincing.

I finished the story right up to the moment where Malachi and Dolus had found me on that snowy road and looked up from the table to the monk, who had remained standing this whole time. He looked impassive, arms folded behind his back, his road-worn tunic's sleeves pulled up. He looked like he was back at Ebon Gables, ready to aid the young pups in washing bowls, not performing an interrogation on someone he knew full well was already terrified of him.

But then, maybe that was the point. Brother Dolus had a lifetime with me already behind us to intimidate, assert his dominance, and make clear what the consequences were of defying him. He didn't need anything more than that.

And yet still, I defied him.

The decision to lie to this man—if not the execution—had come to me so much more easily than I'd ever thought it would. Shame was my constant companion, and it was notably absent here. I was proud of myself, I realized. I felt as though I'd done the right thing by not betraying Darcy to Brother Dolus.

It was strange and somewhat exciting, practicing deception to do what I firmly believed was right for this case. When Cillian had proclaimed I might be willing to lie for God, I don't think this is what he'd envisioned.

I expected a barrage of questions following my account. Or pointed statements, meant to elicit emotional responses from me. Some clever interrogation tactic I did not know of, because I hadn't the high degree of training he had, yet. What I got instead was…

A simple nod. And then a few curt words.

"About what I'd expected, save a few details I will make note of for the debriefing report." He gestured for me to stand, and I did so, trying not to look as confused as I felt. "I'll have Brother Malachi draw up the documents later tonight, and you can look them over to clear up a few points, but I think we have what we need here for now."

"We're done, Brother?" I asked, hardly able to believe my luck. This had been mere minutes. He'd listened, asked next to no questions, and just accepted my recounting of events?

Had I held my countenance that well? Was the story just *that* believable? Or was Brother Dolus simply eager to be done with all of this? He'd seemed impatient to be assigned to this case from the first day he'd arrived in Redcoven, so maybe that really was it.

"We are done," he confirmed flatly. "And you are doubtless in need of rest, Isidor. I'm certain I don't need to say this, but just in case you are in any doubt, the Ministry will send down the official order tonight—you are no longer assigned to this investigation as of now. Any disciplinary action for breach of records will come down from the High Offices when they've decided on whether it's warranted and will pass directly to my or Father Helstrom's hands when the time comes. I expect, though, given how fruitful your investigation into this case ended up being, they will be forgiving. For whatever my word is worth, I will encourage them to be so in my report. It is a formality that you weren't granted access to the Archives, as it is."

He crossed over the side of the table towards me and reached out to settle a hand on my shoulder. Brother Dolus had always been less stiff and formal about that sort of thing, but in this instance, it chilled me even more than it might have normally. It felt strange *because* it had all the appearances of being so familiar. Like an uncanny mask of congeniality. I knew not what it was truly covering.

I tried not to lean back.

"Furthermore, I am going to put in a recommendation for you to be admitted for Inquisition training, as soon as the new semester begins in Amurfolk," he said, smiling. "I'm very proud that such a promising career has come from the ranks of our little Abbey. You are going to honor your Father and me and all of your brothers and sisters when you are admitted to the ranks of the Inquisition, son. And, earnestly?"

He leaned in, lowering his voice. "I am personally *very* glad to see that you've expanded your horizons on methodology and personal restraint. Our quarry do not play by any rules, either the laws of God or the land, and if we are to match them wit for wit, we must not worry so much over propriety, acceptable conduct or even the restrictions faith can put on us. Many proud and self-righteous men of the cloth have failed to serve God and country with the zealousness this profession demands because of fear for their immortal souls. It is a true servant of the Lord who puts himself aside and does what need be done, even if that means our hearts are heavier for it. I worried for you, before..."

And here, he trailed off, clucking in the back of his throat. "Scholarly pursuits are one thing, but this relentless, hopelessly optimistic drive for spiritual purity that Germain pushes... it is not for *us*. Certainly not for any of you foundlings."

"Brother?" I questioned, uncertain I was understanding him correctly.

"We do not share much about ourselves, as your elders. This is done by design," Brother Dolus said, looking me in the eyes in a way I don't think he ever had before. It wasn't intimidation, I realized. This wasn't meant to frighten me. He was trying to speak to me, man to man. For perhaps the first time in my life. This was how he spoke to other adults. Other Templar.

Except, I would always struggle to see him as my Brother. He could take up an earnest, genuine affect all he liked, speak only the truth to me, mean only the best for me—or what he thought was the best for me—but it could never erase the weight of years.

He would always be the angry adult who'd hurt me as a child

because he'd wanted to. Until I could make sense of that, see any kind of justification for it that wasn't simply... spite... I could never accept him as anything other than my tormentor.

"Germain is a low Pedigree, did you know that?" he asked.

I blinked. "I... had suspected, I suppose, but..."

"Small family, I believe he was their only son," he continued. "Devout. No need of a Templar, hardly enough weight in society or fortune that needs be watched over, but *very* devout. He could have lived as a Lord. No one of great renown, but he had enough privilege to be comfortable if he'd kept to his obligations. This vocation? It is his choice. And I've no doubt he sees it as a very worthy call, a martyr is he to have walked away from a life of ease and luxury."

I didn't miss the bitterness in his tone. For just a moment there, he had let something real slip. I remained quiet and continued to listen to him speak. I didn't think it was his place to divulge Father Helstrom's past, but this was an opportunity to learn more about the both of them. And given how enigmatic the men who raised me had always been, I could not conceive of turning that down.

"But for us?" He looked between himself and me. "For the unwanted? A bastard son and a sick runt of the litter? This is our *salvation*. And we are brought to understand—through our limited paths in life—what true sacrifice means. There is no decent or comfortable life for us outside of the Ministry. We are no one—less than no one—without the Church. That is why we are its most faithful servants. No man is born devout through and through. Dependency, the need for survival, compels us in a way it will never compel men like Germain. And that makes us loyal. That makes us *obedient*."

He released my shoulder, stepping back from me by a foot. I needed that foot. Especially right now.

"But most of all," he twisted a slender wrist, reaching into what must have been a hidden pocket in his opposite sleeve, and pulling free something he held in his palm, obscured. "It means we are flexible. Adaptive. Because we don't think ourselves above the *work*, you see. We are humble enough to lie in the dirt if need be and brush it off afterwards, make our amends, and keep serving. Men like Germain?" He reached for my four-fingered hand and placed something, hard but wrapped in leather, long as a knife but thinner. I recognized the feel of my lock-picking tools immediately.

"Men like that lie down in the dirt once and think their hearts are forever sullied," he said, softly. "They become afraid. Hesitant. And then they stop. Doing. The work."

I stared down at the lock-picking set, trying to make sense of all of this. Of everything he'd said, and why he'd given me this—how he'd *gotten* it. I must have left it behind at the Lodge, which meant he'd been there before it had burnt. Which meant Darcy must have already left, which meant…

"I found them wrapped and stowed safely near the hearth fire, of all places," he tutted. "Can't imagine why they may have been there, but then the whole place was in disarray when I arrived. Quite the mess our little thief left us with. And the structure was… unsound. When the fire broke out, I can't even say I was surprised."

My eyes widened. "Are you saying the Heart Thief tried to burn you alive inside the place?"

"That is certainly what will be going in the report," he confirmed. "Coincidental timing, otherwise. But the important thing is you are alive. I am alive. And you've gotten us our best intelligence yet on this feline's possible identity and connections. Brother Malachi may have his faults, but he is a dauntless pursuer, and I have no doubt that with the full backing of the Ministry, along with your accrued knowledge on the target, we'll have her in custody quite soon."

"'Her'?" I questioned.

He merely smiled. "I think so, yes. A feeling, if you will. She certainly seems to have a way with men that I would associate more with a woman's talents than any molly boy."

"If you say so, Brother."

"You'd be forgiven for meeting her and being confused," he waved a hand. "She's a serpent, lad. You were not prepared to contend with a criminal this cunning. Let us take over now. Go home. Rest on your laurels until it is time for your training to begin. What an auspicious start though, aye? Our little southpaw." He looked me over, up and down. "A work of marble, carved from the mud."

I swallowed. "Bless you, Brother."

"And you, young Brother," he said before turning to open the door for me.

I opened the door to see a towering malamute poking his nose around the corner, quickly moving back when we stepped out. I didn't miss Brother Dolus frown upon initially seeing him, but I didn't get the impression he wasn't supposed to be here. He'd likely been guarding the room.

"I've got the reports drawn up and ready for you, Brother Dolus," he said, bowing his head respectfully and handing over the slim, wrapped parcel.

"Very good," the monk nodded, taking them and retreating back towards the table. "Be ready to leave for an extended overland trip in the morning. Have Whitehall commission a stipend for at least a month for you and your mount. We have agents to meet with in Carlidash two days hence and a trail to pick up once we've cleared our final interrogations here."

I stepped out into the hallway to an expectant Malachi, cleaned up and dressed in what must have been his finest: a handsome if inexpensive tunic, vest, leather breeches, and a court blade. I had half a mind to ask him which Pedigree estate dinner he'd be attending tonight, but given he was on an active case, that seemed unlikely.

"You clean up well," I simply said instead and smiled.

"Double fur coat doesn't work well with a cravat," he plucked at the thick ruff around his neck. "But then I suppose you know that, eh?"

"I do," I chuckled, hearing the door shut behind me. I felt more at ease already. "So, what's the occasion?"

"Seeing you off," he said. "Better reason than a funeral, which is what I thought I'd lain these out for."

I didn't need to force the grin that came to my muzzle. "I'm honored," I said sincerely.

"And I'm relieved," he said as he walked me down the hallway, towards one of the reading rooms. I could see Father Helstrom waiting for us there, patiently leafing through his Tome in one of the sitting chairs. "You can't know how much."

"You said you'd lost Brothers before," I murmured. "Partners?"

"And two I grew up with," he said, his tone hard to read. His voice and his whole countenance turned to impassable stone when he spoke on this subject. Trained, I knew. Betraying little. But I could guess at what I'd feel if someone like Nicholas died… for any reason. Whether it be illness, accidental, or the line of duty. It was hard to imagine how I'd be so composed.

With time, I suppose.

"We knew each other only in passing when you came to train here," he said, walking slowly with me, "and you were a child, then. We've not gotten to know one another as well as I'd like over these last few weeks, but I would have felt personally responsible if the Order had lost you. I should have been looking after you more diligently. I was worried I…"

His features were inscrutable for a few moments, the dark mask of fur around his eyes making it all the harder to detect subtle changes in his expression. We canines with masks were preferred by the Ministry for that reason, I'd heard.

"I can come off audacious," he said at last. "Overwhelming, intimidating. Some of it's inherent, but much of the time, I simply do not realize I'm letting my trained demeanor bleed out into my other interactions. I don't intend it, especially not with my fellow Brothers. I felt, at some point, that I must have been frightening you. Unnerving you…"

"No, no," I insisted. "Malachi, I don't know how to convince you, but I swear, you've not upset me." I tipped my nose up enough to be at eye level with him. We were close to the same height, but he was still a little bit taller than me. It was refreshing, honestly.

He stared down at me in silence, one ear twitching. He looked nervous for some reason.

"Not by action or by who you are," I assured him. "In fact, I'd like to come to know you better with time, too. If God allows."

He smiled a little. "I was quite serious about working with you again once you're accredited. You're an up-and-comer, young buck. We'd make the sinners quake in their spats, you and I. I'm convinced of it."

I laughed, because I hardly knew what else to say to a comment like that.

"Isidor," my Father called to me.

"That'll be the cattle call, then," Malachi sighed. "You take care of yourself, alright? My own Father wants me back home tonight to catch him up. I haven't had a chance yet, what with the report. At least I'll look fine for services."

"We'll be leaving early tomorrow morning," I said, ears dropping for a moment, "so I suppose this is goodbye for now."

"For now." He knocked a fist into my chest lightly. "But I haven't gotten on this well with a Brother in a while, Isidor. We'll work together again soon enough, mark my words. God has a way of bringing like-minded souls together."

I thought of Darcy. Of course I did.

"I hope you're right," I said.

I made my way to the reading room, feeling Malachi's eyes on my back for a few more moments before the man headed out. It felt odd, the way he looked at me. Not bad. But like I was meant to be saying more. Like when you've parted ways with someone, but you've forgotten to tell them something important. That's the best feeling I can think of to describe it.

When I entered the reading room, Father was standing, his Tome closed, looking past my shoulder presumably at Malachi as he exited the main doors.

The reading room was a small alcove with no doors, simply two cross-hatched paned windows, a little potbelly stove for heat, a few tables and chairs, some cushioned sitting chairs for the elderly or infirm, and several wall bookcases, nearly full. I breathed in the scent of the parchment and binding, my eyes alighting across unfamiliar titles and authors, stood at the side of my Father, free from the interrogation and facing many unknowns, but feeling for the first time... unburdened. I had made Confession and my Father did not hate me. I had born false witness to the man I feared most in the world, and he had all but confirmed he knew I was not being entirely truthful, but that he understood it to be a necessity of the work, whatever that meant.

I had made a new friend in Malachi.

And somewhere out there in the world, Darcy was headed for safety. And the truth remained ready for my Father and me to unearth it.

Days ago, I was certain I was going to be cast to Ciraberos for my transgressions, and now I wasn't even sure it was wrong of me to consider all the questions the last few weeks had brought. God had given me to Ebon Gables to *learn*, after all. Education was the cure for ignorance, and it was the greatest gift the Abbey had ever bequeathed to me. Perhaps I was meant to seek the truth, even if the answers were upsetting or made me question my superiors. Perhaps *especially* then.

"That poor boy," my Father said, snapping me out of my book-smell-induced reverie.

"What?" I looked to him.

"Brother Malachi," the bloodhound said quietly. "I pulled his files from the Archive and read them while you were being tended to and questioned."

"Oh," I blinked rapidly. "Father—"

"You seem to have made fast bosom brothers," he explained. "I'm entitled to worry whom my son is associating with, and I'd heard rumors that suggested he might be a problematic acquaintance."

"Brother Dolus inferred as much," I said, trying to disguise my minor upset that my Father had gone and looked into the man's past. It was invasive, but I had done the same thing to a stranger with less reason.

"I will not burden you with the grim tale," he said somberly. "And I doubt he would prefer to share it. But he seems reformed. He has made a very concerted effort to discipline himself and worked diligently for nearly a decade, tirelessly and in some very difficult regions of the world, in service to the Ministry and our Lord. Under Bahdren no less, working with... *mercenaries* and scum. One must offer forgiveness and understanding to a young man so bent and dedicated to his own redemption, who has put in so much work to reform."

I looked to him, then to the closed door. I wanted to ask, but I also wasn't sure I wanted to know. And my Father's face, deeply creased in newfound understanding, was warning enough.

"Bloody tragic," he said, shaking his head. "Why God tests the young so ferociously, and whom He chooses to heap such pain upon, I cannot understand. Nor will I ever." He stared down at his Tome. "All we can do is tend to them as well as we are able."

. . .

We weren't able to discuss my Confession or the reason behind the cryptic messages in his letters in detail until we were on the road, alone inside a clattering carriage with the hoofbeats and rushing ambience of the road to assure we were not overheard. I appreciated my Father's wariness, but the wait of nearly an entire night before we could leave had my head spinning with the possibilities. I got very little sleep.

"It wasn't the last I tried to send," he said, still low enough that I had to hunker in to hear him, leaning with my elbows on my knees from the seat across from him. "Two more, afterwards. Although they either went astray or Dolus intercepted them."

"If he did, he did not hand them off to me," I said. "Not even in the day since I've been back."

"I must assume by now he's realized the cryptograph is more than a puzzle game for one of my children," he surmised. "But I rather doubt he can translate it, at least not without aid from one of the more learned monks on ancient cuneiform. You were able to read it?"

"It took me a little while," I confessed, "but yes. I wish I'd read it before I went for the Lodge, but I was distracted."

"So it seems," the bloodhound said, narrowing his eyes.

I hung my head, tipping back my ears. "Forgive me, Father."

"You know and understand your sins," he said, holding to his strict expression for a few final moments before it melted away to one more exhausted. "There is no further need for correction or censure on my part. Isidor... you're a good boy. You always have been. Earnestly, the only reason I've been as vigilant with your discipline and Confession over the years is because you've seemed to desire it, to be settled in Grace and forgiveness. Some children crave correction and moral guidance more than others. Some—like Nicholas—revolt against it if you push too hard. I've always exercised a somewhat lighter touch with him, and he has developed a freer spirit for it. I hope you've never seen that as favoritism."

"No," I said, shocked. "I've never resented your discipline, Father. Or thought it too extreme. It's Brother Dolus... who..."

He only nodded silently, a brief wince—a painful memory, perhaps—moving over his features. I could take a guess at which one, but the two men had raised more children together over the years than just me. It could be any number of grievances.

"I suppose I understand what you mean about my own innate desire for discipline," I said, my ears growing warm. "Even afar from the Abbey, mired in my own sinful decisions and justifications for immoral behavior, I craved absolution. I wanted so badly to know I had not fallen too far from His Grace that I could yet be saved."

"Some part of that is your doctrinal teaching shaping how you think, as well it should be," he said. "The Tome teaches us to walk the righteous path. But you are focusing on the wrong sins, lad. Your deception and bucking the authority of the Ministry are graver crimes by any measure than your yearnings of the flesh," he assured me. "The Ministry will certainly deem it so, and I personally worry far more over your actions there than a young man's natural inclinations of lust and self-satisfaction."

He sounded uncomfortable whenever we spoke on this subject. He was exercising control over his tone now, but I could still detect it. I had long thought it was disgust over the sin itself, but I was beginning to think it may have been something more. He was almost *dismissive* of the sin. He had said many times that he trusted me to temper my desires and seek repentance accordingly, and no part of it seemed to alarm him.

Well. Save one.

"Even..." I stammered, correcting myself quickly. Speak cleanly and with purpose when you are addressing a Holy Man or anyone worthy of respect. I rallied. "Even the yearnings I have had, considering this person to be of the male sex?"

That gave him pause. But at length, he recovered just as I had. Speaking with clarity, pushing through the conversation as quickly as possible. "Given the uncertainty of your unique situation with the feline, I would say it might be normal for the mind to wander to all possibilities. This does not mean that is what you *want*, Isidor. I worry I was never clear enough on this point, and the fault there is mine. This subject can be hard to talk about with any nuance without giving immature minds the wrong ideas. Or worse yet, planting sinful ideas *within* those minds. Young minds are malleable. You may tend to assume that errant thoughts or catastrophic worries are not only possible, but *probable*. Factual. You may then adopt those thoughts as legitimate, integral parts of your being, rather than dismissing them for what they are—confusion. Youth is a frenetic time. Your mind will entertain ludicrous things that a mature mind would know to be nonsense."

I nodded, because some part of what he was saying made a certain measure of sense to me. Like how desperately self-loathsome I'd been at times in the Lodge. How I had thought, known for certain, that I was damned. How close I'd been to losing all hope. Those were feelings of desperation that I could reflect on now—barely a week later—with greater clarity and perspective. My misgivings over my own wanton desires were still present, but felt less world-ending, less pressing even than the importance and gravity of the conspiracy I'd found myself a part of. The concern for Darcy's life and, indeed, my own. Even my fear for my soul had lessened, since it seemed quite undeniable that God had a purpose for me, here and now. And whether I had filthy dreams likely mattered far less to Him than whether I served Him well in this most important task.

But as to my feelings on Darcy...

"But my thoughts on the matter of their sex have not really

changed," I stated outright to my father with some confusion. "It wasn't just the dream. I have considered it much since then, and I have come to the conclusion that... I.... well, I believe I am attracted to them, regardless? Is that possible?"

"The Tome teaches us that the desire for companionship and physical connection is a gift," my Father said, his voice gone rather thin. "And it is not a gift we are *all* blessed with, Isidor, or not in equal measure. You have it in spades, and for that I am grateful. You will be a contented and diligent husband and father to your family, some day. But there are boundaries. Natural laws dictated by God's design for us and additionally for the security and betterment of man's society. We are made by Him to form families and complement one another in a particular way, and revoking God's plan for us leads to disunity and strife. I know you and I debate the scriptures, but this is not merely the interpretations of a Saint or Scholar from ages past, guessing at what He intended for us. It is etched into our bodies from the time we are born. It is binary. It is natural. It is inarguable."

I considered what he was saying, chewing on the inside of my mouth. It was hard to find an argument against his logic, especially when he fell back on what was incontrovertible—the way our bodies had obviously been designed to complement one another. I may have been an Abbey boy, but I knew that much. I understood basic anatomy, and I had endured the brief, uncomfortable talk from my Father when I'd reached fifteen about what would be expected of me on my wedding night.

"But," I could not help but object all the same, "what if someone is... neither? God's plan deviates sometimes. We are all unique. My intolerance of diet is not normal, but you've told me many times it does not mean I am *meant* to be weak or that I was meant to die when I was young. Men become monks, neutren, some women are barren or die as spinsters. Some of them happily so, I think. Do we all need to couple as man and wife and make young in order to honor God's plan for us?"

His creased face went tense and strange, his eyes drifting away from me to the window. It was almost unheard of for Father Helstrom to break eye contact with someone when he was speaking on important matters. I wanted to know what he was thinking, but I gave him time, instead. Maybe he'd tell me.

"That is a complicated question," he answered at length. "God's children are diverse by natural design as well. We fulfill different niches within the world, different roles in society, and altogether we complete His great tapestry. But God is not... fair... Isidor. We are not all created equal nor promised the same happiness in life as our peers. A fact you are not naïve to."

"I think we are all entitled to know His love, and the love for His world," I said softly. "It's just harder for some of us because we carry more burdens than others. I've... I will not lie. I've never understood why. Why suffering is necessary in all cases. Often it seems heaped on those who do not deserve it. I struggle to understand His purpose in that."

"You are not alone," he assured me, reaching out to hold my hand, wrapping his thin, wrinkled fingers around mine and brushing over my missing joint. "I've seen so much evil in the world, Isidor. By man's hand, by the cold, neutral forces of nature, and by sheer happenstance. What I can tell you quite certainly I have *never* seen? Is any cruelty inflicted upon our world by God Himself. Those who say a storm is punishing a port—as an extension of God's will—usually have a petty agenda of their own. Much in our world has been heaped at God's feet, for good or ill. But that ignores the fact that He gave this world to us to forge our own paths, make our own mistakes, and find our own justice with one another while we share in this life. He stands by ready to judge us when we pass to His realm, and there is where the balance is struck. Perhaps those who've faced greater adversity are weighted accordingly when considered for ascendance."

"Ascendance is promised to no one," I said, by route, "but it is impossibly out of reach for any but the Pedigree, at least in this life. I'll need to be reborn... six times before I've even a chance at proving myself worthy."

"Just so," he nodded. "Eternal peace beside Him is a struggle from lifetime to lifetime, as we ascend the ladder towards His perfect form for us. The lowly rat may suffer in his lifetime, but if he makes the most of what he is given and lives a kind, noble life, he will not be so lowly in the next."

"But it's harder to live a kind and righteous life when you're poor and struggling," I said, frustrated. "It's simpler for Pedigree. They don't need to steal to eat or live surrounded by violence in the slums."

"Not everyone is given the same chance at Grace, son," he said, a hint of sadness in his voice.

"Why not?" I persisted.

"Because every cathedral must have a foundation," he said, and I knew the line; I'd heard it before. He was repeating it word for word from an account by Saint Endrys. "That foundation is oft ignored, taken for granted, but without it the people it uplifts would fall. It may sound cruel, it may sound unfair, but that is why our souls are reborn. They will not always suffer."

"But when your current life is painful and difficult, that might be a hard thing to believe," I said.

"People are short-sighted," he agreed. "We are made that way intentionally, remember. So that we may exist in the moment and make the most of the lives we are given. Ciraberos could not cease wanting for more because he was consumed by his regrets and fears, for the past and present. It may be hard to see it, but our limitations are another of His gifts."

He let out a long breath, then pressed on. "That being said.

He does not punish us by building us 'broken.' I meant everything I said to you when you were a little, starving pup. You do not need to be weak and sickly. You are entitled to a good life despite your condition. Everyone is, regardless of their struggles or the circumstances of their birth."

"What about someone like Darcy?" I asked, point-blank.

He paused. "The thievery is inexcusable, regardless of their assertions. But I assume you mean their issues with their birth sex. They... may simply be confused, for now. They're also young, yes?"

"I don't know," I admitted. "I think so. But what if they're just made differently? What if they're *supposed* to be made differently? Where they come from, they believe that is how God intends many people to be. What if they're right about themselves, and... they never change? Are *they* broken? Is..." I remembered his words, clear as day on the subject. "Malachi thinks he is broken. Is *he* right?"

"Malachi is a very troubled man, Isidor," my Father stressed, squeezing my hand. "I have sympathy for him and respect how hard he has worked to reform himself. But he is not contending with simply mundane sins, as you are. He killed someone when he was fifteen years old. Another Brother. Very, very violently."

I leaned back in shock.

"The circumstances were," he snuffed softly, closing his eyes, "tragic and extreme. Were it one of my sons? I shudder to think."

The possibilities of what may have happened, as I considered them, were deeply distressing, but whatever he'd done it had happened long ago and the Ministry had seen fit to reinstate him. He clearly regretted his actions, lived a life of repentance, and that was between him and God.

"There is a difference between being born wrong and being wronged by the world," Father said, his eyes still staring off somewhere, distantly. "And..." he paused for a long while here, obviously deeply considering his words, "… no," he said at long last. "I cannot bring myself to believe any of us are born wrong. To believe that would be to doubt God's plan, and while we all question throughout our lives, I have to trust there are things beyond my understanding. Fates He has spun for us that may not make sense within this lifetime, or to our children, our children's children, but they will reveal their purpose in time. Perhaps generations upon generations from now."

"Darcy said something similar," I murmured. "About being misunderstood in their time, but perhaps understood better in the future. They hope their story will inspire others, some day."

"It sounds to me like your friend is planning to die," the bloodhound stated grimly.

"I hope I've talked them out of that," I said uncertainly. "But I don't know. I think they're a deeply sad person, Father. I wish I understood the full breadth of what made them who they are."

"Thieves tend to be secretive," he warned me. "And deceptive. You cannot be certain anything they've told you is the truth Isidor, do you understand me? I know you're young, but you're cleverer than that. Don't act foolishly because you fancy them. Any more so than you already have, I mean."

"Is it sinful?" I asked him nervously. "That I… like them?"

"I am more concerned that the person my son has formed designs on is wanted for grand larceny and murder, than whether they wear britches or bloomers," he muttered. "Let us tackle one thing at a time here in the order of importance. You very well may find in time that this infatuation of yours is merely lust or obsession fueled by the months you spent pursuing them. And if it *is* something more serious, and the feline is in fact the woman you wish to pledge yourself to, I do not envy you the adjudication or cost of clearing *so* many crimes. The Pardon power of the Ministry for sentence-cleared marriages is generally limited to minor larceny or indecency, hysteria, the sort of things that land women in workhouses. This goes *very* far beyond that."

"Sentence-cleared marriages?" I repeated, my ears going bolt upright.

He groaned. "Lord. Look it up yourself, son. We have graver concerns now, and I'd rather not plant false hope in your head. Remember that I cautioned against it and with good reason. It is nearly impossible in these circumstances."

"Nearly," I said. I could *feel* my claws clinging at the edge of a very precarious cliff.

"The serval is pre-sentenced to be hanged, Isidor," he reminded me. "Let us not avert our eyes from that reality. The best thing they can hope for now is to survive all of this. If you care for them, and you truly believe in their innocence, your firmest hope should be that they are boarding a ship as we speak. They aren't safe here."

"I know."

"I discovered something I am certain I was not meant to know," he said, his voice lowering in pitch considerably, so much so that I had to strain to hear him, "when I began looking into the theft myself after you left. Something very distressing."

"The reason you tried to warn me," I deduced.

He nodded. "As soon as I learned of it, I scented the whiff of something deeply embedded within the meat of the Ministry's paws. A thorn that could become a seeping wound if we try to pry it out into the light. I've seen this before, if rarely. I think a grave mistake may have been made, two years ago. Perhaps a decision made rashly in a moment of panic by the upper echelon. Or perhaps a lone Inquisitor, someone with pull, who decided it ought to be done. Regardless of who was responsible, it is clear to me by the lengths it took me to unearth anything about this that they are burying it. They do not want this looked into."

"The Heart Theft?" I whispered, shocked. "But... no. It's an open case. Even *I* was permitted to investigate it."

"With all due respect to your considerable talents, Isidor," he sighed, "you are nineteen years old. You have not even taken a full House Posting yet, let alone trained for Inquisition work. I believe they may have thought allowing you to pursue the feline was harmless. At best, you'd catch an art thief, at worst, you'd waste a pittance of Ministry funds. You were so passionate about it, though. Did you not ever wonder why you were pursuing the investigation largely alone? Why no Senior Inquisitors were tasked with bringing this thief in?"

"I did," I said, gritting my teeth. "Many, many times. I didn't want to question the leadership, but I felt very alone and as though I was being ignored. Until Malachi."

"I believe Inquisitor Malachi was ordered home from the border territories to take over this Investigation once it became clear to the Ministry that you stood a substantial chance of actually capturing the Heart Thief," he said. "He's a rational choice. He has a diligent track record, he's efficient, dogged, and, most importantly, loyal to a fault. He has to be, or his deferred punishment will be extreme. They hold a sword to his neck. He would never question the leadership as we are doing right now."

"If they're framing Darcy," I stammered, "why wouldn't they initially want them caught? And what purpose does all of this serve?"

"I cannot be entirely sure," he said hesitantly, "but I think your feline friend is the unfortunate but necessary victim of scapegoating, not deliberate framing. The Heart Thief—or however it is they were referred to before all of this—has at least a five-year history that I could find with minimal digging of out and proud antiquities and art theft under their belt. They are known, reviled, and much talked-of. Infamous, I suppose, would be the word. And they are a ghost. As far as I could find, you are the only person who has ever tracked them down more than once, and your predecessors were not successful in capturing them, obviously."

"Apparently one mercenary got close," I said, recalling the conversation. And then the manacles. I still had them. I had a sudden desire to handle them, which I quickly quashed.

But maybe later.

"I do not think the Ministry really intended for the 'thief' of the Heart of Faith to be caught," he continued. "They just needed someone to blame. Your 'Darcy' was the obvious choice. It fit their profile, and their evasion of the law in the past meant little chance they would be caught, tried, and potentially proven innocent. Not that I find that likely."

"But there really was a theft," I insisted. "The Heart is missing. There are *bodies*. *Those* are real. The housekeeper, and the two Templar. They're lying in state. Aren't they?"

"That's what I was looking into," he said, gravely. "I didn't know all of this then. Not even about Malachi, let alone what you've told me since we got you back. But even taking a cursory glance into the report on the theft and murders got me on the scent of something foul. The couriers who accompanied the Heart when it was being moved... I do not think they were Templar."

"They falsified who was escorting the Heart?" I questioned, confused. "Why would they do that? Are they really dead?"

"Someone is," he said, his voice low as distant thunder. "There are most certainly two murdered bodies lying in state at Ministry Headquarters in Amurfolk. Or two *very* convincing Physician's reports and many falsified statements from witnesses. I find that unlikely. It would—as horrific as this sounds—be easier to produce two bodies than it would be to fabricate all of that. Less of a risk to the Ministry, as well. Less likely to be called into question later. I will need to confirm this with my own eyes, but I think the men who were killed are real.

Whether they were killed over this—or indeed had *anything* at all to do with the Heart—is another matter."

"How," I was having trouble maintaining my composure, "h-how—could they—I'm sorry, Father. Why do you suspect all of this? You said something in the reports—"

"I know the Abbey and, moreover, the Priest who is supposedly the man who reared these two boys," he said. "Father Pieter Volstov. It is far-flung in the northern country above the brow line of the contested Kadrush border. They mostly take in wolves and wolfdogs. The report claims that these two boys are brothers, terrier kin. Pieter and I do not correspond often. We did not serve together or work together extensively, but he served in the same several decades as I did. We retired close to the same time. I would not consider him a friend, but an acquaintance? Most certainly."

He lifted his sunken eyes back to look into mine. "If he were raising two terrier boys, I would have known. A pair of brothers, both elevated through the ranks together? He would have been so proud. You don't get many success stories like that up there. Boys that promising, with some breeding, would have been moved once they were even moderately of-age to a more Amur-central Abbey. The Templar forged in the crucible of the North Country are sent immediately to the wastes of the Kadrush, to war, to Crusade. These two boys—as far as their history states—were shipped from up north directly to Headquarters in Amurfolk, where they graduated in precisely as little time as is realistic and were *immediately* given this most important task? No. I think not."

"Who were they, then?" I asked.

"I don't know," he shook his head. "If I had to guess? Petty criminals or mercenaries. People with few or little connections who wouldn't be missed. People whose lives could be rewritten."

"That's unthinkable," I stated plainly.

41

"You aren't a child anymore, Isidor," he said. "I say this not to frighten you, but because you need to know. I have witnessed worse at the hands of the Ministry. At the hands of Templar. I have been a part of it. I have rationalized, I have justified, I have prayed for forgiveness and hoped beyond hope that I have done more good than harm. But nothing about this is as appalling to me as it should be. It is not even surprising."

I stared at him in mute horror.

"When they told you that you were the arbiter of God's necessary but brutal deeds," he looked at me calmly, "what did you think that meant, son?"

"Fighting for God," I said shakily.

"Sometimes fighting for God means killing a magistrate in his own home because he has a little girl locked in his root cellar, bound by a chain to her arm so tightly, that it has begun to decay while still attached to her living body," he said, his voice gutturally hollow. "Sometimes that fight sees you covered in his blood one day, then attending his funeral the next, assuring his family and friends that you'll catch his killer. Because his family has connections the Ministry can still use, and unearthing who he was would forever sully their name and render them useless."

I could say nothing. Nothing would be sufficient.

"I didn't want this for you, son," he said raggedly. "I wanted you to be a house guard. But God made you too smart. Too passionate. And too honest. And now, you have no choice. You are a part of this. And I know you better than to think you'll let this go. All I can do is try to give you guidance as you navigate this. I do not know why specifically they've done any of this, but I know the signs of their work. I do not know who's involved or what their motivations were. I do not know what truly became of the Heart. It's possible it never even left the Ministry's hands."

"Then that means there's a chance it could still be found," I said hopefully.

"Yes," he said, "and I also know you will not stop until that chance has perished. You wish to prove your friend's innocence. Just understand, if they've gone through this much effort already, whatever rot lies at the root of this, they want it to stay buried. Going against them... against us... rarely ends well."

"You're not telling me to give up."

"I should be," he growled. "If I really believed you'd listen to me, I would demand you give this up *right* now! The entire reason I tried to warn you against this case is because I'm worried for your safety. Lives have been lost already, and I'm not certain why. This has all the signs of a dark operation, Isidor. A conspiracy within the Ministry that is meant to remain hidden even from most Templar. I can't even risk putting in a request for information without endangering the both of us. If their belief that our silence is necessary for them to accomplish their aims..."

"But," I said, swallowing dryly, "you're still not telling me to give up. My stubbornness has never stopped you from standing firm and correcting me, before."

"Because you will not listen to me," he repeated. "And I do not want you to run so far from me in your pursuit of this that I lose your trust forever."

"I could never," I gasped.

"If you feel you cannot come to me, I worry you'll act alone. And... you are in the right, here," he admitted, shaking his head. "How could I ask you to do what goes against your beliefs? And my own, I dare add."

"Your devotion to the Ministry," I said pointedly. "I don't fault you for it, Father. But a lifetime spent in their service, your reservations for the work aside, I..."

He smiled, tiredly. "You're my son, Isidor. I devoted myself to you, and my other children when I laid down my sword. The Ministry is my past. All I wish to be now is your father. Do not doubt my dedication."

2

ARRANGED

Seeing and walking the grounds of Ebon Gables again was a blessing, unmarred by the presence of Brother Dolus. Unlike my last return home, I was able to greet the Abbey, and my brothers and sisters this time without fear of censure or interruption by the arbiter of dread I'd long shied away from.

Brother Dolus was still on the trail of the Heart Thief. And honestly, that should have worried me. He had Malachi at his side, as well. A formidable duo they would make, and I'd pray for any quarry unfortunate enough to be their intended target.

But this was Darcy.

Darcy was too clever for them. It was odd how assured in that fact I felt, and somewhat egotistical, too. I'd found and tracked them down multiple times now, after all. But for all that I didn't doubt his determination, Malachi seemed to lack the skill in deduction that had been so essential in my pursuit. He was roundly aware of it, too. Had commented many a time on explicitly that fact. He was right to think we'd make a good team. His grit and tenacity would balance out my hesitation and constant second-guessing.

Dolus... what Dolus lacked was not cleverness, but creativity. I knew that well enough from years spent under his wing, being instructed by the man, and finding my own ways to avoid his scrutiny and deflect his cruelty. If Nicholas and I could rely upon his regimented schedule enough each day to plot a circuit through the grounds to avoid him when it was blueberry season and we wanted to filch extra food, Darcy could run circles around him. I wasn't worried.

Maybe I should have been. But it was hard to be anything other than hopeful, now that I was home with my true Father, I had unburdened myself and still felt his love, and I knew I'd have his help in unraveling the perplexing mystery before us. Dark though it was, this was also a puzzle. The ultimate 'who done it', where the hard work he and I put in might not just unearth answers, but be a fire to burn out the rot that had caused all of this in the organization I still wanted to believe in.

That wholesome feeling of being in the right place at the right time, of knowing I was walking the path God intended for me, while still able to harbor feelings of hope for my future... maybe a future that could include Darcy in some way... it kept my heart light and my spirits lifted.

For all of an hour. And then the bells rang for breakfast on that first day, and I saw my little sister.

She entered the room before most of the other young girls, but after the young men, of course. That was not strange. What alarmed me immediately was that she walked at the front of the procession of girls from the female dormitories. And her manner of dress and grooming had significantly changed since I'd last seen her.

She was a bit taller, but she was also clearly wearing stays beneath her quilted, cream-colored petticoat, forcing her posture more upright and ladylike and further enhancing her apparent height. I'd never seen my little sister wearing a bodice of any kind, let alone one obviously affixed so rigidly. Young

Pedigree ladies might dress thusly from a young age, but Mabel was an Abbey girl. She'd only ever worn stockings and dresses as long as I'd known her. The girls here dressed humbly, not enhancing or correcting their figures as merchant's or noble's daughters might. It was a jarring change to behold.

She must have seen a groomer as well and not just the old monk here who helped us keep our fur trimmed and properly brushed when we were blowing our coats. Mabel was a mixed breed, but her fur was longer and wispy in places around her ears, joints, and framing her face, especially. She probably had some retriever in her. I'd always found the tufty unruliness of her fur charming, in the same way Nicholas's uncropped ears lent him a roguish sweetness.

She'd been shaved down and carefully manicured to an even coat, all over. It lent her cheeks and jaw a more hollow, lean appearance, and what I suppose some might consider a more 'regal' bearing. But to me, it was just so… foreign. So unlike the little girl I'd known.

But she was growing up, after all. The time would always have come, and it wouldn't do for me to hold on to the image of her I held in my heart and expect her to conform to it always. I swallowed my misgivings and smiled at her when she finally lifted her eyes to the room and saw me.

Her eyes widened, and happiness bloomed in my chest, awaiting the excited grin I'd missed so dearly. She hadn't known I'd be getting home today. I'd asked my father to be sure. I was looking forward to surprising her.

The hope died like the greeting that lodged in my throat, when the expression that fell over her golden-furred face was not jubilance, but something like fear.

Instinctively, I glanced over my shoulder to see if Brother Dolus had somehow manifested in the room. But no one stood near enough to me, no one that would have frightened her so, and certainly not the old monk. No, she was… she was looking at *me* with those eyes. Wide, pupils shrunk to pinpricks, her whole body stiff like she'd seen a bird in the brush.

Her gaze eventually shrunk from mine and she filed in behind the Matron to take her seat on the women's wing of the mess hall. And I was left bereft of answers, dropping my eyes from her eventually if only out of politeness, standing frozen in the spot I'd been when I'd seen her, until a hand on my shoulder snapped me out of my frantic inner thoughts.

"Son, you are miles away," my Father's voice, from behind me. Thank God. "Come, you need to eat."

I nodded mutely and followed him, sliding out a stool mechanically and falling into my prayers much the same. I barely considered the words, only recited by rote. When my father placed a plate of warm bread and then a ladle of oatmeal in front of me, my stomach churned. We'd been traveling all night with little to eat since the last carriage house. I'd gotten too few hours of sleep in the bumping carriage, and we'd been crossing the country now for nearly a week. The wheat bread that smelled like our Abbey grains, and the plain but nourishing oatmeal I'd been raised with should have appealed.

But nothing did.

"Are you well?" my Father asked. I could feel him hovering near, nearer than he usually kept to me in the past. Almost like when I'd been young, struggling to eat. Protective. "The carriage ride was uncomfortable. If you're feeling ill, I can brew some tea that may help settle your stomach."

"It's not that," I assured him, staring off across the room again, towards where my sisters sat.

He followed my gaze, seeming to realize immediately. "Ah. Young Mabel. You'll be able to speak to her after breakfast and morning prayer. I know this is the longest you've been apart from your closest siblings. But this is adulthood, son. It is natural that your brothers and sisters make their own way in the world. I know how difficult it can be to see the image of them as pups slip away," he chuckled wryly, spooning himself some oatmeal as well. "Trust me."

"Why is she dressed and groomed like she's courting?" I asked directly, quietly enough that through the din of the room, I was certain only he would hear. I sat at the table with the grown men now, most of which were lay monks. Even Nicholas was away, so Father was my only confidante here anymore.

"She is garbed in the manner befitting a young lady her age," he said, seeming confused by my concern. "And little Mabel has always had a keen interest in sewing and… I suppose you'd say 'fashion,' as most young girls her age do. Remarkable seamstress despite her disability. She'll do well mending garments or assisting in a Tailor's shop eventually if she goes into trade. She's come so far," he said in an uncharacteristically soft tone for him.

"It's not just that," I insisted. "She's been groomed, don't you see? And she won't look at me."

His gaze narrowed when he chanced a glimpse across the room at her and noticed what I had. "Well," he said hesitantly after a few moments, "she is… perhaps experiencing a bad shed, and the monks felt—"

"It's winter," I said, clenching my teeth inside my muzzle. "She is being readied." I was certain of it the moment the words left my mouth.

He seemed to mull over the possibility, but eventually shook his head. "No. I would know if she'd been made an offer. Even despite my time away, she is my daughter. I would have been informed if any man of merit had petitioned for her."

"You are not her only Father," I pointed out, my voice hoarse.

"She is not yet fourteen," he said stiffly. "And, though I think it no blemish upon her worth, she is maimed, Isidor. Be realistic. She is too young, too poor, and too plain to be a target even for the most miserably lonely old tradesman. Have sense."

"If someone made an offer for her," I asked him, throat

aching, "given all of that, wouldn't you be duty-bound to accept? With her chances at marriage so low, wouldn't *any* offer be deemed acceptable?"

"She will need to marry in due time, Isidor," he said, some sternness returning to his voice. "You will have to make peace with that. She cannot be your little sister forever. She will grow up, she will please *someone* despite her damages, and eventually, she will marry."

He stared across the room, clearly deep in thought himself. *"Eventually,"* he pressed out, again. Very intentionally. "We've enough to contend with, now. Let's not worry over things that have not yet come to pass."

But I could tell he was worried, too. My Father could not hide things from me as well as he was once able to, not anymore. The anxiousness persisted through the meal, a shared cloud hanging over the both of us. And when it was time to clear the tables and I realized she'd been tasked with wiping down stools, I stole my chance to talk to her before morning prayers.

Her shoulders hitched when I came near, and seeing her jump at my approach hurt worse than the crop had on my back. I gave her space, standing more than a respectable distance away, but calling out to her.

"Mabel," I said, trying to keep the worry from my tone. "I'm home. I've… I've missed you. How have you been faring, sister?"

She stammered a moment, her arm brushing over her sides, where the stays were pinching her waist in. She looked uncomfortable, as I'd expected.

She stared up at me, seeming cowed by my presence, by my height or my size—I couldn't be sure—for the first time in all the years we'd known one another. "Isidor," she said and curtsied, unable to bend very well at the waist. "Broth—ah. Young sir. I'm… I'm not certain we should call one another that anymore."

"I'll always be your brother, Mabel," I insisted softly. "Even when we're both old and gray. Is this because I've spent so much time away from home?"

"No, no of course not, young Sir," she insisted in the tone she might use when being reprimanded by a monk or another disciplinarian. "You're a Templar now. You're doing God's work in the world, how could I resent such a thing? I-I just..." she stared at her feet, knitting her fingers in her dress, "... I don't think we should call one another brother and sister anymore."

"If that's how you prefer it," I said, trying to disguise the hurt in my voice. I added, afterwards, "Mabel. You... look very fetching in your new dress. Did you help make this one, too?"

She winced, from what I knew not. Oh God, what had I said to offend her? "Yes," she said quietly. "I've gotten better. In your absence. I can even mend your clothes now. The Matron has shown me how to work on embroidered vestments."

"That would mean a great deal to me," I said, tip-toeing through the conversation, wary of *every word*. I didn't understand this. I didn't understand her. I wasn't sure how or why I seemed to be frightening her, every other word.

She stared between the stools and the rag bucket she was meant to be cleaning with, then to me. "I'm not sure," she said softly, "how much time we are meant to spend together now. I have chores, and... I *think* it is permissible for us to talk, so long as we have a guardian present, but the Matron has been very strict about that." She looked quietly desperate for a moment. And when she finally stared up at me again, there was a spark of the sister I knew in her eyes. "I would love to talk to you about your travels. I'm sure you have so much to tell, and I—I *have* missed you, Isidor."

"Mabel," I said, honoring her request to use her name, "please tell me why you seem so upset with me. What's this about spending time together? We've played together since you were a pup with no need of guidance. I'm your elder; it's alright.

Do you want to walk in the garden later, after prayers? I can tell you all about my travels."

"We can't be alone together like that anymore," she whispered fiercely. "Not yet," she trembled.

Trembled.

"Is a man courting you?" I asked her, keeping my voice hushed. I could feel the eyes of the Matron on me, standing in the back corner of the room. She'd been watching us since I'd come over, and I hadn't missed her scrutinous gaze. But oddly, she'd not intervened. She was merely watching us. "Has someone made an offer for you? You don't have to accept it, Mabel. No matter what the Matron says. You have the final word; God gives only *you* that right."

Her golden-brown eyes widened considerably, and she shook as she said, "How could you not know?"

"I've been away," I said, bracing for the news. Who? What man had tried to lay claim to my little Mabel?

"I thought Brother Dolus would have told you," she said, shocked and quiet. "Isidor, it's... it's *you*. The Ministry and God intend us for one *another.*"

"Of course I didn't know!" my Father snapped, his voice reverberating off the stuffy walls of his small office, his footsteps thudding on the hollow floorboards as he marched over to his desk, depositing his cane on the countertop with a clatter before fishing out a set of keys from beneath his robe and noisily unlocking one of the drawers. "Do you honestly think I would have sanctioned this depravity? Good Lord boy, what must you think of me?"

"I'm sorry," I said frantically, shutting the door and swiping my paws up over my ears, scratching nervously at my scalp as I walked in small circles around the other half of the room. "God, the things I said, I-I didn't know. I complimented her *appearance—*"

"Mabel is a sharper girl than anyone gives her credit for," he said, rifling through log books in his drawer at a speed that was careless for the old bloodhound. "She'll not hold a grudge over a misunderstanding, especially now that she realizes this wasn't your idea."

"Good God," I cried out into my palm, muffling my voice. "Is that what he told her?!"

"It doesn't matter, it was a *lie*," Helstrom growled, finally finding the leather-bound book he was looking for and hefting it up onto the desk, sitting down heavily and opening it, leafing through it with purpose.

"Why would he do this?" I asked in a threadbare voice, staring at nothing. "Why would he…?"

"Strictly speaking," my Father sighed out raggedly, "and—I am speaking in the role of an impartial observer obviously, I know the situation and am cognizant of the wrongness in all of this—you are not related by blood. There is a sizable age gap between you and that means you were not raised side by side in the same clutch. It is not unheard of for children raised in the same abbey to marry. It's even… common. He might *earnestly* have thought you two were an eligible match."

"She is a *child!*" I said, horrified. "And my *sister.*"

"I said I was aware of the wrongness of the situation," Father Helstrom reminded me sharply, flicking his eyes up briefly at me before turning a page again and scanning it. "Your relationship is not suited to marriage. Anyone with eyes or ears would understand that. But Brother Dolus does not concern himself overly with the nuances of his children's bonds, and he has been bemoaning the cost of raising so many young girls at once for several years now. We are given far more girls than boys, here. Rural families *keep* boys. But the girls… those more appropriately aged for marriage have trouble finding matches, and then there is the dowry to be contended with. Marrying our charges to one another, especially when the husband has a stipend from the Ministry to support them both on, is way around that. He may see it as an apt solution to several problems at once. Not the least of which, I'll point out, are your own struggles with lust. Which I consulted with him on more than once."

I reeled back as if struck. "Mabel is no *solution* to that problem! And that was meant to stay between the two of us and God, Father."

"I never told him which of my boys was facing those struggles," he said, guiltless and unbothered. "But he could have deduced, I suppose. I know the man has his failings, son, but I cannot aid my flock entirely on my own merits. There are areas —blind spots in my understanding—that I *must* consult with other holy men on."

"You've *never* struggled with lust?" I asked, boldly, disbelievingly. Half a year ago, the mere thought of demanding such an answer from my Father would have sent me into fits. But right now, I was too aghast, too betrayed, too angry, to care. "I find that hard to believe."

"You shall have to have faith in your Father, then," he said coldly and resolutely, matching me angry breath for breath. He was tempering himself better, but not standing down against my barrage. "God constructs us in different ways, Isidor. With different strengths and failings. I have not faced the same struggles as you have, but that does not mean I do not strive to help you, all the same. Sometimes that means asking for help from someone else. Brother Dolus understands certain temptations that I do not, and while he may not always be the most moral man, when contending with sin, you can often learn more from a man who's fallen to its vices before and knows the perils."

"Fine," I snapped, slicing my hand through the air. "It's done, it cannot be undone, you've already spoken to him, but in the future, allow me to seek the confidence of a different more experienced man on the subject, *please*. It wounds me to think he terrified poor Mabel with this prospect... of..." I stumbled over a dozen different things I could have filled in that sentence with, but that sent my mind spinning through half-remembered dreams and yearnings I'd had for Darcy, and to even consider anything remotely similar with my *little sister-!*

"Lord God above, how you've grown," he rumbled, not altogether failing to be intimidating. "Look at you now, young buck, shouting at your Father."

"I'm not—" I stomped down on my tone, gritting my teeth. "I'm sorry. I'm sorry, Father. Truly. I know... you only had my best interests at heart..."

"Your temper has grown in leaps and bounds, since you began finding your independence," he sighed. "Alas, not your *sense,* lad. But I understand your revulsion in this and," here he hesitated, "perhaps I should not have inferred it was your own failings of any kind that lead to this. Especially not given that I may have played an unintended role. I am... I am sorry, as well."

I let my hands fall at my sides, staring at him in shock. "Thank you," I said, my voice quieting. "Father."

He only nodded. "We are as good as equals now, Isidor. If you would prefer to address me as Germain, I would not fault you. Although it would take some getting used to."

"No," I shook my head, crossing the room towards the desk. "You'll always be my Father. What are you trying to find?" I stared down at the book. It looked like a dispatch log.

"Comings and goings, logs of messengers, visitors from the Ministry," he said, eyes back to scanning the page. "I should be able to deduce... yes, there. It was nearly two months ago, right around when you left. Brother Dolus ordered a courier to bring word to the Matron House in Temmiroslyn. Mabel and I spent a week there after she'd cleared her time with the Physician's

Resting House to ensure she was fit for life at Ebon Gables. It's where they perform inspections on the young girls and rate their lineage and prospects. The Head Matron there is the guardian of Mabel's papers and effectively her Godmother. This cannot be anything else. This is when he arranged for the match."

"How could he have done this without my permission?" I asked, my fur bristling over every uncovered inch of my body.

He shook his head. "I do not know the details, but he clearly did not fear your finding out, nor felt any reason to warn or inform you, which is most unusual. If he forged your name, that was bold. But he wouldn't have needed to, Isidor. He is, as I am, one of your Guardians. He can submit a request like this for your courtship to begin, to gain permission from Mabel's Godmother, and then coerce or cajole you to accept through whatever means he deems necessary if he really thinks it's in your best interest. Young Pedigree lads and lasses find themselves in positions like this all the time. The common folk, too. It's a matter of pressure and responsibility in most cases."

"I don't care how much he 'pressures' me," I snarled. "I'm not going to marry Mabel just because it's economically convenient for the Abbey."

"I wouldn't expect you to," he assured me, "and I'll have some fierce words for the man when we see him again, you may be assured. But Isidor, he may honestly just be *dense*. He may truly have thought your affection for her could translate into something more befitting marriage. I don't know. We mustn't assume that his intention here was maliciously-motivated."

"I'm sorry, Father," I murmured, "but I do."

The following week was disquieting in its mundanity. I took the chance to rest, double up on my prayers and duties in the Abbey and focus on self-reflection while my body was kept busy. I made myself as useful to my Father and the other monks as possible.

I rarely saw Mabel. By now at least, she understood this arrangement had not been my idea. I hoped she believed that, at least. But she still seemed to shy from me when we spoke, she looked at me differently, and I could tell she felt less safe around me. Our relationship had been changed forever. In the months I'd been gone, she'd had all that time to see me in a light she'd likely never imagined. Consider me as her potential husband, not her hapless older brother.

I couldn't imagine what must have gone through the young girl's head. How overwhelmed, confused, terrified she must have been. To think I'd been the subject of those fears, those misconceptions… it made me sick at night.

My dreams now were all nightmares. And not the imaginings I'd had before, the yearnings I'd mistaken for daemonic temptations. These were true nightmares, twisted visages of my sister or Darcy, chained and abused by faceless people, torn asunder, and rotting in that cellar Father had spoken of, or hanging from the gallows in a square in Amurfolk.

And my Father, God protect him, had truly seen these sorts of horrors. Not half-remembered dreams, but in the waking world. How did he sleep? How could you live in a world like this, see the things he had, and believe in God's love?

I had not lost faith. I had not even lost hope. I was still certain I was walking the path He intended for me. But I was beginning to doubt God's control over his creation. His authority here. His people—His chosen people—were capable of such terrible works. I had known it, of course, I was well-read. But to read the histories or the news of the day was quite a different experience to living it. Witnessing it.

It seemed at least very clear to me that God needed help. I had never believed in the work I was meant to do more fervently. But I had begun to lose faith in the Ministry itself.

I had my Father, at least. And he was digging. He was poking his nose in places that I, for now, could not go. He was writing letters to many of his contacts, more and more each day, seizing the opportunity to avail himself of the Ministry's couriers while Dolus was still away. I was certain he was being careful in what he asked and how, regardless. I'd already seen he had his ways.

I was somewhat helpless to do much of anything besides digging through the Abbey's books on cuneiform. Something about all of this hinged on the cuneiform, I was certain. It was close to being a lost language, and with the additional artifacts found at Solsforge, we should have been *advancing* our knowledge of what was written on the Heart of Faith. If there was a mistranslation, or if we'd dated it incorrectly... even if in the worst case imaginable, that its' providence was brought into doubt... it was still ancient, and whatever history we unearthed would enrich our understanding of it. *And* our Faith.

I could not understand being so afraid of the truth that you'd kill someone to cover it up. It couldn't be so. It couldn't....

There was no chance that we possessed the knowledge here in our little abbey to decipher any more than the Historical Societies had, but at the very least I could brush up, so I'd have the knowledge stowed in my mind when I inevitably got back on the road.

A week into being home, I had an opportunity to travel again, and it could not have possibly been more welcome.

Father called me into his office, the letter with a freshly-broken wax seal still in hand. "The Ministry sent a request that you pay a visit to young Nicholas and supervise him for a week at the Hudson Estate," he said, offering the letter to me.

I took it, but barely looked it over. "Oh, I'd been wanting to ask how he was faring," I said, tail swaying a bit. "I've asked some of the monks, but none of them have much knowledge, and I know you'd been traveling."

"Last I knew he was doing well enough at the posting," he

sighed. "I'll admit, I worried he wasn't ready for the work, but the Hudsons are good, God-fearing people, and they're a small family. The husband limits his temptations and the wife is steadfastly sober-minded. I know little of the daughter, except that she is nineteen and yet unmarried, but the family is very wealthy. She can afford to wait if she pleases. They liked that Nicholas was unmarried; the wife did not want another young woman living in the house, or even on the adjacent property."

"Honestly, I would be slightly concerned that he might become restless," I said. "The grounds are a good long jaunt from the nearest township, and the park there is lovely, but Nicholas was never all that interested in gardening or nature walks. They have an excellent library too, but—"

He shook his head, giving a rueful smile. "Never quite the reader you are."

"It's not far, and I certainly wouldn't mind getting out for a little while," I blew out a breath. "Especially getting to see Nicholas again."

"The Ministry is just trying to make use of you in the interim before you're sent off for Inquisitor training," Helstrom said, sitting down slowly and stiffly, wincing. "A letter would suffice, if you prefer."

"No, I want to," I insisted. "I *have* worried about him, and I'm certain he'd like to see me."

"Very good then," my Father smiled. "Earnestly, it'll be better you not walk a rut in these halls, anyway. I'm weeks from hearing back from any of my contacts. I'll be sure to write if I hear anything, though."

"And Mabel?" I asked worriedly.

"The Matron of Temmirosyln is one of the people I wrote to." He patted my hand. "That's why I entrusted her as Mabel's Godmother. I am waiting to hear back from her, and then hopefully we can cast off this courtship officially, as well as unofficially."

"Thank you," I breathed out.

"Mabel is a survivor, Isidor," he reminded me quietly. "She has endured more than most of us have in her short life. You'll mend your bond in time, once this is behind us. I'm certain of it."

I stayed silent. I wasn't as certain as he was. What had been done could not so easily be undone. A woman, even a young woman's countenance was... fragile. Her heart, equally so.

"Now, I don't need to tell you to take better care of yourself on the road this time?" he asked as he opened the lockbox on the table to begin counting out what would likely be my travel stipend. I didn't miss as he deliberately stacked three coins instead of two while counting.

"Yes, Father," I said, intending the words as an oath.

"Bring your new cloak," he tutted at me. "I tire of these repetitive colds, Isidor."

"So do I," I agreed. "Of course I'll bring it. I'm fond of it, anyway. It was a gift."

It still smelled vaguely of the incense from the malamute's apartment, the same scent he used on his fur and rubbed into his leathers. It reminded me of him, and even though he was out there right now, likely still trying to hunt down Darcy, I could not find it in me to dislike the man. I rather missed him, in fact. His loud, boisterous voice, and his unfailing protectiveness. I did hope we'd see one another again someday.

"Take Blackbow," Father said, denoting our largest riding horse. "He's bold, but not flighty. Young, still. I think he might make a good permanent mount for you if the Ministry will allow me to appoint you your own. He's too broad for my old legs, anyway."

"No public carriages?" I asked, barely withholding my excitement.

He smiled. "No, lad. God had given you your Crusade. You ought be outfitted like a Crusader, at last."

3

THE SNARE

The town of Hudsonridge was a small, pleasant hamlet dug into the rolling countryside surrounding the Hudsons' vast park. The family was rich in land holdings, spanning most of the adjacent counties for hours of travel in and around. I hardly knew the acreage, but they were the landlords for hundreds of people and in truth did little else. The family was landlocked, and Lordship was their only source of wealth, as far as I knew. They had not moved their resources into industry. Country counties like this held on to an older way of life, less cut up and divvied into slices by the rising mercantile class. It meant townships like this were less diverse, not inviting to most outside financial interests or merchants, but the occasional sporting event or ball—or the fact that a major road passed through these parts—still brought in a steady stream of commerce from the cities, post carriages, and the odd foreigner or two.

The day I made it into the hamlet was a particularly lively day on the streets, owing to several caravans being in town. A lot of people in the east who were moneyed enough to travel casually would leave for their western homes or to stay with family when the north-eastern winds from the Kadrush blew in this time of year. The little town was bustling, and the few local establishments seemed fit to bursting, having trouble accommodating all the visitors.

My intention was to move through town briskly, picking up only a few things from the local bakery for Nicholas, before making the two-hour ride to the Estate. I ended up waiting for the few sweet rolls I'd wanted for nearly an hour, since the poor overworked badger baker there was out when I arrived but swore there would be fresh ones out momentarily. Then he got caught up fulfilling a bread order for one of the local carriage houses and had to check a second batch of rising dough they apparently hadn't been expecting to need, so I... found myself waiting for those rolls for a long time.

I wasn't about to make a fuss. There was no hurry to arrive; there were still plenty of hours of daylight left and the weather had been fair, if a bit cold.

But while waiting, I ducked out of the stifling hot bakery several times to get some air, and while wandering the streets trying not to look as though I were here to question anyone (a difficult task, Templar vestments were white, with the bold lines of the blood striped down them, and *very* well-known and noticeable) I had whispers of a sensation that chilled me and set me to anxious searching.

It was almost primal, a tickling at the back of my ears, a scent unremembered, perhaps. It made me snuffle and sneeze more than once and turn my head to be certain I wasn't being watched. It was like... grease? But more metallic. Maybe. Perhaps just the smell of the tailor's shop leaving dyed cloth out to dry. Perhaps some errant smell from the tanners.

It tantalized and tailed me intermittently, just out of the corner of my senses, like an errant thought I couldn't pin down. I never was able to catch sight of anything or anyone, but the sensation lingered with me until I was on my way out of town, eating one of the warm, steaming rolls. By then though, I all but *had* to dismiss it as a product of my own worries.

The Hudson Estate loomed over the edge of the grasping tree cover, geese cawed in the large man-made ponds, and it wasn't long before the grounds began looking familiar. With it came a wash of nostalgia and an ache I'd been doing a fine job of ignoring for the last few weeks.

This is where I'd first met them. The very beginning of my paws-on-the-ground chase after the 'Heart Thief'. The mysterious feline who remained a largely incomplete puzzle in my mind. My thoughts went to them, got lost in the memories and the ghosts of sensations and feelings, the world around me faded as I pictured the curl of their smile, their fangs peeking out when they laughed, their claws on my shoulders when we embraced…

I could all but hear their amused, tipsy chortle that night we'd shared the bottle of mead. So immersed was I, I didn't realize I'd steered poor Blackbow to the side of the stone bridge I was crossing. When I came to, it was because we'd stopped moving, the horse standing beside the stone rail, the both of us staring out across the grounds.

There was an extra carriage in the carriage house, I took note. A few horses I didn't remember, as well. Family or guests, I couldn't say. Otherwise, the grounds looked the same. I could even spy the top of the hot house from here, and the hint of the dovecote rising out of the gardens behind it.

The shouting, I hadn't been expecting.

It was muffled at first, and when I turned to try to spy where it was coming from, it took me a moment to see the flash of white and red bounding through the woodlands. But in time, his voice was unmistakable.

Nicholas—dashing and bounding through the brush despite being in *full* harness—came panting into view across the browning winter grass, his big dane ears slapping at the side of his face as he ran. He brushed one aside as he finally skidded to a halt on the lawn near the other side of the bridge, and despite the distance, his toothy, boyish grin was unmistakable.

I turned Blackbow and trotted on over towards him, smiling back at my brother, reining the horse in to a stop once we were nearer. "You look like you were out for a run... in full regalia? Nicholas, there's no one here to punish you. Why are you punishing *yourself?*"

"You oaf," he laughed, "I saw you from across the bloody park, up on the daisy hill. Well, right now s'more of a... mud hill. We were up there for the vista. Good view o' the hills."

"'We'?" I asked, before spotting the second figure walking at a far more reasonable pace through the woods, her yellow and white dress and hat catching the sunlight as soon as she'd moved into view. I recognized the young lady of the house immediately. "Oh, Miss Hazel," I said, correcting my posture despite still being in the saddle and the woman being quite far off. Then, quieter, I looked back to Nicholas and asked, "You're out with the young woman... just the two of you?"

"She wanted to paint today," he explained, "and she needed a guardian. Takes 'er *hours*. The Lady of the House don't mind if it's me."

"That doesn't sound like her," I said, suspiciously. My brother was a poor liar. "She's quite strict about propriety."

He sighed. "Not a minute yer here and already you're catching me out. Alright, fine. T'was her idea. She wanted some air, and she really *was* painting. And I really *was* bored as hell."

I sniffed. Then arched an eyebrow. "I smell tobacco, Nicholas. Try again."

"Good *God*," he slumped. "Look, that her, too. I might've... tried a puff. Awful. Don't know what she gets out of it, earnestly."

"The young miss is smoking cigars?" I asked, incredulously, eyeing her as she continued her careful approach, minding the slick hillside. It seemed like they'd had some icy rain the night before.

"Oh, that's not all she gets up to," he chuckled, then when he noticed my glare, blanched. "*What?*"

"Nicholas, I cannot stress this enough," I pinched my brow. "This is. *Literally.* Your job now."

"Ah, ah," he clucked his tongue. "Idn't nothing on my cheat sheet 'bout the particular little toes out of line she steps, so who am I to deny the young miss her mildly rebellious ways?"

"The House Templar," I answered, rolling my eyes. "Nicholas, I… God, I haven't been here *five minutes.*"

"Yeah, and you're being a real stick in the mud," he grinned. "You sound like Father. Life on the road, doin' the good work, s'really turning you into our dad, huh?"

"Stop slurring," I muttered and got down off the horse to greet the young miss as she approached us.

"I was hoping traveling would loosen you up a bit," he grumbled. "Get you seeing there's more out there than the good book and the Ministry's doctrine, you know? You don't seem like you've changed much."

"You haven't a bloody clue," I grumbled, then moved down to kneel before the bull terrier lady approaching us, Lady Hazel Hudson, daughter of Lord Harold Hudson. "Good afternoon, M'lady, well met once again."

"Young Sir Isidor," she said, sounding pleasantly surprised. "I was wondering if I might ever see you again. We shared very few words on your last visit, and I have long thought that quite regrettable. I think we might share something of an interest in reading. I saw you oft in the Library but was hesitant to strike up a conversation."

I stood, brushing off my knee. "I'm glad no such hesitation kept you from friendly discourse with my brother here. But then, he is, I'm told, more gregarious and approachable than I. It's a matter of countenance, I think. I do not mean to intimidate, but my demeanor can lend itself to an air of intensity..."

"Oh, nothing of the sort," she assured me, crinkling her nose when she smiled and twitching her whiskers. "Only that you were here on such a particular task when you came, and I didn't wish to get in the way."

I hung my head. "Yes, I'm... very sorry, Lady. I failed you and your house."

She waved a hand. "It's given mother a good story to share at parties, and no one cared for the bauble that was taken, anyway. Heirloom, passed down... I hardly know. Father thinks it was your presence here that kept the thief from absconding with more valuables than just that, and I'm inclined to believe he's right. But enough of that—I'm so glad you've come to visit! To check in with your brother, I'm assuming?"

"Indeed," I said sternly, staring him down. He made a face at me.

"Oh, just in time, for the poor weather's about to set in again," she sighed. "I won't be able to paint in the park for a long while. And convenient for the servants, too, that our visitors' stays coincide. We'll have a merry party at dinner tonight."

"I noticed the other carriage," I said, nodding. "Friends or family? Or trade, perhaps?"

"Friend of the family," she confirmed. "Perhaps trade or financial, too, I'm really not certain. Father seemed surprised a man of his stature was paying us a visit. Lord Rathborne is a very pleasant young man though, and traveling without his wife, thankfully. Not that I would have minded, but mother would have."

"Excuse me?" I nearly stumbled back into my own horse.

Her ears tipped back at my outburst. "I'm sorry, I... what is it I've said?"

"The man visiting you is Lord Rathborne?" I repeated. "Lord... Cillian Rathborne?"

She brightened. "Oh, you know him! How fortuitous. Yes, he's keeping out of the weather. Shall we call for him?"

"What the hell are you doing here?!" the gentleman demanded of me almost exactly as I asked...

"Why are you here?!"

The all-too-familiar man stood in the doorway of his personal room at the Hudson Estate in the East wing, a posher area of the house I'd not spent much time in during my stay. Almost exclusively for well-to-do guests. It wasn't proper for the young miss to accompany us to rouse a gentleman in his chambers, but Nicholas was still with me, so I had to be careful. He mostly seemed perplexed that I knew someone this wealthy.

"What're the odds you'd run into one of the few gentlemen you met on the road?" he thumped a fist against my shoulder. "Small world, eh? I s'pose we're on the main road to Amurfolk. That where you were headed, Sir?"

"My primary residence is there, yes," the red setter said distractedly, pushing his uncharacteristically unkempt fur back around his neck ruff. He wore only a dressing shirt and slacks, his cravat hung loosely around his neck. I had never—not even the last time I'd met the man when he'd been crying and threatening my life—seen him so undone.

Looking past him, his quarters seemed equally messy. His bed was unmade, a plate of half-eaten food on a dresser stand, and there were books. *Everywhere.* Dozens of them, more than could have come from the small shelves in this particular room.

I stared him in the eyes, saying nothing. We shared a look that asked the same question, though. What the hell was going on here?

"How have you been since our last talk in Redcoven, young Sir?" he asked, glancing briefly aside in the direction of Nicholas, then back to me. "I wouldn't mind... catching up."

"Neither would I," I said, stepping slightly to the side to address Nicholas, so that I might begin to fabricate some reason why he should go back on duty, or why he could not join us. It turned out, it was unnecessary.

He sighed. "Right, I get it. This's Ministry business, idn't it? I know I'm not exactly privy to all that yet. That's fine, honestly... Isi, can I take a ride out with Blackbow? Been a while since I've gotten on a real horse."

"Oh, of course," I said, relieved. "He could stand a brush and the tack could use looking over. Would you mind?"

"Not at all," he smirked. "Turning me into your proper squire, you are. I don't mind at all. I'll be back b'fore supper, alright?"

"Be careful on the trail roads," I urged, as he took off down the hallway. I raised my voice, "And don't run in manor halls!"

When I turned back to the red setter, he was still standing there in the same state, looking softer and smaller out of his fine clothing, and for all the world like any other man. Not the tortured figure who'd come to threaten my life twice in one week.

"So," he cleared his throat. "This is rather awkward."

"Are you armed?" I asked, my voice more tired than I'd intended for it to sound.

"I don't go anywhere without a pistol these days," he muttered, opening the door further for me, "but it won't be pointed at you unless you give me reason."

I stepped inside, and he shut the door behind me, then grabbed me by the edge of my cloak and tugged me backwards through the room, towards a dressing closet. I let him, only because I could have thrown him off me with very little effort if I'd wanted to. Once inside the large closet, he shut the door.

"I don't know how long we have before that boy, or another of your Order, is listening in on us, so we make this fast," he whispered fiercely.

"Nicholas is not a spy," I sighed.

"I don't care how wet-behind-the ears the young man is; he is a *House Templar*," he growled. "He is—in *all* respects—literally a spy."

"There is being careful, and then there is paranoia," I reasoned.

"Why are you here?!" he demanded.

"To check in on my brother," I said. "I swear. I didn't know you'd be staying with the Hudsons. Why are *you* here?"

"Tying up a loose end. Darcy said they left something here during their stay," he explained, quickly. "A half-written letter, tucked into a book. They had to leave quickly after... well, *you* came into their life... and they left it accidentally. Something connecting the both of us together. Incriminating, if it's ever found. Although I'm beginning to doubt their story, truth be told."

"You spoke to them before they left Redcoven?" I asked, hopefully. "Wh—what did they say?"

"You mean about *you*?" he narrowed his eyes. "A great. Deal. You've unlocked some kind of obsession in their heart which I've seen up close and personal before, and it is likely to *burn* the both of you to ash if you don't stop behaving foolishly! Why are you *here?!*"

"I already told you!"

"This is a trap, you realize," he said, glancing around, his breath coming out in pants. "They sent you here to pull Darcy out of hiding. Because you two cannot *bloody* stay away from one another!" He raised his voice near the end of his tirade, shoving me away from him. "You should be on opposite ends of the country by now!"

"I thought we were," I said helplessly. I really had!

"Damned, I knew this was a ploy to get closer to you," he bit out. "I fucking knew they were lying to me, but I couldn't risk it—"

"H-hang on," I held out my hands. "I'm trying to keep up, here. About the letter in the book, you mean? What makes you think they were lying?"

"I have been looking for it for days, and I cannot find it," he spat out.

"Maybe you aren't looking in the right books," I said, glancing across some of the covers in the room. "This house has an enormous collection, where have you been looking? I'm guessing they couldn't remember what they'd been reading…"

God, this was a familiar problem. I knew exactly how it had happened, too. I'd lost *track* of how many times I'd used something I had on hand to mark my place in a book, if it had no ribbon or there was nothing else usable. I'd gone fishing back in the stacks more than once, trying to find a bookmark or a folded letter or prayer sheet sacrificed to the task. And I hadn't always found them.

"It doesn't matter, it's a *lie*, it's always been a lie," he snarled. "An excuse to come back here. They wanted to come themselves, you know. Expected me to head back to Amurfolk and leave them to their merry way to return to the site of one of their own sodding crime scenes. I had to convince them I'd do it if only to protect them… and I know they followed me. I know they're here. I rutting know it. If not here, then in town."

"They're *here?!*" Oh God, how my heart *sung*. But he was right, this was foolish, if he was correct this was the *last* place they should be, but oh—" Why are you so certain they followed you here?" I asked, voice threadbare.

"Because *your* bloody Abbey is two days' ride away!"

"You think they would have come to see me once more?" I asked, hope and reason warring with one another in my mind. It was a losing battle for reason.

"Don't equate cunning with self-preservation," he groused. "Darcy has never made wise decisions, where their well-being is concerned. And apparently, you share that in common."

I thought back on the many times I'd almost died to the elements just in the last two months. "You're not wrong," I conceded.

"This could be arranged," he said. "The Ministry sent you, while I happen to be here? No. Too coincidental."

"You've only been here, how long?" I sighed. "A few days?"

"Long enough to send word to your Abbey," he countered. "They knew I'd be here, somehow, and where I go Darcy tends to be nearby. It's an obvious inference: they know I'm helping them escape. And they sent you because you *always* find them, you two *always* find one another, like frigates drawn towards the same bloody whirlpool." His voice had grown in intensity near the end of his tirade, the frustration evident.

"You're in a frantic state, Sir," I tried to remind him. "And I understand why," I cut him off before he obviously intended to retort angrily at me, "but you have to admit some portion of your worry is paranoia."

"And you're just finding excuses not to panic because you hope to see them again," he bit back. "Overlooking the risk, good god, you think I haven't been *exactly* where you are right now, before?"

I grabbed the manic canine by the shoulders, jostling him until he looked up at me. And I stared him straight in the eyes and asked, "Where. Are. They?"

"I don't *know*," he growled out, shoving me back away from him. "And honestly, there is no point in guessing. Darcy will find you—us—when they're ready. Unfortunately. And there's little I can do at this point to stop that from happening. We parted ways in Redcoven. If I *ever* had a way to know where they were at any given time between when they choose to pop in and out of my life, I'd hire someone to tie them up and ship them off to the farthest reaches of Mataa, where they'd at least be safe from all of *this*. Forcing their hand is the only way I've ever found to protect them from themselves."

"Did you?" I demanded suddenly.

"Excuse me?" he snuffed, his body language going defensive.

"*Did* you hire someone to bind them and force them to leave the country?" I stood my ground. "The bounty hunter who caught them, once."

"Lord above," he nearly laughed, "you're so young, I keep forgetting you're a *bloody Inquisitor*."

"Was that you?" I demanded. "I'd wondered how anyone else could have gotten so close to capturing them."

"How highly you think of yourself," he sneered.

"I never caught them," I reminded him, "they captured *me*. Twice, if we're counting. Darcy writes to you sometimes, when they need help," I continued, certainty dawning, and with it, anger. "You're the only person who'd know how to find them. It really *was* you. That bounty hunter roughed them up to capture them, you know. Probably terrified them."

"You mean like you?" he countered. "Look, the man wasn't supposed to use violence, but a few scuffs would have been worth getting them to safety—you have *no* idea how difficult it is to take care of Darcy when they're in your *care*, let alone at a distance, when they'll hardly talk to you anymore! It has been a lifelong agony for the both of us!"

"You've known one another your entire life?" I asked disbelievingly.

"Very nearly," he said, letting out his breath in a ragged cough. "And if you felt for them as I do, you'd do everything in your power to prevent this slow, painful suicide they seem so insistent upon, too. You agree with me, I *know* you do, because you also tried to talk them into getting to safety. How well did begging and pleading work for you, hm? Do you think whatever promises they made to you, they intended to keep?"

I shut my mouth and considered again the feeling of being watched, tailed, while I was in town. The scent I couldn't place.

Dye.

God, they really were here, weren't they? How foolish could you be? And after they'd promised me that they'd leave the country...

I couldn't find it in my heart to be angry. I wanted to see them again. So badly.

Cillian only nodded, giving a bitter smile. "Yes, I know that look well. I've been where you've been. God, it's not any better looking from the outside in. Why can't I just walk away?" The last part was asked mostly of himself, the words fading into the silence of the small room.

This was the man who'd tried to kill me more than once, I had to remind myself. My back brushed into a row of coats, my sheathed sword bumping the wall. Cillian was still wearing little other than his undershirt and pants, and I couldn't imagine anywhere he'd be hiding a gun on him, so I had no worry at least in here, in the dressing closet, that he'd be a danger.

Looking down on the average-sized man, a bit paunchy but lean-limbed, not unusual for a wealthy man, it was hard to think he'd ever frightened me. But then I looked in his eyes again and remembered. There was an intensity there, a fire brimming at the edges that belied his outward appearance. It was beyond the confidence that came with wealth and status. It was reckless, brave, even. This man was unconcerned for his own safety.

I looked between the two of us, the size discrepancy, at my arms and armor and then his weak leg. He was leaning on his other more heavily, and even without his cane, the limp was obvious. "God has blessed you with a fearless heart, Sir," I commended him quietly.

He gave a sudden, bitter laugh. "Your god has blessed me with very little in life save wealth, and even that came at a cost too steep. I would relinquish it all now if it meant I could get back what I lost in exchange for it."

"You are a Pedigree," I said, choking back any bitterness in my tone and sticking to mostly outrage. "You are not merely wealthy, you are *ascendant*. First in the line. You are the closest to God's Eternal Kingdom and the chance to lay your head down beside Canus and know everlasting peace."

"Ascendance," he chuckled wryly. "The final shining hill upon which all the suffering of the world is decreed a worthwhile march. And what are we promised, exactly? Peace? Slumber? Maybe a dreamless sleep, yes... that would be nice."

"You are *so* close to finding out," I said desperately.

"And how far off are you, supposedly?" he asked, leaning back against his side of the closet, shelves of spats and cravats. "Five lifetimes away? Four? You're an Akita, right?"

"Six," I said, with a glance upwards. I closed my eyes afterwards, blowing out a breath through my nose. "Six lifetimes from His grace, if I do not fail Him."

"How does that make any bloody sense?" he rubbed his nose with his sleeve, quite ungentlemanlike, but it was clear the dust in the closet was affecting him. "You've sworn your entire life to god, you'll live and die for the Church all your days. Why should a heretic like me be closer to his kingdom than you? Because of who sired me? Please."

"You are blessed," I said. "The product of an entire ancestry of righteous men who lived difficult lives. Your soul passed on through many lifetimes. You may not remember it, but you've earned your place. Someday I will, too."

"I'm the *product* of two first cousins marrying," he said, arching an eyebrow. "The *only* child who survived my line. Not my twin sister, not the four litters that came before me. By the time I was old enough to know my mother, she could barely look at me. She was so afraid I'd die like the others, deaf and blind and failing to thrive. What you see before you is the bitter end, not the pinnacle of god's design. By all rights, I shouldn't be alive. The odds were against me."

"I'm sorry," I said softly. What else could I say?

"You've probably led a difficult life in that Abbey of yours, too," he said. "Shouldn't *that* be rewarded? How much have you suffered for something promised instead to your 'betters'? How have you been convinced that's somehow just and righteous, that you should serve us as you do, because of something so beyond your control? It's detestable how they mold you boys like pig iron, battering you into whatever shapes best suit them."

"Watch your tongue," I finally had the chance to stand up for Ebon Gables and my Father, and this time I'd take it. "You aren't holding a gun to me any longer Your Lordship, and I do not need to listen to you sully the names of the people and the place who raised me, let alone my faith."

"Well now, you *do* have some bite to you when pressed, don't you?" He quirked one side of his muzzle. "In your Ministry, don't they call that a spirit of rebellion? They used to drown and burn that out of people, if I've got my histories right."

He wasn't wrong, but I also wasn't about to give ground when he was being so rude. "My Abbey, and moreover my Father, saved me from starvation. My birth family could not afford to feed me. They gave me up to save my life, and if Ebon Gables had not been willing and able to take on a sickly pup, I would have died." His expression twitched, his eyes averted, something akin to guilt darting across his face. "You've never known hunger, I'd wager to guess," I said sharply. "Not real hunger. Not the kind that bloats your belly and turns your guts inside out, where you shit black and choke up bile and would rather die than force down bad meat again."

"No," he said quietly. "I have not. I'm sorry, that shouldn't be a plight any family faces. Why it should be so hard to feed one more child, I—I struggle to understand."

"I can't eat fish or shellfish," I explained, unafraid. If the man wanted to kill me, he had a pistol and a fortune. It's not as if it was an easily exploitable weakness. "My mother and father were poor tradesmen, and meat from the river was about all they could afford to feed their growing brood. It's a miracle they were able to keep me alive as long as they did, but thin broth and bread could only suffice so long. I grew weaker and weaker, and sicker and sicker, until they did the only thing they could to keep me alive. The Abbey was my *salvation*."

"Handing your child over to an order of religious extremist *spies* and assassins should not be the only recourse for the poor," he insisted.

"It was that or a workhouse, and I certainly would not have received the same kind of care at one of those," I said. "I would have died. I don't blame my parents for being poor or for giving me up. They had no other option."

"They should have," he said, "had another option, I mean. Why is it that charity in this country is only dispensed by the Church? Shouldn't aid for the downtrodden be given without theistic strings attached?"

"Then do so yourself," I stated pointedly. "You have enough wealth to save a thousand hungry children, several times over, I'd wager, and still remain rich. You could probably do so yearly if you really wanted to. What's completely out of reach for a family like mine would be a pittance for you."

He sighed. "It's… it's not that simple. Our holdings are enmeshed in estates and trade, factories in Amurfolk… I'd have a dozen different seneschals and solicitors screaming in my ear before I got halfway through trying. It's a tall task to arrange something like that, let alone see it through."

"The Ministry manages nearly fifty different Abbeys and Training Houses across Amuresca," I said. "Each one is home to as many children as they can afford to foster and school. And that's only the Ministry; the Church itself takes in *far* more foundlings, unwanted women, and orphans for its workhouses, which are a fair shake better than those workhouses that function for profit. If the Lords of this country cannot save the poor, it *must* fall to the Church."

"What a miserable world we live in," he shook his head. "I loathe what I've been born to, you know. I doubt you'll believe me. But it's true."

"If you hate it so," I said, preparing to step out on a limb, "then why aren't you with Darcy?"

He froze.

Not in anger. No. The sensation I saw sweep over him, clear as day, was guilt.

"I've unearthed it, haven't I?" I asked softly. "You're married now, but… that wasn't always the case, not even for as long as you've known them. The timing seems right. You wedded your Pedigree wife instead of swearing yourself to Darcy. Isn't that so?"

"Damn you," he rasped.

"It explains everything," I murmured. "The bitterness between you. The way you speak on your wealth and privilege as if it were ash in your mouth. And Darcy talks of trust and promises as if…" I found my paws ghosting over my prayer book, where it was affixed to my belt. I hadn't let it out of my sight since it had been added to. Since they'd written in it. "… as if they've had their heart broken before," I finished at a near whisper. "What sorts of oaths did you make to them that you did not keep, Sir Rathborne?"

He looked up at me, his eyes glossy even in the dark. He tried to speak for a moment, struggled, and then eventually managed in a weak voice, "Everything. I promised them *everything*. And I betrayed that promise."

"Why?" I asked, shaking my head. "You don't seem to care about the wealth. Harder to give it all up than you say it is? You must have been wealthy before your marriage, too."

"You cannot possibly understand the pressure I was under," he insisted desperately. "The shaming, the threats, the sheer, raw *hatred* I endured when I stood before my family and declared I would marry a *servant*, not the Pedigree girl I'd been promised to from the day of my birth."

"You tried?" I was, admittedly, surprised. The mere thought of a Pedigree Lord, regardless of wealth or station, marrying outside his kin, his breed, let alone another *species*... Foreign-born. A worker.

"I tried," he confirmed, the words so quiet as to be nearly inaudible. "I was so desperately, painfully in love. Of course I tried. We were everything to each other, once. *Everything.*"

"Then why not take some of your fortune, whatever you could get your hands on, and elope?" I asked, hardly believing the words as they left my mouth. This was precisely the sort of thing a House Templar would seek to put a stop to. A young lord running off with a servant girl? If I had been serving as his family's House Templar, I would be duty-bound to break him away from such disastrous temptation, and the servant would be sent to an Inquisitor to ensure the secrets of the family and have her moved far enough away that she could never trouble them again.

Or her fate might be worse if she proved to be an insatiable harlot. Or carrying his bastard.

He looked directly at me. "Would you do the same? Leave every person and responsibility you have in the world behind to be with Darcy? Or anyone you loved, for that matter?"

"I have no fortune," I said weakly. "No trade, outside the Church. How could I promise anything in good conscience?"

"Take them and run," he said, vehemently but softly. "Run... far, far away from here, from the Ministry, from the reach of Amurescan Law, from anyone who would hurt them. Protect them. Swear to me on your god's name that you will protect them. Pledge yourself to them however befits a man like you. I don't care if it's marriage or some other arrangement, and I will ensure the two you never want for anything. I have contacts and trade partners, even Privateers I can call upon, if need arises. I *will* take care of you."

I gaped at him. "I..." I stammered, "I do not even know that Darcy desires a future with me. Of any kind."

"I think they do," he said with just a hint of sadness and, yes, envy. He blinked rapidly for a moment, visibly steeling himself. "I'm sorry, you'll have to forgive my obvious bitterness, but I cannot entirely help my tone. Our time together is over, and I've been hoping they'd move on. Truly. Or at least, that's what I've told myself, so that I feel like a better man. I am married now. I have children. And despite that, my inability to release my love for Darcy has bound us in such agonizing circumstances as you now find. Perhaps if I'd been crueler or kept my distance once it was well and truly done. But..."

This was when you let them talk. I could all but hear Father Helstrom's voice in my ear. 'He is as a rose unfurling his petals. Force the man now, and he will never truly open. Wait, encourage if you must, but let him unfold on his own.'

"I couldn't let what we once had rest," he said softly. "Not because I yearned to kindle our passions anew. I *salted the earth* of our love, *ravaged* their heart. I expected no forgiveness, let alone renewal. But what shocked me was the way they punished themselves afterwards, as if it was *their* fault. As if they were worthless. I could not detach us while that instinct for self-destruction so ruled them. I could not leave them to wither and die in neglect of my attentions. I was frightened for them all the time. I kept seeking them out, afraid of what condition I might find them in. Money didn't help. Coin was never what they wanted from me, and all it served was to feed their worst habits. I hardly knew what to do."

"You didn't carry on the affair after you were married?" I questioned.

"It depends upon what you would consider an affair," he said regretfully. "I never took them to bed again, but there were times we held one another. Times we…"

He went silent. I said, eventually, "If your behavior was at all in question, it *was* an affair."

He only nodded, not denying. This would have been a confession in any other setting.

I wished I could stop thinking like an Inquisitor. This man's pain was real and relevant to my own life. This was too personal, too raw to dissect coldly and dispassionately. But I was *desperate* to know more about Darcy.

Especially if they were *here*. I had thought we might not ever see one another again. That had been over three weeks—nearly a month ago, now. A month was so little time in the grand scheme of one's life, but it felt like I'd thought of them every other minute. I was not well without knowing they were well. I had been unable to eat often enough, unable to sleep through most nights. My dreams, once of longing, were now poisoned with visages of what might befall them in my absence. I was sick —quite literally, physically ailing—for the lack of their presence in my life. Withering in fear that I'd never hear their voice again.

Cillian was staring at me, shocked, teeth obviously tightly gritted within his muzzle. I blinked slowly, uncertain why at first.

Then I realized I'd said some of that out loud.

"Good Lord," he breathed out. "Are you certain you're a Church boy? You are… *entirely* too far gone. You sound like someone out of their bloody novels."

"I don't know how to answer that," I admitted. "I *am* a Templar, I believe in the Ministry's purpose still, even though it is all so at odds with what I've come to feel for Darcy. It… is causing such *doubt* to creep into my life. I studied and hunted Darcy as my quarry for nearly a year and yet these feelings persist. I thought perhaps at first that they were demonic whispers, sinful urges I was meant to overcome, or the misbegotten product of obsession over my work. But I am convinced now that they are not. They are the voice of my very soul, and I hardly know how to translate them yet. I don't know what they are or why they seem to overrule all good sense, logic, and I daresay the teachings I hold closest to my heart. I have to believe—I *must* believe—that God has placed this passion and longing within me for some reason. Even if it is simply to be their friend. Their ally. To bring forth justice and clear their name."

"Why give so much credit to your god?" he sighed. "You two found one another. You seem drawn inexorably towards one another. And if you ask me... you *do* sound in love. You do not sound like a man forlorn of lack of a—a book club partner."

"I do not understand love well," I admitted. "Outside of what I feel for my family. But this is... this is certainly different."

He gave a rueful smile. "I suppose, if you need an ear... It will only be *overwhelmingly* painful for me. I shall try not to weep openly."

"How do you know?" I asked, simply. Forlornly. Desperately.

"That you're in love?" He gave a soft 'tch' of noise, leaning his head to the side, staring off distantly. "The poets all have their answers, or they claim you can *never* know. For my own sake, it came on so gradually, I cannot say when exactly I was certain. But I will say that when I knew, I knew."

On this point, his words were solid as bedrock, the certainty in his eyes so resolute, it made me ache with envy. I wanted that.

"It was undeniable," he shrugged weakly. "Perhaps you are simply not there yet. Infatuation and obsession are certainly adjacent, and to someone so young who has never known the difference, it must be quite confusing. I, ah. I would imagine you've never taken another to bed before? We gentlemen are a varied lot, but that certainly sent *me* spinning and confused for a long while. It occupies a powerful place in one's mind. Especially on first blush."

I considered his words, confused. "I've never slept beside anyone other than my brothers when I was younger, if that's what you mean. It was indeed very different to that."

He gave me an odd look. "I would hope so? Excuse me. I, ah. I meant..." He quirked his muzzle uncomfortably, averting his eyes, "... I meant... intimacy. Of the carnal sort. Perhaps I should not have assumed?"

I reeled, when his meaning became clear. "No," I said quickly, vehemently. "I have not... *we* have not."

He put his hands up. "I'm sorry, I meant no offense. You stayed with Darcy at the Lodge for nearly a week, and it's a small dwelling. Apologies. I did not mean to impugn your decency."

"I cannot interpret such an assumption any other way," I huffed.

"It's not because of you," he insisted, obviously choosing his words carefully. "Only that I know... I know Darcy rather well, and they are not... patient on that front."

"Now you're insulting *them*," I said defensively.

"No," he narrowed his eyes, "that wasn't my intention. I speak from *experience*, remember. If you find the thought of an amorous partner unacceptable, it may be better that you benefit from my knowledge *now*. Lord, I fear you may be in over your head. Nay, I'm certain of it. You know very little about them outside of their criminal profile, I'd wager."

"You want me to abscond with them and protect them in some far corner of the world," I said, gesturing at nothing. "Why are you trying to put me off?"

"I am not," he insisted, exhaustedly. "But Darcy is... a complicated person to have as a lover. Perhaps you are better off friends, after all. If it's an ill match, I wouldn't want you to have the wrong impression out of the gate. You cannot *change* them; I will promise you that. If you're hoping to make a demure, complacent, humble little house wife out of them, you will both end in misery. They are *indomitable*. You will find *yourself* the house keeper and they the Master of your home and prospects before long, mark my words."

God, explain to me, please. Why did the thought of that appeal?

"What do you really know about them?" he asked. "Have they even told you about their time with me? How it is they came to be in this country? Their upbringing?"

"No," I answered honestly. "Only what I've inferred. You've said they were a servant. I suppose I can somewhat discern the rest. You had an affair, before you were wedded to the Pedigree woman you'd been arranged with. Your family did not approve. You separated, and now have this tempestuous relationship I've seen. The Ministry knows you had a lover before your marriage, I can say that much. A feline. They never discovered... 'her'. The whole thing was brushed under the rug after you married."

"I promise you," he said quietly, "you would never 'discern' the true story between us from such paltry details. It is far fouler than any decent person is capable of imagining. And, I fear, a dreadfully common tale amongst the elites in this country. How many others must there be out there, like us? Our fates, our truths never known? The Ministry knew all the details of this once, you know. We had a dedicated House Templar. He wasn't even a particularly corrupt old bastard, not compared to some I've seen. Just... average, for your ilk. He knew everything, was involved in fact, but none of this was recorded, obviously. Some things, they do not put to pen. Would have saved them a lot of trouble later on, if they'd not buried their own secrets from themselves."

He looked up at me, asking in a dull tone, "Would you like to know? It is my story to tell as well as theirs."

Every question I'd wanted answered, freely given. The offer

explicit. It would be violating Darcy's most intimate histories to listen to what this man had to say. Their most private sanctum. Their past. But it was also *his* story. He had a right to tell it if he wanted.

I didn't know what to do. I knew what I wanted, but I wasn't certain it was right to accept it.

"To hell with it, ey?" he chuckled grimly. "You already know enough to hang me with. You ought to know what you've become a part of. At least I think you should."

"No," I said, the word stinging my tongue as it left my mouth. It tasted bitter and my chest pounded with regret almost immediately. It seemed to surprise Cillian, too. I looked down at him slowly. "I want *them* to tell me when they're ready."

His expression of mild surprise lasted through the whole silence that followed. When it melted away at last, it transformed into something altogether stranger. He nodded at me.

Respectfully.

"You know, I was wondering..." he admitted, trailing off for a moment. Then he guffawed, quietly. "I was honestly wondering up until this point if this was some kind of strange interrogation or if you were just a *very* deeply embedded spy for the Ministry. Would have been the most advanced tactic they've tried on me yet. And I've been through the whole gamut, believe me."

"We need to find this letter," I said, pressing on to something more time sensitive and a task that might distract myself from what I'd just passed up. "I checked the dispatch logs before I came out here because I've been trying to stay clear of a particular man from my Order. Two of them, really. No other Templar should be coming in or out of this County right now, but Nicholas is here and I'd rather he not get involved in any of this. If Darcy is somewhere close, either in town or—God forbid, at the Hudson Estate as we speak—we need to cover this up as quickly as possible and move them along towards the coast before anyone's the wiser that they were here."

"I've been here three days," he muttered. "As you can tell, I've spent most of every night stealing down to the Library and the reading room, evading the family and servants alike as much as I am capable to look through as many books as I can find. I am not cut out for this like Darcy is. I'm certain some of my strange activities have been noticed by the staff. But damned if I've found anything for all of my trouble."

"Have you looked through any Glaswren?" I asked first-off. "Their spiritual mystery novellas?"

"What, why?" He snuffed. "Ghost stories? That doesn't seem to Darcy's taste. Reading together is about the only activity I could share with them, growing up. It's how we bonded. I know their preferences, generally."

"Preferences change," I said, not so dense as to ignore the subtext in our conversation. "Darcy is a different person now than the one you knew growing up. They may have different tastes. And in any case, reading is like that. You discover a title that becomes the exception in a genre you'd previously overlooked, and then you find yourself more interested in it."

"The First Edition Glaswrens are in the Master's Study," he insisted, shaking his head. "I saw them when Lord Hudson and I talked textiles and shared a bottle of brandy. He locks the study down when he's not in there, and while I doubt that would stop Darcy, that would be unnecessarily risky to nab and return a single book. I wrote off everything in that room."

"There are second-edition copies in the main Library," I said. "When we talked about their collection while we were at the Lodge, they remarked with regret that they hadn't spotted the first edition copies. You're probably right that they never risked going in there."

"You two talked books," he surmised. "Ah. I see. It's all beginning to make sense, now."

"What is?" I asked, opening the closet door.

"I had this wrong," he confessed. "I thought perhaps this was surface-level attraction. But you're not just some muscle-bound head-cracker for the Ministry, are you? You're a book worm who happens to *be* a head-cracker."

"I've never broken anyone's skull," I sighed.

"Are you denying you could?" he asked, looking me up and down.

I made a face and eventually had to admit, "… it would depend on the skull."

"I am beginning to see why they might be attracted to you," he said, pushing uncomfortably past me on his way out of the closet. I was not about to turn my back on the man. I waited for him to go first. "I never had that sharp edge that Darcy needed. They have it, clearly. It was hidden, tucked away, until they began their life of crime. But there is no doubting the grit it takes to do what they do. I didn't have the backbone to fight for my principles. For *them*."

"You've more backbone than you give yourself credit for," I said. "More nerve than most Pedigree sons of privilege I've encountered, at least."

"If that were true," he said, "you'd be dead right now. Allow me to change, if you would. I'll arise suspicion if I go out into the manor looking like this."

I'd been introduced and explained my visit, along with passing along the necessary missive, when I'd first arrived and checked in with the groom. It was a formality—the family already knew I was coming and why. So, it wasn't unusual for me to be taking a turn about the house with Cillian, speaking lowly as we walked from room to room, trying to appear casual. We saw no one other than staff. The family was getting ready for dinner.

"Shit," Cillian cursed in a whisper when we arrived at the

Library. The room was separated from one of the breakfast nooks and the adjoining music rooms by a set of mostly glass doors with ornate framing. For whatever reason, the staff had closed and—we soon learned—locked them. Likely because the Library had large, ground-level windows that looked out onto the front lawn, it was nearly dusk, and the family had been recently burglarized. A safety precaution.

I looked expectantly at him for a moment or two. The man was staring through the glass and tried the handle again, of course to no avail. He noticed me looking at him eventually, then gave me an awkward stare in return. "What?" he asked insistently. "Why are you looking at me like that? It's locked. We'll need to try tomorrow."

"Oh," I cleared my throat quietly. "Alright. I'm sorry. You've known Darcy so long, so I suppose I assumed…"

"I am not their accomplice!" he scoffed.

"I just thought I'd let you handle it. But, ah…"

I fished out my picks and set to work. The red setter watched me, mystified, as I leaned down to get a better look. "Won't take but a moment," I confirmed. "Please keep an eye out?"

He presumably did so. I don't know for sure. I was busy. As expected for an internal door, the lock gave way with very little fuss. I stood afterwards, stowing my kit before opening the door and gesturing for him to walk in ahead of me.

He did, while still looking oddly scandalized. "Does Darcy know you can do that?" he asked.

"Yes." I answered. "I picked the locks on the cuffs they put on me while we were at the Lodge."

"Oh, I'm certain *that* got them hot under the collar," he rolled his eyes.

"Yes," I didn't bother lying. "I think so, anyway. They inferred as much, although I thought it might have been in jest at the time."

"I'm understanding whatever it is between you two more and more every few minutes," he grumbled.

"You are?" I followed him inside, shutting the door softly to avoid any unnecessary noise. "Could you explain it to me, then? Because I am still terribly confused, and I promised my Father I'd stop asking him these things and seek out the wisdom of gentleman more experienced in the ravages of sin."

"You just say absolutely everything that comes to your mind, do you?" he coughed into his palm.

"I assure you, no," I promised him.

He began sorting through stacks. And, bizarrely, answered me. I'm not sure I'll ever know why. "You want the accrued knowledge of a gentleman more experienced in the 'ravages of sin', do you?"

"I truly do," I assured him.

"Alright, then," he took a breath. "Don't chain yourself within the limitations that propriety and station demand of you, especially where love is concerned. I suppose I should add 'religion' to that list, in your case. Be careless in professing your feelings—you never know when you've had your last chance to do so. Don't bed someone until there is *no* doubt in your minds that it is what you both want. Don't do it submerged in water, ever. You might think it sounds romantic, I assure you, it is not. Urinate afterwards, always, and clean your fur and theirs of your spend, or you'll regret it in the morning. Drink water with your alcohol, I find in equal amounts avails me best. Stay clear of the 'Divine' or any powdered drug from Mataa of a similar ilk—they have many different names—and, oh—" he paused and quirked a knowing smile at me, "and grappa and wine are not the same thing."

I flushed in my ears, I'm sure. "They told you about that, did they?"

"As I said, they had quite a lot to say about you," he hummed, before selecting a book from the shelf.

"That was a lot to digest," I murmured, "but… thank you. I shall try to remember it all." I swallowed a moment, then pressed on, "And thank you for being so direct on subjects most gentlemen would consider too crass to speak plainly on. No one's ever talked to me about those… things. Not so openly."

"I've made so many mistakes," he shook his head. "*Someone* ought to be able to learn from them. By the by, if you're hoping to keep your relationship more… *pure* while you figure things out, I wouldn't fault you for that," he said, his muzzle sliding into an expression of regret. "I don't accept the Church's teachings about keeping young people empty-headed on the subject of intercourse until marriage, mind you. I plan to talk to my children—sons *and* daughters—when they're of age. I know far too many of my peers both male and female alike who've suffered disastrously because of a lack of education. But, given the vast disparity in experience between the two of *you*, I'd say it's important you hold to some of your values, or you'll feel as if you've sacrificed too much to be with them."

He closed his eyes a moment, then slowly opened them, staring blankly down at the page he had open. "Darcy is both passionate and persuasive when they've got their eye on something, and the surest way you're like to fall apart is if they convince you to betray your most tightly-held beliefs or rush into something you come to regret afterwards. You don't seem the sort who's afraid to speak your mind. Don't hold back if it really matters to you. Stand your ground. Darcy is not fragile. They'll either push back or meet you in the middle."

"Is this strange for you?" I asked quietly. "Helping me, advising me, about them?"

"Yes," he said without pause, "but I want them to be happy. I always told myself if they were lucky enough to find someone who would help them ease their misery, and perhaps—miraculously—walk away from the grand fucking *larceny*—"

"Yes, that ah," I cleared my throat, "would need to stop."

"In that we're agreed," he sighed. "I don't care that a few Pedigree and private collectors are out their baubles, and I understand why it matters to Darcy, but it is going to get them killed eventually. It's a foregone conclusion. You seem to understand that. Earnestly, I never would have imagined they'd befriend someone from within the fucking *Ministry*, but the fact that you're not dragging me to Confession as we speak after all of this," he gestured between the two of us, "fills me with hope for you." He started leafing through the book again "Whatever snapped you out of your doctrine, I hope you keep at it."

"Darcy," I said. "Talking with them, coming to know them has led me to question a great many things."

"God damn you," he said suddenly.

I bristled, glaring down at him. "What?"

"You were right," he muttered irritably and opened a page to display a creased, single piece of paper. Ink had bled through it just enough on the backside to reveal someone had written on it, at least halfway down the paper, before folding it up to use as a bookmark. "First bloody try. Mother of Canus… I'm glad you're on our side."

He clapped the book shut, shelved it, and carefully unfolded the half-written letter, his eyes scanning the page.

I glanced behind us once, glad the doors into here were glass so I could keep an eye out for anyone coming. "Does it really matter what it says? It's Darcy's, right?"

"Oh, most certainly," he nodded. "I'd know their hand anywhere."

"Burn it," I snapped. "Destroy it. Let's get to dinner and none will be the wiser we were here. We can put the whole of this behind us."

"You're not curious what they wrote, all those months ago?" he teased with a snuff. "You keep denying yourself answers. You're simultaneously the best and worst Inquisitor I've ever known."

"It's private," I said.

"They were writing it to *me*."

"They never sent it," I pointed out.

"Mm-hm," he said distractedly. "And you're certain you don't want to read it yourself? Even though you're mentioned in it?"

"What?" my eyes widened, and I snatched it out of his hand. He snorted out a laugh, even as I began reading. "Why would they write about me, back then? I was barely a fixture in the house, let alone on their trail yet."

"See for yourself," he said, crossing his arms over his chest and tapping his cane against his thigh.

I read.

Cillian,

It's been some time. Two years, nearly? I don't know why I am writing to you now. I'm following the Dressage Circuit and seeing all the young men flaunting their paltry skills makes me yearn to show them how it is done. ~~But of course, without your patronage, I'm reduced to a spectator.~~

~~I miss little about those days, except seeing you in the stands. Feeling the pride I felt representing you.~~ I miss Daylily. I remember braiding her mane. (perhaps I'll keep this part)

~~I miss you.~~

This place is soulless. They do not care for the relic I'll take, earnestly they may not even notice it missing. They do not care for much at all. I feel for the young miss. I saw her drinking far too much at dinner. She is unhappy, that much is clear. The Lord and Lady loathe one another and barely look at each other during meal times, then retire to opposite ends of the house.

The old drunk sin-guard I was expecting is nowhere to be found. The handsome young choir boy they sent in his place is an anomaly and an odd spark of chaos introduced into the droll and otherwise predictable equation that this job could have been. He moved the item into his own quarters, which is hardly much of a wrinkle, but don't they normally keep to a regimented schedule? He spends too much time in there and burns the oil late into the night. I've yet to find a safe opening.

~~When can I come home?~~

I know we cannot go back in time. But I don't know how to move forward, either.

I read it over and over again, awestruck. It was otherworldly, something I never thought I'd have. A look into Darcy's inner thoughts, even those they had chosen not to share with their oldest friend. Aborted longings and honesty too raw for them to commit to.

And… they'd called me handsome.

"Even back then, you clearly caught their eye," Cillian said pointedly. "You warranted a mention."

"Darcy has odd taste," I said.

He laughed. Hard enough that he muffled it into his palm. "Perhaps," he agreed.

"They called me handsome," I muttered, mystified.

"You *are* handsome," Cillian said with the same air of irritation he'd had when he'd found the letter in the book I'd suggested. "Earnestly, I am developing a complex, here."

I looked up from the letter, giving him a dubious look. "By whose measure? Don't patronize me. I'm well-aware how plain and rough-edged I am."

"By whose measure?" he repeated. "Well, Darcy's, clearly. But also my own, for whatever that is worth to you. Could stand someone teaching you how to groom and style that fur of yours, I suppose, but that's all window dressing. Lad, if you've serious designs on Darcy, you need to have some confidence and know your worth, or they'll walk all over you. Eschew this humble abbey boy shite."

"You're no Lady," I pointed out. "Men aren't a good judge of one another. And my grooming is… fine."

"Darcy is also no Lady," he said pointedly. "And enough of this. I've taken my share of men to bed, I'm as good a judge as any woman." He gave me a beat to look predictably scandalized, and then grinned at me. "Ah, there it is. The final ramparts. That revulsion, that *instant* reaction of fear and condemnation, that inner voice that screams 'heresy'. That barrier *must* come down, you know, or this is all in vain. Darcy is *not* a woman, lad. Make peace with that or move on."

I spoke through gritted teeth. "It is not so easy. There are truths that *cannot* be denied or easily ignored."

"Well, you'd best make up your mind, then," he snorted, "or you're in for a rude awakening. Darcy will never conform to those beliefs of yours, nor live in denial of who they are. So, if that's your plan, get a better one. And for god's sake, love yourself a little more. Imagine how miserable a man you'll be if you think all these things about *yourself*. Consider it. You have these feelings for them. Undeniably. Yes?"

"Yes," I said roughly.

"That either means you're a heretic, loathed by god and consumed by sin," he reasoned, "or the bloody book is *wrong*. And the way we are, the way Darcy is, it's just another way to be. Honestly, the whole thing gets easier when you accept it's all tripe. But something tells me you need it. Your faith."

"Everyone needs faith," I said quietly.

"It brought me nothing but pain," he assured me. "I'm fine without it. Happier, even."

"If you're wrong, you lose everything," I said, struggling to understand. "Your everlasting peace. Your afterlife. Your place in His Kingdom. If *I'm* wrong, what have I lost?"

"Well, if you're not careful," he said, looking me in the eyes, "Darcy."

I went silent, my throat constricting.

"And the life you could have here," he continued. "This lifetime. Together. You and I suffer under different masters. Different responsibilities. But take it from someone who let those responsibilities, those arbitrary restrictions and rules dictate their future. It wasn't worth what *I* lost." He gave me a long, sad look. "You'll need to decide for yourself."

I fell into a sullen silence for a time following that and eventually headed back to the glass doors, checking the hall once more before opening them and letting us out.

We locked up, and I took one glance towards the direction of the dining hall, before my gaze swept over the windows facing the hothouse and the garden. My mind suddenly set, I began heading in a familiar direction. One I'd gone months ago, when I'd been looking for somewhere to take my rest.

"Where are you going?" he asked from behind me.

"To burn this outside," I said. "Please tell the family I'm a mite too tired from the road to come to dinner."

"I'm sure they'll hardly notice," he said. "You *will* stay on the property though, yes? No going out there into the wild looking for them."

I only waved a hand at him, dismissing his fears. I heard him heading off towards the dining hall, murmuring something indistinct to himself as he went. It sounded worried.

And maybe he should have been. I had but one destination in mind, and it felt as though I was walking the path to perdition. Uncertainty curdled in my gut, a stab of paranoia came and went, anxiousness settled deep in my bones, like the feeling one got when they were being watched by a predator. I felt—nay, I knew—this was God's last warning. I was forging my way through every misgiving, despite knowing better, despite the alarmed cries of the last sentries of reason within my head.

I could not help myself.

This was what it felt like to give yourself over to yearning. To surrender to passion. Passion: the one element of romantic attraction Darcy had told me I did not yet understand.

I went out into the dusk, into the park, and walked that same path we had. To the Dovecote.

4

TO LOVE, TO LUST, TO KNOW THE DIFFERENCE

I burnt the letter, although it nearly broke me to do it. I read it at least a dozen more times before I did. I sat there on the same stone bench, imagining I could feel them beside me, smell their scent, hear their laugh. I thought about absolutely everything Cillian had said to me.

I thought about God. I thought about my Father, and Mabel, and Nicholas, and… even Brother Dolus. Malachi. Everyone in my life I'd be leaving behind if I left now. If I accepted Cillian's offer. I considered—really, truly considered, for the first time in my life—whether God could hear me or not. What life without Him would be like. It was almost unthinkable.

Was it all real? Of course. Of course God was real. How could I even doubt that?

This was nearly verbatim what my teachers had always warned us would happen when temptation crept into our lives. With it came doubt and the willingness to turn one's back on the Word, to the irrefutable truths of the world. Desire made men blind. It corrupted us, made us lose our senses, leave our families, *destroyed* our faith.

It occurred to me now that the reason it had all been so

accurately predicted was that my situation was not unique. Many, many others had faced these very same challenges throughout the centuries. And they had either redoubled their worship and strengthened their fortitude in faith, or they had left. Been excommunicated, exiled, shunned. Jailed or even executed.

But what exactly was the barrier between those men, or indeed myself, and their faith and families? Was it the temptation that got in the way, the forbidden sin that had caused them to stumble? Perhaps if they fell to drink or callous, evil actions, but in my case the only reason I'd be cast away from the church and my family was... Darcy. The desire to protect a person. To be with them.

A person whose only crimes were the theft of objects, as far as I knew. Things. And not the essentials of life, either. I had an entire mental inventory of every crime the Ministry thought the 'Heart Thief' was responsible for, and not a one of them was essential to any other person's existence. They may have had meaning to the people who'd owned them before, or owned them now, but was the material ownership of any one object worth the lives that had been lost over it? The lives that might *still* be lost?

Even the Heart...

Would it be worth it for people to die to return the Heart of Faith to its rightful place? Did we need *it* or the pilgrimage to be one with God?

God's love could be felt in the bleakest of places, I knew this. That was why I could not doubt Him. I had felt Him. His assurance, His strength, could penetrate the most cloying darkness. I had felt His light when I'd had my story heard and valued for the first time beside Malachi in that Ministry Archive. I had felt a renewal of my spirit when I'd realized Darcy's innocence, the conspiracy we'd unearthed, and that I was precisely where I was meant to be at their side. I had known the balm of His love when my father had—against all odds—accepted me despite my transgressions.

The God that I knew would not want me to lose my family. The God that I knew did not want the innocent to be sacrificed upon the altar of convenience to cover for lies. And the God that I knew did not value the existence of an artifact, regardless of its historical importance to His Church, over even one life.

Either these truths were self-evident or the God I'd been taught was at odds with the God I knew in my heart.

I clasped my hands together and bowed my head. Night fell. Hours passed.

I heard the sound of a distant piano. The family in the music room after dinner. The cold began to settle in, but not quite so sharply as it had near Redcoven. The doves spoke lowly with one another in their nests nearby. The wind whispered in the barren branches and boughs of the many trees in the Park.

An animal moved through the nearby forest. No, not just an animal… a horse.

I'd had my head down so long, when I lifted it, I became dizzy and had to blink the blackness out of my eyes, waiting for them to adjust and catch the early moonlight. I turned towards where I'd heard the distant sound in the forest.

A figure stood at the edge of the wood-line. Silhouetted against the manicured grass. Watching me. Their eyes briefly caught the light. Wide. Feline.

I stood slowly, my body acting of its own accord. Hardly a thought not just as soon unraveled passed through my mind. I stared, not daring to breathe, my muscles seized in rigor.

Then they took a step, and so did I. Another. Another, faster. And we were running. Racing across the half acre, towards one another.

My heart pounded in my ears like cannon fire, my breath puffing around me like a dragon. When I finally clawed my feet into the earth to stop, not two more paces from them, every exhale shook my body.

The words that left me in a torrent were beyond my control and without any fury. I could muster none.

"I am *so* angry at you," I gasped out.

Darcy's dye-darkened features slowly spread into a jubilant smile, and they—always braver than I—crossed the last threshold between us, springing towards me with the happiest little sound I think I'd ever heard them make.

I caught them, gathering them up tightly into my arms, and clutching them close. I don't think their feet touched the ground again for several minutes.

God be praised, there was the feline's laughter. Soft, and pleased, and right against my cheek. No hymn could compare.

I gave a guttural noise of relief and then a sniff muffled by the bunched-up scarf around their neck, and my own knitted by Mabel, the fibers clinging together, testament to how close we were. "Bloody hell, why are you here?! Why are you *here*?!"

"Why are you?!" they countered manically. I could feel their smile against my throat. Their nose was cold and right on my pulse. And there was another rhythmic...

Purring. They were purring.

"God, Darcy," I groaned.

"You smell good," they sighed, closing their eyes. "Like books, and... pine."

"It's the incense from the Abbey," I explained, letting out a ragged breath. "Gets into my fur. Frankincense, mostly. Lord, you smell like that grappa to me still. I can't think of you without smelling it, now. Or the mead."

They chuckled. "I suppose you could associate something worse with me. I'll take it."

"Saints be praised, Darcy, why couldn't you just let Cillian handle this?" I begged. "Why come yourself?"

"I missed you, you fool," they said.

I set them down gingerly. They craned their neck back to follow the angle of my muzzle with their own, keeping us eye to eye. Their eyelids slipped low, still open but shaded as they stared up at me, pupils blown wide in the dark, and good Lord above, something stirred in me. No one had *ever* looked at me that way.

"You couldn't have known I'd be here," I said. "What exactly was your plan? Find me at Ebon Gables?"

Their response to that was to… shrug. And give a lopsided smile. "I wasn't sure, but I'd knew I'd find you, or you'd find me. You always find me. I was so certain of it, I brought your weapons. I stowed them in the dovecote itself, earlier. Under the slab in there, wrapped. You'll find them if you look."

"I almost wish you'd gone to Ebon Gables," I growled. "This is worse."

"I wanted to be sure we found the letter," they said. "Before I leave. No loose ends, especially for Cillian's sake. So, did he find it?"

I glanced aside.

Their smile got more impish, and they blinked slowly up at me. "Oh," they said, realization dawning. "Did *you?*"

"Yes," I admitted.

"He never would have written to you for help," they said curiously, "so how did you find your way here?"

"The Ministry sent me," I said, impressing my worry into the words, "to check in with the House Templar here. He's my younger Brother, and he *does* need guidance, but the timing is coincidental."

"Oh, that's suspicious," they said, ears dropping back slightly.

"Yes, it is," I agreed. "Cillian thinks so, too. You can't *be* here." I put my hands on their shoulders and their eyes fell to where I was gripping them, traveling the length of my arms while I continued talking. "We've burnt the letter. My Father and I are looking into the conspiracy. Cillian will certainly leave soon, and so should you—"

"You two are talking now, are you?" they said, not sounding particularly pleased by the fact. But anything more I could have gleaned from them was soon lost in the sensation of their small, dexterous fingers drifting back and forth over the knuckles of my right hand. My breath caught in my chest when one of their soft finger-pads moved over my missing joint.

"Darcy…" I warned, my voice weak.

"No complaints this time," they huffed with a smile, "you crossed the five-paw distance yourself."

"Darcy," I said again, frustrated and unable to summon forth more than their name. Anything more I wanted to say to them right now, I simply didn't have the words for.

"It's enough already, for better or for worse, I'm here now," they said, tilting their head up, their voice dropping to a furtive whisper. "I was keeping to town, but then I saw you. Don't worry, no one saw *me*."

"That's impossible," I reasoned quietly. "Even with your dye on, you're still a distinctive feline in a mostly canine town."

"I kept to the rooftops," they explained.

"How…" I stammered, trying to imagine that, "… how could you follow me… along rooftops?"

"You've never seen me jump," they said with a grin. "These legs aren't just for cutting a fine figure in trousers, you know."

God help me, the images that summoned.

"I might have seen you jump that stone wall on the patio we met on if you hadn't fired a pistol at near point-blank range at my face," I said, trying to focus on something, anything other than the desire to cross the short space between us with my muzzle. Every inch of their body language said that was precisely what they wanted me to do, but I knew once I did, I was lost.

I had *never* been so close to losing everything in my life all at once, because of *one* decision. And the frightening thing was, I was considering it, nonetheless.

"I know you fell, back then," they said, concern slipping over their features. "Did you hurt yourself?"

"Hit my head," I said, brushing it aside. I didn't want them thinking I was still sore about that. It felt like a lifetime since then, even if it had only been just over a month. "It hardly matters anymore."

I'd averted my eyes over the course of the conversation, finding the intensity of their gaze too hard to hold without giving in to the moment, so when the warmth of their palm slid its way up over my shoulder, carded through the ruff of fur along my neck, and ultimately settled on the back of my head, it caught me off-guard. I blinked and flitted my gaze back down to them, wide-eyed and lost.

Their touch wandered the back of my skull, not specifically searching, but stroking. Petting, I realized. My fur there was dense and choppy, nothing like the sleek, soft locks or velvety fur that crowned most Pedigrees. But it grew harder to focus on how self-conscious I was over being touched there when they kept... touching me. Almost reverently.

"I'm sorry," they said. They sounded genuine. "For hurting you, back then."

"We were enemies at that point," I reasoned.

Their muzzle curled up just slightly. "And now?" they asked expectantly.

"I don't know," I said in an exhale.

"Shall I say it, then?" they offered.

I opened my mouth, hardly knowing how I could argue.

"Thick, is what you are," a voice called out from the lawn. Behind us, and I couldn't place it in the first few seconds, so I panicked, spinning unsteadily, and shoving Darcy behind my bulk. My hand went to my sword, but I'd barely clenched on the grip before I realized who'd come upon us. And then I was only *mostly* relieved.

"You're sodding idiots, the both of you," the Pedigree spat out, his voice hushed. He made his way across the uneven lawn with a wince and a limp on each step, his cane tucked up under an arm. He presumably wasn't able to move quite so quietly if he used it. "If you didn't hear *me* coming upon you, how thoroughly fucked would you be if I'd been a hunter or another of his kin?"

He stopped not far from us, his ears obviously up despite their well-manicured wavy tresses. "I cannot believe you, Dar," he snapped in a fierce whisper. "Him, maybe, the bloke is *nineteen*. You're twenty-four, and you're behaving like a child again—"

"Only content to let me act foolishly when it's with you, Cillian?" Darcy interjected in a steady, cutting tone, their demeanor gone *instantly* cold.

"—and how well did that work out for us?!" the canine hobbled up the final distance to us, his fangs flashing in the dark. "You won't have my family's wealth and the prospect of a fouled marriage to hang over the Ministry like a precarious sword, this time. They will *not* bury this because I ask them to! Not *again*!"

Darcy lifted their chin. "You owe it to me to try."

"You think I haven't?" he said, outraged. "You think I haven't tried to leverage what little standing the Rathbornes still have with the Church to get you off the hook for all of this?"

"I didn't bloody *do it*, damnit!" they snarled.

"They. Do not. Care." He thumped his cane on the earth. "How many times must I say this, Dar? You are the sacrificial lamb for this whole messy ordeal, and they'll *have* you slaughtered just as soon as they can just to put it all to bed!"

"He's right," I said, finally finding my voice. I had one hand on Darcy's shoulder, and I used my grip there to gently turn them back to face me. They fought me, still glaring daggers at Cillian. "Darcy, he's right," I said, putting some strength in my voice to get their attention. "It will be easier to settle the public's outrage over the Heart's disappearance if someone is punished for it. If they're trying to hide it, or if it truly *was* taken by someone else and they can't find it, it's still in the Church's best interest that someone hang for it. It makes the country and the Faith look weak, allowing a crime this big to seep like an open wound. Maybe, if you hadn't kept robbing, but since you have..."

"Listen to him if you won't listen to me," Cillian said desperately. "You cannot remain here in Amuresca, Dar. You should be on a bloody ship or across the border right now. You sure as hell should *not* be within spitting distance of one of the manors you hit *and* the Abbey of the Templar you 'held hostage' not a month ago."

"Why is it safe for the both of *you*, then?" they parried. "The Ministry knows you're involved, Cillian, and *you*—" and here their eyes fell on me, hard, and I was not prepared for that, "-are still within their fold! Why am I being pushed aside while the *men* settle this conspiracy—the one I am on the hook for? How is that right?"

"Because neither of us have an execution order out for us, that's why," Cillian answered before I could. "And I'm still the Master of the Rathborne line, the Ministry cannot *touch* me, and they know it. They can bark, and snarl, and threaten, but my family is too integral to the functioning of trade in Amurfolk for them to disappear me."

"You ought not assume that," I spoke up, my words surprising both of them. I looked between them. "This is a strange and terrible frontier we find ourselves walking," I continued. "The Ministry may have intentionally buried or destroyed our most sacred artifact. Nothing is out of bounds right now. Nothing."

A sobering silence settled over the three of us, but it was momentary. It was Cillian who broke it.

"None of this matters," he said. "None of it. Because all this arguing assumes that you give *any* care for your own survival, Dar. And I gave up on that notion years ago."

"Don't," the feline said simply. A whispered utterance, and most certainly a warning.

"Are you drinking?" he asked point-blank. "What is it this time? What form of false bravado are you imbibing to be acting this unbelievably *stupid?*"

"Grappa," I said quietly. Darcy swung their head to look up at me, betrayed. I just looked back down at them sadly. "I wasn't imagining it, was I?"

"They're careful about it," Cillian muttered, "cunning, like a Pedigree sneaking drinks between social engagements."

"You'd know," the feline said with an underlying hiss in their tone.

"I would, yes," he declared unashamedly, "but I'm not that young anymore and neither are you. And I never *drank* myself nearly to death, either."

I shot a look down at them, alarmed. They were still staring furiously at Cillian.

"This has been a problem since we were children," he explained to me. "You'd never have known what to look for, don't feel bad… but I can tell. I can always tell, Dar."

"How much did you say?" they asked, icily. "About us? Our history?"

"I would have told him everything, but he wouldn't hear it," he said, looking to me. "Your Templar there is the real thing. He stands by his convictions, and honestly?" He snuffed, shaking his head. "He was right to stop me. *You* should be the one to tell your own story. Your life is your own, now. I am not your keeper."

"Strange then that you still act it," they said. "Reproaching me for drinking wine, ordering me out of your presence."

"That's not—that is woefully missing the point!" he said, frustrated.

"It is," I agreed grimly. "The circumstances we find ourselves in... Darcy, surely you understand—"

"I am not your doll anymore," the feline said, baring their long fangs at Cillian. "You got tired of playing with me, remember?"

The setter's tone was frail and tired when he murmured, "I don't think of you as my doll, Darcy."

Not 'I never thought of you that way', my mind supplanted. He was speaking present-tense. As though something, at some point, had shifted between them. If he meant never, he would have said that.

The reality of what was unfurling before me, the twisted tale Cillian had alluded to, was making itself known in small, awful snippets. Glimpses into something truly dark.

"You're being cruel to yourself as well as me, right now," he reasoned softly, "because of the fear, the drink, the anxiety of being hunted. You think I don't know this side of you? You get reckless. You do things that get you hurt or hurt others. And if it's not alcohol poisoning that nearly steals you away from the world this time it'll be the Ministry. You're always looking for ways to end your pain in some dramatic fashion, and I *will not* help you do so again, not even indirectly. I want to help you *live*. Even if that means you live safely somewhere... far away from me, finding your happiness in another's arms."

"Whose fault would that be, Cillian?" they asked quietly, shaking so much that I could feel it through three layers of clothing on their shoulder. When they spoke again, their voice was a rasping whisper. "I kept my oath to you. I never left your side. You cast *me* out."

There lay the messy, unraveled tapestry behind the man's

eyes. The darting thoughts, memories, and whatever tangled web must have led to the outcome that was before me. I didn't need to know it to understand it was more complicated than what Darcy had said. The setter could defend himself against the accusation. I almost wished he would, but I also knew that would air more of their pain. I hurt with him. I hurt with *both* of them. It was impossible not to imagine myself in a similar situation, choosing between love and duty.

In a way… I was.

But he didn't defend himself. I saw the moment he surrendered, cursed my training for being able to pick out every little movement and expression shift in the man's features. I didn't want to intrude upon this. Beyond how intensely personal it all was, it felt like a premonition of my own future. And that was a horrifying thought.

"I did," he said, his voice raw. "I did cast you aside."

Darcy's ears fell back, their body hitching in. They hadn't wanted him to agree.

"And it doesn't matter how gently I did it or how I tried to make amends," he pressed on. "I broke my oath to you. I can never repair what I severed. I don't expect to be forgiven, Dar. I just want you to survive."

He gripped his cane, his leg wobbling unsteadily as he leaned on it, eyes slipping closed in pain for a moment. I knew those agonizing twitches. I felt them in my hand sometimes.

"Please," he begged. "*Please* let me help you, this one last time. I know I have no right, but I cannot… I cannot greet the sun each day without knowing you're well. Please just go. Leave here. Go with Isidor, the both of you find refuge somewhere safe. I would get on my knees and beg if I thought I could get back up."

"Don't," both Darcy and I said at the same time, Darcy breaking from my gentle grip on their shoulder to step towards him.

He held out a hand, warding us off. "I can help you better from a distance than I can close, for so many reasons," he said. He finally looked to me, the conviction and assuredness returning to him. "Isidor, I know what you must be giving up, but you... you seem like a good man, and that means you're as much in danger as Darcy is from your Ministry. And you will not evade them as expertly as we have. You're too honest. For your own sake as well as theirs, *go* with Dar. I understand it's all you've ever known, but this is not the life for you. They will either destroy you or re-mold you to suit their ends, and I shudder to think what a man like you could become if they hollowed out all the good in you."

"Would you come with me?" Darcy asked plaintively from beside me. "If I fled now?" I could feel their eyes on me, and my heart froze. If I so much as looked at them now, it would wound me to my core to turn them down.

But I had to.

I kept my gaze on Cillian, instead. Like a coward.

"I need..." I spoke around panting breaths, "... time to... my family—"

"No," Cillian said definitively. "*Now.*"

I could feel Darcy's resolve weakening in sympathy of my own. "You're being too heavy-handed," they insisted to Cillian. "You're asking too much of him too fast. We haven't even—"

"It doesn't matter what any of us think or what's fair here," he said. "The Ministry won't wait. If they aren't on their way already, they'll be sending out agents to checkpoints, areas you can't avoid. Roads, bridges, wherever they think you'll be forced to flee along. They'll have spies watching me—they likely already do. I've been hopping coaches and traveling without an honor guard because I can't bloody trust anyone anymore. I had to come here without notice of my visit; the house guard nearly rejected me at the gate until they confirmed who I was."

"I'm sorry," Darcy said with some of their earlier venom. "It must be difficult traveling without your usual entourage."

"It is when you're a sodding *cripple*," the Pedigree said, shutting the feline down all but immediately. "I am not bemoaning the fact, but I have made sacrifices, too. My own family doesn't know where I am right now—no one does! I couldn't tell a soul. For god's sake, we have a *House Templar* in Amurfolk. The man is on the take, but coin only buys you so much loyalty, especially with someone as lacking in moral fortitude as he is."

I must have made a face, because he nodded at me. "I told you. This is *not* the line of work for you, lad. Even the loyal ones still bury bodies for their Lords. Is that really who you want to be?"

He couldn't have known what Father Helstrom had confided in me. But the statement struck a nerve.

"Talk," he said to the both of us. "Take as much time as you think you have left on this earth, because it very well could be. I'm going to get together everything I've left in my travel funds, save the bare minimum necessary for me to endure the trip back to the Capital. My wife probably thinks I've absconded with a lover or died, by now. Earnestly, I hope the thought gives her some temporary joy. She deserves it, after the last pregnancy."

"Good bleeding Canus, Cillian," Darcy said, wincing. "What Hell has your life become?"

"One of my own making," he assured them. "Don't worry about me. Just please make the right decision here."

He gathered up his cane, using it this time when he began his trek up the slight hill towards the manor. Watching him make the weary procession made my own legs ache, and suddenly my whole body ached, as the tension began to ebb out of it. The energy within me faded from the nervous, battle-ready, hyper-alert state it had been in, and what followed was exhaustion.

An uncomfortable silence fell between the two of us. I assumed after all that had happened that Darcy would distance themselves again. Pull away. *So* many wounds had just been ripped open.

They surprised me. As ever.

I felt their arm slide down along mine, fingers interlacing on my right hand. They always seemed to reach for my right hand. Where I was damaged. This time, they lifted my paw to their face and pressed their delicate muzzle into the joint, giving the spot a soft, almost courtly kiss. I was dumbstruck.

"You look like you're liable to fall over," they said quietly. "Have you been sleeping?"

"Not well," I confessed hoarsely. "Have you?"

"That's what the grappa's for," they said with a wry smile.

"Are you sober?" I asked, serious as the grave.

"I had my last drink nearly four hours ago," they sighed. "After I saw you in town, I… I *was* afraid to come here—"

"As well you should have been," I said, knitting my brow.

"Not because of the Ministry," they insisted. "Because I was nervous to see you again. After going back to the fold, I-I wasn't certain you'd still… and I was worried what they may have done to you." They gave a fragile smile, unfolding my fingers and placing my paw on their cheek. "But you're still you."

I watched Cillian's retreating figure over Darcy's head, and reason returned to me for just a moment. The Dovecote was in a largely ignored corner of the park here, which was hundreds of acres that wrapped around the manor home. We were closer to the house than I would have liked, but still not an area staff would have any good reason to go, at this hour. I wasn't quite so paranoid as Cillian, but all the same…

If *I* was the House Templar here, and I'd seen a guest split off to head for the gardens this time of night…

"What?" Darcy asked, noting my rigid pose.

"Cillian's made it back to the hothouse," I said.

Their eyes went sharp and they turned their ears. "Then I shouldn't hear breathing other than ours."

"What?" I tried to... but no. Their hearing surpassed mine.

"Someone followed him," they said, going for the pistol on their belt.

I pulled my weapon, laying the flat of the blade over my arming sword glove, my eyes scanning the darkness of the Park around us. I heard Darcy falling in behind me and the soft metallic click as they checked their flintlock. The metal shown in the moonlight as they lifted it to the tree line.

"Don't fire unless you're certain we're about to be fired on," I whispered sharply. "The sound will carry for miles. You'll bring down the whole county on us."

"I *will* kill your kinsmen if they try to kill me, Isidor," the feline said shakily. "Be prepared for that fact."

I caught the outline of someone man-sized shifting near a clutch of wild rosebushes. They were crouched, and I was already on my feet. Which meant...

"I can run him down," I said to Darcy. "Don't fire. Circle. Get around him."

They only nodded, stowing their pistol, and pulling a stiletto, instead. I wasn't even certain where they'd been keeping it. I'd never seen it before.

I leaned back, coiling, hiding my readiness from our spy until the last moment, then lunged into a run. We big lads had to chase like wolves, I could hear my Father's voice saying. Choose a main chaser. Build momentum, put the fear in them, but accept you'd be outpaced swiftly, then count on your fellows to run them down. Circle, exhaust them, force them to reposition...

It turned out, I was overthinking it. Our watcher stumbled back onto his arse in the dirt when he realized we were coming for him, scrabbling to his feet and trying to turn and take off for the house. I was on him before he'd even gotten out of the brush, Darcy's lightning-fast form darting in around him, cutting him off from the only other angle.

I pounced, wrestling the gangly fellow down into the dirt, and the flash of red and white I'd caught in the dim light was soon eclipsed by the confirmation of his face.

"Nicholas, damn it all! I knew it..." I snarled, dropping my blade and fisting both of my hands in the bunched-up edge of the boy's cloak, shoving him down by the neck. Darcy did *not* drop or stow their blade.

The young dane mix panted and shook beneath me, an expression of shock and terror broken across his features. He gave a stuttering sob that was just shy of real tears, putting his hands out, unarmed.

"Why are you here?!" I demanded hoarsely. "Why the *hell* are you out here?!"

"Followed the... Lord," he said, all his composure cracking down to the marrow, his nose running. "I was just... t-rying to... do my job, Isi... H-he was acting... strange."

"Fuck," Darcy whispered. "He saw us. He heard all of it."

"How much did you see, Nick?!" I demanded desperately.

He finally broke down into an actual sob. "Isidor," he whined, "what... what are you doing? What's *happening*?"

"Nicholas, God, I can't—"

"He saw us talking to Cillian," Darcy said, their voice dangerously low. "He'll tell the Ministry *everything*."

"He's fifteen!" I snapped. "And my *brother*. He's just doing as he's trained to. Like I was."

Blessedly, I saw the hard edge soften in the feline's eyes, bleeding off into uncertainty. They looked to me, easing back away from Nicholas's prone form, some.

"Oh God, she's the one, isn't she?" Nicholas glanced up once, the whites of his eyes visible. "She's the one you've been after? Isi, I swear, I won't tell no one I saw 'er, but... I don't understand…" He swallowed heavily. "What's going on with you? Are you going to leave us?"

I released him, lifting myself heavily to my feet. "Get up," I commanded.

He did, not bothering to clean the mud and leaves from his vestments as he stood, unsteadily. He warily looked between the two of us. I could feel Darcy's heated gaze like a fire at my back. They were scared. Uncertain. But holding their blade for now, which is all I cared about.

"This isn't Ministry business, issit?" Nicholas asked like a damned fool. "You're… you're turning?"

"Nicholas, shut *up*," I bit out.

"He's right, you aren't helping assure me any," Darcy said with a dark chuckle.

"I'm not going to sell out my Brother," he insisted. Then he looked to me, swiping a gloved hand over his nose. "But… really? Isi-I… I never… this isn't… you're the most pious man I *know*. We all thought you'd make Inquisitor before you were twenty. What *happened* out there on the road?"

"It's just you, right?" I pressed.

"Wh—yeah, of course," he said, sounding earnestly confused. "Who else would I be with? I don't bloody know anyone well outside the Abbey."

"Go back inside," I said, gesturing to the manor. "Wait for me. We'll talk."

"Are you leaving the fold?" he asked persistently. He sounded particularly emphatic about wanting an answer on that.

"We are not talking about this out here," I growled out. "Go. Back. Inside. I will find you in your quarters."

He slumped, then quietly nodded. He brushed off a few of the leaves on his tunic, glancing behind me to Darcy once more, his expression still so totally lost. My chest hurt, guilt eating through me. This was a disaster. I couldn't think of anyone I'd want to have seen this any less than him. No one would have questioned Mabel or assumed she knew anything. Father Helstrom could have kept it secret.

"M'sorry for scaring you, Lady," he said to Darcy, giving a brief, polite bow.

"You didn't," Darcy assured him defiantly.

He bowed once more, the mysterious feline obviously making him nervous, then walked slowly in my direction. He stopped only briefly to look at me and mouth a silent, 'She's pretty', before dashing off into a jog back towards the house.

I know Darcy caught it, so when I turned to them again, I said in a sad tone, "He's a very young fifteen."

"I got that," they said, their body relaxing, stowing their blade somewhere hidden beneath their one-shouldered corset. "Even having overheard us, he doesn't seem to understand how serious this is." They sighed. "Now what?"

"Nicholas just made my decision for me," I said. "I'm sorry Darcy, but I need to stay with him—at least for a while—to make sure he doesn't share any of what he saw. More than that, to ensure he doesn't give them a *reason* to interrogate him. Because he won't stand up to an Inquisitor. Not for long. And I wouldn't expect him to. It's one thing if I considered taking off with you if it would only endanger me, but now—"

"No, I understand," they said, doing a fine job of hiding their sadness. "I never wanted to ask you to make that choice, anyway. That was Cillian."

"Will you please honor your original promise to me and get to safety without me?" I asked.

"Now that you're even *more* in danger?" Darcy scoffed.

Something snapped up in the trees and Darcy and I both stiffened, before realizing with a flutter of wings that it was just a large bird. Likely an owl, judging by the noise.

"I am getting very tired of all of these eavesdroppers," Darcy said, annoyed.

"Well, we picked a bad place for our rendezvous," I said, arching an eyebrow. "Or rather, you picked it for us."

"I'm sorry there wasn't another rustic hunting cabin or charming cottage in the countryside I could seduce you at," they said pithily. "I'm on the run from the law, and you're… the law. It's rather hard for us to meet at a neutral location."

"Did you burn down the Lodge?" I asked them suddenly.

"No," they said vehemently. "I saw the smoke when I was leaving. I swear to you."

"That means Dolus did it," I said, lost. "I don't understand."

I felt a thrum against my palm, and something cold touched my fingertips. When I looked down, Darcy's eyes were closed and they were nuzzling into my hand, purring again. Their nose was chilled in the early night air.

The weakness from before returned threefold. I must have swayed, because fast as a bolt, they shot both hands out to steady me. One hooked in my belt, the other my cloak.

"I'm fine," I insisted. "I just—"

I began to move to my knees, giving in to the urge to prostrate myself, as I did so many times a day to pray. Right now, it had the added benefit of maintaining my balance.

Darcy released my hand, watching me as I settled at their feet. Without any need of asking, they reached out to stroke their palms over my head, brushing back my ears and whispering a soft, "It's alright. You're alright."

I grasped upwards and wrapped an arm around their hip, my hand settling on their lower back, holding fast to them like a lifeline. Their palms continued to pet along my head in gentle, calming circles, the ministrations centering me somewhat. But whether I was able to stand or think clearly hardly mattered. What I needed was an answer.

"I'm so sorry," they murmured. "This isn't right. Look, Cillian isn't the final word on anything. *I'm* not asking you to choose between me or your family. That's insane. I can take care of myself, alright?"

"But you'd leave," I breathed out, "if I left with you now. Not just here, but the country. You'd go somewhere safe if I went with you. Wouldn't you?"

A long pause. Then a quiet, simple, "Yes."

"We know so little about one another..."

"We'll learn," they said with certainty. "I'd give you every chance if you gave up everything for me. It's only fair."

My mind raced. If I could ensure Nicholas was safe, would he and Mabel be better off if I was gone? No arranged marriage to negotiate our way out of. No connection to me any longer that might endanger either of them. Would Father give up looking into the Heart? He'd be safer. I'd leave a hollow space in my wake, they'd pray for me for all their days, but would their lives really be worse if I weren't here?

Was I being selfish, trying to have everything? Or was I being selfish, considering *this*?

God help me, I just didn't *know*.

I looked up at Darcy slowly, my jaw resting on their hip. "You'd trust me that much? With your future?" I asked.

When they smiled again, it was trembling. "No one's ever chosen me over anything important to them," they said. "I don't know if I can ever fully... trust... anyone. Ever again. But I would be willing to try."

I felt the same, weak words I'd said so many times in dreams, in reality, bubbling up out of my throat. But if I couldn't be weak with Darcy, how could I even be considering this?

"I don't know what to do," I whispered against them.

They grabbed up both of my hands suddenly, then slowly pulled me backwards. I found myself dragged off with them as they walked backwards into the forest itself.

117

"Darcy," I said, huffing. "Come now… Darcy, please, what on earth are you doing?"

They found a particularly girthsome tree and thumped back against it with their back, tugging me to them until our bodies bumped together. When they looked up at me in the dark, their expression promised trouble. I couldn't help but feel a Confession was in my near future.

"Is this any better?" they asked playfully. "At least it's a little more private. Not from the owls, but…"

"You should be leaving," I said softly. But I leaned in, all the same. Braced myself on the tree on either side of them.

They craned their neck up towards me, mouth slightly parted. Their hands crawled up around my cloak hood and into the thick fur along the nape of my neck. "You'll find me again?" they asked, but there was no doubt in their voice.

"Always," I said, aware on some level of the underlying twisted nature of the promise, given our history. It didn't make it any less true. "I'll always find you."

"Then what does it matter where I go?" they said, their eyes catching shine in the dark, gold as sunlight. "Promise me you'll come find me, Isidor. Wherever I go. Swear it, and I'll… I'll try to believe you."

"You'll go somewhere safe?" I repeated. They didn't answer, but I knew that's what they were inferring, so I steeled my expression. "I swear it, Darcy. I swear it on the Good Lord Above, in God's name. I will find you. I will come to you, wherever you are. We'll be together again."

They smiled at me. Their arms drew them up onto their toes, and they whispered against my whiskers, "I believe you."

The moment went on, the tension slowly bleeding from the air, and they remained poised, waiting… until at long last, they lowered themselves back to their paws, their expression hard to read. Disappointed, I think.

"Why won't you kiss me, Isidor?" they asked directly, sounding just on the edge of hurt.

I let out a long, staggered breath. "Because... I never have?" I said, guessing. "Because it's a promise, and I failed to promise myself to you today. Because you just had a vicious argument with the love of your youth, and you're still upset? This... this just isn't how I want it to be, Darcy."

"Isidor, I like you," they emphasized, stroking one of my ears. "Very... very much. You're smart, you're *passionate*, you're strong in your convictions even when I press you on them. You're not afraid to debate with me and speak your mind. You don't treat me like a lesser. You treat me like someone whose thoughts and opinions are *worth* something. And, for whatever it matters to you... I like looking at your face. I'm fair certain I'd like the rest of you, too."

I flushed, stammering, knowing I should say something. "I'm supposed to compliment *you* now, I think," I said. "But I'm bad at being courtly."

"I don't need you to compliment me," they assured me. "The way you treat me, the way you talk to me is how you show your regard. I know that."

They drew themselves up again, but this time rather than pulling our muzzles closer, they nuzzled their nose into the hollow of my throat. It felt no less intimate, although I'd never kissed anyone, so it was hard to say. But it was not very different to how they'd nestled in when they'd hugged me before. And the fact that it was not a new threshold made my racing heart calm a few beats. I reached up slowly to cup a hand on the back of their small skull, my rough-palmed, oversized grip feeling far too brutish to touch the seemingly delicate feline.

But I knew better. Even through both of our layers of clothing, I could feel the cording of their muscle, the hard planes of their small, strong body. Darcy was no delicate creature. And I was far more at their mercy here in this glade, alone with them, than they were mine.

"I like you," they repeated, muffled against my fur. "I think you like me, too. If it's not to be romance between us, then... what is this? Friendship?"

"I wish I knew," I said weakly. "There is so much happening, and I'm... I'm having trouble finding certainty. This is important. I don't want to make an oath to you I cannot hold."

"That's refreshing," they said with a tilting smile, "but you may be overthinking it."

"I do that," I confirmed.

"You've already made me promises."

"Of protection, of standing beside you through this," I said firmly. "I don't require your hand to promise you that. I'd do so out of sheer regard for you."

The feline gasped out a breath that was both exhausted and overwhelmed. "Isidor, my goodness. I *adore* you. Do you know how you sound sometimes? No one has ever made respecting me sound so sensual," they chuckled.

I groaned, crushing my nose down into the crown of fur atop their head, inhaling softly. "Whatever it is between us is far more than just respect," I assured them.

Their heat was bleeding into mine. Their arms had sunk into the gathered fabric of my—of Malachi's cloak—around my shoulders. Their cross-belts pressed into my thigh, the edge of their pistol pressing as hard into me as my pommel was into them, I was certain. We were both in our traveling clothes. Hardly the ideal outfits for an indecent embrace, but nothing about this was ideal.

I cursed myself silently for eschewing my heavy gambeson today, but it was beyond uncomfortable to ride in. The padded cotton one did well enough to keep the cold out, but it didn't fasten all the way down and it did little to conceal my failure of virtue. All that separated our bodies was cloth. *This* is why you didn't cross the five-paw distance, my mind screamed at me.

The edges of their claws pricked into my shoulders, through cloth and fur alike. I exhaled slowly, my breath puffing out around us in the winter air. Their steady gaze on me said they knew what they'd done, and that it had been intentional.

"I could leave you marks to remember me by," they said against my ear.

"Darcy…" I warned toothlessly. We both knew I wouldn't stop them.

"I want to be with you, Isidor," they said, the words vague enough and yet… completely clear. Even to me. "We don't need to court. We don't need to kiss if that's a bridge too far."

"And this isn't?" I countered. But their legs were slotted between mine, and I wasn't pushing them away. I wasn't letting them go. One of my hands was on their hip. I didn't even remember putting it there. I was holding them there, my weight doing the rest.

"I've never been in love with anyone, other than Cillian," they said softly. "And that wasn't… it wasn't right, what we had. We were young. Deprived of experience. We almost had no choice but to fall for one another."

"Why are you telling me this?" I asked, voice raw.

"Because I need you to understand this is foreign to me, too," they said. "I have no idea what I'm doing, either."

"Oh, no," I closed my eyes. "Darcy, that isn't *good*."

"I know," they said, a laugh bubbling up out of them. "But, do you know what I *do* understand well enough?"

Something sharp and sudden tugged at the edge of my ear, and I nearly jumped, the sensation startling me before I realized the feline had *nipped* me. First the soft edge of my ear and then the scruff of my neck, beneath my fur.

I panted out an open-mouthed gasp, my forearm flattening against the tree trunk, bracing my weight on it. Darcy coiled against me and leapt. Their legs wrapped around my waist, arms tightening around my shoulders. When the shift in weight caused us both to fall back against the tree, our bodies fit together at the waist, their thighs around my belt line, calves curling underneath my surcoat. Before I could do so much more than take stock, they deftly undid the main loop holding their cross belts together, and they—along with their pistol—slipped off and fell to the forest floor.

We were both still fully dressed. But my clothing could have been gossamer, for all that it mattered. They could *feel* me through my trousers, that much was painfully clear when their eyes fluttered shut, and they rolled their hips against mine.

"Ha-ah…" I dug my claws into the tree, the hand on their hip clutching tighter into the soft leather of their riding britches.

They brushed their whiskers over mine, leaning their muzzle up against my cheek, speaking softly again, right near my ear. "I heard you in the Lodge," they breathed out. "I wanted you… and to know that you wanted me, too? I had to fight every urge to come through that door…"

Humiliation burned through me like a grassfire, swift and cleansing, leaving me clean in its wake. It was almost relieving. "How did you know what I…?"

"You said my name," they whispered. The swift answer shut down any further confusion I may have had.

"I didn't realize I'd said anything," I confessed.

"You ramble in your sleep all the time," they said, smiling. "I'm tired of listening from the other side of a door. I don't want to just touch myself thinking of you again. I want to touch *you.*"

I groaned gutturally when the crux of their thighs slid against me, crushing heat and leather together, their legs *squeezed* around me. What in the hell even was this we were doing? We were dressed, we were… *certainly* not fornicating, at least not insofar as I knew it, but we were… it still felt like….

I squeezed my eyes tightly for a moment, then forced them

to ease back open, and found myself nose to nose with Darcy. The feline's mouth was slightly open, panting into mine. Their eyes looked as hazed-over and far gone as my own must have. "I-I feel..." I stuttered, "... like we're doing... this out of order."

They gave a breathless laugh and pressed their nose to mine. "What a thing to say at a time like this," they teased. "Do you want to stop?"

"No," I said, most moral fortitude I had left long since stamped down by the burning needs of my body. This, even alone, satisfying this urge, had felt *so* wrong back at the Lodge. Like my own body was betraying me and forcing me to sin to relieve myself of the ache. Why was it any different now? Why had I agreed to continue so readily, yet the shame was not eating at me as it once had?

Because this time, I knew we both wanted it.

The realization was so obvious and came unbidden, as if my soul simply... knew. The relief the moment of enlightenment brought was immediate. Cleansing. The clarity it brought...

It hadn't been the desire to touch my own body that had been what made it all feel so wrong. It was the fact that I'd involved another in my fantasies. A person I didn't know then could feel for me this way.

So, this didn't feel like damnation any more. It was something else. Lust? Love? I'd never known either. How would I know? What now?

"I don't..." I stammered, "I-I've only ever done this... alone. I don't know..."

"We don't even need to disrobe," they assured me, grinding down into me and tracing the *shape* of my sheath (and what was very fully emerged by now out of it) with a roll upwards, looking almost dizzy for a moment before they gasped out a surprised, "*Lord*, Isidor."

"I am as God made me," I said haplessly.

They nuzzled my jaw line, then nipped again, this time at my throat. I hadn't realized there'd be so much *biting*, but something told me that was for my benefit. They'd discovered my weakness. Every little successive tease of their teeth made my heart skip and a pounding body-wide thrill move through my blood.

"You're perfect," they groaned. "I want you... God, I want all of you..."

My fingers splayed around the bowl of their hip, pressing into the taut expanse of their backside. I used the grip as leverage, while I steadied myself against the tree, and I tried to move. To answer their own motions.

The first thrust of my hips tore a happy and surprised moan from the lithe feline, and their claws cut into the flesh on the arch of my neck, dragging down to where it met my shoulder, pulling the hood of my cloak taut with it. They left the claws sunk in, holding fast to me like a swaying branch.

"I-I don't... was that alright?" I asked helplessly, worried their tight grip on me meant I'd hurt them, meant I'd gone too far, meant I hadn't done *enough*—

"Yes," they sung, their voice pitching high and almost lyrical. "Just—right th—like that, again. God, don't be too gentle, now."

Where was this even headed? Why were we..? It must be... like how I'd... on my own....

They clung tight to me, one hand shifting from my shoulder to my back, up underneath the cloak. Their claws couldn't possibly penetrate the padded gambeson, but I could feel the ghost of them there, and the tension and *want* that must have compelled them to dig so deeply. It was cathartic, it was relieving—*so* relieving—to know I wasn't alone in my yearnings. They'd even said they'd... while thinking of me?

I wasn't some filth-dwelling, sin-eaten lost soul. Or at the very least, I wasn't alone.

Their little gasps and moans, echoing my own wanton,

shameless utterances, were proof of it. It was mutual, this thing between us. Whatever it was.

Maybe it wasn't love. Maybe it *was* just lust. But if we both wanted it, and none other could suffer for our actions, was it so wrong?

My thoughts were in a tailspin. I gave a hitching breath and a rough grunt as I made the feline's body shudder with the next inexpert thrust, but it seemed to strike a chord. Their muzzle twisted up in pleasure, lips peeling back to reveal their porcelain fangs and pink tongue, and something in my body swooped, wound up, came a hairsbreadth from snapping. My limbs stung and my tail uncurled, my painfully restrained manhood twitching in warning.

My whole upper body shook, breath coming out in a prolonged rattle. Somehow, Darcy seemed to just *know*, and they unhooked one arm to shove their nimble hand down between us, unbuckling my belt and shucking it off me faster than I ever had. I let them, powerless to do anything but hold tight.

"You need to go back into that manor, unlike me," they said softly, somehow more in touch with common sense than I think I *ever* would be in any situation like this. They slipped a hand past the lower half of my tunic, undid one of the buttons on my trousers, and then another, their eyes darting to mine before the last came free. "Can I?" they asked, breath still ragged.

I nodded. Words were beyond me right now.

They gave me a sultry smile, then tugged free their cravat, holding it in their teeth before slipping their palm up beneath the hem of my shirt and down the trail of fur under my navel.

When their palm finally touched me, it was searing. I nearly lost my grip and dropped them. I had to ease them back down to their feet, bowing my body over theirs while their fingers softly trailed the length of me, feeling out the shape before just outright *gripping* me.

I whuffed out a deep-throated, final gasp, unable to bear more than a few moments of their touch. With my buttons undone, they spared my clothing, and quickly snapped up their cravat to enfold their grasp as they stroked me through my end.

I watched the whole of it, even as the evidence of my sin bled through the thin fabric into their palm, even as some of it streaked up their arm. Even as their lithe hips ground up against my thigh, hand remaining shakily clasping my length and the ruined cravat as their own breaths came closer together.

I was spinning, glad for the support of the tree, wave after wave of relieved bliss crashing over my shuddering frame. The feline's motions became jerky and uncoordinated, which had been me the entire time, but was unlike them. They leaned into my chest and gave a keening cry, bleeding off into a longer, lower moan. They pressed tightly to my thigh, their hips going still at last, save a few final twitches.

Their hand slipped away from me eventually. I didn't know what they did with the cravat, and I didn't care to.

I dropped my muzzle, nosing at the soft tuft of fur between their ears. I wanted to comfort them, and I didn't know why. I felt sleepy, satisfied, and completely certain I would regret this when I regained my senses, but for now all I wanted was the affirmation of knowing they were alright.

"How do you feel?" Darcy asked, their voice quiet but still far more cognizant than mine.

"... tired," I answered honestly. "Like I could sleep for days."

"Now that I've 'satisfied your sin,'" Darcy said, speaking playfully, but they were in fact quoting scripture, whether they realized it or not, "how do you feel? Do you think... this is it? Do you see me any differently? Is the bloom off the rose, as they say?"

I genuinely thought on that. Scripture aside, lust and love were not the same thing, and I truly believed that. Now that I'd satisfied one with another person, were my feelings any clearer? Or less so?

"I feel the same," I confessed into the darkness.

"Mmhh," they agreed, folding their arms around me tightly. "So do I."

"… what does that mean?"

"I think it means we need to keep trying this until it makes sense," they reasoned.

I sighed, embracing them in return. "Maybe not in the woods next time."

They laughed, and I committed the sound to memory. The same way I would a verse of a book I liked or scripture that spoke to me. You can't always have the book at hand. But you can remember and find those feelings again.

5

BREAK THE CHAIN

T he manor was quiet when I surreptitiously crept my way back in, choosing to avoid any of the front entrances in favor of the hot house door. I found it locked and briefly considered whether breaking and entering into the Hudsons' actual home at this point was really any worse than what I'd already done. Considering everything that was at stake, I decided it was still the better option. If I went in through the front, I'd have to contend with staff. My arrival would be put in a ledger, and even if the only one who'd really look it over was the Head Housekeeper, I didn't want to arouse any undue suspicion.

After deciding I'd pick the lock, I found—much to my dismay—the door to be deadbolted. I could still easily make ingress if I was determined enough. It was glass, after all. But that was a bridge too far. I opted for one of the servant's entrances instead, after going around the back of the house and finding one of the doors near the laundry lines not only unlocked, but ajar. It seemed odd at this hour, but given there was not a soul in sight, I had to assume someone had stepped out to smoke or get up to something untoward, something…

… like what I'd just done? Oh God.

I shook my head, resisting the urge to murmur a prayer as I stepped inside. There'd be time enough for that later. I couldn't even begin to know how I was going to ask forgiveness in good faith this time. These transgressions were not mere errant thoughts. They were actions. Taken willingly, and if I was being honest with myself, with very little regret or guilt to be found. No matter how deeply I probed.

I found myself, instead, overwhelmingly… relieved. And a bit befuddled. No matter how many times my mind reminded me of scripture, of damnation, I could not summon forth the same kind of aching guilt I'd felt in the past whenever I'd surrendered to the mere thought of these passions. Now that I'd experienced the sin, I… I earnestly wasn't certain why it had ever terrified me so. It seemed a brief, awkward, and benign affair, certainly not worth so much condemnation. Why it would ever offend God or even be worth His concern, I could not say. I suppose if it were a breach of someone's virtue that offended them, hurt them, or in the worst of cases, sired bastard offspring… but given it was possible to engage in these passions without threat of that…

I just didn't understand. *This* was what I'd been warned would sink my soul into the depths of Hellfire my whole life? How? Why?

I needed to talk to my Father about it. He'd have answers. Maybe not answers I'd like, but I needed to be ready for that. I wanted to understand. I *needed* to understand.

In the meantime, I didn't *feel* damned. So that was good?

I walked the narrow servant's corridors, ready to duck or dash my way past any occupied rooms. It seemed like most doors were shut; the staff turned in for the night. There should still have been late-night help turning down the kitchens though, so I readied myself for that.

I passed one of the kitchens, noting the lantern light pooling out from the doorway. That signaled someone should have been there, so I kept quiet and listened, but heard no one. When I eventually made it up to the open doorway and peered around the corner carefully, I saw... no one.

Actually, there were *several* lanterns lit in the room. As well as the hearth. Pots and plates sat un-scrubbed. The area had already begun to smell of souring leftover food.

That would be the first of many signs that something was wrong. Dreadfully wrong. Disturbed, I found the nearest exit from the servant's halls and ducked back into the main house, coming out close to one of the parlors. I knew the house well enough from my brief stay here (before I'd met Darcy) to get my bearings quickly enough.

I passed the main dining hall, finding it cleared out, suggesting they'd at least cleaned up after dinner. But obviously this late, no one was still using the room. I might have expected staff at least milling about conducting their final chores for the night, but the house seemed and sounded empty.

The staff may have all retired to their quarters early, but if so, why leave lanterns lit and the kitchen in a state of disarray? The feeling of unease grew within me.

When Cillian had come back into the house after we'd spoken, I might have imagined he'd join the family in the music room rather than retire directly to his quarters. At least to excuse himself for the evening. But when I next came upon the music room, I found it empty, the piano unattended but left open.

The place did not seem ransacked or rifled through. But I was growing increasingly certain that the family was in danger. Something had happened here.

The fur down the whole ridge of my neck and back was rigid beneath the crush of my cloak and gambeson. The scents in the house were too much of a confusing cavalcade of different canines, servants, food, wax, and lamp oil, but amidst them all was a pervasive and shifting undercurrent of strangeness. A waft of the outsider, of someone not of this place. Maybe dirt or mud from the road outside. Too much fresh air, like doors had been opened repeatedly or left open. The place was cold too, fires left untended, but lanterns allowed to burn out their reserves.

I fought the urge to run. Not only would it do no good—whatever or whoever had descended on this place had come quickly and would certainly not allow me to leave now that I'd returned—I also had an obligation to this family that I was not willing to put aside simply because my term with them was up.

I wanted so badly to be wrong. I wanted there to be some banal reason for all the increasingly-distressing things I was finding. But then I finally made it into the same hallway I'd been in with Cillian earlier that night and saw the glass doors to the library open and two obviously-armed men standing at either side of them, their tunics emblazoned in the same red, white, and gold as my own.

Beyond them, sitting collected in the library like they were seated for a portrait, but smelling of terror and anxiety even from here, were the Hudsons. And far more angry than frightened, unwilling to sit but needing to rest his weight against one of the shelves, was Cillian.

He saw me about the same moment as I saw him. The entire family did. The guards—Templar, I should say, because they very certainly were—seemed to have heard me approaching from farther off. They barely regarded me, except for a nod from the shorter of the two. Nothing condemning. Just an affirmation that we were in one another's presence.

I swallowed, trying to measure my external emotions. I took stock for as long as I was able without appearing to be pinned down on the spot. The family looked frightened, but not hurt. The Templar were keeping them in one of the most central rooms in the house, somewhere they could see all areas of approach. I didn't recognize the Templar guarding them, but they had no special insignia. They were not Inquisitors.

I didn't see Nicholas.

How could I ask? Or rather, how could I ask without making it clear I was not a part of whatever was happening here?

Did I run, right now? I might outrun these two, at least. I needed to warn Darcy... they were leaving, but the Ministry was here. They'd cordoned off the family. They were tightening the snare. There might be another Templar or two outside.

How had they found us? God, Cillian was right. They must have had a tail on him.

The man in question was staring icily at me. But, no, that wasn't it. There was bile there, certainly, but also an imploring gaze dragging me back to it. When I chanced to lock eyes with him, he very intentionally darted his irises to the left. No, down the hallway. He was compelling me to follow his gaze. Or to go there?

I had no justification to demand entrance to the area the family was being kept, and I wasn't about to attack my kinsmen just to talk to Cillian. I continued, haltingly, down the hallway, trying to put some confidence in my steps so as not to appear lost. What was down this way? A reading room and the Master's Study.

The door to the reading room was open. And I smelled blood. Sharp, irony, and fresh. It hit me like a wave of nausea, evoking about the same sensation in my gut. It was so powerful once I had it in my nose, it wiped out all other scents. It was *all* I could smell.

And worse yet, I recognized it. It was a terrible thing, associating anyone's blood with the person. But I'd smelled his blood before. We trained together, we'd grown up together, made mistakes, and had accidents together. Slipping on icy paving stones, falling off a broken tree branch, a nose busted by a wooden sword...

Nick.

He was laying splayed on the ground right at the entrance of the reading room, just inside. His chest rose and fell. What blood he'd lost was spattered across his muzzle and forming a small semicircle on the floor in front of him, collecting in the round patterned crease at the center of one of the tiles. The floor in here was alabaster, and I could not help but see the crimson waxing crescent we all wore on our chests, haloed in blood.

His brows twitched, eyes fluttering open to white slits for a moment as he struggled to grasp at consciousness. I drug in a breath sharply and held it, trying to make sense of what had happened to him. His face was swollen and battered, and he'd clearly fallen, but it didn't seem like the hit to his head had come from his impact with the ground. A scattering of loose papers and a black stain creeping down the leg of a nearby desk brought my gaze to the area of impact—the workspace area of the desk, a miniature battleground. The inkwell was not only tipped-over but broken, pieces of glass seeped in black sparkling in the low candlelight. Whatever blood was there was hidden by the spreading stain.

"My Prodigal son, once more rejoining the hunt."

The voice was every nightmare made manifest, spoken from the hollow darkness of the room near the only window. I was halfway towards Nicholas by then, but I stopped as if yanked by an invisible chain. Years of ground-in obedience compelled me.

"Finally deigning to make an appearance, are you?" The senior man turned from where he'd been standing, his eyes catching red in the lantern light. It wasn't a reflection. Their hue in the dark was and had always been red, a rarer pigment of night shine than gold or green. It meant nothing in the modern context, but some ancient scribes spoke of it being a mark of Ciraberos and of mothers drowning pups who'd been born thusly, after their eyes opened on their first night alive.

If any part of that ancient superstition was true, then we were both damned. Because it's one of the few things Brother Dolus and I shared in common.

We stared at one another, we potential demons in the dark. And then his features came into view in the candlelight. Piteous, not angry. Unerringly normal and mundane as he'd ever looked. One of the most off-putting things about the man was how humble and regular he seemed, even when his presence made you quake in terror.

"God have mercy on you, child," he said, striding across the room, his steps measured but assured, "look at your face. That fear does not become you. The gall of you, horrified *now* by the consequences of your own actions. It's a little late for that."

I gestured at Nicholas, who'd begun to moan quietly in pain. I could barely manage but one word, and it was a breathless, "Why?!"

"Time was of the essence, and the disobedient bastard was being stubborn as ever. I don't need to tell you this, you know how he is," he said almost dismissively, pushing into my personal space. Alarmed, I had to grit my teeth to stand my ground, trying not to let him crowd me back away from standing guard over Nick.

"Discomfort them, force them to take a submissive posture."

"If you wanted the boy to avoid the discipline and the questioning meant for you, *Isidor*," the lurcher said, muzzle peeled back to reveal just the hint of his fangs…

"Use their name. Use it as an accusation."

"…then you should have shown me the respect of honesty, weeks ago… or escorted your young Brother back to the manor, rather than choosing your liaison over family."

I'd been roughly the same height as the older monk for years, now. But somehow, his presence still felt towering. I *still* felt like that little boy, cowering from him.

"Use your body to speak louder than your words can. You can damage resolve far before it becomes necessary to damage flesh."

I could hear Father Helstrom, could all but feel his presence. It occurred to me now and only now that these lessons he'd taught me so long ago... they were not merely for me to wield. He'd been preparing *me* for being subject to Inquisition. Warning me of the tactics I'd one day face. Even without knowing all that would transpire, we subjected our own to scrutiny constantly. He'd known. He'd wanted me to understand, too.

My Father was with me, bolstering me, I reminded myself. And he would have my back, no matter what happened here. He would love me for who I was and try to understand what I did here tonight.

And so would God.

It was time to take a stand against this man. I was *so* tired of being afraid of him.

I took a step forward, closing what little distance remained between us, bringing our faces inches from one another. I could smell his breath, feel the presence he exuded, calm and collected but with a frenetic anger always lying *just* beneath the surface. His temper was well-known in the Abbey. Rarely wielded, but when it was....

My eyes fell to Nicholas again. He was clawing weakly at the ground, trying to get up.

"You know," I said quietly but without weakness. I hoped. I lifted my chin, staring eye to eye with the man. "About Darcy and me. You've known since the Lodge."

"Why else do you think I had to burn it down, you dim pup?" he retorted coldly. "Germain thinks you are some kind of prodigy, but it seems like many a scholar, your mind is feeble in the ways that truly matter. You are *nineteen*, child. I shouldn't have to clean up your messes anymore."

"Why?" I asked—demanded. "Why not just confront me then? If you're going to turn me in regardless?"

He shook his head. "Isidor, my dear boy, when will you eschew this childish aversion to me as some sort of overbearing disciplinary figure—that was Germain and *always* has been—and see me for what I truly am? For you and all my children?"

"And what are you for us?" I asked softly, the tang of blood in the air filling my nose on every breath.

"Your savior," he said, smiling in a way that showed most of his teeth, very intentionally. "And now, most especially to you, your *only* ally."

"What?" I breathed out.

"Do you have any idea what the Ministry would have *done* with you—where you would be right now, as we speak—if I hadn't covered your filthy tracks?" he barked out. "God restore me, I do not balk at my responsibilities, Oh Lord," he clutched at the rosary around his neck, "I know you only deliver unto us as much hardship as we are capable of managing... but Isidor, how you have *tested* me. Such a difficult child, so needy, so frail, so requiring of our precious *time*," he spat the last word out. "I thought we'd gotten past all of that, but here we are, and you are once again our *special case*. You exhaust me, boy."

"I cannot help the conditions of my youth," I said. "I was born with them."

"Mmhh. Germain has a knack for finding the most despoiled, unwanted, broken little wretches and taking them within our gates," he said, deliberately barbing me, I was certain. To what end, I couldn't be certain. Perhaps simply cruelty. "Never a care for what limits there are on our resources or our own personal capabilities, I dare add. Hewing down a functional blade out of the pig iron we find ourselves saddled with thanks to his bleeding heart is a trial, and it does not serve God as He deserves. He would be better pleased by His House taking in the functional, the capable children of the world. Just as deserving of His Light and His Grace, but more readily shaped for His Army. And a fair side less expensive to *feed*."

He snorted mildly when he must have seen the hurt on my face. "Don't look at me like that. The truth is not always pleasant. The fact of the matter is, we could have raised three healthy young lads to become soldiers for God's Army in your place with the funds and time it took Germain and me to nurture you back to health and manage your upbringing. The same could be said for Mabel or the other sickly babes he keeps bringing home, and all of the young... rats, and mice, and other such vermin... none of whom have any prospects for trade, marriage, or worthwhile service to the Abbey or the Faith."

"That should not be all that matters," I said, trying to keep the quiver from my voice. "They are still faithful. They will still serve God, and live righteous lives."

"The Ministry is not a charity, Isidor," he said. "Our purpose is correction. To serve as stewards of the powerful and a reminder of their oaths to God and the Crown. Oaths you swore your very soul to when you were ordained."

I bit my tongue, my outrage stagnating. On this point at least, he was right. I had not forgotten the vows I had taken when I'd been sworn as a Templar. It was not so very long ago, and I had every intent then to honor them until the day I died. Even now, I still believed in what this organization stood for. An independent, communally-run brotherhood of holy men, sworn not to King and Country but to God Himself. We turned our gaze inwards towards our own ranks as well as the elites of the ruling class and prevented the whole fabric of our society from collapsing to sin, vice, and corruption. We were the check upon the Pedigree. We were their worst enemies and the protectors of their souls. We did not exist to be loved, respected, or to enrich ourselves. We did not even serve to elevate our own salvation. The work we did was not holy. It was unpleasant, disturbing, and more often than not, adjacent to sin. Templar were, in many ways, martyrs. Spiritual protectors, as well as house guards and holy warriors.

I believed in it still. And I'd been considering giving it all up. I still was. I could hardly see a way in which this day ended where I stayed within their ranks. But I would mourn my excommunication, not celebrate it. I still thought the work was necessary, and my quest to clear Darcy's name was a part of that belief.

"I am not your enemy here," the monk said, his voice evening out to his usual calmer, soothing timbre. "Someday, if not now, you will understand that. I want nothing more than for you to hold to your oaths. To fulfill your potential, which we so *painstakingly* germinated within you. I have been *protecting* you, Isidor. This entire time. Since I smelled that wench on you and knew with painful certainty that my son had fallen to her expert seductions."

He leaned back, curling his nose, then giving a long-suffering sigh. "You are young. Naïve. I do not fault you as Germain would, if he knew. I am not so divorced from the realities of the world, of the temptations of banal sin. God will judge you, Isidor. It is of little value for me to do so. I am just attempting to salvage what I can of this situation you have *put* us in."

"You don't understand," I insisted, pressing, "they aren't guilty of this crime, Brother. I am attempting to uncover—"

"Please spare me whatever lies they've fed you, son," he cut me off, sharply. "Surely even you realize that whatever excuses you are making for your behavior—however salient they may seem to you—you are *biased*. As would be any man we were steering away from certain ruination in the arms of a conniving criminal. The feline is a *succubus*, Isidor. She has done this before, most certainly, and she nearly ruined that man's life, as well. I am trying to *save* my son. Not just your soul, but your very life."

He tipped his head up, staring down at me from the bridge of his cheeks. "You may not prefer the hardened love I show my children, but we've seen how Germain's approach has borne out. I poured a decade of my life into raising you, for better or for worse. I will *not* surrender you to re-education, to some work camp where they'll brow-beat you to uselessness or starve you to death, and squander everything we worked so hard for. I am not so weak as Whitehall, giving up on my children thusly."

"*You* beat on us!" I said, desperately gesturing to Nicholas. "What the hell is the difference?!"

"I have the right," he answered unfalteringly. "You are my pups, each and every one of you, and I feel no shame for the viciousness with which I must protect my family. Even from themselves, if need be. It is not punishment. It is... correction. And some of you require more of it than others."

"You hurt him so badly," I said, wincing as I looked down at the young Templar, struggling to get to his knees.

"I... sh... dor," he mumbled, blood drizzling out from between his teeth, mixed with saliva. He was trying to speak around a swollen mouth, and I wanted to tell him to stop. But he looked desperate, even through one swollen-shut eye and another nearly stuck together with tears.

"Don't talk," I urged him.

"I would listen to him," Dolus warned, a resting growl in the back of his throat. "In fact, I would hope a lesson has been well and truly learned here today. You will not be talking to anyone other than myself about any of this going forward. Will you, Nicholas?"

Even through the pain and the obvious light-headedness, I could tell by the way the dane's brow crinkled that he was about to disobey the man. Again. I weighed the situation for half a moment before speaking up, "No."

Both of them looked to me. Dolus, expectantly. Calculating.

"No," I repeated. "Neither of us will speak a word of any of this. I…" swallowed back my bile, is what I did, "… I appreciate what you've done for me, Brother. I understand what risks you must have taken covering for me."

Buy more time. Darcy was on their horse, taking to the roads, as we spoke. I needed to keep Dolus here, he and the other Templar he'd brought. As long as possible.

"It is not merely for you," the lurcher assured me. "I cannot allow your youthful follies to sully our Abbey's name either, Isidor. You understand. So many other children's hopes and futures rest on that name. Redcoven's sons suffered for years in the humiliating shade of their Brother Malachi's actions. Think what you'd be inflicting on your entire family. Never mind how you'd break old Germain's heart."

He didn't know I'd been honest with Father Helstrom. That made sense. A man like him couldn't fathom that kind of trust.

"I understand," I assured him, "I…"

Nicholas grabbed at my ankle, yanking at me. About the same time, I realized something I should have earlier.

"Malachi," I tried not to shudder as the folly of my choices here struck me. "Where is Malachi?"

They'd been traveling together. Pursuing Darcy together. They were still, as far as I knew.

Dolus smiled, ever-so-slightly.

"That's the thing about you scholars," he clucked through his front teeth. "Deductive reasoning and book smarts are all well and good, but you need to be able to think on your feet too, lad."

A few young Enforcers wouldn't be able to run Darcy down, if there even were any outside the house. But Malachi….

"M'sorry, Isi," Nicholas wheezed, squeezing both of his eyes shut as he dragged himself, finally, to his knees.

"I thought I was clear," Dolus threatened the boy.

The young dane belted out defiantly, all the same, "I… t-told'm… where I s-aw… you two." He gave a wet, pained sob.

"Him'n the big fellow. I didn'wan'to, but... f-fel-like... e'was breakin m... m'skull... M'so sorry, Isi!"

Fire rose in my throat, my body alight with panic. I whipped my head to stare out the window, to no avail, of course. Even if it faced the right side of the house, I'd see nothing. Darcy had been out in the Park, last I knew. It was acres of countryside, small roads, and forests. It was night.

"*Isidor*," the monk moved his threats to me, cutting me off before I could make a move towards the door. "You have *one* chance here to assure me this grave chapter of your life is over. Cut your losses while you can and choose wisely. Let the foregone events here play out and comfort yourself in knowing I've taken care of the rest. Thankfully, the malamute had his head caved in a few too many times, and he isn't particularly sharp. He was willing to believe the shite story I fed him about this being an intentional operation."

"Nicholas," I leaned down, keeping my eyes on the monk the whole while, gripping the young man by the arm, "can you get up? I need you to get up. Can you move?"

"Can... move. Can even run," he said, keeping his sentences short. His legs wobbled as he stood, the tilt of his body suggesting he was dizzy. But he looked determined, nonetheless.

"Don't throw your bloody life away for what is already signed and sealed," Dolus pressed, affecting a tone meant to sound concerned and sincere. It had a whiff like bad meat. The man spread his arms wide, palms out, "You caught the Heart Thief! You led us straight to her, once again... and that is all the Ministry need *ever* know. This will write you into the annals of history, you and our little Abbey, and you will forget this infatuation in short order and come to see the good all of this has done. The *limb* I have stood on for you!"

"Did you ever really even look for Darcy?" I asked him as I pulled Nicholas unsteadily to his feet and looped his arm around my shoulder. "Or did you just follow Cillian directly from Redcoven?"

He looked briefly shocked and then—of all things—laughed. Broad and near manic. "Simpering *pup*. I sicced the malamute on the craven lordling. I followed *you*, Isidor."

My voice caught in my throat, unformed words on my tongue.

"I sent for you to come here when Malachi informed me where the Rathborne man was headed, after his last carriage hop." He smiled presumably at my expression of shock. "Oh, lad. I know. You checked the dispatch logs. You realize Germain pens those, yes? You think I report everything I do to him?"

My ears burned. My nostrils flared. I hated how naked I felt before him.

He waved a hand as though my turmoil meant nothing to him. "Don't feel too bad, son. You'll learn this soon enough on your own. People are predictable. Especially those caught in the thrall of swindlers and seductors. And the Heart Thief is arrogant enough to be as stupid as her victims, apparently. No part of me is surprised, any more. In time, you'll be able to figure out how people work as well as I do. It isn't complicated."

I glanced back behind me through the door and the hallway beyond. Dolus crossed his arms patiently in front of his chest, cocking his head at me.

"Here, I'll show you," he said. "Go, if you're so desperate to. I won't stop you. But you'll do nothing to help her. *Nothing*. And not just because the odds are against you, but because that is how people are. No amount of infatuation is worth losing what you believe to be yours. No matter the pull of lust, or real regard, whatever it is you've convinced yourself you have. You lack the nerve to risk…"

His voice fell off into a strange pause, and I followed his eyeline. To Nicholas. I swung my nose back to glare at him, disbelievingly.

"... leaving your family behind," he finished, with a click of his teeth. "I was hoping to spare you the pain of seeing the Heart Thief in chains, of realizing you aren't the man you think you are when you ultimately choose your life over hers, but if you must torture yourself..." and here he gave me a knowing look, "... consider it penance."

I felt myself moving backwards, through the door. There was no world in which I didn't take this chance, however small.

"Go," he gestured again. "Time is wasting, lad. That wolf-born Heretic is nothing if not a good hunter. It's in the blood. You can always rely on them as Enforcers, if nothing else."

"Isi..." Nick pleaded, wanting to leave no matter the reason, no doubt.

"You'll make the right choice," he assured me, with nerve-wracking certainty. "You are not as strong as you think you are, Isidor. Not of will, nor of faith, or conviction. None of us are. We've all been humbled at some point in our lives. I think this may be your moment."

The woods were a dark and murky blur around me, swiping and clawing at my face and arms whenever I cut too close to trees or hedges. Blackbow's hoofbeats echoed the thundering in my heart as I clung tight to the reins, standing in the saddle. I did not ride often at a breakneck gallop, let alone in a wooded Park I didn't know well. Every moment, I ran the risk of cutting into a trench, or divot, or upturned root, endangering the both of us. My thighs burned, my lungs protested the cold air, and I'm certain it was no better for my steed.

I worried for Nicholas, left hunkering in the hay loft of the stables, assuring me he'd stay clear of our own people while I did... whatever it was I intended to do out here tonight.

I still didn't know.

There was no guarantee I would find Darcy or any of the

Templar out here hunting them. I didn't even know how many Dolus had called upon, *none* of them, none of *any* of this, had been in the dispatch logs.

But neither I nor Father Helstrom had even known the man was tailing us. Not Cillian, not Darcy, but *us*. God, everything about the timing made sense, now. Cillian had arrived here three, almost four days ago. He'd hopped a carriage two days before that, at which point Malachi had sent word to Dolus. Then the monk has sent the 'order' down to Ebon Gables, and I'd...

I'd come here, exactly as anticipated, and drawn Darcy out of hiding. I could see the chain of events playing out, could imagine how I might have thought and acted if I'd been pursuing the investigation as an outsider and the man in my role had been anyone else.

Years now, the Ministry has ostensibly been after Darcy. But it wasn't until I began encountering them and reporting it back up the chain that they'd assigned real Inquisitors to the task. And now that they had, in less than a month, they'd cornered the feline.

I wasn't some prodigy. I was just about as good at the job as Dolus, Malachi, and likely most other Inquisitors. This was just the first time they'd really made a concerted effort to capture Darcy. And I'd been the one to light the fire.

And now I'd lead the Ministry right to them. Pride goeth before a fall.

Worse yet, I wouldn't even be punished for all of this. Dolus would bury it all to avoid embarrassment for Ebon Gables and likely himself. He'd protect me all the way up through my rise to the Inquisition as well, I was certain. And he would *never* let me forget that fact. He expected me to see this as a favor, as something he'd done for my own good.

And a small part of me wondered if he were right.

It was extinguished quickly, but the niggling echoes of

scripture, of every sermon I'd ever sat through that warned of the ravages of sin and the temptations they'd offer... *they* persisted. Persisted and warred with the new enlightenment I'd been contending with. The challenges against dogma that recent events had led me to consider. The doubts, the *doubts!* And the feelings that had been blossoming inside me, the hope that they might not be wrong-felt, that they may in fact be God-given and *right*. How I wanted them to be permitted, these things I was feeling. How deeply I ached to be relieved of my guilt, and yearn freely, *love* freely....

The forest was alive at night with the sounds of birds and beasts, but when the agonized whinny of a horse split the air, it could be mistaken for nothing else. I reined in Blackbow abruptly, circling him in a clearing, tipping my ears in each direction to discern where the sound had come from. It could echo through a glade like this, but...

There again, but weaker, whining in pain. Crows cawed in the treetops, rustled from their slumber. A strange bird called out into the night.

My ears shot up towards the direction of the call. No, that was a man. A Templar call. Shrill, loud, and meant to carry. Two... three... four, and then five...

Five calls answered it.

I loosed a soft moan of fear as I turned Blackbow towards the noise and spurred him into a gallop once more. The horse took off with a grumbling huff into the cold air, pushing into one of the thicker areas of the forest fearlessly. I could never repay the stalwartness this animal was affording me this night.

We rode for less than a minute, the calls coming closer together. Then, there were shouts. No gunfire, no sound of steel. Only voices. One of them gruff, commanding, I began to recognize as I got closer.

Malachi.

I broke through a thick overgrowth of holly brush, clutching tight to my mount as the first of the other Templar arrived on the scene as well, lighting a fiercely-swinging lantern. The flare of light briefly blinded me and sent wild shadows dancing across the clearing. But it didn't take long to see what had transpired.

It was Darcy's horse. The chestnut mare they'd been riding at the Lodge. I'd taken care of that horse. Fed it, brushed it, even talked to it for a time while Darcy had been out hunting.

It was on its side, collapsed in a roughed-up patch of game trail, where it had clearly gone down mid-run. The animal was suffering, crying out what would likely be its last struggling breaths. A crossbow bolt was lodged in its ribs, deep. Blood poured down its chest and flank.

And alongside its death throes, tearing through my heart like hot iron, was the panicked, desperate crying of its rider. I could see little more than their left arm and part of their ear, as they struggled in vain to pull themselves free of the dying animal. They were pinned. Likely hurt. I could not guess at how badly.

The towering form of the leather-clad malamute was already stepping over the prone animal, hunkering down with something held in his main hand. A simple wooden club. He put his hand through the loop affixed to the handle and then raised it over his head.

I screamed. I screamed his name. And it didn't matter.

Malachi brought the club down precisely and viciously, the wood resounding against the feline's skull with a sickening thud. The thief gave no further twitch, going limp where they lay.

I watched, horrified. I gasped in each breath, trying to steady my body before I fell from the saddle. The man stood slowly afterwards, clutching the feline by their bodice strap, the very same one I'd felt under my paws earlier, and dragged them out from beneath the still dying animal.

"A moment!" he called back towards me, as he focused on his task. He didn't seem to realize who I was, yet.

One of the other Templar, on Malachi's orders, pulled a pistol from his belt and aimed down into the horse's skull. The shot split the clearing and jogged my body somehow back into the realm of reality. This was no dream. This was happening, playing out before my very eyes, and I had very little time to act.

No one thus far even seemed to realize I was not meant to be here. Three other Templar had arrived, more incoming... but that was four men, including Malachi. All armed and ready to take down a dangerous criminal. Could I lie our way out of this somehow? Take custody? God, were they even alive—

I clumsily clambered down out of my saddle, trying not to stumble as I got closer to the scene. Darcy was... they were breathing. Of course. Malachi was nothing if not obedient to the Ministry, and they wanted them alive.

"Gave us a merry chase," I heard the man saying in that melodious timbre of his I'd found so endearing. It was blood-curdling now in this context.

"Good shot there," one of the others, a short, wiry man I didn't recognize said to him, patting him on the arm.

"Good running 'er down," he said in return. "Choke point worked out w—"

His eyes caught mine in the dark. And what followed was a horrifying moment I'd never forget. The malamute I'd come to regard as a friend and respect... grinned at me in the dark with those wolfish features and long fangs, with Darcy's blood spattered on his glove and the club he still wielded. Standing over their prone body. Their life very much in his hands.

Three... four of the other closed in, two on horses by the sound of it. I couldn't fight my way out. I couldn't....

"Decided to join us for the take-down, after all?" he asked me. "Your monk said you'd... well, it doesn't matter. Hot damn, young buck. This worked. You've got colder blood than me. Respect."

I stared down at Darcy, the crushing realization pressing in on me from all sides, just as surely as we were surrounded by my fellows. If I did... anything but what Dolus wanted of me... I would die here.

We would both die here.

Or be dragged off to the Ministry, separated immediately, and then sent to our fates.

But it was all that was left to me. Was I that man? Was I the same as Saint Rapheus of Olminster? Would I die for my principles? Would I fight to the last for a cause I knew to be lost, already?

Would I die for love?

I felt that fire rage inside me once more, filling my chest like billowing sails. Was it His or my own? Did it matter? It compelled me towards only one course. I would meet God today, I consoled myself. I would meet Him, doing what I felt in my heart *had* to be the only righteous path left to me.

I had the element of surprise, at least. I'd make my way to them, attempt to stun Malachi, and then we'd fight our way out of here. I could try not to mortally wound...

Something compelled me back to the world, to focus on what—or rather who—I'd been looking at this entire time. Darcy's prone form, lying at Malachi's feet. And for just a brief moment, I saw those beautiful eyes open.

And they shook their head at me. Barely an inch of movement. Hardly noticeable. But it was undeniable.

They looked at me for one last moment, tears streaked down through the dye on their face. And then they closed them again and played prone, once more.

"God is surely with us this day, Brothers!" Malachi said, raising his arms to the sky, crossed at the wrists. "Under His guidance, we have brought this elusive demon to its proper reward! Ready the gallows, oh Holy Ministry! We, your Sons, commit this Heretic to thee! Praise Canus!"

The stables of the Hudson Estate were clean and spacious, the structure well-tended, the lanterns safely hung and boxed in by glass. It was a far finer stable house than any I'd ever spent time in prior to serving the Hudsons. When I'd been briefly stationed at this manor, I'd come to them sometimes to care for the horses, even though none of them were mine. It was quiet and peaceful in here, especially at night, save the rustling of the animals and the occasional barn owl.

It was also one of the few places on the property I knew of that Nicholas and I would be left alone. At least for now. Until Dolus inevitably found us.

There would be no hiding from my rampaging thoughts, though. Especially not the fresh memories replaying repeatedly in my mind, as if on a loop. Darcy's limp body, bound, gagged, manacled even at the ankles. The Templar had turned every part of their garb inside out searching for possessions, stopping only barely short of completely stripping them.

It had taken every fiber of self-control and reserves I hadn't known I possessed to stand by and watch... and do nothing. Especially knowing that I was proving Dolus right.

But there was no disputing what I'd seen. What Darcy had asked of me, with or without words. And as the minutes ticked by and the blood pumping through my body cooled, reason began to return to me, and I understood it more and more.

As things stood, I was still... inside. In the fold of the very Organization that held Darcy and would try them for their crimes. As cathartic, as romantic as it may have seemed, now was not the time for reckless self-sacrifice. Because it wouldn't only be me who suffered for it. Darcy was not dead, yet. In fact, if the lack of pained sounds from them was any indication, they were either possessing of unfathomable amounts of self-control or they had somehow taken that fall without breaking anything major. And given the rough handling they endured from Malachi and the other Templar hunters, I hoped the latter was true.

If we were very, very, extraordinarily careful, brilliant, and lucky, we might find our way out of this. Somehow. I could not imagine a workable scenario yet, and the knowledge that, even now, Darcy was being loaded into a wagon for transport, bound for I-knew-not-where was…

… absolutely terrifying.

It felt hopeless. I could not even accompany them to the wagon. I'd followed the procession as long as I could, focusing the entirety of my energy on keeping my expression neutral and trying to formulate responses to Malachi's few comments that did not betray my utter devastation.

The malamute was beaming. I don't think I'd ever seen him smile this much, at least not so constantly. But we hadn't much time to talk… which was for the best. He was all business once the other Templar began looking to him for guidance on escorting their prisoner and keeping them bound properly.

There were six of them altogether, fully-fledged Templar hunters. Malachi seemed to be the only Inquisitor here, save Brother Dolus. The rest were what the Ministry would call a 'Hunter Unit', which was precisely what it sounded like. If they were posted within a house or a place of worship, they'd be an Honor Guard. It was the fate of most Templar who either were not fortunate enough to, ill-suited to, or chose not to accept a permanent posting as a House Guard. They traveled wherever the Ministry had need of them, even internationally on mission work, if called upon.

Counting the two in the manor and Dolus, that made ten Templar here, two of whom were Inquisitors. And that wasn't even taking Nicholas and me into account. The Ministry had *finally* committed itself to this mission. And they'd gotten what they wanted out of it.

I could waste away punishing myself for all of this… and maybe eventually, I would. But the one who'd ultimately suffer the most if I allowed myself to be consumed by self-loathing and indecision was Darcy, and I simply hated the thought of that more than I currently hated myself.

There were too many of my own kin here, committed to guarding their prisoner and keeping close watch over them, to free the feline. Allowing them to take Darcy somewhere I wouldn't know the location of seemed a foolish prospect and a sure way to lose them forever. But I simply had no choice. I had to trust Darcy had a plan. Perhaps to escape while in transit?

Whatever they intended to do, I would not be sitting on my own hands. I wasn't certain how I would aid them yet, but acting rashly was not the answer. I would have time. How much, I wasn't certain, but the Ministry would want to conduct some kind of show trial for Darcy. Even if they sped it along, I'd have months, not hours. I'd studied many trials and Inquisitions of the past. Darcy may not be able to hire a solicitor to plead their case, but the Ministry was obsessive about procedure when it came to legal outcomes as serious as execution. They'd had to be since the era of Heresy Hunters had finally come to an ignoble close some decades ago. For instance, it was bad form for the Church to execute Heretics by burning any more, at *all*. And especially given how infamous as the Heart Thief was and how many Pedigree families they'd stolen from, it would seem heavy-handed for us to rush to sentencing without allowing the Council of Lords to weigh in first.

We had some… limited… time. The problem was, in the interim, Darcy was….

"What're you gonn'do, Isi?" Nicholas asked me, an arm clutched across his midsection, where I had him holding a piece I'd broken off from the ice block in the cellar, wrapped in sack cloth. I was cleaning his face with a rag as best as I was able. He'd be better off seeing a Physician for a roughing-up this severe, but I knew better than to think Dolus would allow that. He never liked us seeing anyone else to be treated if the welts or scratches were his doing. Both of us boys knew that very well by now.

No, as hypocritical as it sounded, he would be more likely to insist *he* be the one to look over Nicholas's wounds later. Probably while reminding the young dog of his oath of discipline.

How had I never realized how wrong this all was? Brother Dolus was more lacking in discipline than any of us young men or even the children at Ebon Gables. He was a grown man. A *disciplined* grown man would not lose his temper so often nor take it out on children and young adults. Especially not his own flock who were meant to trust him.

I chose not to answer Nick's question, instead dropping my muzzle down and staring into my lap after putting the bloody rag back in the bucket I'd been using. "The swelling will get worse before it gets better," I told him.

"He's beat on me before," he said, his words still muddled by the damage to his muzzle, "but never this bad. Never so bad I thought I'd die. Isi." He reached out for me, tentatively taking my hand. I let him, without protest. So much closeness and touching between us would have been unthinkable just a few months ago. Not since we'd become adults. Now, I hardly noticed any more. "I'm sorry," he repeated for about the dozenth time since everything had happened. "I couldn'hold out…"

I shook my head. "He would have kept beating you if you hadn't talked. I don't think he would have stopped until something broke."

"I only said you was in the Park behind th'manor," he said, sounding angry at himself for even that much. "I don'know how much it mattered. But I'm sorry if't made the difference, if s'why they caught up to her."

"I don't know that they could have escaped once the Templar closed in on this place," I said. "Darcy shouldn't have been here, and I shouldn't have let them linger as long as they did."

"I don't want to do this anymore," he said after a pensive, quiet beat had passed between us.

My brows lifted. "What do you mean?"

"This," he said, his voice pained and shaking. "I don't want to serve God this way. There has to be somethin' else out there for us. I hate this. I don't want t'spy on people like Hazel n'rat on them to people like bloody *Dolus*. Don't that feel backwards to you?"

"It does," I agreed softly.

"Was that really the Heart Thief?" he asked, dropping his voice to a near inaudible whisper.

I considered how to answer that. "They're..." I chose my words carefully. I didn't want him knowing about the conspiracy, but I also didn't want to lie to him. "...they're the person the Ministry calls the Heart Thief. Yes."

"An'this weren't... an op. You meetin' with her like that?" He blanched a little, averting his eyes. "You were *real* close."

"No," I said, more evenly this time. "It wasn't a ruse. We are... close. That was real."

"Damn," was his simple, eloquent response. Then, "How'd tha'happen?"

"You already know too much of the story for your own good," I said, shaking my head. "I'm sorry. I just want you to be safe, Nick."

"M'not safe in the Ministry," he said, stubbornly. "Never will be."

"I think," I said quietly, "you might be right."

Heavy footsteps into the barn caught both of our attention, Nicholas going rigid and frightened. Seeing the way he reacted made me ache inside. Everything I was going through right now paled in importance to protecting my Brother, as far as I was concerned. If Dolus had any more violence planned for him...

... I'd kill him. I'd kill him if I had to.

"Isidor?" a familiar and intimidating voice—but not the one I'd feared—called up towards us. "You're here, aren't you?"

I leaned down over the edge of the loft, ensuring first that the malamute was alone before climbing down the ladder, bracing myself inwardly.

I could not wear my feelings on my face right now. For Darcy's sake, I had to keep calm.

Malachi turned, seeming mildly relieved as he crossed the aisle towards me. "I'm sorry, I wasn't trying to track you," he assured me. "I just wanted to ensure you were well before we go, and we're not lingering here long. Brother Dolus said you might need some... time," he said the last part haltingly, as if treading carefully around my feelings. "I've never fished a target out before, so I don't know how it feels. It must be confounding to the senses."

I gritted my teeth inside my muzzle and only nodded. I could barely find the will to speak right now. I prayed I would not have to.

"I suppose you didn't have a choice," he said, quirking his muzzle uncomfortably. "No one will fault you for using whatever tactics were necessary to survive your capture. At least I won't. I just wanted to say, what I... what I said in the woods... that was careless talk. I didn't mean what it sounded like. You're not cold for appealing to someone who held your life in their hands and talkin' your way out of that. It's alright to use deception for survival's sake, aye? And you must've truly won him over because the incubus came to you again of his own accord."

I was beginning to understand Darcy's frustration over being defined by their gender, whatever anyone thought it was at the moment. Dolus seemed to assume they were a woman because of how duplicitous they were, and Malachi's opinion changed frequently, but always because he attributed the worst assumptions of either to them.

"M'sorry your handler pushed you to go through all that," he continued, "I'm guessing 'twas his idea anyway, cause he's the domineering sort, yeah? You mostly seemed like you wanted to head home, last I saw you."

I nodded and meant it. Dolus was wrong; Malachi was *not* dim-witted. In fact, he was showing more insight here than the monk was. I had spent most of my time at the Lodge slowly winning Darcy's trust, and part of that had certainly been because I was worried about survival. Especially in the beginning.

Dolus had both admission and proof of my transgressions with the feline, but Malachi had simply been able to infer a version of what had happened by reading the situation. And he wasn't that far off from the truth. The malamute wasn't an Inquisitor for no reason; he was clever and had made more of an effort to understand this case and the people in it than either of us had given him credit for. Dolus didn't seem to *care* what had happened between Darcy and me, which was terribly incurious for an Inquisitor. Now that the task was done, all he wanted was to bury and forget it. And he clearly assumed the sword he could hold over my head would keep me in check, force me to do as he wanted and bend the knee, regardless of any regard I had for the feline.

I would show him what it was to be humbled.

Malachi, though... Malachi actually gave a damn. About me, about the investigation, and I suspected he held to his oaths more vigorously. He wasn't on my side—let alone Darcy's—but he didn't know that. He was trying to understand what had happened to me. And that, unfortunately, made associating with him even more dangerous right now than being with Dolus.

"Isidor?"

I quaked, trying to force something—anything—out of my mouth. Words. I needed words.

I felt him move in closer, could see the edges of a worried expression on his muzzle out of the corner of my eye, but I was still stammering. Still failing to play the role I so desperately needed to.

I could smell Darcy's blood on him, this close. On his gloves. The memory of him bringing that club down on their skull played over and over again in my mind, like a horrific chorus.

"Oy," he piped, loud enough to force my attention. My head shot up, spine going straight out of habit, like one of my elders had corrected my posture. But when my eyes met his, I only saw sympathy there. And concern.

I began to say something, finally, but I barely got out an, "I..." before one of his big arms had wrapped around my shoulders and pulled me in. He'd embraced me before, but this was less careful, less uncertain. He'd crossed that boundary with me already and clearly had no hesitation doing so any longer.

I couldn't explain to him why it was jarring me so badly. Why the whole of this was so... strange. He didn't see me as fallen, as an enemy of the Ministry. He didn't know what was in my heart right now. He just knew I was in crisis.

"You didn't have the training needed to get that close to a target, let alone one so wily," he said, his palm moving gently over my back. I could feel its heat even through the cloak he'd given me. "It's gonna feel strange for awhile. You got to know him, got into his head, ey? They'll tell you when you go for schooling... the bleed goes both ways. With informers, too. You've got to shield your heart. However works for you. I go cold. That isn't right for everyone, but it might work for you."

He pulled back, looking me in the eyes, intensely. "You're all fire and passion, Isidor. For the work, for the Lord. It's obviously what feeds your soul, but it'll leave you raw. Trust me.

I didn't know how to quell those fires when I was young, a-
and..." his irises paled, un-focusing. When he spoke again, his
voice was tight, nearly choked. "... near burnt me up inside.
That kind of Hellfire, it's not what God wants for us, and it's not
what the Ministry *demands* of us. You've got to learn to douse it
out, smother it, before it roars out of control."

His claws tightened on my shoulder, and I wasn't sure what
we were talking about any more. But I nodded, swallowing
heavily, because agreeing seemed to be all I could do.

"Those fires, they'll *come* back," he said, sounding almost
manic now. "They *always* come back. But the Ministry—your
Trainer—he'll teach you how to fortify your spirit. How to step
back and set yourself apart from what you're doing, like it's
someone else going through the motions. It gets easier, then.
When passion doesn't get in the way, things become clearer.
Even sin." His eyes swept down my chest, resting there, as he
clutched my shoulders now in both hands, bowing his head.

"You'll even see your own sins for what they are more
plainly," he pressed on. "Everything gets easier, once you learn
how to suppress that fire. And these moments of confusion will
be in your past and your past only. You'll face the coming tasks
with a bulwark around your heart."

"I'm..." I said shakily, "... not sure that I want that."

He leaned back, looking confused. "No?" he asked
uncertainly.

"I want to be able to let things *in* my heart."

He stepped backwards, seeming to realize how close we
were. His voice had gone thready, strange. "That isn't always a
good idea."

I stared at him, feeling tears prickling in my eyes. "I don't
care."

It would have been impossible to know what was going on
in the older Templar's mind then, but something shifted in his
expression. A point of recognition, a repressed jolt of

awareness, and then worry. Whatever he'd just worked out, I felt certain it was something that troubled him.

I wouldn't know then, and perhaps ever, because an even more unwelcome guest had manifested in the open barn doorway. I smelled him before I saw him, and so did Malachi, judging by how he snapped upright and put five paws' distance between us again.

Dolus was, like most monks, fastidiously clean and innocuous-smelling. But what was doubtless an attempt to mask his scent to blend in better when he traveled and more efficiently become a ghost wherever he went would stand out to you over time if you knew (and feared) him well enough. He used some kind of soap or perfume in his fur that neutralized him, to an extent. But its mellow, almost cucumber or leaf-like scent was distinctive if you had a good enough nose.

"The Hudsons are demanding we take the prisoner off their property," the canine said when he realized he'd been noticed. "And even at a straight shot, with carriage and horse changeovers, it's five days in good weather. We need to move."

Malachi seemed surprised. "Far more than five days, even on fair roads."

"We will not be taking our rest," Dolus said, moving into the barn and casting a glance upwards, likely at the loft where Nick was watching from. He was supposed to be staying out of sight, but it wouldn't have mattered. He was still bleeding, and Dolus had a keen perception for blood, as did most hounds.

"At *all?*" Malachi balked. "The men will exhaust themselves. Is that wise?"

"She has too many connections we don't know of," Dolus said. "And several we *are* aware of that are beyond monitoring or control. The men will sleep in shifts on the road. We'll determine our route as we go and allow her allies," his gaze flicked briefly to me, "no time or consistent information with which to mount an escape."

Malachi lifted his chin and nodded resolutely, back straight, arms clapping out to cross at the wrists in front of him. "Yes, Brother. I'll keep the men on a tight schedule. These lads are on the road all the time, they should be used to it by now."

"They had best be. All eyes will be upon us for how we handle this most important task. There will be Hell to pay if anyone steps out of line, mark my words," Dolus growled. He was speaking to Malachi, but his eyes were on me, now. And had been for some time. "Now, if you are quite finished saying your goodbyes to your *junior* Brother here, please see to the men and ensure the prisoner is secure once again before we set out."

"Yes, Brother," Malachi repeated in the same practiced, fiercely obedient tone he'd been addressing the monk with this entire time. I wished he knew what the man had said about him behind his back, but honestly? It probably wouldn't have mattered. Whatever lay in the malamute's past, they'd expunged his 'spirit of rebellion' in the re-education camps. He was only loose with the rules so long as it was minor infractions.

The fact that I could reflect on all of this, feel rubbed raw by it, rebel against the man's sad reality even internally... I'm not sure what that meant, but it certainly said something about whatever change was taking hold within me.

God help me, I didn't want this. I didn't want to be like *him*. I wanted no part in whatever kind of education could allow you to set yourself apart from your actions and accept doing things that felt wrong. It was all so antithetical to what I understood God's justice to be. Being willing to lie, to obfuscate certain unhappy facts from the masses, to use force and even bring death when necessary to the enemies of the greater good... all of that, I was willing to accept.

But Dolus and whoever was passing on orders to him within the Ministry didn't *care* what the truth of all of this was. Dolus himself was working counter to the Ministry, hiding my own indiscretions because of… essentially vanity. His reputation and the reputation of Ebon Gables. If I was in the wrong, if Darcy truly was the demon they were accused of being, and I was being led astray from the path? What then? He was compounding lies upon lies, false information upon false information. No one involved in the upper echelons of the Ministry would have the right intel to find the truth in whatever chain of events played out here because he wasn't giving it to them even when I'd tried to offer.

And we were already working with information we knew to be false. Everything about this case was compromised in a mangled web of deception that probably all had similar petty causes at the root of it. What if the reason all of this had happened—the reason two men had died—was also to cover up someone's reputation? Or just some other convenient lie? What if the entire motivation behind our Faith losing its most sacred artifact and Darcy being executed for a crime they hadn't committed was because one person somewhere had made one self-indulgent mistake and was seeking to cover it up?

Months ago, I would never have believed it possible. But now, I was watching it play out. I was watching one of the elders who'd raised me, someone with considerable weight and experience within the Ministry I sought to serve, intentionally manipulate the situation and feed lies to every person involved in the case—including his superiors, who would Archive those lies for all time into the record—all to save face.

And I'd found myself a part of it, against my will.

Malachi cast me one last long look as he left, and I hardly knew how to feel. There was such an earnest expression of regard for me there. The man cared about me. I could tell. He was worried for me.

But he was also the sword arm of the man I feared most in the world right now. And he'd do as he was told. Up to and including killing Darcy.

Or even potentially… me.

I couldn't imagine any way to change that. Telling him the truth wasn't safe. And it wasn't even remotely possible aside from that. Especially given…

The ladder beside me creaked and my heart leapt into my chest. Dolus briefly glanced upwards but seemed to give the young man descending towards us little mind.

Nicholas was not willing to let me stand alone with him. My Brother was hopelessly brave. And that fact scared me, now more than ever.

"Well enough that I address the both of you," Dolus said, as I felt the other young man move in beside me. He was still clutching an arm across his midsection but was otherwise trying to stand to his full height. Not out of respect. The ire and defiance were all but *radiating* off him. I silently prayed for God to calm his spirit.

"This is your crucible," the monk said, addressing me. "The next few months will forge you into the man you are meant to become. Treat this time as such. A difficult time of loss and reflection, but necessary. God is testing you. Do not let Him—or the Ministry—down, or your waking life will become an agony, and your next a fall from Grace. Ascension is not all there is, young Brothers… we can descend, as well. Never forget that."

It was Nicholas who spoke. The young man could not seem to stop himself, despite his battered state. "I've never balked at suffering in His name, Brother. I put my time in same as everyone else, making penance and training 'til my paws bled. But some of this pain seems… avoidable. Un-bloody-necessary, if you ask me. I don't see what point it all serves. What'm I meant to be learning, here?"

Dolus gave a slim, humorless smile. "My dear lad, life isn't a seminary. You aren't always going to learn from your experiences. For some people especially, there is a… cap. A natural end to learning. You cannot teach someone to be more than their God-given limitations."

I felt Nicholas step forward and shot a hand out to steady him on his bicep, holding him firm in place.

"Besides," the monk said dismissively. "I suffered, and lost, and was denied, again and again at your age. It forged me into the man I am today. Why shouldn't you be willing to endure the same? I promise you, there is a fulfilling life ahead for both of you. You'll find your triumphs, your satisfaction, your little pleasures. And you'll look back on this moment and thank me for protecting you and guiding you."

He turned partially, then seemed to think the better of it, looking back to me. "I've appointed a two-man honor guard to take you both home. Rejoice in how liberal-minded I am being in not reporting either of your behavior here. The forbearance I am showing in favor of promoting your careers and seeing my sons succeed. This is a second chance for both of you. Nicholas, you will return to your studies for a further year until you can prove you are ready for another posting. Isidor... you've proven yourself more than sufficient as a candidate for the Inquisition. I'll see to it you're shipped off within the month. Ready yourself for this new chapter."

"What about Mabel?" I found myself asking suddenly.

The question caught both Dolus and Nicholas off-guard. Nicholas in particular looked worried. "Wait, what *about* Mabel?"

Dolus gave me a puzzled look and a shake of his head. "Take her as your wife if that is your wish."

"What?!" Nicholas jerked back, staring at me in shock.

"I never," I spat, "ever would have—he's the one who arranged it!" I stared icily at Dolus. "Why? What on earth possessed you to think it was acceptable to arrange such a match? Let alone without either of our consent?"

"Her consent is hardly a consideration," he said with a snort. "But yes Isidor, I did put in the request on your behalf."

"Why?!" I asked emphatically, stopping just short of shouting. I could only contain my outrage so much.

"The young lass needed to reassess her value to potential suitors," he said flatly, seriously, despite how ludicrously venomous the statement sounded on its face. "Sometimes it's necessary to offer youth a worse alternative to what is best for them, to force them to put their choices in perspective. Say... sending a child who is acting out to bed without dinner, so that whatever their quibble, they'll remember next time how much worse it was to go hungry than pitch a fit. In this case, even less harm was ultimately done. I didn't expect you to accept her as your potential bride, Isidor. I just wanted the young lady to know her worth. If even her closest Brother does not deem her a suitable match for him, she will consider *why* that might be. Her poverty, her maiming... the fact that she is not pure... all things a potential groom will consider in selecting her. All things *you* considered, I'm certain."

"Ciraberos take you," I gasped through my teeth.

"I'll ignore that," he said evenly. "I think we're all a bit emotional right now. In any case. Young Mabel received an offer from a widower, a tailor, several months ago. She was not receptive. The man was aged, granted, but it would have been a very eligible match for her, given her interest in being a seamstress. He was willing to overlook her body's deficiencies, her impoverished state, and seemed enthusiastic to have a young woman in his home again, with his daughters recently married. But there was no convincing her, and while I could have forced the issue, an unwilling bride is a misery to most men. I thought it best I treat the situation more delicately and nudge her back towards such an obvious windfall once she'd been brought lower. Humbled. I take it you've already turned her down?"

"She is thirteen and my *sister*," I said, dragging a wet breath through my nose. "Of course I did."

Dolus tutted. "My southpaw, such a heartbreaker. I never saw it in you, I must confess. But it suits you well, Isidor. You *can* do better, and some day, you shall. I look forward to seeing more devastated women in your wake in the meantime. Germain may be content to raise a generation of impotent scholars, but I prefer more arrows in our quiver, even if they're born out of wedlock. *Do* let me know if you ever sire a bastard or two. I'll be happy to take them on at Ebon Gables."

I'd been worried about Nicholas all this time, but I was the first to swing a fist. No fiber of my body obeyed me; I was propelled by sheer, unyielding fury. When Dolus had told me long ago that men could lose themselves to their passions, he'd been right. But lust was not the sin that would undo me.

It was wrath.

Brother Dolus seemed to have expected the outburst of violence. It was possible he'd even elicited it on purpose. The man was the monk most responsible at the Abbey for our grappling and small arms training, and his reaction to my reeling back for a swing was immediate, calm, and efficient.

I didn't connect. I didn't even get *close*.

He swayed to the side and brought his forearm up in the gap, shoving with little effort at my wrist while I was over-extended and forcing my bicep wide to the left to open up my chest. Then he popped his knee up into my stomach, pounding the air out of me, and brought his main hand down at a cross into my jaw. He didn't even punch me. He just slapped me. Hard.

Hard enough that I tasted blood in my mouth, felt my lip split on my fang, and had to stumble back lest I fall to the ground completely. I whipped my head up, snarling at him through tears.

He looked impassive. Unimpressed.

"Isidor, you are still capable of learning," he said, "so let me impart one last lesson before I have you children carted back home. Do not think you can cross me without consequence. And consider for a moment that you may not be the one I take my pound of flesh from. The feline is in *my* care until the time of her execution."

My muzzle fell back over my teeth, my heart freezing mid-beat.

"I will be conducting her Inquisition," he continued, "and I am permitted to do so by whatever means I deem necessary, provided she is intact by the date of her hanging. I take particular pride in my creativity as an Interrogator, but I was planning to keep things simple, this time. For your sake. Please don't make me reconsider."

I hung my head, if only to hide my face from the man. No nightmare I had before now compared to this moment. I begged God to wake me up.

Nicholas's hands fell on my shoulders, and I eventually realized the injured young man was trying to help steady *me*. Keep me on my feet.

"Good lad," Dolus said, then began to pad away. He must have heard something though, because a moment later from the entrance to the barn, he muttered an irritated, "Lord help me, what now?"

I heard it too, after a moment. Shouting, one of the voices most definitely Malachi. And…

… Cillian.

The scene outside when we all arrived, Dolus ahead of us, Nicholas and I hanging back, was less pandemonium and more just one very loud argument. But both men were worked up, belligerent, and easily two of the most fiery people I knew, so it was intense.

Malachi had the upper ground physically, but that was hardly a surprise. He had Cillian pinned back against a fence, the Pedigree Lord using his cane to put what little distance he could between himself and the larger canine. No one had weapons drawn, but tempers were high and I knew both men were armed, even if Cillian didn't seem it. He was still in his coat and dinner wear, with plenty of room to hide a pistol on him. Malachi had a big hand fisted in the man's shirt and cravat, nearly lifting him off the ground, with the cane pressed into the malamute's chest, keeping him a foot back while they screamed at one another.

We came in on, "-I am not now, nor have I ever, been bloody afraid of you, mongrel! Go ahead and strike me down, lay your claws through my flesh, and see how swiftly the Council of Lords has you *tried at The Arches!*"

"Brother Malachi, do not touch him," Dolus said as he approached the scene, his voice more tired than angry.

"I caught him lurking about, spying on his wretched paramour's carriage," the malamute spat out through his fangs. "We should take him in, too."

"Absolutely not," Dolus said calmly. "Now let go of him."

"This is the same lane to the Hudsons' Carriage House," Cillian snarled, "and I have every goddamned right to walk it, moreso than you jackals rotting do."

"You think I don't know the difference between spying and walking?" Malachi roared, shoving at the man again. "Don't *bullshit* me, you inbred cocksucker!"

He did shove him one last time, but stepped back and away, as Dolus had commanded. Cillian took a moment to recover against the fence—barely a moment—before giving a spiteful grin that showed his teeth. "Oh, projection, the weakest weapon in the arsenal of the clergy! I grew up spending my summers in Redcoven, you think I don't know your story?! It was fodder for every society high or low for *years.*"

Malachi's hackles rose and something like panic grew in the whites of his eyes. For a moment, I thought he'd draw steel right there and then, but Dolus stepped between them, his voice deadly low.

"Enough," he warned. "He is untouchable. Do you understand?"

Malachi was still snarling, his breath puffing out between his teeth. The monk grabbed him physically by the lower jaw and forced him to look his way instead of the Pedigree's. "Brother. Do you understand?"

"Yes, Brother." He turned with a scrape of his claws on the ice, whirling off and departing the scene without so much as a glance our way. I'm not certain he'd even seen us.

Dolus did give the both of us one last look, before heading out towards the waiting carriage. But that's all it was. A look. And really, that's all it needed to be.

I found myself at Cillian's side, unsure if I should be helping the man or how. But as soon as I got close, I became the next victim of his ire.

"Well, there you have it," he snarled at me. "The inevitable, miserable end to this whole tale. Are you quite satisfied now, young Templar?"

I glanced back in Dolus's direction. The man wasn't a fool. He was near enough that he could overhear us still.

"I told you to avoid my mistakes," Cillian continued, and wisely chose his words. I was bitter with anger, hurt, scared, and confused, but I still had my senses enough to discern how carefully he said what he said next. "I warned you about Darcy. About all of this. It is well and truly over, now. Rejoice in your freedom. Go home."

He said the last part very intentionally, while staring me in the eyes. He wanted me to listen.

"It isn't over until the trial's over," I reasoned, my voice raw. "There is still a chance to appeal. You could—"

"I am *done*," he said so finitely, I almost believed him. "My association with them nearly ruined my life, and it will ruin yours if you pursue this any further, mark my words." His shoulders fell, his whole body sagging against where he clutched his cane. "It's out of your hands, now. You'll only make things worse by intervening."

He was scared for them, too. He didn't want me risking their life, going after them now. He couldn't be any clearer.

"The winter storms are coming down from the Kadrush," he said. "They'll arrive here soon. I can't meet them head on, which means I can't go home yet. The roads into the Capital are a trauma, this time of year."

The statement was odd, but I searched my mind to make sense of it. He was leading, he wanted me to ask... "Where will you go then, Young Lord?"

"Redcoven," he said, "I've family there. I can winter with them."

He pushed himself up off the fence, straightening his coat and staring once more off in the direction of the carriage. We both did. I'm not sure which of us looked more pained.

"I thought the Heart Thief was cleverer than this," I said, keeping my voice low. If Dolus could hear anything, I still wanted to keep our conversation neutral, but I had to know....

"I thought they'd have one final... plot," I said. "One last act of defiance."

Cillian raised a brow and slowly shook his head at me. "Young Sir, this *is* their last act of defiance."

"What?" I blinked.

"I would think a zealot would understand. They intend to die," he said. "Like so many before them, proclaiming their beliefs from the gallows."

I looked at him in mute horror.

"You thought they'd try to escape," he said in a soft, sympathetic whisper. "Oh, lad... no. This is what they wanted all along."

. . .

We had no choice but to return to Ebon Gables, escorted by the 'honor guard.' It was hard enough for me to shake them for a few minutes in the intermittent hours between Dolus leaving and our own group setting out, that I could find a chance to go to the dovecote and get my weapons. They were exactly where Darcy had said they would be... for all the good they'd do.

The journey home would be a long and somber march that took the better part of two days.

Two days.

Two days between Darcy and me, and further still, because we were headed in opposite directions. I felt at every moment that I should have been fighting. Drawing steel on my brothers? Or somehow slipping away from them in the midst of the night? We couldn't discuss it openly, but Nicholas and I shared a common anxiousness and many worried looks.

Distressingly, I think if I'd made the irrevocable and potentially life-ending decision to turn on our two armed Brothers, he would have joined me. And that, more than anything, stayed my hand. If we were going to do anything drastic, we'd be home and only under the watch of monks and our Father soon. That would be the time to slip away. The men who escorted us never let us out of their sight, as was their duty. Not even the one night we encamped on the road.

Breaking from them would mean a confrontation. And the odds were not in our favor. I earnestly wasn't certain where my skill level lay, but these were seasoned Crusaders, warrior Templar. And we were evenly matched in number, but Nicholas was still a youth, and injured.

I also got the feeling Dolus had told them something. They did not treat us as though we were trustworthy. They hardly spoke to us, and when they did, they weren't what I would call 'amicable.' I was certain he hadn't told them the truth, but he must have informed them we were being sent for discipline. They were on-guard. We'd not get the drop on them.

The eponymous black iron gates of Ebon Gables loomed before us in the evening of the second day, and never before had I felt such dread coming home. It wasn't that I was afraid of what awaited me here, it's just that I knew I could not call this place home for very much longer. And the desire blooming in my chest, the voice that cried out for escape, sang the song of the spirit of rebellion I had been warned would come my entire life. But its words rang like a bell in my heart. Like His Truth, His Word, was in chorus with them.

Was it arrogant, foolish, or both to assume God wanted what I wanted in this moment? Did it matter? God would not speak to me directly. I had to have faith in myself in addition to my faith in the Almighty. Otherwise, I had no mind with which to follow Him. There was no escaping the self.

I still wasn't entirely certain what I would do. But one final conversation, one innocuous interaction, with Nicholas sealed it for me. We were walking the cloisters, our guard at our back, taking us to the Physician for our check-in. The evening meal bells were tolling, the familiar sights, sounds, and smells of my childhood home surrounding me, and Nick asked:

"That girl you fancy…" He glanced sidelong at me as we walked. "Y'know… the pretty one. You gonna marry her, you think?"

I looked briefly at the two men, but they didn't seem to care about our idle chatter. So, I turned back to Nick and said as casually as I could, "I don't know. We haven't even started courting yet. I'm not sure if we're right for each other."

"I think y'are," he said with enviable certainty.

"How would you know?" I asked, quirking half a smile at him. "You've hardly met."

"I saw you two together," he responded, smiling more easily than me, despite his still swollen face. "Never seen you look at anyone like that, Brother. You were so… soft. Didn't know your face could even *do* that."

I shoved him and he snickered, and went to shove me back.

"Enough," one of the men with us snapped, then gestured to the infirmary doors. "Ahead."

Thankfully, our guards didn't follow us inside. In fact, I saw them through the tinted glass windows of the infirmary, turning and walking back down the cloisters. They were leaving. Hopefully for good.

"Oh, lads," the familiar and somewhat disappointed voice of the Abbey Physician, a Jack Russel fellow in his mid-sixties who had retired his practice to become a monk late in life, spoke from behind us. "Both of you returned to us so soon? And with an escort no less."

Nicholas and I turned to address him, and it must have been then that he saw Nick's condition. His expression softened immediately. "Lord, I'm sorry. I thought this was disciplinary... that swelling's really set in, young fellow. I'm sure you'll make your report to Father later. For now, let's just see to you, aye?"

"I did my best for him on the road," I said as I began stripping out of my gear. "I'm glad to have him seen to properly, though. I think he might lose a tooth..."

"Certainly feels like it," Nicholas confirmed while tonguing at the molar in question.

The Physician looked me over briefly while I got undressed, before turning his attention back to Nicholas. "Still slimming down, Isidor? You'll be within your acceptable range in no time at this rate. Whatever you're doing differently, keep at it."

I felt my brow crease, trying not to show the irritation I was feeling. This was the second time now the Physician had checked me in and complimented me on this very fact. What I hadn't said—what I really wanted to say—was that the cause of my weight loss was the fearful nights, anxieties, lack of appetite and the occasional inability even to keep basic, bland food down. I was eating half of what I had before, all in all, and I felt weak and exhausted all the time. What's more, I felt certain that must have been obvious on the outside. This man was responsible for monitoring my health and assuring I'd be in serviceable order to work as a Templar. Why was he focusing on something so paltry when I was clearly falling apart, otherwise?

Ever since my time at the Lodge, my entire vision of the world and my faith had been thrown into question. That had certainly not improved over the last two days now that I knew Darcy was with Dolus. Awaiting execution.

I was wasting because I was ill inside. I was in agony. And all this man could see was that I'd look less portly in my uniform.

Bit by bit, it was like a shroud was falling. My Father would know when he saw me, he would see that I was suffering. And he would care. My brother cared for me. All my brothers and sisters, even the little ones, were my family. But to the Ministry —at least to men like the Physician or Dolus, who viewed me as a resource—what mattered was not my person or even my faith. It was about appearances.

It was lunacy too, because I'd be more useful to God, and thus to the stated purpose of the Ministry, if I were healthy. If Nicholas were healthy.

It was sitting there in that chair, holding my brother's hand while the Physician donned his bib and played his part as an amateur barber surgeon, extracting my brother's broken tooth, that I saw the visage I'd long believed in fall before my eyes. Utterly and completely. And I came to one final, inarguable decision.

The Ministry was a mortal institution. It was not the arm of God I had long thought it to be. It empowered men like Dolus to hurt us, to lie for the sake of vanity and appearances, and sabotaged itself in the process. It was corrupt.

And it was not my future.

6

I HAVE BECOME THE INCUBUS

Father was in town that day, and I was honestly glad for it because Nicholas and I spent the next few hours after the check-in with the Physician trying to speak furtively about what our next steps were. I say 'trying' because Nick was in a lot of pain and a not-insubstantial amount drunk after the tooth extraction. But the young canine still rallied admirably.

We were both agreed at least on a few things. For one, and perhaps most importantly, what Cillian had tried to infer to us before our departure from the Hudson Estate.

Redcoven. They were taking Darcy to Redcoven. Some parts of what he'd said, I wasn't certain if they were code or not, like the references to the storms coming down from the Kadrush. That *sounded* like it may have been some kind of message, but he'd probably had to think fast and if he'd intended something secret by it, it was lost on us.

But one thing I knew for certain from my talks with Cillian was this—he wouldn't abandon Darcy. If he was going to Redcoven and mentioning his journey there to us, it meant that's where they were headed. Dolus would know he was following them too, but I'd heard him say aloud that someone of Cillian's station was 'untouchable'. He'd stayed Malachi's hand. Cillian could afford to risk following them and being seen in Redcoven, openly. Regardless how suspicious it looked… unless he did something overt, his family name would protect him.

We couldn't.

After poring over exactly one law book in the library on Inter-Governmental-Ministry procedures for trying prisoners who'd committed crimes that straddled both civil and Church jurisdictions, we were fairly certain we'd deduced why they were taking Darcy back to Redcoven, despite risking Cillian's connections he'd doubtless bring to bear in the area. The crimes Darcy had committed in Redcoven were proven by witnesses and recent events, and were a more certain conviction than the lengthy Inquisition and public trial they'd undergo for the theft of the Heart. They'd discharged a firearm on private property, attempted murder of the intended target—namely myself—which made it a crime against clergy, and what would most certainly be a charge of imprisonment of clergy, and destruction of private property: the Lodge.

They'd need to deal with the Magistrate in Redcoven and present Darcy before him, try them for their crimes there, before moving the feline off to Amurfolk for their major crimes… and eventually if sentenced, execution. If they didn't, Dolus would be committing astounding levels of overreach and flouting jurisdiction, which did not strike me as risks the man would take. Not for no reason other than expedience.

I didn't understand the complicated dance the Ministry and the Crown partook in, but I knew from studying this case before I'd begun my chase that there were political complications higher-ups like Dolus would be contending with, if they executed or maimed Darcy before the Crown and the Council of Lords got to weigh in on the case. The Theft of the Heart had become a national incident, and even before I'd talked with my Father about the potential conspiracy, there'd been rumors abounding that it had been a foreign attack on our most holy land, or a plot by the Jarls of the Kadrush as some sort of saber rattling. If the Ministry mishandled this, the King himself might decree our Inquisitors pay for the mistake in blood.

Very rarely had the Ministry and the Crown faced such conflict with one another that it threatened the stability of the nation. But there had been tumultuous battles between the two major powers in the past, and the collateral damage this could mean right now, with the nation already destabilized by so many collapsing colonies...

The Ministry would be careful here. They'd want to avoid angering the Lords, especially when there was no reason not to. They would both want this show trial in the Capital, anyway.

Darcy would need to be kept alive and safe in Redcoven for some time in order for the civil authority in the city to be satisfied. We didn't have *much* time, but this wasn't something that would be resolved in a few days.

But as to what would happen when we made it to the city, I... I didn't know. Something 'utterly insane', Nicholas had said around a drunken smile, and I was forced to silently concur. I wasn't even certain what I was capable of at this point. But Redcoven would be our best chance to free Darcy before they were transferred again, likely with an even heavier guard this time.

And then there was the matter of them being subject to Inquisition. The less time I left them in Dolus's care, the better.

The only other option in all of this was to unearth the conspiracy before they were executed. But we still didn't know the facts involved. Father Helstrom was working on it, but....

No. I couldn't wait that long. I could not sit idle and investigate, dig, and hope. Not only hope that I'd uncover the truth behind what had really happened to the Heart, but hope that the Ministry would *care*.

Try as we might, with the few hours we had, we were not able to come up with a workable idea as to how we'd free a prisoner being held by the Ministry. Neither Nicholas nor I were educated or experienced in the art of crime. Unless you counted lock-picking, security measures employed by our own Ministry, Estates we were meant to guard, spying, covert communications….

Alright, we were perhaps a bit… educated in skills tangential to committing crimes.

But breaking someone out of prison? We might need to play that one by ear.

"Isi?" Nick asked, after a long quiet stretch had passed between us. We were both exhausted but unable to sleep, so we were watching snow fall through the honeycomb-patterned glass panels in the windows of the library. We'd need to get some rest soon, especially given what we were considering, but we were waiting up for our Father. We'd both decided that no matter what, we couldn't leave without speaking to him first.

What we would say, I still didn't know.

"Hmm?" I uttered back, still reading slowly through the only book I'd been able to find on Redcoven's Ministry Architecture. It was mostly information about the Church itself, but there were some records about the construction of the Ministry Office as well. It wasn't guaranteed that's where they'd be holding Darcy, but it was an option.

"Are we ever comin' back home?" he asked, turning his head to face me. He'd been resting it—the cheek opposite the tooth he'd had extracted—on his arm.

I closed my book, then closed my eyes. "I don't know," I said. "As things stand now… likely not. I should have run with Darcy when I had the chance, and I didn't." I shook my head slowly. "I won't make that mistake again."

"Who *are* you?" he smirked, then grimaced, letting his head loll tiredly. "If you'd asked me a month ago, I'd've never guessed *you'd* be the Brother who'd elope."

"I'm not—"

"No, 'course not," he chuckled. "You're just breaking this woman outta prison, this *famed thief*, 'cause you want to carry on a monk-like, platonic *friendship* with 'er."

"Is that so hard to believe?" I sighed. "I told you how we met. I have a high regard for their wit, their intellect, their..."

"Why d'you keep referring to her that way?" he asked, puzzled. "And Isi, it ain't that I think you can't get on well with a woman you don't fancy like that. Ah'mean, Miss Hudson and I was like that. We got on famously, and I liked spendin' time with her like I would one of my sisters. I liked watchin' her paint and talk about court, about places I'd never been. She was real traveled, compared to most people I know. Funny, too. She made me laugh a lot. I hope I did the same, but I wasn't as witty as she were."

"Nicholas," I warned, "she's a Pedigree Lady. You weren't inappropriate with her, were you?"

He made a face, then flinched, then made a face again. "No. Like I said, it wasn't like that. Courtly or nothin'. I mean, I've never courted. I guess I don't know what it's supposed to be like 'cept for etiquette. But I've thought a girl's pretty before, and it's not that I didn't think Miss Hudson was beautiful, but I don't know. I guess I just don't think I fancy rich girls. M'not ready to court or marry, anyway. She was just nice to me and made the posting a lot less boring." He gave me a slight smile. "But you and the Heart Thief weren't actin' like mere acquaintances."

I swallowed a bit. "You're not wrong."

"Isi, you were all but kissin' her."

I opened my mouth, but the moment was broken by a gasp that both Nick and I heard, despite someone's obvious attempt to cover it up. We turned towards the stacks, ears perked.

I settled a hand where my sword would be if I were armed. And with a warning growl in my tone, I said, "Come on out, now. We know you're there."

The gold-furred head that poked around the corner confirmed my worst fears. I'd thought it was Mabel based on the sound she'd made alone. I knew my sister's little noises well enough by now.

"Mabel, no," I cursed in a whisper, hanging my paws over my knees. "How long have you been here?"

"Since it got dark," she confessed, stepping into full view. She was wearing one of her loose-fitting, simple dresses again, like she used to. Her fur had grown out a little, too. She looked like my little sister again, not the manicured young wife-to-be the matchmaker was grooming her into. She had her sleeve pinned up on her missing arm with the ribbon I'd gotten her.

"Lord, that must've been over an hour ago," Nick mumbled. "That's more shame on us than her, I'd say."

"You should have turned in by now," I said, standing. "Why are you skulking about in the library after-hours?"

"Isidor," she ignored me completely, her body trembling slightly as she stood her ground and demanded, "are you going to leave us and never come back?"

I went stock still, cowed by the young girl completely. I had no better an answer for her than Nicholas, of course. I struggled thinking of how to justify all of this. She knew next to nothing about what had happened to me the last few months.

Actually, if she'd been here for over an hour now listening in on us, she might know more than she ought to.

I should have predicted Nicholas would find some way to make this whole situation worse. I could not have imagined *how* much worse he'd make it in a single sentence.

"This is why I was askin', right here," he said, "cause if we're not coming back, we should be taking her with us!"

"Nicholas!" I snapped. "Bloody *think*, man!"

"Yes!" Mabel raised her voice, trotting over towards us and grabbing me by my tunic. "You can't leave me here, Isidor! Or you can't leave at all!"

"Mabel," I adopted a pleading tone, going to move to my knees, but realizing before I did that the young girl was nearly to my collarbone, now. If I knelt, we wouldn't be face to face. So, I stayed standing. Addressed her as I would a young woman. "I always would have left the Abbey eventually," I reasoned. "You knew this. And it isn't as though you'll be without family. Father will be here. Your brothers and sisters...."

"Leave me here, and I'll find my way to you somehow," she swore to me, the young woman's expression more intense than I'd ever seen it. I believed her.

"Mabel—"

"No!" she balled her one fist, lifting her chin up at me. "I'm tired of watching you walk out those gates Isi, never knowing if I'll see you again! If I'm an adult now, I get to choose whether I live here or not. I don't want to live here anymore! And if you two are leaving, I want to, as well!"

"Where is all of this coming from?" I asked, easing my hand down to cup hers and hold it. "Please. Tell me what you're feeling in your heart right now."

"Why is it you think I'm safer here than anywhere else I might go with you?" she asked, glancing back towards the darkened doorway. "You're... you're my intended. I should go where you go, anyway."

"Mabel," I said, after unclenching my jaw. "I told you that wasn't my choice. I've spoken to Father about withdrawing the engagement, and he's assured me it will be done. I know that it isn't what you want, either."

"I thought it was what you wanted for *months*," she said, her eyes glossy. "Because you weren't *here*, Isidor. Because Brother Dolus was speaking for you."

"He orchestrated all of this for reasons of his own," I said, stomping back the desire to explain the whole situation to her. She wasn't ready to understand that kind of thinking. I wasn't even sure I was.

"If you leave me here, you don't just leave me with Father and our brothers and sisters," she said. "You leave me with *him*. And he'll be angry, Isidor. Because of everything you were just talking about. I don't understand… I want to, but I don't understand what's happening… but I want to!"

"She's right," Nick said. "Even if all we do is run, the two of us—your Heart Thief aside—the monk's going to be *furious*. When he inevitably returns here…"

"He's so scary when he's angry," she said, her voice cracking and falling to a near whisper. "Isi, he's going to make me marry that man. Or he'll send me to a workhouse because my intended left me despoiled and unwanted before we've even called off our engagement."

My breath hitched, and I stared at her in horror. "Mabel, you're not—"

"Despoiled?" She stared up at me with those wide brown eyes, her features not scared, not pained, but shockingly calm. Resolute. However it was the young girl saw herself, she'd come to terms with it long ago. "Yes, Isi, I am. Despoiled, maimed, unwanted. But you love me anyway. Right? Like Father loves me. None of that matters to you. Right?"

I breathed out and squeezed her hand tightly. "I don't believe… I don't believe any of that is true, Mabel. Those words are just terrible ways to say you've suffered throughout your life. Like the saints. Like Canus himself. They weren't 'despoiled' by the trials they endured or broken by the terrors they lived through, and they all bore scars, too. But they were the best of us. And you have as great and meaningful a life before you as they did, mark my words."

She leaned up, her small fingers clutching tight to my palm. "Not here," she said.

I felt my mind and body surrender. The young woman's wisdom was impenetrable, and I could not deny her forever. The truth was, I loved her too much to hold out for much longer. And I'd lost every battle against my heart's interests, so far. I was beginning to feel it wasn't worth the fight.

"Besides," she said a moment later, her expression going just a bit impish, "I heard a lot of things I think I wasn't supposed to… but mostly, Isi?" Her eyes went wider. "Are you in love? Are you running off with a girl?!"

I sighed.

"I want to meet her!" she said, finally smiling a little. That, at least, felt good to see.

Nicholas twisted his ears, a second before we all heard it. The gate bell.

"That has to be Father," he said. "Come on, we should get our things together," he glanced at me, and then her, "all of us. Before we're missed."

I had rarely seen my Father reduced to such a state of shock.

"You're… all… leaving the Abbey?"

Each of us eventually nodded.

He hadn't looked well when he'd come in, and seeing both Nicholas and me, *and* Mabel waiting for him in the hall to his chambers looked like it might have felled him on the spot if not for his cane.

He ushered us inside quickly, moving with the same vigilance he had when he'd been rushing me into the Ministry building in Redcoven. As if even he was afraid of being watched.

To be fair, those two rogue Templar were still here, as far as we knew. And I had no idea what Dolus had told them. It was unlikely he'd shared his secrets with them, given how intent he was on protecting his Abbey's reputation, but he may have given them an entirely different, condemning story about us. They certainly seemed to think we needed looking-after on the way here.

"My children," Father Helstrom murmured, as he ambled towards his desk, eventually settling down heavily in his chair, so clumsily that it squawked backwards with his weight. He said it again for some reason, a moment later. "My children...."

I moved up towards his desk slowly, bypassing the respectable distance we were meant to keep when we met with him in here. More hesitantly, Mabel and Nicholas followed in my wake. They'd never seen our Father like this. I'd seen him in many a harried and depressive state over the last few weeks, but this was easily the worst. It hurt to witness.

The bloodhound had been the central pillar of my life, after God. And more so in many ways, because he was physically present, my caregiver, my leader, my preacher....

To see him so carved-out, so worn and worried, shook my own resolve in ways I couldn't begin to grapple with right now. I knew what we were doing—even just the act of leaving the fold, let alone actively working against it—would have been madness to the man I was not two months ago. But to the man who'd raised me, it must have been horrific.

"I will walk with God wherever I go, Father," I promised him, moving up to his desk and placing my palms down on the surface, gently. I wanted to reach out to him, but I wasn't certain that was wise, right now. "But as things stand with the Ministry now, I feel certain that my path forward will be dictated almost entirely by a man who..." I steeled my nerve, "... I believe... is not right with God. And I do not think the Lord wants me to follow a false prophet any more than I do."

"If you leave the fold, I cannot protect you," he emphasized, bracing his palms on the desk. "And Isidor, what you're involved in right now..." he looked briefly to my siblings, obviously uncertain what they knew. "You cannot possibly wish to involve your younger siblings in such troubles, and that will be unavoidable if they follow you. They are *children*—"

"Father, whatever awaits us out there, it idn't worse than the danger we're in every day we got t'answer to Brother Dolus," Nicholas said, still speaking around his injuries and a freshly-swollen jaw from where he'd had the tooth extraction. "I'm tired of being hurt by that man. He keeps takin' pieces out of me, there won't be nothing left to serve God or anyone else for that matter. If I'm man'nuff to get my skull smashed into a desk edge, why aren't I man'nuff to make this choice for m'self?"

"He wants to sell me like a sow to bear children for a man thrice my age," Mabel said calmly, but with a seriousness that belied her age.

"I will not let that happen," Father promised her, fiercely.

"But if I'm old enough to marry, why can't I decide to leave and take my chances out there?" she countered. "We won't be alone. We'll have each other."

"We could have you all transferred," the bloodhound said with an obvious grimace, the thought clearly giving him great pain. "It shouldn't... it shouldn't be like this. This Abbey is meant to be a cradle of safety for lost children, a place to raise and groom righteous young lives, not what it has become... Brother Dolus is just not suited for the work..."

"Why is he like this?" Mabel was the one whose voice lifted our Father's gaze, at last. The question was so simple, but so pertinent. She swallowed once she realized she had everyone's attention, and added, "He did what he did to Isidor and me just to hurt and confuse us. Why does our elder monk hate us so?"

"Brother Dolus of Cuthbert's Abbey," Father said, his voice low and gravelly, "hates the whole of the world. The man feels he is owed a debt he can never collect on, and he is full of bile over it. Hate like that poisons the heart. It makes a man sick."

"Why?" I asked.

The bloodhound hesitated only a moment, then visibly

steeled himself. "You are all correct. You are my children—you always shall be—but it's time I stopped treating you as such. You're grown, now."

We waited, trepidatious. At length, he spoke evenly, "Dolus was the second, younger bastard son of an infamously vice-sick Baron from the Islands who kept several mistresses at his Estate. *In* his employ," Father said. "I wish I could say it is uncommon, but it is frightfully not-so. The Ministry buried the existence of the first well enough by taking him within their fold young, and then the girls… I do not know what happened to the girls… but Dolus lived within the walls of the Estate, serving the very family he shared blood with, for *eleven* years before the Baron realized his resemblance was too uncanny to hide any more. He was shipped to the Abbey then, but not before the boy witnessed the life he was but one parent away from having."

The room was silent. I'd never known the monk's history, nor had I ever wanted to, but I had to assume if Father was breaking his confidence now, it must have served a reason.

"The lurcher has struggled with his envy and wrath throughout his entire tenure in the Order," he continued darkly. "He is rather infamous for his bouts of temper and proclivity for violence. But he is also—on the whole—obedient. And perhaps one of the most skilled and meticulous Inquisitors in the art of information retrieval that the Order has ever had. He's been disciplined, written up, and sent for censure many times. You wouldn't even be the first children who've reported him as the reason why they've chosen to leave their training and give up room and board here for life on the road or in a workhouse."

I blinked, shocked. "Other Brothers and Sisters took a workhouse over remaining here because of Dolus?"

"This place, believe it or not, is part of his penance," he said, knitting his fingers on the desk in front of him, his whole body tense. "He is still a working Templar. He could be serving in

Amurfolk or out of a Ministry Office or Archive. But someone, somewhere up the chain, thought a posting like this would mellow the man. Humble him. Perhaps even make him more kind. He was here before even I was, and he… struggled with retaining trainees as they grew older. I was posted here because when I retired, I asked for an Abbey I could spend my final years in, where I might do the most good. I had Mabel, she needed a safe place to grow up, and the previous Father had left due to his own disagreements with Dolus. It seemed God's purpose for me was clear. Reformation of this place."

He squeezed his eyes shut, and my chest ached. I don't think I could bear watching my Father cry. But he did no such thing. Perhaps he knew.

"I am so sorry," he said at length in a near-whisper. "I failed you all. I failed to reform Brother Dolus and I failed to protect you from him."

"There is no reforming that man," Nicholas growled.

"You're the reason I'm alive," I said emphatically.

"Me, too," Mabel said. And, braver than Nicholas or me, she dashed around the desk suddenly, to jam herself into the bloodhound's side and wrap her arm around him.

He eased himself up to more of a sitting position and slowly extended a robed arm, wrapping her in it. He kissed her brow, stroking back her ears, and opened his sunken eyes when he looked at her. "You're the bravest child I've ever known," he told her, forcing a wrinkled smile, edged with pain. "And you shouldn't have to be. Not anymore. You deserve a life you can choose for yourself, where you need not be afraid. You…" he turned his head to look between all of us, "… all of you… are not resources to be bartered over or a burden to be shucked off. You are not ours—you never were. You belong to God, and He alone will dictate your futures. And I believe each of you hears His voice more clearly than Brother Dolus. Or even me. You must go where that voice leads you. Even if it is…"

His head fell, his ears shrouding his eyes. "… far from me."

"Come with us!" Nicholas pleaded, brushing past me to go to our Father's other side. I stayed where I was, not merely because I did not want to crowd the elderly man, but because I wanted him to be able to fully look me in the eyes.

Mabel tugged at Father's sleeve, nodding. "We need you," she concurred. "I need my Pa." She said the last part haltingly, and it wasn't the first time I'd heard her call him thusly; it was just the first time she'd done so in many years, since she got older. Dolus and the other monks used to snap at her for the informal term of endearment.

Helstrom smiled, his eyes crinkling around the edges. He put a hand on her shoulder and gave it a light squeeze. A truly bold gesture of affection for the man. "You have everything you need in your Brothers, your faith, and yourself. I would very much like to be there for you, Mabel. For you all. To guide you, to see you grow, perhaps even to give you away, some day. It pains me to think I may not be present going forward in your life, but I will be awaiting you in the next life, and, ultimately someday, in His Kingdom."

"No…" Mabel said weakly, starting to cry.

Nicholas dragged a wet breath through his nose, crossing his arms over his chest and hanging his head. We were taught to do so as men when tears threatened.

I was envious of women, sometimes.

"I must remain here and unearth what Dolus has done," Father said, looking finally to me. His eyes were hard, unyielding. The strength I knew was there, even when he looked weak, fed my own. I straightened my back and looked my Father in the eyes—as I'd promised myself I would—and received his orders.

"Isidor, you are the eldest," he said. "You must lead them in this pilgrimage. You must be prepared to protect your brother and sister, even from your kinsmen, do you understand?"

"Yes, Father," I said.

"Dolus will act immediately once he realizes you've left the fold," he said. "You hold too many secrets. More than you know, in fact…" he paused for a moment, clearly considering something, then shook his head. "No. It is better for now that you focus on getting to safety."

"You were in town," I said, suddenly realizing. My fur stood on end. "You've heard from one of your contacts—"

"I will be in correspondence," he said. "We cannot speak here. We haven't the time, and honestly, until you are clear of danger with someone I know I can trust, it is better that you know as little as possible."

"With someone you trust?" I quirked my muzzle. "Where— who on earth can we trust, right now?"

"A man who is more an enemy to the Ministry than we are," he said, quickly pulling out a quill and wetting it in his inkwell. "Your prayer book, Isidor."

I withdrew it from the leather loop on my belt and handed it to him, uncertainly. He searched the psalms towards the back half for a few moments, before settling on one I had not written much in the margins of.

"More cuneiform," I said curiously, watching him etch characters into the page.

"We must prepare for all eventualities," he said, glancing up at me briefly. "It wouldn't even be the first time someone has gotten their hands on this book, and if they do, I want none other to know of this location."

"We're going to Redcoven, Father," I declared quietly.

He didn't even look up this time. "I know," he said grimly. "The two men who came with you assessed me of the situation with the Heart Thief before I came to my quarters. I suspected you'd be leaving us to make chase as soon as I heard."

"That confirms where they're headed, at least," Nick said.

"I wish you'd reconsider, but I know better than to talk you out of following that feline around at this point," he muttered as he continued to write. "I have been concocting my own thoughts on how to handle the situation in Redcoven since I arrived. I'd ask at least that you stay downwind of the Ministry until you hear word from me. I will help you as much as I can from here. I'm waiting on word from several of my sources, and I can uphold the façade that the two of you are still here for as long as possible."

"How?" Nicholas asked.

"By informing the Ministry Central Archives that you are on a disciplinary hold for a month, while informing the monks and our Ministry Parish that you've been sent to Amurfolk for training," he answered. "A shell game that will only hold for so long, as I'm sure you can imagine."

"You agreed to allow me to take your children to Redcoven too quickly," I finally just outright stated what was on my mind. "Into the waiting mouth of the lion. Even Mabel? Father, please. What do you know?"

"I'd rather know where you all are than order you somewhere you will not go," he barked. "And I know better than to argue with young love. The fact is—all of you—if you are *hell-bent* on leaving the Abbey, you will be safer together. *You* are the one choosing to endanger your siblings, Isidor. Carry that burden and feel its weight because I do not want you to forget it."

I closed my muzzle, fighting back any other objections. But one last retort slipped out, softer and more plaintive than argumentative. "It just doesn't seem the time to keep secrets, Father. Even if you think you're sparing us something."

"We *need* to get your feline clear of the Ministry," Father said determinedly, "and far, far from the Courts in Amurfolk. This theft has political implications now. If they transport the Heart Thief to the Inquisitors in Amurfolk, they *will* force confessions from them that will have dire consequences. Regardless of the truth."

"Darcy is strong," I said softly, trying to believe it as much as I possibly could.

My Father's slow shake of his head was not encouraging. "I'm certain they are, but I have seen how a person can be broken, Isidor. Whatever your thief thinks their imprisonment will be like, I promise you, they are wrong. There will be no gallows manifestos, no holding to whatever beliefs they deem sacred. They will use the serval as a means to ignite an old powder barrel once again... to confess before a Court of influential Pedigrees, Navymen, and Armed Forces that the Faith's most sacred artifact is in the hands of a Kadrushian Jarl."

"What?" I balked, trying to understand what I was hearing.

"I don't know how this all began," he said, pausing, "not for certain... but I have enough friends amongst Pedigree circles that I've had four confirm the same rumors being circulated all over the country. That means the Ministry is allowing this seed to be planted, potentially even fostering it. The common belief now is that the Heart Thief stole the Heart of Faith on behalf of a Kadrushian Lord. A Jarl."

"Why would they want to foster aggression with the Jarls?" I asked, aghast. "That could lead to—"

"Another wave of border disputes and trade wars in the borderlands and cold seas." He nodded, looking exhausted. "The waters are still slick with blood and gunpowder from the last attempted ripples outward, and yet, we begin again. Tens of thousands of men lost their lives over my lifetime to this eternal conflict. It feeds the demons of wrath, and they grow fat on our dead. It is horrifying to imagine what could result from this."

The room went silent, Nicholas and I looking to one another. The poor lad looked as lost as I felt. Mabel hugged a little closer to Father Helstrom.

"Why would anyone *want* a war?" she asked the question we were all thinking aloud.

"The same paltry reasons that have always existed," Father shook his head. "Sea routes, trade roads, naval power, herring. There's even talk that the Wolves' Trade Cartels have cornered exclusive control over *coal*, of all things."

"Coal?" Nick arched an eyebrow. "That's worth a war?"

"None of you have ever traveled on a steam-powered carriage or ship, I'd wager," Father said. "They're something of a novelty for the rich now, but I've heard intelligent men claim they'll power every ship on the seas in twenty years' time."

"Were those 'intelligent men' puffing on a pipe full of powder from Mataa?" Nick asked dubiously.

"Lord, what did you learn at that Estate?" Father sneered. "Listen to you. I thought the Hudsons were a decent family."

Nick shrugged. "Better I know it than not, isn't it? Hazel said it's always better to know what you're puffing on than not."

"I... I do not have time to address all of that," Father said gruffly. "You were too young for a posting, Nicholas. That much is clear."

I made a noise that wasn't quite an 'I told you so', but it was close enough.

"I'm certain I don't need to say this, Isidor," he turned his attention back to me, "but *do not* involve your Brother or Sister in any crimes against the Ministry. For God's sake. When you swore to me to protect them, that means *above* the life of the thief. Do you understand? If something *can* be done in Redcoven, it may be the time to act. But until you're certain you have a window, you lay low in the mountains and wait for word from me to move. Avoid the city limits; Dolus will be there."

He closed my book and handed it back to me. I didn't bother trying to discern the cuneiform he'd written in it yet. That would take some time. But I did ask, "Once we've gotten Darcy," and at that he gave me a hard look, but I pressed on, "where are you sending us? Where can we be safe? Outside the country?"

"You aren't safe from the Ministry outside the borders of Amuresca, Isidor," he almost laughed. "It doesn't matter if you're in Carvecia or the Ministry's back bloody doorstep... in fact there's the element of incredulity in the latter. No."

He shook his head. "What you need to be safe from them is leverage. This is a game of information, held at bay like the tip of a spear. Pointed at one another's hearts, poised to strike. I am sending you to a man who has accrued more Ministry secrets than anyone who yet draws breath. Although for how much longer, I am not certain. He will protect you because he will want to know what you know. For his bloody... reformation thesis...."

I knew immediately. I knew who he meant. How could I not?

"The Heresiarch?" I felt my blood go cold.

"The very same," he said.

"Isi, why won't you tell me about your paramour?" Mabel whined, letting her head thunk back against my gambeson. She stared up at me upside-down, giving me literal puppy-dog eyes.

I sighed, spurring Blackbow into a trot now that the road ahead looked a little clearer. The sun had been out a few hours on our second day on the road, and it was melting what little snow had fallen days ago. It felt more like autumn today, albeit with bare trees and a long-dead carpet of crunching brown leaves scattered across the carriage road. You could say many things about the eastern country of Amuresca: that it was rural, remote, isolating, rugged, but you could never claim it wasn't beautiful. The horizon all around us was ringed by distant, snow-capped mountains, heralding the trade roads that eventually led to the contested borderlands of the Kadrush region.

We were two days into what was easily the most emotional journey of my life. Father had been right to call it a pilgrimage. From the tearful—and hopefully not final—goodbyes with the bloodhound who'd raised us, to stealing away in the night with my brother and sister bundled up against the cold and as frightened as I was beside me, to now retracing the very same roads I'd taken to hunt down Darcy in the first place. Back then, when we'd first met with three inches of hardwood between us, I'd offered to be their salvation. Hopefully this time, I'd make good on that promise.

For the sake of expedience, Mabel was riding with me. I didn't mind of course, but Father's reasoning had made Mabel sore. She knew how to ride side-saddle, but she was still a child, and a young woman, at that. Father feared she would lack control and stability in the saddle if we had to flee pursuers and he was probably right, but I understood her frustration. She'd not had the training Nicholas and I had due entirely to her gender, not just her disability or her age. And earnestly, I would have preferred she have her own horse or pony, as well. It would give her more autonomy on the road.

Darcy rode their horse as a man would and had an excellent seat from what I'd seen. They'd even done so in a dress. At some point they'd been taught to ride as a man, and regardless of where they fell… anatomically… I was starting to wonder if the Physician's and the Church's teachings on feminine delicacy and the need for side-saddle riding were another fabrication. It wasn't as though a man's body was any less 'delicate' in the areas of note.

"Isi…" Mabel thudded her head back again, begging my attention and giving me a playful smile.

Honestly, I'd loved every moment of traveling the roads with my sister, the cold aside. Seeing the world together was a privilege I'd never thought we'd have. But *this* kept happening.

"They aren't my 'paramour,'" I cleared my throat uncomfortably. "Darcy is just a friend."

"He's lying," Nicholas clucked, trotting his horse up beside us and shooting me a wicked grin. "I saw them bumpin' muzzles, huggin' in a wholly unseemly way. How uncharitable o'you, Isidor. You ought repent! We're your brother and sister; we deserve only honesty from you."

"Isi!" Mabel elbowed me in the ribs. Thanks to the gambeson, I hardly felt it.

"Bold claim," I snuffed. "I'll admit I fancy them then. Is that enough to clear my name? We are not promised, we are not courting. They are not my paramour. Besides, that word suggests something… illicit between us."

"Well you *were* kissin' on her out of wedlock," Nicholas accused.

"No, I wasn't!" I prickled.

"Look, it was hard t'tell exactly what was going on while I was hidin' in the bushes, but—"

"You spied on Isi?!" Mabel squeaked, laughing.

"Hell yes I did," he declared proudly. "Lad was too distracted t'notice. And I didn't exactly have the best angle on the action, but Brother… her scent was *all* over you when you came back in lookin' for me."

"I wasn't," I stammered, "we weren't kissing."

"Then what were you doing out there in th'woods so long?" he asked dubiously.

I couldn't hold eye contact. I also didn't answer for a suspiciously long time. "Not kissing," I finally said.

Whatever my younger brother took away from that, I'd never know, and that was probably for the best. "Well, it's not like that's the main point, anyway. She's a bona-fide criminal, Isidor," Nick reminded me with an arched eyebrow. "And you're still a Templar, s'far as the Ministry's concerned. That's pretty damn—"

"You shouldn't swear when a lady's present," Mabel tutted at Nicholas, smirking at him.

"… my apologies of course, Lady Mabel," the young man said, overly formally, smirking right back.

"If you rescue her, are you going to marry her?" Mabel asked, staring up at me again.

I averted my eyes, looking back to the road and the horizon instead. "I don't know, Mabel," I confessed. "But probably not. Don't get your hopes up."

"Why not?"

I felt my brows pinch. "It's just… there are a lot of reasons. But mostly, I do not think they would want to marry me, even if it was possible."

"That's silly. Who wouldn't want to marry you?" She quirked her muzzle a moment. "Well, other than me. But—"

"I do not reproach you on that score," I assured her, releasing one hand from the reins to grip her own hand comfortingly. "The feeling is quite mutual, I assure you."

"Good," she said, relieved. "I was… I think that's what scared me the most, Isi. That you'd feel… u-uhm. Unlovable. If I didn't want…."

I shook my head, smiling. "There are different kinds of love, Mabel. And maybe that's the main thing, honestly. I don't know if Darcy loves me. Or I they. Like that. It's complicated. Confusing."

"That's what they say love is like," she said.

"Who are 'they'?" I asked.

"I don't know," she mumbled. "Poets. The older girls?"

"Love is for rich people," Nicholas muttered, brushing a few leaves out of his horse's mane. "S'not for paupers like us. You marry so you have someone to keep house with, raise pups with, grow old with. A friend is fine. Better if you think they're pretty, but that in't always a given either."

"You already said she's a friend," Mabel counted off on her fingers. "You can't have pups with cat-kind, right? But Father isn't our blood-father, and that didn't matter. He's still my Pa. So that just leaves… is she pretty, Isi?"

I opened my mouth, but Nicholas cut me off.

"Yep. She's *real* pretty, and if you say otherwise Isi, you're lyin' again."

I sighed, relenting in a soft tone, "Darcy is… breathtakingly beautiful, yes."

"I want to meet her!" Mabel said again, excited. "Do you think she'd let me dress her or do her fur?"

I paused. "I think they might actually enjoy that. They're much more, um, fashion-forward than I am."

"Good, *someone* needs to tidy you up on a daily basis," Mabel snorted.

"I have impeccable hygiene," I grumbled.

"Your spats don't match."

I blanched, shooting a look down at my legs, and the cloth spats I was wearing beneath my guards. She wasn't wrong.

"I got dressed in the dark," I complained. "And they're not— cream white and eggshell white are close enough."

"What would your feline friend say if she heard you say that?" she teased.

I tried to imagine it. Darcy fussing over me in the mornings when we dressed. Maybe… together. We wouldn't be wealthy if they gave up their life of crime. We'd only have one bedroom. We'd share, well, everything. It would be like at the Lodge, but we wouldn't be pretending we didn't want to be with one another.

I knew they wanted that for certain now. Not being domestic together, necessarily. But at least sharing a bed. Maybe sharing a room for a time. In the past when I'd thought on things like this, my mind had gone right to the sins I'd been warned against, the way my mind and body would fail me if I made myself vulnerable to the temptations of the flesh.

But now that I'd crossed that line once, it was like the ripples on the surface of the water had dissipated. I knew what lay below the waterline, or at least had dipped my toes in those delights. It had been pleasant. Wonderful, in fact. But nothing— ultimately—had changed. And it felt less frightening, less anxious, to consider something like sleeping beside them. Sharing a space with them. If it happened again, it happened again. God had not struck me down yet. And more importantly, no one had been hurt.

I felt certain I would be able to control myself. All this time, I'd been warned I would transform into someone I wouldn't recognize, would surrender to these passions as though possessed. But Darcy had brought me along time and again past those barriers, those lines I had been warned not to cross, and I had never once felt I was beyond control. I had given in to my wants, certainly, but only when the feline had all but begged me to, and I knew without a shadow of a doubt that what I desired with them was permitted. And even then....

They'd lead. I'd followed.

One could make an argument that I was being led astray from the righteous path, and they'd have a good argument there. But I didn't feel as... lost, any more. If anything, I felt more certain than I had since this had begun. If I was off the path, I was finding another.

And so much of that biting self-hatred and recrimination had cooled. Whenever I thought of Darcy and me alone together, it brought me peace. I would consider some impossible future. My imaginings of them were purer, if anything. With the fears of losing myself to lust because I'd seen a part of their body I wasn't meant to or shared a touch that should have been reserved for marriage... with those anxieties gone, I could think about them more clearly. Consider the practicalities of what living or even just traveling with them for a time would be like. Whatever we were to one another.

If it were possible, would I want to be with them like that? For a long time? Possibly the rest of our lives? Would they want to be with *me*?

"I think," I said quietly, after a long time spent thinking. "Or I'd like to believe, at least, that we might be able to find happiness with one another for a time. Come to know one another more deeply. But marriage is forever, and… I—I don't know… we are so different in many ways. I'm not even certain we'd be *allowed* to marry, if we free them or exonerate them and all else is somehow settled. Even then…."

I looked down at my sister, who was staring up at me, entranced. I could feel Nick's eyes on me too, bewildered, and curious. I had to keep reminding myself that they'd never known this side of me. To them, I was the same man I had been when I'd been ordained months ago.

And, they were both essentially still children. Nicholas at fifteen, nearly sixteen, Mabel thirteen. If not for the very real threat of danger they faced staying at Ebon Gables any longer, I'd feel like a butcher leading lambs to slaughter, involving them in this. But there wasn't any choice.

Sometimes we aren't given easy roads to travel. Between a treacherous climb through the mountains and a fragile, swaying bridge, how did one choose? You went with your gut.

Right now, my gut was telling me to be honest with my siblings. If no one else in the world would understand what I was facing, they would. They would at least *try*.

"Alright," I said, reining my horse in to a stop, near a clutch of bare apple trees on the roadside. Nicholas came to a stop as well, haltingly, and began looking about for signs of trouble. "We're fine," I assured him. "I just need to consider my words for a moment."

They both waited for me to do so, silently. A bird sung nearby, the wind bit at our noses, the scent of hay from a nearby field clinging to it.

"Firstly," I began, "Darcy is not a woman."

Nick's eyes widened. "I just thought—I mean she was wearin' britches, but I thought—"

"Isi," Mabel blinked up at me, "you're in love with a boy?"

I swallowed. "The world's not all we were led to believe. The rules we know, they're not... they're not true everywhere. They may not even really be true here. It's just the way they want us to think of people, but people are more varied than the Church says. You know how, say, Brother Dolus taught us that mice can't work with lumber, only stone and brick, because mice only build down, not up?"

Both of them nodded. We all remembered the lesson.

I brought in a breath, then said, "I thought that was true until I went to Redcoven. But the mice and rats there built half the *city*. They own butcher shops, inns, bakeries, and they even work as law clerks."

"And people don't get sick from their food?" Nick asked, aghast. The vermin kind at Ebon Gables weren't even allowed to cross the threshold into the kitchens.

I shook my head. "Those 'truths' aren't true. I think a great deal of what we've learned may be ill-informed, or at least not always true. Even—maybe especially—what we learned about men and women."

"So, what is," Nick seemed to struggle, "sh-he?"

"They," I said, "are neither. I suppose I'll explain it the way they explained it to me...."

We made good time, all in all. Father Helstrom's decision to send us off on horses rather than hopping carriages was made by necessity—not financial this time, he'd given us a small fortune from his own personal strongbox, and even eating well, we'd not exhaust it any time soon—but because of the independence and lower profile it granted us. Traveling by saddle was harder, more taxing on the body especially in the cold, but we were all young and it was early winter, yet.

All the same, the light downy snow that came in from the north this time of year was little trouble for a well-appointed, surefooted Templar's steed, but murder on carriage wheels. In addition to the anonymity it granted us and the lack of a paper trail, it was also a more reliable way to travel if one could weather it. And weather it, we had.

I was proud of my siblings. Nicholas especially. He was still recovering from his injuries and hadn't complained the whole of the trip, remaining stalwart and bright-eyed. The dane was tough, healed fast, and seemed aware of the need to keep the group's spirits high, which he excelled at far more than I did. He filled our long days on the road with stories of his time at the Hudson Estate and the many antics he and his friend—the apparently sly, secretive troublemaker Hazel Hudson—had gotten up to. Honestly, the young Pedigree heiress sounded like a handful and none too keen to marry at nineteen, which did not bode well for the family's prospects.

It had worried me at first, but after so much talk of her, I didn't detect a hint of any romantic yearning from my brother. Earnestly, I think he may have just been... lonely. And she as well. After I'd gotten into more intensive training to be ordained officially, I hadn't been able to spend much time with Nicholas. And most of the other boys at Ebon Gables were either far younger than us or older and moved on to postings or other jobs by now.

Hazel Hudson and Nicholas were four years apart, but both young adults by most people's standards. It would be an absolute scandal if it had ever been known how much time the two had apparently been spending together. Conclusions would be drawn. But the more I listened, the more it sounded like a friendship. There was nothing flirtatious or lascivious in the way my brother spoke of her. Perhaps months ago, I would not have trusted my own experience. But at this point, I had at least something of an idea what to look out for.

Could a young man and woman of courting age be confidantes, and nothing more? I was certain that people who didn't know my brother as well as I did would not think so.

Mabel was frightened, exhausted, sore, and trying to put on a brave face. But we all were by the end of the trip. If anything, the young girl seemed to rebound better than the two of us at the start of every day, and slept more soundly through the nights, even the few we spent in common-room boarding houses.

Nicholas and I boxed ourselves in with her between us at night, a proper family sharing the same bedroll or straw mattress, like the family I'd grown up in. We'd been raised in communal bunks our whole lives, but always a blanket tuck away from our brother or sisters, preparing us for proper society and the rules of separation that bound it. I had somehow forgotten that this is how the common folk all lived. Sharing body heat and nearly every space we occupied together.

This is how I'd grown up. It was distant, barely scraps of memories now, but I could recall the sound of my mother's voice lulling us to sleep, the jab of my brother's paws in my ribs at night, the smell of our damp home. I'd lain in that straw bed through many days, watching the sun slat through the windows, sick again, unable to eat. My mother crying, unable to understand why I was ill so often. Why I was wasting away....

Returning to life as a commoner wasn't sad, though. Rather, it was nostalgic, making me grateful to my parents for having the wisdom and being able to put their own wants aside long enough to do the right thing for me. Cillian had been right, it *shouldn't* have been so hard for them to feed me, but... it had been. And what felt like an error in God's design had led me here to this point with my new family journeying across the most beautiful corners of the country I called home to do what I hoped would be His work. Bring Salvation to the Heart Thief, as I'd long hoped, and perhaps in the process avert a war?

As terrifying as it all was, I'd never known such certainty of purpose. And that kept me focused. It kept me strong. I found myself able to eat again because I needed to in order to build my strength back up. I slept through each night, despite the aches of the road. I kept us on task during the days and managed to navigate our trip without getting lost or misdirected once. It helped that I'd taken these very roads once before, but also…

I had my family. Through all of it. I could scarcely believe how well my brother and sister were holding their countenance, given that we'd all unmoored ourselves from every promise of safety and security we'd ever known in one week's time. But we were survivors, each of us. Relentless.

We'd known hardship before and during our time at Ebon Gables. But we'd also had a good teacher, who—we were finding more and more, day by day—had been preparing us to be self-reliant, and when needed to trust in one another to cover our blind spots. That was, after all, what the Ministry at its most righteous was meant to be. A brotherhood.

The importance of that became clear on our tenth day in the northeastern country. We were barely a few hours from Redcoven on horseback, staying at a woodcutter's lodge and trade post that sat nestled at the edge of the Dyre Wood. Waiting here for nearly two days had been agony. We were close. We were *so* close to the city, and Darcy was most certainly here by now. But I wasn't sure how to approach without running the risk of being seen by Ministry Agents, and even if I *could* disguise or sneak my way inside the city limits, what then? I didn't know where they were being held.

There was the Cathedral itself, which was unlikely. No Church I knew of save those from the ancient ages had cells or fortified areas to keep a prisoner. The Ministry building, of course. That would be the most obvious location. Fortified, familiar to them. But that was also to its detriment as an option. While I doubted Dolus suspected I'd do something as severe as... what I was considering... trekking across the entire countryside, relying on my father to lie for me to mislead the Ministry back home, and attempt a jail break *here*, somewhere I was *not* meant to be....

Dolus was a calculating man who considered his options carefully, but I don't think even he'd expect one of his sons to go against him in such a way. With so little hope of success. But I also hadn't foreseen that the man would have followed me all the way from Redcoven to Ebon Gables, with a second on Cillian's tail, and orchestrate us to meet in the middle and draw out his quarry.

And he had.

I had to be prepared to be out-maneuvered again. However I acted here in Redcoven, I had to be unexpected. He would take the protection of his asset seriously. I couldn't just go in alone and expect I'd have the element of surprise on my side. That wasn't guaranteed and even if it was, Darcy would be under heavy guard. I'd be setting myself up for a fall.

And we didn't even know where they were keeping them. Redcoven had a prison, but as far as I knew it wasn't inside the city walls. They wouldn't risk keeping them so far from the Ministry and their center of power. There was the Ministry building itself, but that would be obvious. It was, like all Templar structures, fortified and built with security in mind. There would be interior rooms with no easy ingress, suitable for holding a prisoner. They wouldn't hold Darcy within Saint Rhine's itself, since it was consecrated earth.

Each option had its downsides, but any of them were

ultimately possible. And there was also the wildcard: a completely neutral location. One I'd not thought of.

And now I was reflecting on how impossible this all was again. I'd been fighting off waves of hopelessness, trying to clutch to my strength of purpose. It was a battle I was still, for the most part, winning.

But the fact was I was running up against the limitations of my training and lack of resources. When I'd been pursuing Darcy, I'd been a Templar. Now I had my uniform and patents, but if I tried to wield them in Redcoven, even amongst civilians, I'd almost certainly be in the Ministry's crosshairs in no time.

I knew how to find someone when the odds were against me. I could track Darcy to wherever they were keeping them, I was certain of it. But not with my hands tied behind my back. How could I find them when I couldn't even enter the city without risking ruining our element of surprise?

I'd considered disguise, of course. The primary issue was my tail. It was noticeable even from a distance, and I couldn't keep it uncurled for long periods of time to hide it beneath my cloak. Something like Darcy's dye might avail me at least to be less obvious in a crowd, but I was a large man with a distinctive bearing. The training was hard to shake. We were taught to carry ourselves a certain way. I couldn't disappear amongst the masses like the feline did.

I just wasn't very good at this. And I didn't have the time to learn.

Our opponent here was a man who knew how to disappear, who had followed me and my Father across two counties without either of us being the wiser, and I simply wasn't skilled in that way. The way Dolus dressed down and changed how he carried himself, becoming no one of concern so *effortlessly*... it made much more sense, now. He'd cultivated that humbler persona, like he'd cultivated his softer, more charismatic demeanor. It was a mask. One he wore most of the time honestly, and I wasn't even certain I'd seen it fully slip away, yet. The well there went deep, into a blackness I'd only just begun to glimpse.

We hadn't heard from Father Helstrom yet. And we were running out of time. It might take weeks for them to try Darcy here in Redcoven, but every day was another they spent subject to questioning.

To Dolus. And God knew who else.

A frontal assault—some kind of quick pierce into the city, and a swift surveillance of the possible locations they could be at, until I found the right location and just as swiftly broke my way in—might be my only option. I was finding ways to rationalize it more and more as time wore on.

Nicholas and I spent our days primarily in the taphouse of the inn we were staying at. We had enough coin to have a shared private room for the three of us, a luxury that both Nick and I considered essential at this point for safety's sake. We were in one of the rural townships of Redcoven on the outskirts. Far enough from the city that I couldn't imagine the Ministry sending someone here when they had no reason to, but close enough still that I wasn't comfortable dropping our guard in a public place. Unless we wanted to keep a watch, I preferred a room we could close ourselves in at night.

"That's your third beer today," I said, not looking up from my prayer book. The cuneiform Father had left me with this time was complex, and without a key or a library to reference, I was left with my memory and trial and error. It was a puzzle, but not one I resented. It had kept my mind busy over the last few days, at least.

"They water the shite out of them," Nicholas muttered, downing the last of his mug. "I've my senses, Isi. Never you fear."

"Then we're wasting coin," I said pointedly. "I hope at least they're filling."

"M'supposed to drink alcohol 'til my gums heal," he reminded me. "Spirits keep bile an' pus at bay. Physician said so."

"I've always wondered at that," I confessed, sighing. "The pain-numbing properties are obvious, but why does it help with infection?"

He shrugged. "We aren't Physicians. Trust the men with learnin'; they know their craft."

I bent my nose back to my book and hummed thoughtfully, pouring over the same line I'd been trying to decipher all day. My humming became the opening chords to a hymn—Bow Before the Pack Lord, Oh Faithful—as I considered the characters in front of me.

I'd sung this song with Darcy at the Lodge. It felt like a lifetime ago. Lord, I was worried about them.

Nick's elbow bumped mine, and before I could look up, he said over the rim of his beer mug, "Nah, keep your head down. I think we've got someone here lookin' for us."

"What?" I asked, alarmed but quiet.

"Yeah, don't look up, but they're to our left, back of the bar," he said, reaching for one of the biscuits we had at our table and breaking off a piece of it for himself. "Wolf, for sure, an'... I don'know. Some kinda big cat. Long tail, lots of fur. They look northern, the both o'them. Thick coats."

"Foreigners?" I resisted the urge to turn around, but flicked my eyes to the side to catch the barest glimpse of what must have been one of them. Nicholas was right about the tail. Long, white, gray, maybe spotted? A Kadrushian feline of some sort, maybe.

"I don't know, they aren't *dressed* foreign," Nick shrugged. "Least not that I can tell. They've been here a few hours now that I've noticed, an'they've floated by us a few times. The wolf keeps looking us over."

"God, I hadn't noticed," I said, ashamed. This place was a busy post, there were a lot of people coming in and out, almost all of them an eclectic mix of men of various walks in life. I'd seen a few dozen species since we'd started staying here, including a few folks that may have been from the north. The tiger from the other day, for sure. Some kind of hunter. He'd stood out primarily due to his size but had moved on quickly.

"Mmh, well you've had yer nose in that book all day," he said, grinning a bit. "Never you mind, Isi. I've 'ad a look out."

"Clearly," I said. "Good lad. What are they—"

"Just drinkin', right now. 'Ang on and stay put, alright?"

He stood suddenly, pushing his chair back. I sat bolt upright and tried not to whirl or react in shock any more than I already had. I whispered a fierce, "Where are you—"

But by then he was gone. I glanced behind the table only once to watch him pass through the crowded hall... past the men... and then up the stairs? To our room? Why?

I most certainly saw both of those men this time and watched their heads follow my Brother. I snapped my focus back to my prayer book, hitching my breath. Nicholas was right. They were definitely watching us or taking note of us for some reason. Without his sharp eyes, I never would have noticed. I'd been too lost in thought, too focused on the cuneiform, and....

It couldn't have been more than a few minutes before Nicholas returned. I heard the distinct sound of his rosary beads rustling where he kept them wrapped thrice around his wrist. I wore mine under my shirt because I wore my family's bracelet around my wrist, but Nick liked to toy with his.

He pulled his chair out and slid back in to sit beside me, as casually as he'd gotten up.

"You're better at this than I am," I said quietly, below the ambience of the room.

"At what?"

"Acting nondescript," I said. "What did you just do? Try to listen in on them while you walked past?"

"They've been watching us, they would've shut up when I got close," he said. "I talked to Mabel. She's coming down in a few minutes, long enough so's we don't seem connected. I don't think they've seen 'er, yet."

"If they're from the Ministry, they might know her," I said.

"They're secular agents if they are," he reasoned. "They probably won't. You'n I have more of a file in the Archives."

"That's true enough," I relented quietly.

"She's th'only one who can get close."

I went silent, worry seizing me. I tried not to let it show in my posture, and it helped that my back was to them.

Nicholas had a better angle from where he was sitting, so he kept me apprised. "Alright, she's headin' to the bar. I told 'er just to hover about, but she had the idea to order food so she'd have an excuse to wait for a bit."

This went on for nearly ten minutes. Occasionally I caught glimpses of my Sister, idly waiting while she drank from a steaming cup. Tea with sugar and cream, if I knew her. She was awfully close to the two men, but from what little I could tell, they did not *seem* to be taking note of her.

There weren't many young women here, but she wasn't the only one. She was alone, which was suspicious, but my sister was tall enough to pass for a married woman, and she had covered her head in order to sell that image. Whenever anyone had asked, we'd told them she and Nicholas were newly-wed, and I was their brother-in-law. The differences in our kind hardly mattered amongst the lower classes. Families of dogs did not always resemble one another. And no one was going to probe too deeply.

"She got her meal... oh hells, she's coming over," Nick said suddenly.

"What? *No*, now they'll connect us," I turned, unable to fight the urge. But Mabel was already upon us by then, setting her bowl of soup and bread down at our table.

She looked puzzled. But not worried, exactly. "Isidor," she said, setting the bowl she held in her one hand down, then reaching to receive her mug of tea from the bartender who'd brought it down for her, "didn't you say... your friend, or rather Darcy's... the Pedigree fellow. What was his name? Wasn't it rather... unpleasant-sounding?"

"Rathborne," I said, arching an eyebrow. "Cillian Rathborne."

She nodded. "That's the one. They said it—the last name there—at least once. They were speaking lowly, but I heard. They said his name, and that he'd only mentioned one Templar." She paused, then continued, "Oh, they know you're both Templar. Even without the red and white, I guess it *is* kind of obvious, huh?"

"It is?" Nicholas asked obliviously.

"I don't know," she shrugged. "The way you stand? The rosaries. Isi hides his, but you can still sort of see it around his neck. Maybe they saw Isi outside with his cloak on, taking care of the horses."

I was already getting up. They both looked up at me, alarmed.

Head-on. That's the only way I knew how to meet the challenges ahead. And I had an inkling, on this one.

I strode across the room towards the two men, taking them in as I went. They did the same, seeming not at all surprised to see me approaching them. Perhaps they'd been trying to be seen surveilling us. They'd certainly let it go on a long while.

The wolf was close to my build with ashen black fur and blue eyes, wearing practical and comfortable traveling clothes, not expensive, but well-made, and a fur-lined cloak that currently covered most of his torso. I couldn't be certain if he was armed or not, but his build and relatively young age suggested he wouldn't be a pushover if it came to a fight.

The feline was white, gray, and spotted in exotic rosettes, like no cat I'd ever seen except in books. He was one of the northern leopards, I knew that much, but I'd never met one in person before. He was tall—not as tall as the tiger the other day—and intimidating in his dark leathers and long coat, tailored especially for him judging by the fit. Unlike the wolf, he openly carried a blade. This place was lenient to allow it, but the short sword at his side was peace-bound, tied about the hilt with heavy twine. Like mine.

I hadn't any idea what I was walking into, but the stage had been set from the time Mabel had come to sit beside us. I'm glad she had, though. I didn't want to risk us passing these men over like ships in the night. Not if….

"Hail," the feline said, leaning back against the bar and jutting his white chin up in my direction. His tail thrashed behind him, betraying some level of anxiety his otherwise cool demeanor was masking.

"You've been watching us a great deal," I said, putting authority into my voice.

The feline stared out the window a moment, while keeping his ears tipped in my direction. When he spoke again, he did so quietly, for some reason. "The winter storms are coming down from the Kadrush," he said. "They'll arrive here soon."

Memory sparked.

"Cillian Rathborne sent you," I breathed out. "Didn't he?"

The wolf's expression twisted into one more suspicious. "That isn't the code phrase, Ravus."

"This is the sixth township we've tried and the first where we've found an Akita sporting prayer beads and a silver fortune band," the feline snorted. "Who else could he be? Rathborne said things were harried when they parted ways… he never gave you the full phrase, did he?"

"Or I cannot remember it," I confessed. "I didn't even realize what was happening at the time." I paused. "Fortune band?"

"Your wrist," he pointed at my silver bracelet. "You don't know your own lineage?"

I glanced down at the keepsake. "I was young when I… it's all I have left from my family."

"It's Kadrushian," the feline explained. "Almost like your prayer beads, but a blessing by more ancient Gods. The Gods your ancestors worshiped, *Lokushan*." I didn't recognize the word, but I could tell by how easily his accent slipped into more comfortable pronunciation that it was a Kadrush term.

I watched the bracelet slide down my wrist to settle into its usual resting place above my palm, seeing it in a whole new light. "I… I'm wearing the prayer artifact of a heretical religion?"

"No," the wolf spoke up, speaking bluntly and without pause, "you are wearing a blessing from your ancestor's spirits. *They* worshiped what you Amur call heresy."

"And it sounds like you've been wearing it your entire life," the feline said with a fanged grin. "Let us not curse our fortune now, when it's led you to us, *ayoah*? And with so little time to spare. We had begun to think we would have to do this alone."

I felt my brother and sister moving up to flank me. Bracing myself, I asked, "Do what?"

"If you wish to free this person our employer does," the wolf said, again speaking frankly, with an unyielding affect to his tone, "you'll need to come with us. Now. We are short on time, and our opportunity is closing. We will not have a better chance than tonight."

"I don't know, Isi," my brother said worriedly, pulling my gambeson strings tight where they laced at my back, "these're mercenaries. Whether they're workin' with your man or not, this is a hell of a gamble you're taking. Usually Brothers're only forced to work with hired blades under Bahdren."

"We've essentially excommunicated ourselves," I reminded him. "Bahdren pales in comparison."

"I still don't see why we can't be along, at least nearby," Mabel said from where she was sitting on the bed.

"I made an oath to our Father," I said, looking to her. "I promised I'd keep you two out of this."

"You also said you'd await instruction from him," my brother said, tugging tight the buckle on my harness, perhaps with a bit more force than necessary. He was angry, I could tell. Not just worried, like Mabel. "And you're not doin' that. This isn't smart, Isidor. You're smart. You oughta' know better. We don't even have good proof these men're who they say they are."

"Cillian sent along his signet ring," I said, looking to the opulent golden ring with the man's family crest on it, sitting on the end table in our humble room. He could have just used it to stamp something, but he'd sent them with the ring itself. Less easily forged.

"They could have him," Nicholas said needlessly.

"I know," I whispered. "I know the risks, Nick. I know this could be a ploy, but if it is, it's a damned good one, and I can't sit on my hands any longer. Not knowing there's finally something I can possibly do."

"*Possibly*," both of my siblings said at once.

There was a firm rap on the door. I'd heard them approaching in the hall, but I still stiffened. So did Nicholas beside me. Mabel, boldly, just called out, "Come in, mercenaries! It's unlocked."

The door opened slowly, the feline ducking inside. I'd caught by now that his name was 'Ravus', but the wolf had been less forthcoming with his.

"Why is it so imperative you all do this as soon as possible?" my brother demanded, first-off.

"Warm welcome, I see," the feline said, as the wolf shut the door behind them. "I told you, we've a narrow window. Also, this isn't particularly 'soon', by our measure. Our intermediary contacted us nearly a month ago, back when the job was an escort past the border. This only became a rescue when you lot made a mess of things, the way I hear it. We were trying to make contact with our employer in Bellridge when we'd heard it all went south. Bloody bounced us around the country, he has. Lucky he's got deep pockets."

"We only confirmed the thief's location because of a hearing they had to produce the accused for, yesterday," the wolf said, more calmly than his friend. "When they moved the target, I was able to shadow the procession back to where they'd been keeping them. A nondescript residence over a shuttered shop. Odd, but low-key, I suppose. We never would have found it. Our employer mentioned knowing of the location after the fact, but he hadn't considered it as an option for hiding our quarry away."

"The Archives," I swore. "Why didn't I consider… it just didn't seem bloody likely. It's the residence of a Templar from this City. But it's also a reinforced structure with a windowless, tamper-proof basement."

The feline grinned. "Nothing's tamper-proof for me."

"No, you don't understand," I shook my head. "There's an Interrogation chamber beneath older Archives, for Inquisitors to use when their target is too dangerous or unholy to be brought on consecrated ground. They used to employ them for exorcisms. Archives are not hallowed earth. Ministry offices are almost always on Church land. I don't hold to this, but there was a belief that the possessed could not be brought past the bounds of consecrated earth, or their host would die."

The snow cat arched an eyebrow. "And you lot think our Gods are archaic?"

"Demons are very real, sir," I said intensely, "but I don't believe in possession. Neither does my Father. He told me the reason the Archives were fitted with these rooms was because too many people had died during exorcisms. The blame was put on the hallowed earth, rather than...."

"Whatever they are doing in that place to your serval comrade," the wolf spoke up, leveling his blue-eyed stare at me, "it is... unkind. Our employer was at the hearing. He said they looked *very* unwell. He didn't elaborate past that, but he has been fervent since that we act as soon as possible."

My heart ached, and I saw Nick's expression soften sympathetically towards me.

"There are two ways in and out of the lower building," I said, pressing on.

"Two?" Ravus leaned in. "We canvassed the building and saw but one. Well-guarded, I'll add."

"There is a staircase from the apartment down into the Archives," I said. "I've been inside. But once you've gotten downstairs, the hatch to the old cellar, the chambers they must be keeping Darcy inside... well, I never saw it. It would have to be beneath a bookcase or some of the Archive boxes for me to have missed it."

"Are you certain this place exists?" the wolf questioned, narrowing his eyes.

"The apartment above is not secure enough," I shook my head. "Nor is the Archive. If you saw them take Darcy in there and not come out, it's a safe assumption that apartment was built over an older pre-war structure. Many of the Archives were. And it would make sense to hide them away there. Even if you did get past the guards, if you didn't know the history of those places, you could search the whole building and still not find it."

"This feels like the piece we've been missing," Ravus agreed, nodding. "Alright. I prefer we go about this as clean as possible, and our employer seemed to think you would, as well. No bodies. No grievous injuries if we can manage it. The Ministry takes no prisoners when you claim one of their souls. If we can make these boys look like fools instead, and still claim our prize, I'd be a happy leopard."

"How?" I asked the obvious question. "You said we had some kind of window tonight—"

"Well, the monk is out dealing with the local magistrate tonight," Ravus said. "The purse was *real* intent on us avoiding a run-in with him."

"How do you know all this?" Nick asked, crossing his arms over his chest.

"Because the hearing yesterday and the sit-down he's being dragged before tonight with the local moneyed and powerful," the wolf said, "are public forum. Our purse is permitted to attend, and he has. Making your monk real uncomfortable too, I hear. They know he's putting his capital to bear to make this process as hard on them as possible. But your Ministry can't duck out of these formalities, and the monk is their face for managing the bureaucracy involved in all of this."

"Our employer's going to keep him very busy tonight, giving him hell at that public forum," Ravus grinned. "There are two guards on the house at all times, several in the vicinity patrolling the nearby street, and probably one at least *with* the serval. Our aim is misdirection for as many outside as possible and a *kon-shank* projectile for the door guards."

They must have seen the confusion on our faces because the wolf explained, "A Huudari weapon we've employed before. A tightly-packed pouch that bursts upon contact with the ground and sprays the area and all those unfortunate souls within with a combination of ground dust from Mataa chilis and the dried essence of, ah... our skunk kin's most formidable natural weapons. It renders most canines unable to put up a resistance, but we will need to shoot it from a distance before moving in. Masks will not be enough."

"Someone lives upstairs in the apartment," I said.

All eyes locked on me. "Are you certain?" Ravus asked.

I nodded. "He'll be there, too. *He* is why Dolus feels confident leaving Darcy in that place. However many Templar are guarding that door, however clever your tricks, *he* will be the final impediment to our success. He is dedicated, tenacious, and fearless. I have no confidence I could best him in a fight, either. He has far more experience than I."

"And you do not *wish* to fight him," the wolf guessed astutely. His sharp eyes bored into mine.

I nodded slowly. "But I don't see how it can be avoided. He'll be inside, in residence, so your satchel will not disable him. Do you have more than one?"

They only shook their head. Ravus eventually asked me, "You know this man, ya? You sound as though you do."

"I do," I said regrettably. "We were close."

The snow cat smiled. "Then do not fight him, Templar. Talk to him. Keep him occupied. Use whatever you must. We only need distract him for a time."

I looked between the two men and then my siblings. In their eyes I saw my own worry reflected back at me. This was tenuous. I knew it was. Our chances were...

... better now than they had been. And the fact was, if I did not seize what was even a slim possibility now, I might not have another. I would always remember failing them in this moment. Failing myself.

To hell with overthinking. To hell with strategizing. Dolus had been right about one thing: I approached my problems too much like a scholar and lagged behind my instincts.

They were hurting Darcy. That was honestly all that mattered.

I checked my blade, unfurling the peace-binding on it. "I'll do whatever I have to," I said. "Lead on."

We stole into the city at nightfall and traversed the streets casually on horseback. Just three travelers making their way to the temple district.

The two men I was attempting this with were essentially strangers to me. But I had to trust. I had to trust in God and myself and keep my wits about me in case I was wrong. That was all there was to it.

If these two fellows were working for the Ministry, they were *deeply* undercover. They spoke to one another occasionally in mixed Amur and Kadrushian words, translating for me intermittently, I suppose so that I didn't feel they were hiding anything from me. The snow leopard—he had by now told me that's what his kin preferred to call themselves—had what I recognized to be a crossbow case lashed to his saddlebag. It worried me. That was a weapon of death, however you looked at it, but it was also the preferential weapon of Templar assassins. It looked like a foreign design, as did the weapons I eventually saw both him and the wolf checking over. Their clothing was meant to pass as civilian garb, save the leather surcoat the snow leopard wore, but everything from the way they rode their horses to the way they tied their spats said they were foreign.

What they had told me so far rang true. Right down to Cillian knowing the location of Malachi's residence. And when we drew nearer, they had their first chance to prove their loyalty. And they passed spectacularly.

"Eagle's eye on the second story balcony there," the wolf said suddenly, not pulling his horse to a stop, but making some kind of motion with one of his gloved hands at his side that the snow leopard seemed to catch immediately.

"Fifty degrees and to the right," he said to me. "You know fir sign?"

"No," I shook my head, "but I wouldn't mind learning."

"After this is over," he said. "We use it in the fir forests in the north. For ambush, hunting, or whenever you need to be quiet. They can't hear us this far away, but once we get closer, just follow Sig, alright? He's got the best eyes."

"Back guard," the wolf I'd just learned was named 'Sig' said, "and two stories up? Not worth it. Just don't go around back. We're behind the apartment now. Once we 'round this corner we'll have more to worry about. There'll be front eyes, too."

We walked beneath and past the balcony in question, leaving the man be. How we would have gotten up to a second story without alerting the man, I couldn't say. I only hoped the guards around front would be street level.

When we took the right to round the block, we found the street slightly more populated. And by that, I mean there were four or five people, a man lighting lanterns, two gentlemen hustling down the street after walking out the front door of a law clerk's office, and two people huddled around an old brazier in an alley between businesses.

"Lantern-lighter?" Ravus guessed uncertainly.

"No," I said. "It's the two in rags around the brazier."

"I'd have guessed the lantern-lighter, too," Sig said, scanning upwards along rooftops and balconies. "Reason to be out at night, civil job you'd overlook easily—"

"The two around the brazier are wearing clean spats," I said. "You can see the white from here."

"Sig?" The feline looked to his friend. "Eyes above?"

"Two lit windows I don't like," the wolf growled. "Closer to the apartment, though. I don't think they'll be able to see into the alley. Open, though. At night, in this weather? They'll be on us if we jump the door guards alone."

"We need to distract those two before we bomb them," Ravus

said, tugging something free from beneath his cloak. A club. "Give the Templar lad here an opening. Maybe we can kill two birds with one stone."

I eyed his club. "Let me approach them," I offered. "What's the signal for 'attack'?"

The snow leopard showed me the configuration with his hand, a two-part gesture with his fingers at his side, and I committed it to memory.

I broke away from the two of them on foot, walking the street in no rush, and made my way first across the opening of the alley, before I actively paused and then turned, and made my way towards the two men.

They looked to be a dark, ruddy-furred fox and a mutt dog of some sort with a bushy beard of fur. They might have been mistaken for a few fellows down on their luck, if you didn't know what to look for. But I remembered this tactic from shadowing. Their clothing was bulky. Not just layered rags, but rags over quilted clothing. Likely padded armor. One of them was even visibly carrying a knife with a silver handle, catching the light from the brazier.

I didn't know either of them, nor they I as far as I knew, which was good. Secular agents most certainly, given their species. Essentially just mercenaries like the two men I was working with, except on permanent hire by the Ministry.

"Fellows, it's a cold night," I said, fishing in my coin purse as I approached them. "You ought not have to suffer when Saint Rhine's is right down the way. They have bunks—"

"Aye, for a day's labor," the fox said, bristling visibly. "We didn't ask for no charity, pup. C'mon now. Get."

I put up a hand, walking closer towards them, deliberately using the opposite-side building wall from the direction my companions were in. "Then, a rooming house? It's not charity to offer aid in times as these; it's salvation. There may be a storm soon. I only want to help—"

"He said 'get', and he meant it, boy," the dog threatened, his voice calm and authoritative. "We don't need your help; we just need you gone. You aren't a local, are you? Don't know your face."

I signaled with my hands and got a little closer to them, despite their bristling. "Some food, then," I offered instead. "It's not much, but I've some biscuits."

The dog's expression became suspicious at how persistent I was being. His hand ghosted down towards his blade, but he held off, opening his mouth instead to ask me something—

—and a dark figure rose up behind the fox, striking him solidly on the back of his skull. The dog's mouth opened further to bellow something, and I knew that'd be it, he'd sound a warning and—

I brought my fist across his jaw in a southpaw hook, stunning him stupid for just long enough to leap up and wrap an arm around his shoulders, pulling him over backwards with my bicep crushed into his windpipe. Whatever he intended to shout, it came out a wheezed gasp. And then the snow leopard materialized out of the smokey haze around the brazier, aiming carefully for a moment, before bringing his own club down with a visceral thud.

Only the fox went unconscious. And not for long. The two stunned men were, however, very easy to bind and gag. A cursory search of them confirmed what I'd been all but certain of already, but it was a relief to know I hadn't been wrong. In the pocket of the fox was a distinctive key with semi-circular crescent hole in the head.

"That's an Archive key," I said, handing it up to Sig. "I doubt it opens more than the front door, which wouldn't be a hard pick anyway, but it will save you some time. They've been using it to go in and out."

"We can't launch the projectile before Isidor goes in to talk to the Inquisitor," Ravus said, setting something down on the ground. The crossbow case. He clicked it open and pulled out the weapon, engaging the bow release and started going about the process of stringing it. "The bomb's contents won't settle right off, and he'll smell them on you. Let Sig and I get the door guard and the eagle eye's attention and then head in to do your part. Keep the man busy as long as you can. And speak loudly if you can get away with it. The projectile makes a popping noise he might hear from inside."

I nodded. We'd gone over it once already, but I didn't mind the refresher.

"I don't know how long it will take us to find this hidden room," Sig said. "The place is not large. We may need to move furniture, and there will most certainly be another guard down there, so—"

"Intense conversation, whatever I can fabricate," I said, my heart lurching in my chest. I had no idea what I was going to do. I would have to adapt in the moment.

"Or you take the man out," Ravus said. "If you think you can. If he comes upon us while we are down there, we will be trapped."

"I know," I said, swallowing. "I know."

The two men guarding the little patio entryway to the nondescript Archives Office were on guard for suspicious activity, and it turned out that dousing several of the lanterns that ringed the road here, in a row, consecutively, with packed balls of snow, counted as suspicious. Also, Sig had remarkably good aim.

I left my horse with the others in the alleyway and slipped through the shadows on the opposite side of the street, watching as one of the door guards—a Templar who looked familiar, likely one of the men who'd been at the Hudson Estate —moved towards the oddity while calling something back to the other man. The remaining man similarly called up to the window and stared off in that direction while holding his position.

I had to hope the man up-top was also looking curiously out towards the disturbance. This was the best chance I'd get.

The door to Malachi's apartment was above the Archives, but the staircase and landing were off to the left, with a recessed atrium and several supports between the two in our eye-line. If I could make it to the door without being seen, I could potentially get inside covertly, as well. I couldn't knock, the sound might alert the remaining door guard below, even if he was walking a bit down the street to see what was happening. And I couldn't count on that for long, either.

I waited for my moment and stole across the street when all eyes were turned away... I hoped. If I was wrong, I was wrong. The man above was a wild card.

I made it to the same steps Cillian had nearly fallen on. I foolishly sped up them, nearly losing my footing in my hurry on the very same ice and colliding softly with the door. I managed to muffle the noise, or at least I thought I had. I steadied myself, then reached for my pocket, before realizing I already had my key in hand....

... Malachi had given me one, long ago. When I'd stayed here. I had to pray the lock had not been changed.

I'd barely gotten the key in the lock and turned it when I heard heavy footsteps. He must have heard me fall against the door. Freezing in place, I withdrew the key all but immediately, stowed it, then held my paw up as though to knock. I cast a glance down the staircase and saw no guard. They were still investigating the lanterns.

The door swung open.

The air left my muzzle in a billow of steam. Warmth flooded over me from inside the small apartment, seeking to equalize the cold on the landing and the scent of blood stung my nostrils.

Blood, and his smell... his fur... leather, and incense, ink, and paper from the Archives....

Malachi looked down at me, shocked.

"Mal—" I began.

"You shouldn't be here," he growled. Before I could do anything, he grabbed me roughly by the shoulder and yanked me inside, slamming the door behind us.

Once I was in that apartment, everything happened so fast. *So* fast.

He spun me into a wall with a force like a bull. Pinned me by *both* shoulders, and I was struck with the immediate certainty that if this became a fight, I stood no chance. The man was so unbelievably strong and certain in his movements, in all the ways I wasn't. Unhesitating. A seasoned soldier of God. The disparity between us was *vast*.

"God damn it Isidor, what are you thinking?!" he demanded right-off, already loud. That part, at least, wouldn't be hard. I would not need to encourage him to raise his voice, only match it. "The monk sent you back home for a fucking reason! You're compromised—take the out, man! I know how much you wanted to see this to its rotting end, but trust me, you do *not* need the last chapter of this one burning a hole in your mind 'til you die. It's going t'be a right mess. It is *already*."

I didn't want to consider what he meant by that. I would know soon enough.

I just had to stand my ground against the malamute. I had to surge back in retaliation with the very same intensity. I couldn't allow myself to be cowed or charmed by him. Not this time.

For some reason, what came to me in this raw moment, where I had no game plan except to keep the man talking, to do so loudly and vehemently and for as long as possible... was my training. Mere conversation, asking and answering questions, would not be enough. He was going to interrogate me—he was already, if ineloquently—and he had good reason to. I had to turn the tables. I had to interrogate *him*.

"Why do you *think* I'm here? To see you," I said, wrapping my hands around his wrists and clenching my paw-pads tight around them. "I came... to see you, Malachi."

I heard the creed again. *Use their name.*

The malamute's mouth opened, just slightly. His eyes widened, pupils shrinking in the dim light of the hallway. It was honestly incredible how quickly it had an effect on him.

"Use their name. Use it as an accusation."

"Malachi," I said again, pressing past my boundaries and leaning in closer to the man, forcing him to either meet me nearly nose to nose or lean back away from me. "Why are you so angry to see me? I thought you said I could come to you?"

"I'm not," he paused, "angry... not, no. I'm just—"

"I know you well enough by now, Malachi," I said, keeping a defiant edge to my voice, but threading with it enough of a plaintive lilt to make the man think he was scaring me. It wasn't hard. "I can tell when you're angry. I thought you'd be happy—maybe the only person I know who'd be bloody happy—to see me at their doorstep in the middle of the night. I didn't know where else to go."

I remembered Darcy's skilled, bold hands, reaching out to me to seek connection when I'd still been warring with the part of myself resistant to accepting any kind of comforts like that in my life. Malachi was still there, I knew. He'd betrayed himself enough times, reached out for contact enough times, in emotional moments that I knew he wanted it. But he was wary. I'd seen him pull back from me in the past whenever we'd gotten too close for too long. He was frightened of the very same things I had been. Any kind of intimacy with another man, even a fellow Templar, must have harkened back to—

I swallowed heavily, letting my claws unclench and stutter in their path up his arms, catching on the bunching cloth of his thin sleep shirt. It felt clumsy and inelegant, like I was stumbling in the footprints of another, a pale imitation. I was bad at this.

But maybe that made it all the more genuine. The line here between fabrication and reality was *so* thin, I was having trouble separating myself from it. Malachi's thick, sturdy arms were real beneath my palms. Warm and bracing me on either side, like he'd protect me. This man would stand at the gates of Hell for his Brothers. I did not doubt that. Myself included. I remembered embracing him in the past and the safety I'd felt, then. I really *did* wish to embrace him again. Now, if he'd let me.

He watched me, an inscrutable look in his eyes.

This comfort we both clearly wanted to have, to find in one another's arms. This was the only thing I knew of that frightened the man. And I also knew *why*, no matter how I tried to bury the knowledge under layers of denial in the back of my mind.

I knew why Dolus reviled him. Why he worried Father Helstrom. Why he'd nearly been excommunicated. Why he'd been sent to reformation camps for so long.

Why he hurt himself even now and spoke of demonic whispers and lifelong battles against sin.

"Discomfort them, force them to take a submissive posture."

I firmed up my touch and my resolve. Wrapped my arms around him, held him like he was family. And just as reliably as every other instruction had proven itself, his body slumped against mine. Uncoiled and went weak in my arms.

"I *am* happy to see you again, of course I am," the large canine insisted, his jaw quivering. His body was shaking. And not just because I was overwhelming him with all of this. I could smell the blood, it was fresh. He'd used his lash tonight. He was tired, raw, vulnerable in the wake of his self-mortification, even lightheaded. His shoulders clenched inwards, and he was using the wall for support a great deal. I had him on the back foot.

I could probably fell him if I had the nerve to strike. Like the mercenaries had the men outside. Not kill him, but disable him. He would not see it coming.

But I couldn't bring myself to hurt him. I couldn't inflict violence on a man who was scared to hold me... *because* he'd allowed his barricades to drop long enough to hold me. The thought was unbearably cruel.

"Everything has been so wrong since the Lodge," I choked out, choosing words, instead. Words. Words were where I excelled. They would be my weapon here, and they would mean the difference between harming this man or leaving him intact, as he was. Perhaps not well, but... words were better than violence. Weren't they?

"I can't just go home and return to training and life as it was, Malachi!" I said—acted, with just enough truth that I knew he'd believe me. "They asked me to do this, *made* me do this thing for God and the Ministry, and they left me with the remnants of it. Boiling in my mind at night, tormenting me with dreams!"

"Alright, alright," the malamute eased, leaning in closer, sliding an arm around my shoulders. I pressed my head near his neck, talking almost right against his cheek. It wasn't hard to bellow my words emotionally. Most of what I was feeling was real.

"Use your body to speak louder than your words can. You can damage resolve far before it becomes necessary to damage flesh."

I could use my body as well, to sell this lie. Without hurting him in the flesh.

"I don't understand anything anymore," I said, tightening my arms around his broad torso. "And I thought... I thought you'd be the one person who might... who could. You understand what this is like—"

"You did right coming to me, first," he nodded. "Bloody hell,

I knew. I mean, I think we can feel the sin in one another, Brother. I thought I knew when we met, then you told me...and then that serpent got ahold of you and sank his little fockin' teeth in, and I *know* what somethin' like that would have done to me. And then they sent you *back* to him, baited him out..."

Oh, God. That was *envy*. That's what I was hearing. So, every time he'd spoken about Darcy and I, he'd....

I gritted my teeth inside my muzzle, every interaction between Malachi and I lit as though by stark sunlight suddenly, when they'd been in shadows so long. God, how had I concealed the truth from myself this long? Malachi had known me through the most dangerous paces of this, sharing the emotional highs and lows, while worrying for me, caring for me, fighting beside me. I hadn't been honest with him with all that had happened to me, but he trusted me. As far as he knew, we were Brothers-in-Arms, caught in the same troubles, with what I now realized were very similar struggles....

He wanted to be my partner in the Ministry.

He wanted us to serve God together.

He wanted to be at my side.

He wanted....

"M'gonna take care of you, alright?" he promised against my ear. "You ain't told no one, right? I told you *never* to confess any of it to anyone else. You did as I said, right? Came to me. You came to me...."

"I didn't know who else to come to," I said, shaking my head as I felt his paws close in on either side of my cheek ruff. "Something's changed in me, and I don't... I'm frightened. I don't think I'm strong enough to suffer the way you suffered. And I don't think I can shake these sins, Malachi. I don't even think I want to, any more."

I was still being honest. He just didn't know the real reason why.

He stared at me, blue eyes as deep as a midnight sea. "Then

don't," he said in that timbre so deep, I felt it rumble against my chest.

And then he kissed me.

7

REVELATION

I had been saving my first kiss. I suppose everyone does to a certain point in their lives. But I had known—I'm not certain if it was arrogant to claim as much—but I had *known* it would matter. I had known I would never have given it up except in a moment that meant a great deal to me with a person who meant a great deal to me.

I'd never considered that it could be taken from me.

I don't know why. Perhaps because I was a man. I'd wrongly assumed I was the master of my own destiny in this arena at least. How arrogant I was.

But the fact was... this *did* matter. I'd just never have assumed this is how it would be. Not in a thousand lifetimes.

And not with him.

It was more shocking than unpleasant at first. The surprise quickly gave way to fear though, when the larger man's body boxed mine in against the wall, enveloping me and gripping my cheeks tight enough that he could tilt my head. I felt trapped, frozen, uncertain what to do. He was quick to guide me, until what had been an awkward crush of muzzles with my teeth pressed almost painfully to the inside of my mouth softened into something more pliant. With his guidance and a careful shift, a re-angling, the pressure eased. His whiskers and the bristle of his muzzle mouthed against my own, his scent filling my nostrils, and for the first time in my life, I tasted the breath of another.

Clean, like my own. We were raised to take very good care of our teeth. No mint or luxurious pleasantries. Whatever powder he chewed to clean his teeth at night was odd, though. Different to my own.

That and many other strange things went through my mind in those long seconds. Chief among the unlikely revelations was...

Unlike me, Malachi had clearly done this before. Which was odd, given he'd never married. But he knew how to make it... work. I would have been fumbling in the dark, whether I'd done this willingly or not. And while I hadn't been expecting *this*, I'd certainly laid the groundwork, so was this unwilling? Had I invited this? I didn't *want* it, but that didn't mean I hadn't essentially asked for it.

I was dizzy. It was hard to think.

When I felt the coolness of the hall air pass between our muzzles again and he leaned back, it was a relief. I cracked open one eye and found myself staring down the canine's large nose and wide, blue eyes. It was somehow less terrifying to *see* him in this moment than just feel him. The close proximity lent an innocence to his usually fierce features.

I must have given a nervous smile, or at least that's what it felt like I'd done, because the man seemed assured. Whatever remained of his hesitance melted away and he released a sigh, carding his fingers through my cheek and neck ruff. "God be praised for bringing you to me, Isidor. We were meant to find one another, you and I." His lower jaw trembled a moment, and then he surged in again, but not before murmuring heatedly, "You're so bloody handsome, mate. Brilliant, too, fuck. Ah'm naught but a broken soul, but I'll take such good care of you, if you'd let me...."

His muzzle was on mine again, knocking my head back into the wall with the force of his approach. But, once again betraying his experience, his paw was there to catch the back of my skull, his fingers splaying through my thick fur, claws curling into my scalp. He found the 'right' angle first try this time, and I couldn't breathe for the depth of it. My nose was in his whiskers, my mouth consumed by his.

One kiss, I had not been prepared for. Two was overwhelming. For many reasons.

For one, he was more assured now. I hadn't rebuffed him, after all. I'd even smiled. I think. His muzzle was more insistent, like he could meld our mouths closer together than they already were. Which would be impossible, wouldn't it?

But secondly and perhaps most distressingly, my body had begun to react as though this was something I actually wanted. I felt betrayed, almost approaching the panic and loss of control I'd felt when I'd first begun dreaming of Darcy. Did that mean...? No. I'd *never* thought of Malachi this way. Not once.

But Lord help me, if the passion released now was any indication, the malamute must have been pining for me this whole while, and I hadn't seen it. Or had I? God, how could I be uncertain about something like that? Was I lying to myself? I'd known he'd wanted to be closer and I'd used that tonight. I think as I'd approached the point of no return, I'd even realized what this was. And I'd still done it. I hadn't known it would become *this*, but I'd obviously invited these affections without realizing it.

And it was still happening. Close... too close to the front door. This building was more fortified than it looked from the outside, the entire first floor an older stone construct. If we were in the apartment, he'd have a hard time hearing anything below. But close to the front landing....

Clarity was returning. Darcy. The mercenaries. This breakout was still happening. The stakes could not *be* more real or more grave. I had surrendered myself body and soul to this sin, this deception, and I was sunk in the mire of it, now. I had to stay the course. I had no choice. Our lives were at stake. Whatever I endured here, it was nothing compared to that. I had to survive. I had to free Darcy, so that they would survive.

Something like a distant, muffled bang snapped us both from our reverie—mine guilt-stricken, his presumably ecstatic —and I caught the shape of one of his ears twisting backwards as his muzzle pulled away from mine again. He started to turn his head, distracted curiosity passing over his features, before I reached up and grabbed him by the scruff of his neck, pulling him back to face me again.

"I 'eard—" he began.

"Someone slamming a shutter," I said quickly, heatedly, forcing myself to sound impatient. "Mal…"

His eyes fixed on me where I wanted them, muzzle curling up, but a moment later his ears turned again and he seemed uneasy.

So, I kissed *him*.

I didn't know what else to do. And it seemed to be the right call, because it worked.

It's alright, my thoughts spun. *You are doing this to save a life. To save yourself. It isn't cruelty, it isn't selling your soul or your body, it is no different than fighting to defend yourself.*

He gave a contented groan and settled some of his weight against me, gently stroking his fingers where they were still seated at the back of my head down my neck to the edge of my —his—cloak. I still didn't know what I was doing save the most basic practicalities of this—pushing muzzles together. But a few moments in, he chuckled against my teeth and mouthed out a few words before fixing what I'd begun. "Don't worry, young buck… y'get the hang of it with enough practice."

I wanted to ask him how he knew that rather than kiss him any longer. How someone who'd called us 'broken' for even considering sin like this could possibly know that. I'd begun to shake and my guts were coiling, my body was confused, I wanted this or something like this, but not with him. And every moment, I was lying to my Brother. A man whose well-being I genuinely cared for, although you wouldn't know it given what I was doing now.

More than anything, I had to get him away from the door. Deeper into the apartment. He'd nearly heard something already.

"Shakin', there..." he eased back, brushing our whiskers together.

I saw a chance.

"Cold," I said, not hiding the shivering for a moment, "near the door. Been out traveling."

"Shit, I got caught up." He backed away, keeping an arm around me, and guiding me down the short hall towards his sitting room, where I could feel the heat from his stove. More importantly, this room had only one window and it faced the building nearby, not the road.

"Sorry," he apologized when we got there, picking up a few scattered possessions of his from around the room and moving them off the settee. The room was small as it was, but it was currently heaped in what must have been his travel gear, harness, weapons, including an open crossbow case and the disassembled weapon itself. (It was in the midst of being cleaned and re-tuned by the look of it. The wood expands in the cold.) "Wasn't exactly expecting guests and it's been... busy since we got back," he said, sounding off when he said that. "Rough times. This whole ordeal."

"Malachi?" I asked, both because his stilted words were troubling me and because I didn't want any silence between us.

"Can't you be done with it, already? All of this? Shouldn't you? Shouldn't *we?*"

"The case?" he sighed, moving around behind me as he spoke, his hands reaching for the clasp of my cloak to remove it. He seemed to note with some pleasure that I was still wearing it. "You, yes. Myself, not until I'm discharged. Which might be sooner rather than later, the way the monk's handling things. *Messy*," he said with a brief twitch of a snarl. "I don't understand the risks he's taking. But I don't make the calls on this one."

"Not just the case," I said, tilting my head somewhat away from him when his paws lingered on my neck and shoulders. He must have taken it differently than my body had intended, because he moved his claws to card through my neck scruff on the opposite side, petting me there while staring down at me.

I hesitate to say it, but... adoringly. I'd never seen the man look so soft. It was heartbreaking.

"What do you mean, then?" he asked. "Speak plainly, Isidor. You know you can confess *anything* to me, and I will keep it between us."

"You're an Inquisitor, Malachi," I said pointedly. "You were trained to say that. And if I do as Brother Dolus wishes, very soon I will be as well. How can I believe you? You're keeping secrets from them, you've told me to do the same, I can only assume many others do, too. How can I believe—or trust—anyone in this Order? My Brothers? What kind of Brotherhood is that?"

"Poor lad. You've come to all this later in life than I did," he said. "But then, maybe it's better that way. You haven't had the time to make... mistakes... in the most foolish years of youth. Learn from the benefit of my experience, lad. You don't want that. It's a bloody shock, isn't it? To realize your latent heresy, the sinful nature you were born with, when you'd thought yourself a righteous person until now. But we all have the awakening, eventually. You'll settle into the feeling soon enough."

He gripped my neck by the scruff suddenly, not painfully, but vice-strong. Domineering. And when he leaned in, his eyes and his voice were as intense as a preacher's, cadence zealous as a sermon. "We'll go over this again. And again. However many times it takes. We're all *broken*, Isidor. Some of us are given heavier burdens to carry than others, but carry them we must. God demands it of us. We walk through the ravages of life and all its temptations and pain, and we succumb when we can no longer stand it... but we pick ourselves up, we pray for forgiveness, we pay our penance, and we move on with the work. Because the work *must* be done. And it *is* cleansing. You'll feel it yourself in time. How agony—yours, or the suffering of another—is a purifying fire inside you. It will always hurt, but God intends us to feel that pain. That shame. To humble us before Him."

He smiled like a man in the throes of a zealous fire for the Lord, but what he was speaking on so ecstatically was not The Word. It was agony. "It doesn't mean the temptations or the pain ever end. Oh, Lord, no. They *never* end. Even those we think we've left behind us, you'll relive in your dreams. Until the day you die. But that, too, is our martyrdom. We suffer for the Lord. Carrying on, doing this day after day, no matter how weary, how wrongly we feel, is all part of our testament. Do you know why?"

"No," I breathed out, staring at him in horror. I could tell he meant every word. And that's what was so truly frightening. "Nothing in the Tome tells of any of this."

"Men like us are too blasphemous to be committed to scripture," he said. "The Tome gives no instructions on Heresy as deeply-ingrained as ours. Some men can deny these whispers, Brother Isidor..." he slowly released the scruff of my fur and gingerly stroked my cheek with the back of his knuckles. There were unshed tears in his eyes. "But not us. God knows, I've tried. I've prayed, fasted, spilled blood, and flayed myself raw, cried to God for help, and all I've ever heard is that *silence*. There is no salvation for souls like ours, not in this lifetime. Only the work. If we do the work, we are permitted to live, until such time as we can be reborn, clean."

I wanted to hold the man's heart in my hand and protect it from all this. From his own beliefs, somehow. In it were flickers of the dogma I knew and found comforting, but it was twisted so terribly into this cage of condemnation. It must have been what they'd told him, how the false teachers who'd re-molded him had justified his existence and service within the Ministry to him. How they'd justified the things about himself he felt were wrong but couldn't deny. It was so easy for me now to see it for what it was... but if I'd been taken and taught all this when I was younger? Under penalty? I don't know.

Unfortunately... I *was* holding his heart in my hand, right now. And I was no gentle steward, either.

"God loves you, Malachi," I reminded him in a shaken voice. "He is just hard to hear, sometimes."

"No," he insisted breathily. "But don't you see Brother? He *has* spoken to me through His most ardent teachers. The men who retrained me, who showed me how to live with this... this *burden*. It nearly unmade me once, Isidor. And I am *so* glad you will never need stumble as I did. In fact I... I finally see why it is I was spared. The work has never seemed near enough to make penance for all the wrong I've done. But this? To guide another Brother by the hand, and for God to lead us to one another, to share this struggle together?"

"God did not make us to suffer," I said vehemently. "What kind of learning convinced you of that, Malachi? What purpose could it possibly serve Him? He is not malicious."

"It is not cruelty," he insisted, pressing his cheek against mine. "It is not exacting a vengeance upon us for *this* life. It is a punishment we endure because of a transgression in a previous existence. A previous life. That is why we were made as we were. This life *itself* is our penance."

"Rebirth is meant to be a clean slate," I said, knitting my brow. "Ciraberos was lost because he could not separate his past from his present. We are not meant to remember, let alone beg forgiveness for our past selves. Whoever told you this wasn't just wrong, they were speaking heresy."

His thoughts visibly stuttered for only a moment before he gave a fragile smile. "I… thought so too, at first. I remember thinking as you do now. But all struggle is part of His Design, all pain must suit His purpose, and this… it is the only reason that could be logical, and there *must* be a logic to it, Isidor. It is God's will. He does not make mistakes."

"Your reasoning is self-reinforcing," I pointed out. "But that aside, there's a possibility you're not considering. Maybe living this way, not suffering for it, not paying penance for it, just living as we are, *is* God's will for us."

"Yes, exactly," he said, "the point *is* the struggle. It is like flagellation of the *spirit*—"

"No, Malachi," I said, gripping both of his hands in mine and holding them tightly, drawing his eyes to my own with the most unwavering stare I could muster. No matter what came of tonight, no matter what he thought of me after this, I wanted him to know I meant this part. That it was not a lie. "I mean, I think God wants us to be *happy* living as we are. God loves His children, and I must believe He wants us to know love, comfort, and prosperity. I must believe He wants us to remain with our families and share our lives in good health with one another… not split our flesh and suffer loneliness in His name because of some transgression we cannot remember. If we are made this way by Him, it *cannot* be entirely to suffer, every unique difference we are born with serves a purpose in His plan for us—"

"No," he boomed suddenly, vehemently. The word was spoken with such power, loudly, intimidatingly, but it lacked conviction. They taught you how to find the hairline cracks in someone's countenance, raised as we were. How to search for weak spots. In this case, it was glaring. He was speaking in the same manic timbre he had been this entire time, but the one word was upturned at the end, his tone shifting to reveal its fragile edges. He was overcompensating. He was questioning. And he was trying to shut down the conversation.

Panicking.

"You don't understand yet," he pressed out more softly, kneeling down to guide me with him to sit on the settee. "That's all, you just... you haven't had your education completed. You don't understand what comes of sin like ours if we live unrestrained and unrepentant."

I knitted my brow. "No, I don't," I agreed. "Malachi... who exactly would be hurt or harmed in any way if we loved one another as... like a husband and wife might? If we lived together or... shared our bed...?"

His hands had wound their way around me again, one up over my shoulder and the settee's back support, the other at my waist, his palm stroking circles just above my tail on my lower back. I was still wearing nearly all my clothing and armor, but the touch even through three layers made me shake.

This time, he did not lack confidence when he answered, "You would."

I blinked at him, confused. He leaned in to kiss me again, and I let him, but it was a brief affair. He lingered close afterwards, holding fast to me. "I won't hurt you Isidor, don't worry. Stay tonight and... I'll show you. I can make things good for you, for both of us. This is my second chance, and I know how now... how to find ourselves in the shadows and bleed the sin from our bodies when the morning comes without anyone being the wiser. What we do is between the two of us and God, and the Ministry won't ever need know if we're careful."

"If you're going to hide who we are to one another anyway," I reasoned, confused, "then why stay in the fold at all, Malachi?"

I glimpsed a light through a distant doorway. A path ahead, perhaps the only one imaginable, where he and I did not need to be enemies. Where Malachi was released from whatever compulsion they'd put in his head to live in this cycle of suffering where he could not deny who he was, but forever shamed and punished himself for it.

A future where he, too, broke the chain....

"Brother," he breathed out, brushing his muzzle over mine intermittently. The heat from his body was making me drowsy, the weight of him nearly atop me making my chest feel tight. I swallowed, wetting my constricting throat. "There's no life for men like us *without* the Ministry. The fold is what protects us. It's the only reason I'm still alive. And it's the only way I can keep you safe, too."

"What?" I blinked rapidly.

"I killed for the first time when I was fifteen," he said, voice eerily calm. "You really never checked my file, 'uh?"

"No," I said, shaking my head. "You're not a target, Malachi. You're my Brother."

When he spoke again, there was no denying the pity there. "Lad, you're too honest for this filthy fuckin' world. If it chewed you up like it did me, you'd never survive, so enjoy the benefit of my experience, alright? Just trust me. The only reason I'm here beside you and not rotting in the ground is because the Ministry had use for me. And even still..." his eyes glazed over, "... I was the lucky one."

"That is hard to conceive of," I admitted softly.

His gaze suddenly snapped to mine, sharpening. "I don't want that for you. You are just going to have to bloody trust me, alright? This doubt, these questions... you've *got* to just put that in a place you don't think about too much, or it'll drive you mad. They kill men like us on the outside. The Ministry will kill us too, if you aren't careful, but I know how to be careful. I know how to get right with God, so the Priests can't see the sin on you. Toughens you up like squash skin, so they never reap you up. They've left me out in the field for over a decade now, despite knowing. Because I *do the work* and I pay my penance. That is the *only* way this works. Otherwise…."

"They'll make us punish people like ourselves," I said, my thoughts cascading towards whatever fate had befallen Darcy in that basement. Even Malachi had seemed shaken by whatever had transpired recently. I was terrified for them.

Maybe that was a loose thread I could pull at.

"They're heretics, Brother," he said, voice hard. "They don't pay the price for their transgressions as we do. They revel in their debauchery."

"And that's the counterbalance?" I choked. This whole conversation was making my throat ache and seize, like I was having an attack. But, of course, I hadn't eaten in hours. "We get to live on together in sin, hiding who we are and what we do, only ever confessing to one another… because we harm ourselves? Because we are Godly enough to feel ashamed of who we are, but not Godly enough that we *can* be any different?"

He gave a weak smile. "You're beginning to understand."

"Malachi, that is mad," I insisted. "You must realize that. You cannot possibly believe this is how it's meant to be."

"If it isn't, Brother," he said, his voice empty, "I have bled and killed for nothing, all my life. Because there's nothing else for us without the Ministry. Without purpose. Nothing but pain."

"We could escape to somewhere," I said, my voice gone quieter than I wanted, hoarse and thin, "somewhere… I don't know. Somewhere in the world we wouldn't be required to *hurt* ourselves to justify our existence. They might have told you there's no other choice in that work camp—"

"I felt as you did, once," he interrupted me, stroking his claws over the shape of my shoulder blades and up over the collar of my surcoat, drifting just below the edge to trace the leather of my harness strap. "Longed... as you did... but there is a narrow band where we can survive this life, Brother, and I've seen what happens when you think you can have more." He shook his head, pressing our foreheads together, speaking between his clenched fangs. "Not you. Not this time. If I'm going to watch another of my Brothers die, it will be at his side."

He was so close to me like this with our heads pressed together, our muzzles resting alongside one another. I had my eyes open, unlike when we'd kissed, and I could see every criscrossing scar and dark pockmark in the shorter fur around his features. Some of them were from injuries he'd sustained in the field or in training, some of them unmistakably from his own lash, but all of them were the result of this life serving the Ministry. The life he was defending with all he had.

If all this pain had not been enough to convince him to leave, what chance did I really stand?

"I'm here and alive, right now," I said to him. "And I don't know what we could be beyond the Ministry. But I know what I'll be within it because I know *you*. I see you. I see what they've done to you and what misery you must endure. I know you're trying to protect me, Malachi... but I am trying to protect *you*, too."

He gave a quirk of his muzzle, his nose brushing over mine. When he spoke again, his voice was bitter, but fond. "You sound like Eli."

"Who?" I queried softly.

"The boy I loved growing up," he answered. "My Brother, one of the other boys Father Whitehall raised at Redcoven. We grew up together."

Like Nicholas, I realized. Malachi had a Brother he was close with? Perhaps even romantically, once. Maybe that was something I could—

"He died when I was fifteen," he said, and my heart fell through my ribs into the pit of my stomach. "He was sixteen. We were young. Not very good at hiding our love for one another. We tried. We failed." He gave a false smile. "He thought we could have our Faith and our love, too. He asked me to leave, too. Wouldn't shut his maw about it, in fact. Nearly ran on his own once, but I was afraid to lose him, y'see. I told our Father, and nothing came of it, except that he got real mad at me for a while. You remind me of him. Your optimism… your hope. It's no failing of your character, Isidor. It just isn't the way of things. You can live, cursed as we are, as long as you bear the scars and the shame with dignity. As long as you practice your sin in the dark, where none can see. But deny your guilt? Deny God's punishment for you, and man will find his own for you instead. And it will be worse. Much worse. That's why I wouldn't run with Eli. I'd seen them hang a molly boy in the square, once. Didn't want that to be him. I guess in the end, God's judgment found us regardless. You can't hide from God, Isidor."

I did not ask him what had happened to Eli. Fifteen was when Malachi had killed another young Brother and been sent for re-education. The litany of horrible possibilities that drummed up were too frightening in this moment to consider.

But it was hard to think the boy he'd killed was Eli. There was an agony in his eyes when he said his name, deeper than any I'd seen when I'd found him flayed and bloody. I did not doubt that he'd loved this boy.

And one other thing was certain. Achingly so.

He would not leave. Not tonight, likely not even if I had a lifetime to beg him to.

This was all meant to be a distraction, a compelling conversation, to keep the man busy while the mercenaries found their way to Darcy. But at some point, I had really begun to hope I might be finding another unexpected ally in our cause. Malachi was right—I *was* optimistic.

And I was a fool. The malamute was partnered with Brother Dolus and firmly committed to bringing this case to its bloody conclusion. He was in no way conflicted by that, either. He hated Darcy. He knew they were suffering, seemed disturbed by how Dolus was handling them, but he was complicit nonetheless. He didn't *know* the feline well, obviously, but he did not seem—like Nicholas and Mabel—interested in changing his opinions on them or the case. He had spoken with nothing but contempt for them from the beginning of our acquaintance, and he loathed Cillian, as well. He had been hostile and hateful every time they'd met.

He might have been in love with me. But he was still very much the Ministry's servitor, and our relationship, I had to remind myself, was based at this point on a series of lies and concealed truths. I had not been honest with him since the time I'd gone off on my own to the Lodge. He loved the version of me he'd built in his own mind... not who I was.

I could not offer him salvation. I had none to give save false promises based on even more lies, and what little I had to give that was real, he would not want once he knew the full truth. I was being arrogant, thinking I could undo what the Ministry had forged this man into... in one night.

They'd had him his entire life.

And while I firmly believed Malachi did not deserve the twisted, shameful, painful existence he lived through at their hands... I was no better than the Ministry. I was manipulating and hurting him right now. And soon, he'd realize that.

And then he would hate me. Rightfully so.

I could not help him. The realization was stark, rending through me like a blade. I could barely breathe.

God help me, why did it feel like I was having an attack?

This was more than just anxiousness. I was physically feeling the symptoms... the constriction of my throat, the painful itch....

"I'm not certain what you'd planned on doing, Brother," he was saying, his big, rough paws again cupping my cheeks. He would kiss me intermittently on the side of my muzzle or my nose. I was so used to it by now, every brush was dissolving into the whole confusing swirl the night had become. "But we'll settle it all in the morning. Maybe I can still convince them to send you off for training in Amurfolk. I'll go with you even, if they'll allow it. If it's the two of us, doing God's work together, maybe it's alright." His voice was thready, desperate, longing. Even he didn't believe his words, but he *wanted* to. "Maybe we're permitted to live in sin—Brothers in sin—if the good we can do as... partners? Mates? If it outweighs the wrongness."

"You want me to serve God with you," I said rasping. "At your side. Working together... living together... and this..." I put a paw up to push his muzzle just an inch away from mine, so I could look at him. "That just sounds like marriage or love to me, Malachi. Why must it be so different for us?"

"I'm sure you don't need me to explain the reason."

"But it's *not* different," I said emphatically. "That's just my point. The privacies of a home aside, which are no business of anyone's but the family's and God—"

"It's heresy," he said, his voice low as he leaned in. "If you'd chosen to become a House Templar, your entire purpose in life would have been to guard your Patrons against their own sin within the confines of their home."

"Sins like violence," I said, "adultery, abuse of servants, drinking, and drugging... even financial crimes... I believe in our purpose, still. The powerful in this country need curtailing, a reminder of their role as models for the rest of us, as leaders. But just as often, I've heard stories of the men I respect and love being ordered to cover *up* sin and vice for the families they serve."

"Sometimes that sort of thing is necessary for the stability of our country," he sighed.

"If I let you take me to bed right now," I said, trying to recover my voice, to not sound as offput by the concept as I truly was, "would you really consider what we did together to be the same as a man harming his wife? Or cheating his servants of the coin they need to survive? To feed their children?"

"It doesn't matter what I think," he said automatically.

"The Ministry permits, even covers for one of those men and not the other," I declared. "Why?"

"The Ministry covered for me," he said, quietly. "Once."

"They punished and re-educated you, that's not the same thing."

"I deserve to be punished," he said, eyes lost in some far-off place. "But," and here he looked back at me, "you don't need to be afraid, Isidor. I won't make you live as I live. I can pay the penance for both of us. Just..."

He curled his fingers around mine. "Stay with me," he pleaded. "This will all be so much more bearable together. I promise you. It's hard alone."

I swallowed, wincing at the pain in my throat. There was no denying it, any more... I was....

"Malachi," I asked, clutching at my chest, my claws tugging at the straps of my gambeson a moment, loosening them as much as I was able. "Wh-what do you clean your teeth with?"

The question seemed to catch him off-guard and deservedly so. "Ah... a ground powder I purchase from an herbalist in the city."

"Your herbalist, are they an otter?" I asked, fearing I already knew the answer.

"Bloody hell, that's *witchcraft* man, how did you—?"

"Otters make teeth-cleaning powder from ground oyster

shells and charcoal," I said, standing slowly, and reaching blindly for my cloak where he'd set it over the nearby chair. "I was given it once before, instead of the kind made from bone meal. It... took me awhile... to remember the taste...."

His eyes widened, and he shot up to his feet, following me as I stumbled into the chair. "God—fuck, I'm sorry mate. I—I didn't even think of... I saw the allergy in your file, but that was months ago—"

"I—I need to leave," I said, trying to keep my mind straight and on-task despite the clenching in my chest and the thinning of my breath. It felt... like providence. I was certain it would be unpleasant, but I'd had much more severe reactions when I ate the wrong kinds of food. Maybe because the exposure was minimal this time, I could keep my wits about me?

I had to. I *had* to.

I had never before in my life felt my affliction served any purpose, despite Father assuring me God did not make mistakes, when He made us. But here, it was a window. An escape. A means to flee this man, before this all went terribly wrong.

"I'm coming with you," he said, snapping his coat up off the nearby table, where it was crumpled alongside some of his other clothing he'd been cleaning.

"No!" I wheezed out, then coughed. "You need to stay."

"Why?" he asked desperately.

My mind raced. I danced around several lies. I couldn't tell him he needed to stay to guard the prisoner, I wasn't supposed to know Darcy was *here*. I couldn't tell him to stay put while I, suffering an allergic attack, went for help. That wouldn't make any bloody sense. How was I meant to use this?

I seized on the only thought I could find. It was imperfect. I had to hinge my hopes, once again, on his vulnerability and his love for me.

"Better if I move... less," I said, sitting back down. "You go...

down the road, left… towards Saint Rhine's. There's an apothecary at the end of the street."

The opposite direction of the stoop. If he went left out of the apartment steps, he'd likely never see whatever had gone down with the guards in the front of the Archive building below. Unless that was still ongoing, or it was an utter disaster. And if that was the case, I had larger problems.

"What do you need?" he asked, his footsteps thudding inside the room as he grabbed up his satchel and quickly closed his surcoat, belting it.

"Mullein leaf," I said, answering honestly even though it wouldn't matter. "As a tea, it helps open my lungs."

He nodded and quickly knelt at my side, reaching up hesitantly for my cheek, before withdrawing and keeping his muzzle at a good distance. "I'm so…" his jaw trembled, "I promised I wouldn't hurt you, and I've hurt you. I'm so sorry, Isidor."

I shook my head, feverishly. My voice came out sounding almost like a sob when I spoke again. "You've never hurt me, Malachi. I don't deserve your friendship."

"I'll do right by you going forward," he promised, standing. "Don't worry, Isidor. I've put in the time, walked this path already. I won't let you suffer as I have."

I leaned forward and rested my head against his torso, wrapping my arms around him. I trailed one hand up his hip, reaching for him, and he eventually took it in his own, interlacing our fingers. I could feel the fondness bleeding off him.

I sniffed and pulled away from him, trailing my paw along his belt line. "Thank you, Malachi."

"Don't thank me yet," he said. "Just hang on." He looked down at me forlornly and worriedly for a moment longer and then moved off down the hall, determinedly. I waited until I heard the door slam shut, then I got up and pursued.

I was still able to walk, still able to get air through my throat, albeit not enough. I could keep going a while longer.

I opened the door of his apartment, staring down the street at his retreating form. He kept his horse at Saint Rhine's, so he was running.

I could smell wafts of the bomb, and I'm certain he could, too. But he was too distracted to stop.

I unclenched my paw, feeling the cold iron key ring dangling free into my waiting fingers. I wasn't sure if we'd need it, but it had been on his belt....

I made my way down the precarious steps halfway before realizing they weren't as badly iced-over this time, I was just letting the haze of the last half hour in that apartment cloud my senses. I was hardly present, my mind going back, over and over again, to our furtive words, the confusing and conflicting sensations in my body, the remembrance of his whiskers, his fur, his muzzle on mine....

I had stopped feeling as though my allergy was a punishment from God when I was seven, because Father Helstrom had dispelled that notion for me. But tonight, it was so many conflicting things. My salvation, but also His retribution. A punishment meant to remind me of my guilt. The cost of doing what I'd done here, made physically manifest.

The door to the Archives Office was closed, but the scent of the bomb hung in the air, almost dissipated by now, but still strong enough to be cloying to a canine. It stung my eyes and further irritated my throat, bringing forth several wracking coughs. The last saw me stumbling and leaning on the heavy, reinforced door, before trying the handle. It was open.

More than just open. When I tried to turn it, it groaned, and nearly came away, loosely. I stared down at the scarred, frothing brass, warped and indistinguishable from what it had been, especially around the keyhole. I hardly knew what I was looking at.

I didn't have time to wonder. I shoved inside, coughing again. The door jammed against something, and I shoved again, slowly sliding something with it as I forced it open.

When I managed to shoulder my way inside, the familiar room was dark, but still obviously in serious disarray. And the crumpled obstacle at my feet was a man. More specifically by the red and white vestments he was wearing and his somewhat familiar features, a Templar. One of the men who'd been guarding the door. His eyes were blood red and fully open, glaring heatedly at me. He was bound, gagged, and looked to have taken an injury to the leg. The room smelled like his blood, but it was mostly masked beneath the more overwhelming lingering scent of the bomb.

I had pulled up my hood, but it felt pointless. It was useless to hide my identity from these men. Malachi would obviously realize I was involved, very soon. Whether he still felt fondness for me then or not, he would report on my identity. And then he would hunt me.

I wasn't prepared to consider having him for an enemy, inevitable or not. I shook my head, pressing on into the small, cluttered building. It had been a maze down here originally, but the mercenaries had made a right mess of things, shoving over furniture, and pushing aside the cabinets and strongboxes the archives were kept in. Some were even spilled open.

I passed the table Malachi and I had sat at when I'd first come here and he'd looked over my findings. I had a flash of that warmth I'd felt, finally being listened to. Understood. Valued.

That feeling disappeared when I nearly tripped over the legs protruding from under said table. They'd stowed the second man there, and he was sporting an obviously broken nose and a bloody ear. He'd been hit severely in the head and was unconscious, but they'd still bound him. The wound looked bad, but he was still breathing. With a stuttered breath, I stepped over him.

This was insanity. I could hardly believe what I'd become a part of. I was a heretic. Beyond a heretic, I was an enemy of the Faith, now. A criminal. Involved in what could be multiple murders. Of my brethren.

My thoughts were twisting, and panic was rising in my gorge, my mind was atrophying from too little air reaching my lungs, and I still couldn't find—where were they—

I saw a light.

It was dim, yellowish and dingey, as though filtered through dirty or tinted glass. I followed the slim trail of light around an immovable stack I remembered rifling through for books and found...

... the lopsided, rolled up mass of an old, circular carpet, and beside it, the small writing desk that had, to my memory, been standing upon it. This was a corner of the Archives room towards the back that I'd seen Malachi use when he needed to pen something quickly or get ink from one of the desk drawers. And beneath where the carpet and the desk had concealed it, was a wooden hatch in the floor, pulled up by its heavy iron handle ring and left ajar. The light was spilling out from somewhere down the hidden entranceway, tinted by the visible dust and mold drifting in the air from some kind of underground current.

I heard a distant noise like voices and quickly tucked myself down the hole, my feet finding purchase on a foldable ladder. As I lowered myself into that place, still struggling through my body's weakened state, a paralyzing fear crept over my limbs from my toes up.

Darcy was almost certainly down here. But I had been expecting a cell in the local prison or a room at the Ministry Office. This was even more covert, and the history of these places was a dark one. They'd been used for years before and after the last Crusade to torture and interrogate political prisoners, to perform exorcisms, and even sometimes to examine the dead. They were places our Order used exclusively to hide our goings-on from local authorities... and sometimes the Faith itself or local Priests who were not part of the Ministry.

I found myself in a short, cramped underground corridor, leading into a lantern-lit single room, where I could hear the snow leopard, at the very least, quietly talking with someone.

And I could smell Darcy.

This place was suffused, soaked, in their fear. Fear scent was unique to everyone, but in Darcy's case it was sharp, astringent. It burnt my nose worse than the lingering pepper scent upstairs had. I snuffed out, coughed, then grabbed at both sides of the narrow stone walls for purchase, pushing myself forward into the small, underground chamber. Bracing for what I'd find.

The room was almost entirely empty, save the people in it. Sig and Ravus were alive and well, save that Sig was coughing through a cloth mask, and both had tears in their eyes. They'd clearly not avoided all the effects of their own bomb. But they'd gotten the job done with little injury to themselves otherwise, as far as I could see. They were both hunkered over the only piece of furniture in the room... a chair. It sat over a grate in the floor that could charitably be called a drain, and directly underneath a stove pipe in the ceiling that must have led outside, based on the chill wind filtering down through it. A ventilation pipe and the likely source of the strange wind I'd seen blowing out the hatch earlier.

The mold was more obvious. This whole chamber was cold as a cellar, and the floors were oddly wet and slippery. Most of the water was collected in a ring around the drain, stained... black, for some reason. Not red, not brown as if with old blood, but black. And it smelled like—

The dye.

I rushed forward, Sig noticing me and going for the blade on his hip, before realizing who I was and stepping aside for me. And that's when I saw—

"Darcy!" I rasped, clinging to the back of the old, moldering chair and nearly falling beside it, before Ravus's hands caught me about the shoulders.

"Easy, there," he said, pulling off his cloth mask and looking me over, the patterned brows above his eyes looking concerned. "You injured, singuard? You don't look well."

I reached out shakily for the slumped figure sitting splay-legged in the chair. The feline was... I hardly knew what had befallen them. They were recently unbound by the look of the complex, frayed remnants of ropes cut at their feet and around the chair. They'd been stripped to the waist, left with little more than their smallclothes on, and they were soaked thoroughly through, the dye running down their body in rivulets, clotting in their fur. It wasn't quite cold enough in here for the damp to freeze, but very close, and all the worse directly under the vent.

They weren't moving, their eyes weren't open, and their breathing was worrisome. Shallow, quick pants, like they were overheated, not frozen to the bone as they should have been.

"Why haven't you covered them?!" I demanded, quickly unshouldering my cloak.

"We will, comrade," Ravus said. "We only just got them unbound. Y'see the fellow there in the corner?"

I turned, seeing the man for the first time, now. Another of the Templar I'd seen at the Hudson Estate. He looked stunned and out of his senses, writhing on the floor and clutching at his gut. He was lying in a puddle of his own vomit.

"We didn't even take time to bind him," Sig said, reaching down to tug pointedly at something around Darcy's neck. A collar, metal, and closed with a box lock. It was connected to a chain that led down to the grate in the floor. Sealed into the stonework... immovable.

"They were bound up in some of the most complicated knotwork I have ever seen when we arrived," Sig said, growling around a fang. "It took us minutes just to get them free of all of that—we had to be careful, the bindings tightened when we struggled with them, and they were already nearly garrot-tight when we got here. We were afraid undoing them hurriedly would make... whatever has been done to this cat... worse."

"Darcy?" I leaned in, gripping and patting their cheek. "Please, I need you to wake up. You need to tell us what's wrong, what's..." I looked between the two of them, desperately, "... what's been done to them?"

"Other than the dousing and the cold, I do not know," Ravus confessed. "The bindings they were left in were terrible, though. Perhaps it is an issue of blood-flow? I am no Physician."

"The bigger issue is that Tompkins box lock," Sig muttered, lifting it up with one finger, again. "We've been trying to pick it, but we can't—"

"Just use the acid," Ravus gestured to his belt.

"It's too flush, it could burn them."

"We are running short on time," the snow cat said worriedly, looking back towards the ladder. "Isidor. The man upstairs. Did you fight him, or is he still there?"

"I sent him several blocks away," I said, reaching to my belt. "He went quickly, though. We won't have much more time...."

"How did you manage that, you sly fellow?" Ravus asked, arching an eyebrow.

"Don't ask," I said, producing the key ring and sorting through the few keys on it quickly.

Both men goggled down at me when I produced the keys. Even the implacable wolf seemed impressed. "From the same man?"

"Got them off his belt before he left," I said, finding the key based on the general size and shape and quickly working it into the box lock.

"When this is all over, if you're looking for work..." Ravus led off with an impressed purse of his muzzle.

The collar opened with a metallic scrape as the lock separated, and I tugged it off the feline, throwing it aside onto the stone floor with a clatter. It had been the last thing holding Darcy upright, but I caught them as they slumped over, quickly gathering them up and bundling them in my cloak.

They were real. They were real, and warm—not as warm as they should have been—but alive and in my arms. My body was screaming for air and choking on every other breath, but they felt like they weighed nothing.

I tucked their head and their crumpled ears against my throat, swallowing back tears only halfway successfully. I could feel the echoes of pain in this place, the overwhelming terror so intense, it clung to their scent even now. I wanted to wash it all away. I wanted to go back to that moment at the Hudson Estate and agree to run away with them. I wanted to take it all upon myself, somehow. To bear it for them.

But all I could do was hold them. And this time, we would run. Cillian had not run. Malachi had not run. But *we* would run from all of this. And I promised myself, I would never regret that choice.

"The man at the window," I suddenly remembered, as I led the way back towards the ladder. "Is it safe out there?"

"Ravus shot him in the gut."

"I was aiming for the hip, I think I hit his hip," the snow leopard sighed. "He moved. I'm sorry comrade, I know he's one of yours, but little else could be done. If he dies from his injuries, know that I tried to honor your request—"

"*Benelostra de malydictum, toa solnustre vidae,*" I said quietly, pausing at the ladder.

"Come again?" Sig asked.

"It's part of a psalm," I murmured, bitterly. "'In pursuit of good purpose, blood may be spilled'. Someone go up before me, so I can lift them up to you."

"I'll go ahead and get the horses," Ravus said, swiftly climbing the ladder and dashing off out of sight.

Sig followed behind him, saying as he passed me, "Our purse has a safehouse ready for us with a Physician waiting. He said they'd need tending to after he saw them at the hearing the other day. Try to stay focused. We are not out of the woods, yet."

I nodded, and coughed into my elbow, hitching Darcy up against my chest and readying to lift them up the ladder above me to the waiting wolf.

We rode for hours, taking a circuitous path through the city through side streets and alleys, even a few yards we were able to cut through on horseback. The mercenaries had planned a route, but I ended up guiding us through most of it, using a city map I'd taken from the Archives before we'd left. We avoided every major road, carriage post, guard house and anywhere there might be suspicious eyes on us.

And of course, we avoided the Church, the Ministry, and anywhere near the courthouse Dolus was apparently at tonight.

After that, we rode through dark forests and countryside, across fields and farmland, taking deer trails and wagon roads alike, putting as much distance between ourselves and the city as possible.

I kept Darcy close to my chest, trying to warm them as well as I was able. My breathing did not get better once we were galloping through the night air, but the attack began to lessen once we were outside the city walls. What remained in the wake of it was a hollow exhaustion I could not allow myself to fully feel... not until we were somewhere safe. I tried to be mindful of my condition, lest I grow so weak I might endanger the two of us on horseback, but my body did not fail me in the end.

We made it to the safehouse, a cabin tucked away near a dilapidated mill, deep into the night. The place was lit by dim lantern light, and a small trail of smoke curled out from the chimney. A horse was tied in the stables, but I did not take the time to tie my own up. I left Blackbow to the mercenaries and swiftly carried Darcy inside.

The door opened before I'd even lifted a fist to knock, and the fellow who greeted me was a sharply-dressed black and silver fox of mature age, based on the additional silvering along his thin muzzle. He didn't bother asking me who I was, only gestured for us to come inside with a flick of his orange-gold eyes and made way for me to carry the feline in.

"Set them down in the bedroom," he said, pointing towards the doorway to the only other room in this small place. "I've my things in there."

I huffed, nodding and doing exactly as he said. He followed at my heels, glancing briefly up at me before moving towards an end table, where a bulging black leather bag sat.

I recognized him. I recognized the bag, even.

"Sir Mandrake," I said, slowly lowering myself into a nearby chair and feeling the last of my energy boiling away. Good Lord, I was dizzy. "I'm sorry, I…"

He glanced only briefly at me, but was more focused on his work, laying out a small kit on the bed as he hurried to uncover and look over Darcy.

"I looked up your file… once…." I murmured.

"Don't talk," he said. "You're not doing well, are you? Are you shot? Wounded somewhere? Oh," he looked to me, and quickly stood. "You are about to—"

The visage of the man split in three, and I slid out of the chair, as everything spun and then went dark.

8

SANCTUARY

"I'm sorry."

I had been dreaming when I heard those words. Nothing so well-formed as my dreams in the past. I'd been in a chapel, the very same I'd seen many times before. It was—as then—a shifting mirage of stained-glass visages, crumbling artifice and impossible sunlight that shone down in brilliant cascades over vine-covered tile floors and walls, beautifying what was ancient and decaying.

But this time, Darcy had not been the only one there. My family was waiting for me. My Brother and Sister, Nicholas and Mabel, stood at the foot of the altar, where roses bloomed through the crumbling stone all around it. Darcy was resplendent in the sunlight, waiting for me as they had been many times before, wearing an ethereal gown whose hues moved through the whole spectrum, as though rainbows danced across the gossamer fabric. And at their side in his simple country vestments, like he was here to give a sermon… my Father. The moons of the Faith emblazoned in crimson across his robe seemed to wax and wane with each passing moment.

I couldn't remember what had happened in the dream. Except that I'd been happy. Not merely content, but joyous. Overwhelmingly blessed.

When I opened my eyes, the face that greeted me was not one of the ones from my dream. But perhaps, he should have been. I'd been dreaming of the people who meant the most to me in the world right now. And though we'd gotten off on rocky footing (to put it mildly) Cillian may well have earned a place in that circle.

I blinked hazily up at the man, who was seated beside me in an old, padded chair. He looked like he'd been slumped, perhaps even sleeping. He was obviously tired, damp, dirty, and dressed-down for once, wearing only a plain cotton shirt. His fur was askew and poorly-groomed. Like he'd had it under a hat or cloak, possibly both.

But he looked peaceful. I had rarely, if ever, seen the man look truly happy. The expression he wore now was at least comfortable, contented, and genuine.

"Cillian Rathborne," I grumbled in a disused voice. Why did my throat hurt so badly? "Why are you… where…."

"Turn to your right," he said with a soft smile.

I did so, slowly and with every muscle in my body protesting at the movement. I expected my siblings. Or a window view of where we were.

Instead, the sight that greeted me was perhaps the most relieving, blissful visage I could have possibly imagined, given recent events. Darcy's cunning, fierce features, innocent in sleep. The feline was still stained partially in their dye and their nose and muzzle were chapped with cracked skin and traces of abrasions, but they were there, beside me. Breathing steadily, their slim shoulders hunched in, an arm protruding from beneath the blankets, fingers clutching at the only pillow on the bed, which we'd apparently been sharing.

"You're bloody heavy, by the way," Cillian huffed, stretching out a mud-covered leg, wincing.

"I know," I said, perhaps betraying some hint of the inherent shame my lack of discipline with food naturally brought out in me, because the Pedigree arched an eyebrow for a moment, taking note of my reaction. "It's hard for me, I have to eat a limited diet—"

"Oh, can we not with the self-loathing?" he snuffed. "I wasn't calling you *portly*, just big. Anyway, what do you have to complain about? You're built like a bloody Royal Guardsman. Got boulders in your arms, I'm fair sure. I'd trade my bad leg for a few extra pounds any day. I only mention it because when I got here, Mister Mandrake was still tending to you on the floor. He couldn't get you up here on his own, and the hired help had since shoved off to give any pursuers the runaround and keep eyes on the roads—"

"Darcy should… have their own bed…" I mumbled. "Why am I even…?"

Cillian laughed, of all things. "This cabin only *has* one bed, choir boy. Give up the prudishness, already. It's one of your least attractive qualities."

I sat up slowly. Memories flooded back to me, at last. This place. The break-out.

Malachi….

My mind came to a stunned halt at that, and it must have shown on my features, because Cillian leaned and tilted his muzzle to stare at my hung head, then snapped his fingers at me sharply.

"Enough of whatever *that* was, too," he said. "Now's not the time to get mired in your—I'm guessing guilty, judging by that look—thoughts. Make your peace with your inner demons or God another time. Right now is a time for rest. And I need to know you're with us in fighting form."

"I'm with you," I said, nodding insistently, if stiffly. "I'm just… during the break-out, I-I had to…."

"Whatever you did out there, it was to free *them*," he reminded me, nodding in the direction of the slumbering feline.

I turned again to look at Darcy, and this time I didn't look away. They were curled up at my side, mostly a lump beneath the blankets, but even based on the little I saw, I had to swallow back my anger. It distracted me from my regretful thoughts on Malachi, but the feelings that replaced it were no better.

There were raw patches around their wrists and something similar up their arms, criss-crossed in patterns that made little sense. The marks were rope burns. I knew their like. Restraint injuries from being tied and bound in stress positions.

I'd only ever learned basic knots and restraint binding, but Dolus had promised me I'd learn far more once I was formally trained. He seemed particularly keen on the subject and was infamously skilled with rope use and knots, himself. To the point that the kids had long wondered if he'd ever been a sailor.

He had never been a sailor, as far as I knew. It was just… a hobby.

The feline's neck was raw pink and patchy beneath their fur, especially around the collarbone where the collar had been digging into them when I'd unlocked it. Restraint positions that involved the neck were forbidden for the sake of practicality as well as decency. It made it hard for a prisoner to talk, for one, but it was also notoriously responsible for accidental deaths.

For what would certainly not be the last time, I wondered at Brother Dolus and his ways. What motives could compel him to act as he did.

Cillian and I both looked Darcy over in silence for a time. Just listening to their soft, steady breaths. I wanted nothing more than to touch them, even just on the hand, to confirm to myself that they were real. But the feline was sleeping, so that wouldn't be right.

"I said this already, but doing so when I thought you were unconscious was cowardly, so I'll say it again," Cillian took a breath. "Thank you... for what you did. I am not unappreciative of everything you just gave up, believe me. Nor how hard or how terrifying it must have been for you."

I looked slowly back towards him. He met my eyes and continued on quietly, but earnestly. "I was wrong about you. I let my personal issues with the Church color how I saw you, and, honestly, that's as short-sighted as the people who assume what kind of man I might be based on my breeding or my relations. You are... more than your Faith. Far more."

"All it took to impress you was doing something that could and *will* get me excommunicated, at best," I said with some bitterness.

"I'm a hard man to impress," he said ruefully. "It's not because I expect better of people; just the opposite. The world disappoints me so often, I've come to expect it. I wrote you off before I came to know you as Darcy clearly did. I wasn't willing to see what they saw in you. At least not until it was clear you weren't abandoning us."

"And you'd given up on the idea of killing me," I muttered, letting my head thud back down on the pillow. I coughed, clearing my aching throat.

"That, too," he said, not masking the guilt in his expression. "I mean it when I say this, Isidor—and I am not Darcy, I am not prone to emotional declarations, so you know. I have no appetite for dramatics the way they do. But...."

He looked down into his lap a moment, then said, "If I had killed you that night, it would have snuffed what little light is left in me and frightened Dar away from me forever. You said exactly what was necessary then to stop me from making a terrible mistake, and I'm grateful for that. Knowing Darcy is alive and well in the world is genuinely more important to me than my own happiness, and my hired men made it quite clear to me that this breakout would have been unsuccessful without your help."

"I hadn't any idea where to begin looking," I confessed. "We were all but sitting on our hands when we arrived. It was your men who shadowed Dolus to the Archives. Your men who handled most of the guards. I was hardly much help."

"They would never have known about the bloody torture cellar if you hadn't told them," he said while shaking his head. His hands were clutched together tightly, fingers wrapped around his knuckles. I understood the feeling. "We needed a turncoat to save Dar. They said you kept the big fellow busy, too. Sent him away, even. And the key. They told me everything. So, none of this humble shite. You won't impress anyone with it here."

"You set all of this in motion," I said. "Kept your head about you enough at the Hudson Estate to give me the information I needed, too. And you've been keeping Dolus busy, the way I hear it."

"Oh, that?" he snorted. "I attended a public forum, and I may have begun the inquiry that necessitated it. One of Darcy's 'crimes' occurred on my extended family's property, after all. But that is literally it. Look, let's just agree to disagree and give credit where credit is truly due."

"God?" I said at the same time as he said—

"The money."

We paused, and then he began to laugh first. A low chuckle that I soon joined, although after a few moments, I found it gave way to coughing, again.

"Good Lord, man," he pushed himself up from his slump to a more alert sitting position, reaching out hesitantly to settle a hand on my back. "Are you ill again? The Physician seemed to think you were just suffering from exhaustion. He couldn't find any injuries—"

"Not injured or ill, no," I insisted, steadying my breath into my palm. "I... it is just a weakness I was born with. An intolerance. An allergy."

"Oh, say no more," he sighed. "Hay fever sees me wheezing half the year, and it often makes way for an illness taking hold in my nose or lungs."

"It's not..." I let the words bleed off. If I explained it, I'd have to explain *why* I had an attack, and I wasn't prepared to do that right now. "It doesn't matter," I relented, looking back towards Darcy. "All that matters right now is them."

"The Physician is not entirely certain what was *done* to Darcy," Cillian said, anger evident in every word. "They have no serious external injuries, nor broken bones. Not even a fracture he could find. Nearly frostbite in their extremities, but he seems certain they'll not lose anything. Whatever your brethren did to them in that place, it was—"

"Careful," I said in a ghost of a whisper. "He wanted Darcy intact, otherwise they couldn't stand trial."

"Then why interrogate them *now*, at all?" he asked the same question I'd been asking myself. "He needed them to stand trial here, first. The monk brought them to the public hearing just the other night, and even cleaned up, even from across the chamber, I could see how poorly Darcy was. Hell, they needed to transport them across the bloody country after this to stand trial in Amurfolk. Why risk their health?"

I stared down into my lap, my mind inexorably going over the possible answers to his question.

"I am asking you as a Templar," he pressed. "Help me understand. I don't know much about this case Dar's become embroiled in. What do they want? Dar insists they never took this artifact, and I can't imagine why they'd lie to me about that. They're usually proud of their capers."

"I don't know for certain," I said softly. "Their motives might have been for swift information retrieval above the importance of a show trial. But that would infer that whoever is directing

Dolus believes Darcy truly knows the location of the Heart of Faith."

"And?" he pressed, confused. "That seems likely. That's what this whole bloody thing is about, is it not? They think Dar took their holy relic."

I was silent.

He leaned in, his eyes slowly widening. "Don't they?"

"I did," I said, barely above a whisper. "Most… everyone in the Ministry likely still thinks that. Possibly even Dolus."

"I don't like your tone," he said with a hiss of breath. "That haunted look… you think they're framing Dar." He gave me a beat to confirm, but I didn't need to. And that had him spitting out, a moment later, "Why in the hell?! They've stolen plenty of rubbish legitimately!"

"That *is* why," I said, snapping my eyes back to him. "Darcy's crusade to reclaim antiquities and treasures made them the perfect scapegoat, don't you see?"

"I know it's frustrating to watch someone so marvelous waste their talents on what seems like petty thievery," he sighed, "but Dar's purpose is… noble, in a way. The only reason I rail against it so is because of how dangerous it is for them. *Intentionally* so. I wouldn't even care if they were just more careful, but the letters and the high society targets…" he shook his head. "It is like watching someone walk into the sea in slow motion."

"Darcy and I spoke on their purpose behind the crimes," I said. "I know. I am of two minds on the matter, but that's hardly important now."

"You couldn't fully understand unless you know them as I do," he said. "This isn't just about reclaiming antiquities. It is about reclaiming *themselves*. When they wake, talk to them about it. Please."

I nodded. He was honoring my insistence from weeks ago that he not share the feline's history. I couldn't imagine anything more personal... and I still wanted to hear it from them when they were ready. So, it stood.

"If your Ministry is setting them up, then why interrogate Darcy for information they know they do not have?" Cillian pressed helplessly.

I bit the inside of my mouth. "You are assuming cohesion within my Order that you ought not to. As I said... I didn't know. The Ministry and all my direct superiors still allowed me to pursue the investigation, and when I got close, they assigned me senior Inquisitors to ensure the capture was handled by those they preferred. But even still, I cannot say for certain that Malachi or even Brother Dolus are part of this conspiracy, if it is in fact a conspiracy. Their superiors may not know. The only reason *we* suspect the truth is because we believe Darcy and because of information my Father has found out from some of his contacts. If this was a conspiracy, it was formed far from here, by Templar we also do not know, for reasons we do not know for certain. It may not be as well-organized and meticulous as you're imagining. There may be broken links in the chain, confusion within our own ranks, wasted efforts and mistaken action being taken, even now. Interrogating Darcy might seem counterintuitive, but that doesn't mean there is some ulterior motive. It... may just be an ill-informed decision based on bad information, or because my own Order is lying to or falsely informing itself within our own ranks."

To say he looked horrified would have been an understatement. "You're saying," he stammered, "they may have done this—all of this—to my Darcy, out of... incompetence? For no reason?"

I hesitated before nodding slowly. "Cruelty does not need to be the product of maliciousness. It can result just as often from negligence."

"Or maybe you believe that because it comforts you," he reasoned, pinching his brow. "Believing all of this is some bureaucratic mistake, rather than your archaic, dark-ages Order acting with evil in their hearts."

"Perhaps," I agreed sadly. "I... do not know. The only other thought I have is monstrous, and it cannot be the sole factor."

"Enlighten me," he said darkly.

My mouth felt dry. I stared at the wall, counting the cracks in the aging plaster. When I found ten, I had the strength to speak again.

"Brother Dolus, the lead Inquisitor tasked with this investigation—"

"The older one. The lurcher who dresses like a monk."

I nodded. "The one who orchestrated Darcy's capture. He had no interest in this case before he... he was brought into it, I'm fair certain, entirely because of my involvement. He is kin to me. He was one of the two holy men who raised me."

"Alright," he said uncertainly. "And?"

"He likes to hurt people," I said, the words feeling true to my soul, to my experience, but saying them aloud to another still somehow made me twinge inwardly. Like I was breaking some covenant, hanging our filthy sheets out for all to see.

"It may not have been an interrogation," I found myself continuing. "He might have been breaking them for the eventual trial, but I don't think that would take the monk months to do. The point may simply have been to cause pain."

He was looking at me with his mouth open, the edges of his fang tips visible. "I don't understand it any better than you do..." I said hoarsely.

"You're saying this monk hurt Dar because it... pleased him to do so," he said, his tone curdling with revulsion. "Like a... like a *hobby*."

"It doesn't make any more sense to me than it does to you," I murmured, "but it's the only reasoning I can come to for how he has acted through the years."

"When I told you there at the Hudson Estate," he said

bitterly, "when I inferred that you must wait, not act rashly, I had *thought* that we had more time. I would never have hinged our hopes on Redcoven if I'd realized what they'd do to Dar here. While awaiting the most paltry of their charges," he snarled, "I thought, 'they wouldn't dare.' They wouldn't torture or interrogate them until they were ready for the main trial. I never thought they'd risk such savagery so *soon*."

"Darcy is alive and intact," I said, trying to keep my voice neutral. "Whatever was done to them was done with great care to keep them so, until such time as the real... work... could begin. This was the forward. The savagery would have come later."

"Speaking from experience?" he asked. *Also* keeping his tone forcibly neutral.

"No," I said emphatically. "Just training. And because I know that man personally. Dolus hurts people. It's what he does. But he's also a consummate professional. I have no doubt he knows just how far he can push someone before he is risking their life."

The Setter sucked in a breath. I was turned away from him, so I couldn't see his face. But I could imagine it. His tone was concerned and demanding.

"Settle my spirits, please," he begged. "Tell me you are done with any aspirations of continuing to serve this Order. I'm not asking you to give up your faith, but—"

"Yes," I said simply. Resolutely. The word hung in the air between us, but I felt no need to follow up with any more.

It was enough on its own.

"This man," he said at length, "he was one of your Fathers?"

"No," I insisted between my teeth. "He was just there. I'm sure he would consider himself a part of my upbringing, but I can hardly remember a time in my life when I wasn't afraid of him."

"Did he hurt you, too?" he asked.

I didn't answer. Only held up my hand and the missing digit.

"Good God," he breathed out. "I know you must have had *so* few other options, but if your life and limb were literally at stake, why not leave?"

"It's hard to explain," I said, my voice meandering, my thoughts following. "There was love at Ebon Gables, too. Family. A future I genuinely believed in."

"You have nothing anymore," he said, realization dawning. "You gave up everything for this. You have nothing—no one— outside the Ministry. Do you?"

"I have the Brother and Sister who ran with me," I said. "A Father who gave us his blessing to leave, the clothes on my back... and that is more than I thought I would have. More than others in my position have been offered. And I have all of you. And God's love, I pray. It is everything I will ever need."

He was shaking his head. "You know," he murmured, "I do understand why you stayed, believe me or nay. Why you pledged yourself to this brotherhood despite it all."

"With all due respect," I closed my eyes. "You couldn't possibly."

"I nearly walked away from my life once, too."

I turned towards him. He gave me a troubled quirk of his muzzle, but it never became a true smile. "I didn't, in the end," he sighed. "As you know."

"I didn't run away with Darcy at my first opportunity, either," I said.

"You've known them a season," he said. "I knew Dar most of my life. I made promises to them... in my youth, but still. I should have honored the person in my life who loved me. The person who gave themselves freely to me, in body and soul. My allegiance should not have been to those I was unfortunate enough to share blood with."

"It's hard to leave everything you know behind," I eased. "I cannot understand the pressure you must have felt any more than you can understand where I came from."

"But in your case, some of the people you consider beloved kin are still part of this leviathan," he said, troubled.

"Inextricably." I thought of my Father.

"The brother and sister you mentioned," he said. "They're also 'out'? They aren't with you."

"Yes," I said gratefully. "They await me."

"Then I'd say take what you can," he said, blinking slowly, exhaustedly. "While you can."

"I've been given a grace," I agreed. "I know. God is truly standing at my shoulder, right now. I hope I can preserve and protect the family He has given me."

The chair creaked, and he stood stiffly beside me, propped up by his cane. He reached for the handle and twisted, withdrawing a shimmer of silver steel from within it, before sliding it back inside its hidden confines. A cane sword.

"You and I both," he assured me.

"Will you come with us too, then?" I asked, before I really thought about it.

He gave me a tired, but genuinely amused smile. "Are you asking if I plan to abandon my wife and children and flee the country with the person... *you* love, Templar? Such a devil on my shoulder you've become."

"No, I'm not—" I blinked rapidly, stammering. "Lord, I don't know. You obviously mustn't do that, but... but...."

He chuckled. "Calm down. I can't imagine the conflicts this is drumming up in you, and it was cruel of me to egg that indecision on. Rest-assured at least, I have no intentions to leave behind my wife and pups, however ill-suited our match was. She is a decent woman, and my children are innocents in all of this. They deserve to know their father as... I never did my own."

"Your mother was a widow?" I asked. I hadn't seen that in the file.

"No, my parents were merely... distant," he said after a long pause. "Their marriage was fraught and their repetitive failures at producing an heir very painful, especially for my mother. I think by the time I had been the lone child to survive my infancy, they were too scarred to allow themselves that attachment. They were rarely in residence at Rathborne manner; I was raised almost entirely by servants."

"That sounds lonely."

He inclined his head towards Darcy. "It was. Until it wasn't."

This puzzle was nearly complete. The image it was forming was disturbing, but whether I wanted them or not, I would soon have answers.

"In any case," he said, "I will not abandon another family. I've made that mistake one too many times in this life as it is. I will help you all I can, however. As I have been. With connections and resources. What the hell else is it all for?"

"I'm hoping to hear from my Father soon as well—"

"Holy Hell," Cillian breathed out suddenly, cutting me off. For a moment I thought he was staring intently at me, especially when he came to lean over the edge of the bed, but then I followed the line of his eyes.

When I turned over on my side, Darcy was moving beneath the blankets, their face pinched in pain or discomfort, it was hard to say. But they were certainly rousing or moving in their sleep. A breathless mumble whispered into the pillow....

"What did they—" Cillian began.

My heart sung a chorus I thought it had forgotten. The second time they spoke, I heard my name, clear as day.

Cillian must have as well, judging by the fleeting look of loss that crossed his features before he quickly replaced it with a forced smile in my direction. "Maybe I should leave you two?" he offered. "I have a rented room in town, and I really *should* start making preparations."

"You look exhausted." I reached out a tentative hand to resituate the blankets so that they would cover the feline more modestly. They were still wearing little other than smallclothes, judging by their bare shoulders.

"I can sleep later," he said. "And anyway, this chair is murder on my back. There isn't a place for me here."

It wasn't lost on me, the dual nature of his words. I felt a stab of pity, or maybe sympathetic pain, for the man.

"...Isidor..." the feline's murmur was louder, more intelligible, this time. Both of us leaned down to watch as the dimmest wet crescents of their eyes opened. Their beautiful color was lost in bloodshot crimson and crusted tears.

I looked up to Cillian at the very moment that he clearly had the same idea, nodding and shoving himself up to a standing position with his cane. "It's fine, I've got it," he said, hobbling over to the wash basin.

I reached down and—with the briefest of hesitations— gingerly cupped the ragged fringe of Darcy's furred cheek. I made sure to avoid the rawness around their neck with my claws. The bindings hadn't broken skin, but they must have stung.

"I'm here," I breathed out as quietly as I could, sensitive to their ears.

The feline's eyes opened enough and slowly came into focus in the dim room, and it finally felt like they were truly seeing me. They sucked in a rough breath, then let it out in a labored cough that bled off into an exhausted sob. "M'such a... dull-witted thing..." they wheezed, as fresh tears boiled in the corners of their eyes. "I didn'know... it would... be like th... m'not strong like I-I thought... I was...."

"Yes, you are," I assured them, swallowing painfully. "You don't need to—"

"I'm so sorry," they cried, dragging an insufficient breath through their nose. "What... must you have had to... to do—"

"You don't need to strain yourself speaking right now, least of all to apologize," Cillian said from the right of us. His voice briefly startled Darcy, and I found claws suddenly gripping into my bicep. I let them hold fast to me for the few moments it took them to come down. I could hear their heart beat, feel the minute shivers of their body.

I wanted to hold them. But I let them hold me, instead. As much or as little as they wanted.

When the fear and no small amount of delirium subsided in their frantic gaze, their eyes widened further, and they leaned up to greet Cillian's wash cloth. He brought the bunched corner to their lashes, carefully dabbing. Darcy eventually just closed their eyes, surrendering to the treatment, swaying a little where they were sat.

Cillian nodded to me after a while, offering the cloth out to me. "Basin's on the counter there. I'll leave you be," he said quietly. He began to stand again, but startling us both, Darcy's hand shot out and gripped his shirt tail.

"No, no," they said insistently. "Why are you going?"

"I'll just be in the other room—" he said.

"Please don't leave," they said, their words almost slurring with their evident exhaustion. "Please… a'least… stay until I can sleep again."

Cillian looked between the two of us for a moment, helplessly. Then, with a defeated slump of his shoulders, he began to settle back down in the chair.

Darcy tugged on him again, setting him off-balance enough that he had to put out both hands on the edge of the bed to steady himself. "Dar…" he warned, frustrated.

"Stay," they said, as their eyes slid closed.

"I can't—there isn't room—" he said long-sufferingly.

I was already getting up. He began to say something, likely to stop me, but I shook my head. "It's fine," I said as I clambered over the feline less than gracefully to the other side of the bed. I slid to the edge on my side, then tugged Darcy in my direction. They went along with a contented mumble, indicating presumably that they approved of what I was doing.

Cillian stared down at his palms and the space we'd left him. Then looked back to me questioningly. Disbelievingly.

"We'll make it work," I said with a lopsided smile.

"I'm not the man to balk at climbing into bed with another fellow," he said pointedly. "Are you certain?"

"I think we're well past decency and propriety," I answered, stifling a yawn. "Just stay a while so they can sleep. If… that suits you?"

"Suits me fine," he said softly, finally yielding and leaning down into bed, sliding in beside the serval on their other side. There was truly not enough room for us all, but that just meant Darcy moved closer to me, their breath puffing on my neck, and I suddenly couldn't imagine doing anything other than letting sleep take hold of me. I was so tired.

I vaguely remembered Cillian curling an arm around Darcy before I lost my fight with the waking world. Crammed in as we were, we all had no choice but to hold one another.

"Thank you, again," Cillian's voice drifted through the last of my conscious moments. "Please take care of them better than I did."

When I woke, Cillian was gone. In his stead was the Physician, rummaging through his bag near the table at the corner of the room. Darcy continued to slumber on the bed beside me, unaware.

I gently eased their arm off my chest and pushed myself up to sit. The bed creaked and the fox's ears twitched in my direction, but he didn't turn around.

"The Young Lord returned to Redcoven, lest he be missed," the fox explained before I could ask. "He needed to show up at the next public forum as if nothing had happened, or it would look suspicious."

"I thought this might have been an unspoken agreement for you," I said. "Services rendered, without questions asked... that sort of thing. But you know the whole of it, don't you?"

"If it's all the same, I'd rather not confirm how much I know," the black and silver fox said, turning with a mortar and pestle in hand, grinding something pungent-smelling. Now that I was getting a better look at him, it was clear he was more aged than I'd originally thought. Most men of his years would have retired. Then again, it was possible he had.

"I understand," I said.

"Aloe," he explained, "for their abrasions. Reapply it for as long as it lasts."

"As you say," I replied, scrunching my nose at the unfamiliar smell and name. Something foreign?

"You already know I've worked for the Rathborne family for some time, I'd wager," the fox said, arching a silver eyebrow and continuing to grind his medicine patiently. "Suffice it to say, I have a deep and abiding regard for these children. Not the family per se, but then I suppose young Cillian is the bitter end of what once was, so... that's that."

His expression seemed naturally severe, but it softened when he looked down at Darcy's crumpled form. "That poor feline, I have known from the very day they set foot on our shores. The society that trades in people as commodities is a brutal and uncivilized one."

"You mean Mataa?" I guessed. Slavery was still rampant across the border.

He scoffed. "No, lad. They call them 'service contracts' here. 'Indentured servants' elsewhere. It hardly matters. It is all the same, in the end. Even the workhouse poor, the day laborer, is a slave to their wages and their landlord. But to enter into service as an adult is one thing. As a child..."

"Darcy has never told me how they came to be in service to the Rathbornes," I said softly, not wanting to wake them, "but I've long known that must have been the arrangement that led to all of this."

The fox only nodded, walking towards the bed. As he did, he picked something else up from the table and eventually held it out, offering it to me.

"My tome?" I took the book, running my thumb down the spine.

"We removed your harness and belt," he explained, "and set them aside with your cloak and other possessions. I think your tome was in your shoulder bag, and everything got rather wet when the snow and ice began to melt. I left it on the table near the hearth to dry."

"Thank you," I said, touched. "It's leather-bound, and it's certainly seen worse, but I appreciate the thought."

He smiled, his muzzle crinkling the fur along his cheeks. "I am also a man of learning, albeit a different... path. I know if my own favorite books were damaged thusly, I'd be inconsolable."

I felt warm suddenly in the man's presence. Something was familiar about him.

"You spent a good deal of time with Darcy and Cillian when they were growing up, didn't you?" I asked.

"The Young Lord suffered a great many afflictions in his youth, as I assume you already know," he said unhappily. "I suppose I can speak on my own work with the family, since your Ministry recorded the whole of it already. I work as an on-call Physician for many Pedigree families, as well as common folk. I was nearly always on-call and stayed many weeks at a stretch at the Rathborne manor. I saw them more often than my own children, sometimes. After years of diligence at their bedside, it was impossible that I not form an attachment. I read to them, even when Darcy's grasp of

Amurescan was minimal. I worried for them when I wasn't there. And then, fortuitously, the parents decided the mountain air might benefit the Young Lord, and they began taking their summers in Redcoven. And no longer did I need choose between the children in my charge and my own children."

"The Lodge," I said in understanding.

"A rented home on Main Street, at first," he said. "The Lodge was my own idea, when the parents stopped accompanying the children during their stays out here. It was safer than the city, more secluded, and I could spend the summers there with my youngest in tow, as well."

"You said 'fortuitously'," I repeated his odd word choice from earlier. "It *does* sound convenient."

"I may have recommended it." He winked. "The manor was an empty tomb, save its servants. Young Master Rathborne's health improved greatly in a smaller, more comfortable home in the country. Cleaner air, no staircases."

"I'm so glad they had you," I said earnestly. I hardly knew this man, but it was clear how safe Cillian must have felt with him, to entrust him with Darcy. "I think you may have inspired a lifelong obsession with reading, at least in Darcy's case."

"Good!" he said with a laugh. "But I can't take all the credit for that. Books are an escape… and those children *both* needed an escape from the unfortunate circumstances of their lives." His muzzle twitched, then fell again, as he looked once more at Darcy. "It pains me to see that fact has not improved with time."

I didn't know what to say to that, but he didn't seem to require me to say a thing. He moved back towards the table and began laying out whatever he'd been working on.

"I'm confident that whatever roughing-up the patient has endured," he said, "it is non-fatal and has done no serious long-term damage that I can find. No broken bones, swelling or bleeding beneath the skin, no infection or signs of laceration or tearing. I worried at first there might have been internal ruptures, but there is no evidence of depraved assault, either."

I felt my breath stop at the mere implication. I wanted to snap at him. I wanted to yell. The urge to defend my kin, my Order, rose inside me like a reflexive instinct.

But I didn't. And I quaked at the thought of what that meant. Did I think his concerns had merit?

Yes, I realized after barely a moment spent thinking about it. Yes. I did.

"They will need a warm, but not overly-hot bath, to cleanse the filth and dye from their fur," he said, turning to look back at me. "They *do* have abrasions, and an infection now when their body is weak could take hold like a forest fire. They should be capable of managing it themselves when they wake, but only keep close and be certain they do not fall."

"Yes, sir," I nodded.

He gestured towards the door. "There is a well out back and a kettle on the hearth. I'm certain a big fellow like you can handle filling a bath, yes?"

"Yes, sir," I said again.

"I'll check in again with both of you once more before you depart," he assured me as he closed his bag. "You should rest as well, lad. I know little of your own circumstances, and it is better that I not," he held up a hand, "but you appear to be suffering from exhaustion and a lingering lung affliction. Remember that you cannot take care of another if you do not first take care of yourself."

"I understand," I assured him. "And you should take care when you travel. I'm certain you're trying not to be followed, but… in truth, I followed you once before. My kinsman know of you, and they'll try to do the same."

"I was warned," he said uncomfortably. "I have an escort through the local deer trails this time. I trust they will know if we're being tailed."

One of the mercenaries, I assumed. Good. I felt more assured knowing that.

He left us after that, and I watched Darcy while they slept for a while. I hardly knew what else to do with myself. The moments seemed precious and precarious. Each second like sand slipping between my fingers. The persistent knowledge that one wrong move from any of us could mean they'd be taken away again. That my life, and my siblings' lives, and possibly my Father's, would become a living Hell of interrogation and separation. We had to be so bloody careful, now.

And as soon as Darcy was able, we had to run.

"Mhh-hhwas that... Mandrake?" a voice half-muffled by blankets asked from beside me.

I smiled down at them. "Yes," I confirmed. "How... how are you faring? I'm sorry. We were trying to be quiet."

Darcy sat up slowly, but with more dawning clarity in their eyes than last time. Their expression was hard to place, though, and instantly worrying. Their eyes were unfixed, looking nowhere, their motions stiff and pained. They were still not wearing a blouse, or anything over their upper body, and they either hadn't noticed or didn't care. The blankets were bunched and slumping over their torso, covering by a thread.

I could have reached down and tugged them up for decency's sake, but that would mean touching them, and I wasn't sure what was worse. So, I just turned my head aside.

"Why won't you look at me?" Darcy asked, after a few moments of silence passed between us.

I spun to look their way as if I'd been slapped. Caught and disciplined. I felt a stab of guilt, realizing I'd made the wrong choice. Darcy was looking directly at me, but their eyes were so utterly hollow and sad. Imploring me for something... I knew not what. I would have given them the world, but I wasn't certain what they needed from me right now.

"I'm sorry," I said because it was all I could think to say.

They craned their neck and stared down at their lap, hands gathering the blankets around their legs. "I should bathe, like he said," they mumbled. "There's dye all over the bed."

"The Physician told me it's not good to leave it on you. It's been bleeding out of your fur," I agreed.

"He used… water," Darcy whispered raggedly.

I knew they were talking about Dolus. I didn't have to ask.

"I couldn't breathe," they added almost silently.

Suddenly, I couldn't either. I got out of bed, grabbing for the kettle. "I'll get that started," I said.

I went about the process of getting the bath filled and the kettle boiling almost mechanically, glad for the distraction and some means to make myself useful, but simultaneously ashamed of how cowardly I was being. I was here—the only one here with Darcy—in their moment of suffering and shock, and they clearly needed me to give them…

Comfort. Aid. Something beyond a bath and a silent, helpless man to share a room with.

This did not seem the time to profess my love or vow myself to them in some grand romantic gesture, like in all those books Darcy seemed so fond of. But I also knew they needed more than I was giving, and that knowledge ate at me the entire time I made my trips in and out of the small cabin. I barely noticed the cut of the cold air in my throat or the strain of the bucket. My thoughts were all Darcy and how I could possibly make any of this right.

And the guilt. Oh, God, the guilt. I could have prevented this. If I'd only left with them then, before….

"Isidor," they called to me from the bed, while I emptied the last bucket I'd carried in. "I think that's enough."

I made the mistake of looking at them when they called to me. They were sitting on the edge of the bed in nothing but their smallclothes. They looked diminutive in a way I'd never seen in them before. Darcy was a small person, but I'd never have said they *looked* small until right now. They were also having trouble meeting my eyes. Staring mostly at the ground as they slid free of the blankets and stood rigidly. I didn't miss the wince when they put pressure on one of their legs.

I wanted to help them, but everything in me screamed to look away, to leave the room, to let them be. I wasn't supposed to *be* here. Even if we were intended, which we *very much weren't*, I shouldn't be seeing them in this state—

"You found me the way they left me, I take it," they said, their tone shaken, but becoming more resolute with each word. Like they were settling something for themselves.

Whatever I did next, it would matter. For better or for worse.

"Yes," I answered honestly. It was the least I could do.

They squeezed their eyes shut, tipping their head down for a moment. They forced their eyes back open shortly afterwards and stared at me across the room. And then they deftly, and with their jaw clearly clenched inside their muzzle, unlaced their smallclothes and tugged them down their legs.

It took everything I could muster not to succumb to a lifetime of conditioning. And even still, my mind wanted to compel my body against my wishes. This was wrong. Look away.

But it was clear they wanted me to look. So, swallowing thickly, I did.

"I'm..." they literally shook as they spoke, "... not sure what you were ever hoping for in me. If *this* is what you were expecting, or... if it's what you were fearing. But I am as I am. And... and...."

I stood frozen on the spot. Should I go to them?

"I held you, when we found you," I said softly. "I had to carry you, and... there was... little barrier. I-I knew you as you were, then."

They were silent, staring firmly at the hardwood floor.

"But," my mouth was dry, "that doesn't mean I'm entitled to see you like this, you are *due* your decency, and I am *so* sorry my kin took that from you. I can never make up for—"

"Damn it all, Isidor," they sniffed wetly. "Enough with the apologies! Don't think I don't know you just gave up *everything* for me! I need to know if you're going to leave me now. If you're disappointed, i-if you're regretting—"

"Darcy, I have dreamed of every version of you my mind could conjure," I said, finding my words finally. I forced them out with the passion I'd held back all this while. "And every visage I imagined paled in comparison to this moment, I swear to you, I just... I—I do not have the words. I do not have the words for how much I yearn for you, and I want to kiss you, I want *everything*, but I don't want to *take* from you right now, when so much has already been taken from you! I am withholding myself, I am not *disappointed*. I just *don't know what to do!*"

They sobbed fully through their body and stumbled across the room towards me. I met them and caught them before they could fall, holding them while they swayed and sucked in great gasps of relief against my shoulder.

When they lifted their nose to mine, I saw the want in their eyes, clear as it had been in the forest. I asked, "Now? Is... is now the time? Y-you're hurt, and crying, and—"

"If you don't kiss me this time, I'll never let you live it down," they insisted almost angrily.

Right or wrong, I did.

9

SACRAMENT

Two of my first kisses in one day. With two different people. What was this life? Surely not mine.

I had not expected it would be, but kissing Darcy was nothing like the exchange I'd had with Malachi. It was briefer, gentler, precarious as testing hot tea on your tongue.

I worried I'd done it wrong, but I couldn't deny how much better it felt, despite the comparably mellower passion. I was able to breathe afterwards. There was no fear. No seizing in my limbs. None of the panic I'd wrestled with, then.

I think... I think I'd been worried it would be the same as it had been with the malamute. That the overwhelming feeling of wrongness and tension I'd felt this whole while had come from within. Everything leading *up* to the kiss had been fraught with worry and uncertainty, after all.

But when I opened my eyes and it was Darcy's gaze meeting mine, their small nose twitching and tickling my muzzle with their whiskers, an awkward but genuine smile tugging at the corners of their mouth, my doubts bled away. It occurred to me that they had been the first to drift apart and were lingering near, but not pressing in for another when it seemed likely they very much wanted to.

They were holding back. Probably for my sake, because of... a whole number of things. My inexperience, my vows, or just my overall countenance. I knew I must have seeped my discomfort in all things physically intimate. It was no great secret.

"Thank you," I said softly.

"I don't think I've ever felt this relieved," they admitted, their voice still hoarse, but happy. Honeyed with a bliss that hardly suited our situation. I was glad to have had any part in that reprieve. "I should be the one saying thank you," they said in an exhale, then cast a glance aside, "for so many things, obviously. But, can we... I don't want to...."

I shook my head. "We don't have to talk about any of that right now."

They smiled again, their eyes slipping to crescents, and leaned up to bump our noses together, their arms winding around my shoulders. I asked, so they didn't have to, "Do you want to do that again?"

"Yes, please," they said, stepping up on their toes.

The press of their muzzle to mine this time was more assured, and I tried to answer it in kind. They sighed against my mouth, and the soft sound made something shake its chains inside me, surging free. I parted my muzzle just enough that I could better cup the curve of theirs in mine, and reached up with my hand, finding their cheek with the flat of my palm. Any species fundamentalist who argued kind were only meant for kind had clearly never seen how well the serval's cheek fit into the palm of my hand. Like I'd been waiting my whole life to hold them, just like this. Even my missing digit felt right... a fourth finger would have gotten in the way, surely.

Was it folly to imagine we were literally made for one

another? I was probably just lightheaded, but the thought made me happy, so I indulged it for now.

Whether or not I'd intended to, some manner of learning had wedged itself into my mind over the prolonged, misbegotten communion I'd shared with Malachi, and when the feline tilted their head and slipped apart from me for but a moment before pressing back in, I knew what I was meant to do next. I tipped my muzzle in the opposite direction and found better purchase. And without my teeth clamped shut, I experienced a revelation.

I felt the curl of Darcy's warm, small tongue for but a moment, and it set my spine alight and my toe claws curling into the hardwood beneath my feet. I gasped noticeably enough that the feline parted from me, sucking in a short breath before managing to ask. "Are you alright? Was that... I know mine's rough, maybe... not what you were expecting. I should have asked—"

I slid the fingers splayed over their cheek to around the back of their head and pulled them back in.

Their jaw went slack against mine, and I briefly saw the whites of their eyes as they slid backwards, before I closed my own. Like retracing my steps down a now familiar—if unexplored—path, I eased our muzzles open together. Or they led and I followed; it was hard to say. I found I didn't care who was initiating and who was answering, not while we were tasting one another's breath and their strange, wonderful tongue was nudging my own. They tasted of copper, like they'd bitten the inside of their mouth at some point, but the knowledge of yet another unseen injury did little to suppress the gasp-wrenching thrill of feeling them nipping and lapping at my mouth.

By all rights, this should have been... revolting. This isn't how I'd ever imagined kissing would be. When Malachi had tried to initiate something *like* this, I'd balked at the mere thought. God, I needed to stop thinking of him. Enough.

But I liked this, I decided rather quickly. Despite how strange it was, it felt right, fed upon itself, building like a blaze inside me. Each roll of our muzzles against one another, each brush of their tongue against mine, drawing me in somehow deeper, before the tug of a fang against my lower lip made me worry I'd gotten carried away.

But then they were purring, open-mouthed into me, and that nip became two, three, their teeth leaving scalding lines against the edge of my muzzle each pinch and release. I knew by now that I had a complicated relationship with pain, but this wasn't truly painful, it was more... teasing. I wasn't sure I could replicate it. The feline was so delicate with their mouth, so skilled in all the ways I was clumsy.

Our second kiss had become a dozen. At some point, my loose hold on them had wound its way around to a tight grip, palms brushing over the nape of their neck and their lower back. It occurred to me only then that they were nude. I'd done a good job of ignoring it until now. Lord knew how I'd managed that. But, pressed against me as they were, it was... I was only wearing my underclothes, the line of their body was against mine, and things were happening. Things I wouldn't be able to conceal for long.

This fact only became more acute when they tugged themselves up higher to chase my muzzle with theirs and used their grip on my shoulders to do so. I'd forgotten that the feline kept their claws fully untrimmed, for purposes of climbing, I could only imagine. Right now, they were climbing *me*. The sharp hooks dug in past the paltry barrier of my thin shirt, through the cushion of my fur, and clung briefly into flesh.

I dropped their muzzle from mine with the force of my gasp, and my jaw fell open. They seemed to realize as soon as they'd done it and eased back down onto the balls of their feet, their claws slipping free. An obvious apology was in their eyes, but it died on their tongue when they saw how I fared.

I gave a stuttered breath, brows drawn up, my body uncoiling as though I were in prayer. Darcy's fingers soothed where their claws had dug in, eyes searching mine knowingly, while their whiskers ghosted past my muzzle again in several chasing, almost-kisses. "My beautiful, penitent choir boy," they said in a husky, lower register than usual. "I think I have you figured, and then you remind me how uniquely strange you are."

I began to say something, but the little laugh they gave settled my under-confidence immediately. "I like that you're more complicated than you seem," they assured me. They leaned in again, pressing the shapes of our bodies together. "I like that I've been privy to your inner, secretive chambers. I look forward to exploring them further. They're mine, now... all of these furtive hours between us... you're safe to be yourself with me, Isidor. I don't like sharing my secrets. I promise you that."

"I'm well aware of that fact," I said ruefully, running my fingertips—and my far more ground-down, blunted claw-tips— over the bumps in their spine. I felt their tail shiver and thrash, and it was briefly relieving to know they were not as cool and collected as they seemed on the surface.

I tried it again, finding the two little divots above their tail, and their previously soft smile up at me turned sly. With a clutching at my neck, they rolled their hips in tighter against mine, sighing softly as their stomach pressed against my—

"Ahh—" I winced my eyes shut a moment, before cracking just one to look back down at them, caught and embarrassed. "I'm sorry, I-I'm...."

"You're not alone," they assured me coyly. They leaned their nose into my chest, nearly disappearing in the crook of my breast and the thick fur there, as they dragged in one long breath, in and out. "You know, I have wanted you since I saw you chopping wood in the paddock at the Lodge. Probably before then, if I'm being honest. I dared not entertain except in lurid, private fantasy, but when I came to know of your mutual desire, I... I could hardly bear the fact that we'd never partaken. When I was being held down in that place, the thought that I'd never again feel the warmth of you, the crush of your arms around me, the heady scent of your fur and incense intertwined... that was the hardest thing."

"Such theatrical language. The fear of *death* wasn't what primarily occupied your mind? You've got your priorities well-settled," I teased, stroking their neck. We were talking about their imprisonment, and I didn't want to divert the conversation if that's what they wanted to speak on, but it felt like raw territory.

They shook their head, not removing their muzzle from my chest. "Do not judge me," they murmured, "but no. I don't regret risking death for my vocation, my regrets recently have all concerned you. I could face the gallows contented if I knew I was wanted. If I'd been filled of your need for me, if we'd consummated this affection for one another that night in the wood. I would rather face my end with passion in my heart than the yawning emptiness of loneliness."

"Darcy," I lost the teasing tone and all good humor, in seconds.

"It's hard for me to be this forthright with feelings I know to be disturbing," they pressed, finally lifting their gaze to mine. "Do not *judge* me for these feelings, I beg of you again, Isidor."

"I don't," I eased softly, cupping a palm around one of their ears. "I swear it."

"Is it so wrong that I yearn to be wanted?" they asked, the

question seemingly asked as much of themselves as me. "As valued and as promised-to as a wife, a mate…? I have been led by the waist to the water before, and I could have died happily then, too. I just wanted to be his—to be someone's—beloved. To know I mattered to him and that I'd exist in his heart past my end, if it came to that."

"I have no doubt that Cillian will think of you all of his days," I said. "But everything else was a hollow promise. And you lived on, despite that."

I knew even as I said it that the situation was more complex than anyone but the two of them could ever comprehend. I was speaking on a dynamic I still didn't fully understand.

I didn't want to be angry at Cillian any more. It had been easy, once. I obviously had my convictions about men making false promises to women… to lovers, as the case was here… but additionally, and perhaps most importantly, it was clear how much the betrayal had wounded Darcy. I would never know the person they were before it had all transpired, but I suspected they'd been more open, then. More trusting.

Whoever the feline had been then, they were no longer. That didn't mean I couldn't learn what they were willing to share. What shaped them. I had fallen for who they were *now*, but their past would always still be a part of that. Sunken ships still posed hazards, whether you could see the wreckage beneath the surface or not.

My feelings on Cillian were more complicated than they initially had been. They likely always would be. I didn't hate him, but I found it hard to forgive him for a myriad of reasons. I couldn't imagine how much worse it must have been for Darcy to contend with it all.

"If *you* swore yourself to me, it wouldn't be a hollow promise," they said softly, eyes darting up plaintively to mine. "Would it?"

"No…" I agreed, sighing. "But it still doesn't comfort me that you'd go more peaceably to the noose, simply because you've secured my affections, Darcy."

"I don't want to die alone, knowing no one will grieve me. What's so wrong with that?"

My heart skipped a step. I tightened my hold on them. "You won't," I said. "Even if you'd died in that basement, you'd have taken a piece of me with you. I don't need to lay claim to your person to promise myself to you. You don't need to justify our bond by that measure. And I…" I stammered, uncertainty taking hold for one tenuous second, before I dashed it aside, "I *am* promising myself to you, Darcy. How could I deny my dedication to you at this point? I think I must be in love with you… God, I must be. I do not know how it is meant to feel, but—"

They leaned up and kissed me again, albeit briefly. When they pulled back, they brushed their nose against mine, quirking a charming, lopsided smile. "I believe you," they assured me. "I do not think anyone who's seen what you've done, what you've gone through on my behalf over our acquaintance, would doubt you're besotted with me."

"If the poets are to be believed," I murmured, keeping my voice low because of how close their large ears were to my muzzle, "love can be a fleeting, fickle thing. I've never known love like that. I would prefer to think of what I feel towards you as… loyalty."

They tilted their head at me inquisitively.

"I *will* try to love you as you deserve," I continued, stroking their cheek. "I cannot say how good I shall be at it or even if it will remain welcome as you come to know me. I'm not a romantic. But, loyalty. I am very practiced at that. Until this past year, I would have said it was one of my strongest suits. Things… have not shaken out as I ever would have imagined with my relationship to the Ministry, to the law, even, but—"

"They betrayed *you* first," Darcy pressed.

"No. They betrayed the values they are meant to stand for," I said, hanging my head slightly. "That's part of why this is so hard. They would still be my allies were they right with God and the moral principles I thought we stood for. *My* principles have not changed. If anything, my faith has grown. I have learned—have widened my understanding of the world and the nature of man's influence on the Word of God—but I still feel Him in my heart, guiding me true. It can get murky sometimes, but I do feel... I do feel I have done the very best I could to walk the path He has put before me. The right path, or as close to it as I may be able to come. I've stumbled, I've had my hand forced, but to fault is mortal. I can be forgiven, if I recognize my mistakes. What they—what the Ministry—are doing is so far beyond the pale. I do not honestly know how I could have navigated this clean of sin by their measure. And I am becoming dubious of *how* they measure."

"We are not always given easy choices," Darcy said, their eyes gone distant, before they wiped an arm across their dye-stained lashes. "It's folly to live in regret."

"Even the worst things I have had to do throughout this trial," I said, biting back the memories, "have all brought me to this moment. I am where I am meant to be." I firmed up my resolve and reached down to take their hands in mine, squeezing their small fingers tightly in my palms. "I am here because I'm in love with you, Darcy, but not only that. I will be loyal to you, will remain at your side for so long as you wish because we are meant to do this thing together, I believe. God wills it, I am convinced. But it is also *my* will."

The feline's ears splayed shyly, eyes closing for a moment. "That's as beautifully-worded a promise as ever I've heard, your religious convictions aside."

"You... don't believe me?" I asked, trying not to sound hurt.

"No! I mean, I do," they clarified, looking up at me again. "I believe every word, Isidor. I believe... you believe it. I don't know how I feel about a God that decrees I'm a lesser being—"

"That doctrine was written by canine men," I insisted, "and I don't believe it anymore—"

"—but that's a conversation for another day," they pressed on. "What matters in a case like this is how *you* feel about your faith. About us. I know your passion. I know you'd not swear something so earnestly if you weren't absolute in your certainty, especially as it concerns your faith. I just... have no equivalent certainty to promise. I should reply in kind, but I'm just...."

I gave them time. When it seemed they were truly lost for words, I tried to fill the silence with an assurance. "I was hesitant to say any of this to you now, anyway. I wouldn't have if the conversation had not naturally turned this way. After what you've been through, this is too much, right now. You should be resting—"

"No," they said stubbornly and severely. "I wanted, nay I *needed*, to hear you say something like that. Because I felt so bloody guilty from the moment I woke up and saw you, knowing what you must have *lost* going against your kin for me. I need to know this was worth it to you. That I..." they brought in a shaky breath, "... that I was worth all of this to you."

"I would not have gone against the Order if I was uncertain about you," I said, "or how important all of this is to me."

"But that just makes it all the crueler that I cannot find it in me to speak aloud a similar promise," they spat out, shaking their head. They swiped their palm over their eyes again, sniffing. "I'm such a bloody coward."

"No, you're in *pain*," I said seriously, "exhausted, frightened, and possibly ill from exposure. I expect nothing from you right now except that you care for yourself, and even in that case, I will be happy to do it for you. We need to get you into the bath before it cools..."

"It's a few words," they whispered hoarsely. "Why can't I do it?"

"A few words can mean everything," I said, letting my tone go softer. "Darcy. Darcy, please, look at me."

They did, in time. I was not used to seeing so much guilt mirrored back at me. It was as though we'd swapped roles.

"You do not need to be making promises to me right now, when you're this frayed and your mind and body are too exhausted to think clearly," I said, rubbing the pad of my thumb over their cheek. "You have been laid low. Now is not the moment for life-altering declarations. I have had a great *deal* of time with no impediment other than my own thoughts to consider what you are to me, and to air the truth, I am still uncertain what our future together might be. It's fine for us to take our time considering. That's… what courtship is for." I sighed. "I'm only sorry I said this now. I did not mean to pressure, I just thought, in the moment, it would help somehow."

A slight smile tugged briefly at the feline's muzzle. "You want to court me?"

"Well," I gave a weak shrug, "we've surpassed that, wouldn't you say? The rules of etiquette and propriety hardly apply, any more. I don't know what courtship will be for us, but that is also not something we need decide now."

"Does courtship between us mean… you'll…" they paused, glancing down at themselves, "… help me bathe and get the dye out of my fur?"

I felt the heat go straight to my ears, and I had trouble maintaining eye contact, "It, ah," I cleared my throat, "it could. I'm supposed to help you if you need it. Physician's orders."

They dropped their voice, the slightest thrum of a purr entering it when they spoke so lowly. "Does that mean you'll be sharing my bed…?"

"Well, there's only one," I stammered. "So—"

"Isidor, please," they sighed, "I need clarity. Men of your Faith have very strict rules about sex and marriage. I need to know honestly if I'm overstepping."

"My Faith also demands I marry a canine woman and father pups," I said pointedly. "And considers things like what we did in the woods as serious missteps, absolutely life-altering failures of moral character in the case of a woman or a man of the clergy. Of which I am, I'll remind you. But then, I'll be excommunicated as soon as they know I was responsible for releasing a prisoner of the Ministry wanted for Heresy, so…" I let my arms fall at my sides helplessly. "I was under water past my ears long ago, Darcy. At this point it is my own reservations and anxieties that keep me from indulging in hedonism. And even still…"

Their ears perked, and they gave me an expectant stare.

Lord, I honestly wasn't certain if I was ready. But the last thing I wanted was for them to think that was somehow their fault.

"It isn't overstepping, if it's you," I said, at length. "Only let me see how I feel in the moment. And do not blame yourself— do not ever blame yourself—if my nerves get the best of me. I am forging a path here for which there is no map in the book I based my life upon. Permit me to navigate all of this at my own pace?"

Darcy smiled quietly at me and nodded. I didn't really understand it then, but there was a knowingness in their eyes. A surety based on wisdom, experience, and, I daresay, common sense.

The fact is, we were sharing tight quarters, the both of us were a bowstring drawn taut to snapping in our highly emotional states, and we were alone together for the first time since the Lodge, when we'd still been enemies. And I was about to spend an extended period of time laying hands on the serval in the warm bath.

I had drastically overestimated my resolve to take things slowly. *And* my nerves.

The waxing and waning cycles of guilt and release had long since abated, where my affections for Darcy were concerned. In their place was a scorching, unreasonable passion that cared not for concerns like my own physical state, the practicality or privacy of the place we found ourselves in, or what God or my Father might think of me if I gave in to it.

I did not feel, as Brother Dolus had long warned, that I might lose control of myself. If anything, my mind was working very hard to justify every choice, every slip further down the embankment. Passion was a fire, indeed. But it would burn no other, at least not in my case. It burned inside *me*. Hotter, and more intensely until it was impossible to ignore, and all that remained was scorched earth. My mind was empty, singularly fixated on the elegantly freckled, lithe feline basking in the steaming water of the old wash basin I was leaning over. And nothing stood between us. My resolve was ash.

It would have been a tight fit for me on my own, let alone the both of us, so sharing was out. Which was for the best, given how far-gone I was simply sitting outside of it, helping them scrub the dark pigment from their fur.

The water was blackish indigo now, which they'd explained helped cover some of the warmer colors from the gold in their fur. Dragging the wash cloth over shoulder blades, the curve of their rib cage where their skin folded when they cocked their hip, their right breast where the fur bled to cream, *I yearned.*

I knew it before the puff of air and a sound like the softest keen left their muzzle, when the pad of my thumb had accidentally brushed over a bump, the small ridge of one of their nipples. I felt it through the washcloth, and then saw it peeking through the light, plush fur normally covering their chest, plastered down by the water. It was dark like my own. Small, nearly hidden. Beautiful as the rest of them.

"I'm sorry," I whispered.

I was *so* hard in my trousers. It was impossible they hadn't taken note of it by now, I was only wearing my undergarments and they may as well have not been there for all they covered my shame. I could feel the outline of my own manhood, *aching* against my thigh where it was trapped. The fact that I'd gotten quite a bit of damp on myself aiding Darcy in cleaning themselves hadn't helped matters. You could probably have seen the *color* through my soaked whites, at this point.

"Don't be," Darcy said, not hiding their eyeline as it roved over me. "It would have been difficult for me to be as thorough, and I smelled like death. I don't honestly know how you tolerated me. You're so polite sometimes, it is mind-boggling."

I had to chuckle at that a little, at least. "I'm a canine, Darcy. Very few scents put me off. I'll admit, I don't like the smell of blood and fear on you, though."

"There was worse filth on me than blood," they said bitterly. "That place was a tomb, and he wouldn't let me—"

I leaned down and kissed one of their shoulders. "You aren't there anymore," I reminded them, then slowly squeezed out the wash cloth, leaning back. "Let it wash away."

"I like that," they said, eyes slipping closed a moment as my hand found purchase on the nape of their neck, where their fur was broken by the line of one of the raw, abused patches from their restraint bindings. I kneaded it gingerly.

"Isidor..." they moaned quietly, reclining their head. I thought to catch them when they leaned against the edge of the tub, resting their neck against my chest, just about level to them while I knelt.

I leaned my muzzle down over their shoulder, releasing a

breath I hadn't known I was holding. I hadn't meant for it to come out sounding so labored, so stuttering… and they noticed.

"Take me to bed?" they asked in a whisper. Their neck craned back against my chest, eyes slipping open as they looked upwards towards mine.

"Darcy…" I don't know how I'd meant the utterance of their name to sound, but not *that* desperate. Not as yearning as it came out.

"I'm not near so uncertain what my body yearns for as my mind," they said. "I'll give as little or as much as you desire. Just tell me what you want, Isidor."

"I… want to get you out of this chilling water and get you dry," I said, because that was the easiest answer.

They huffed, then gave a smile and turned, the water sloshing with their movements. Much to my surprise, they stood before I had the chance to and carefully stepped clear of the tub, their foot-paws settling wetly on the hardwood not inches to the right of me.

When I looked up, they had their arms spread, palms clutching the edge of the tub, body leaned back just slightly against the lip. But they were standing nearly over me, as I was still kneeling. I had found myself knelt at their feet again, somehow.

I looked up slowly, leaning in before I'd realized it, pushing first my nose and then eventually my whole muzzle into their soaked, silken fur. I traced the outer line of their ribcage, and then the jut of their hip bone. At some point, their fingers found the fur between my ears. I began lacing kisses into the path my mouth was taking. I ended somewhere on their thigh, where I closed my eyes and bent my neck as though in worship.

"You're so good, Isidor," Darcy purred, their fingers rubbing over the softest spots of my ears. "Please tell me what you want, right now. I want to give it to you."

"I don't know," I said, voice thready. "You."

"I want you, too," they said, and let their fingers trail down my cheek to my neck. I wasn't certain what their aim was until I felt something go tight into the fur along the back of my neck, tugging at me upwards.

My rosary. It was on, as ever, beneath the collar of my shirt. Darcy's dexterous fingers had found it and were tugging me up by it. They weren't exerting much force, likely worried of breaking it. But the command was clear.

I stood and was set upon all but immediately by the slender feline. They claimed my mouth with their own, hungrier than they'd ever been, and all I could do was pant and give in, letting them nip their way inside. Our tongues curled, my chest churned with unbridled excitement, and their weight fell against mine. Our arms followed, gripping for purchase on any available curve or angle on each other's bodies. My palms found and clutched their rear—not their lower back this time, but very distinctly their rear end—and sunk into the supple expanse. Each mound seemed somehow perfectly sized for my corresponding palm, a fact which I certainly took note of.

Darcy had gripped and tugged up the loose ends of my shirt, before pulling the whole of it up over my head and peeling it down my arms. I did my best to help, but mostly I was catching my breath during the brief reprieve from the heated kiss. I was forced to think again, I had spent an *entire* lifetime misunderstanding what kissing was, apparently. The last few days had been an education.

"Oh, Good Lord, I'd nearly forgotten what you look like bare-chested," Darcy gasped, giving a wild smile and an obviously admiring gaze over my body.

I took the moment to retrieve the drying cloth from where it hung nearby, so that I could wrap it around the feline's shoulders and begin rubbing their fur dry. Darcy seemed happy for the doting and closed their eyes while I tended to them.

"I'm losing some of my gut," I said. "I doubt I'll have as much trouble eating now you're here, but I can try to keep it up."

"Don't you dare starve yourself for vanity," the serval's eyes snapped open, and their hands were upon me suddenly, brushing up through the soft fur of my abdomen and midsection, rumbling their contentment as they petted at me there. "I like bigger fellows."

I gave a soft, "Hahh..." and then a, "whatever pleases you, I suppose. I don't think time and age will give me much choice in the matter, anyway. Better you like it than not."

"I want you to put me under you," they nearly slurred in their wanton state, "hold me down with your arms, grind me to *dust* with your hips—"

"Darcy, God—"

"I want to take you inside me, Isidor," they said intensely, locking their eyes with mine. "I want that so badly. Lord above, you have no idea...."

I released a haggard breath, because their palm had slipped beneath the hem of my trousers, and they'd found me. They would have been hard-pressed not to, with how I was filling them out. Their paw was soft, claws tucked away for now, rubbing along the length that they'd slowly teased out from its confines. When had they unlaced me? It hardly mattered.

I dropped the drying cloth, losing my footing for a moment and reclaiming it unsteadily on my back foot. The room was small, and at some point during all the kissing they had maneuvered us back towards the bed. Which was for the best, as I was steadily losing my fight to stay standing.

Some part of my mind not muddied by months of pent-up need and my burning affection for this person was mocking me, asking why I'd made such a production of waiting, of taking my time, if I were just going to acquiesce this very night, anyway. They weren't forcing me. I could be the voice of reason.

It was hard to remember, in this moment, why I'd thought

we should wait. We both wanted it, and God, or the natural order, had clearly given us the means to pursue our pleasure with one another. It would satisfy us both, I had to imagine... was that not the point? And Darcy at least knew what they were doing. Even if I was miserably poor at lovemaking... was this even something one could fail at? Could I do this *wrong?*

Darcy would show me how. I could not imagine this under any other circumstances. I was so *very* glad in this moment that I was not contending with a virgin bride, expecting me to know the steps. What a disaster that would have been.

"Tell me what you want," Darcy asked, pressing in close when the backs of my knees hit the edge of the bed. "You said you imagined me in your dreams? Tell me what you imagined."

I glanced down their body again, wetting my muzzle with my tongue. They seemed to see something in my eyes, and briefly followed my gaze, a bolt of uncertainty crossing their features.

"Are you," they paused, "unsure because...."

"No," I said firmly. "Just... I-I don't know how to talk about these things."

They put a palm on my chest and pushed me lightly. I thudded to sit on the bed, and before I could get my bearings, the serval was climbing over top of me, straddling my waist. I caught the vaguest hint of a wince when they put weight on the wrong leg, and then again when their thighs spread over the expanse of my own.

"You're hurt," I said, some clarity snapping back into my consciousness. "We shouldn't—"

My reason held out until exactly the moment when their hips pressed to mine, and I felt them, skin to skin. The shape of their sex against my own, warm and slicker than the rest of us, had me panting a punched-out groan, my tongue lolling between my teeth like a beast on the hunt. It felt feral, primal, reaching down inside and pulling out the guttural noises of my ancient brethren. My hips gave a half-aborted buck, bouncing the feline's splayed thighs where they were spread around my lap.

Darcy bit their lower lip with a long fang and a shudder passed through their fur, their stomach tensing with a roll down into me, grinding where we met together. "It wasn't enough, in the woods," they whispered. "I want to *feel* you."

I gripped their cheek in my palm and pulled them into another kiss, and we both moaned into it, this time. Their hands gripped at my biceps, claws clutching in, not digging, but holding fast.

I would make them dig their claws into me in time, I promised myself. I would earn it.

But tonight, no... God, this couldn't last. I could feel wetness pearling at my tip already, and we were barely moving against one another. Most of the times this had happened to me, I hadn't even been conscious. But I still knew what that meant. I couldn't imagine how I would even make it inside of them before I was done for. And also....

They were hiding it, perhaps even from themselves, but they were in pain. I could feel it in the occasional halting jerks between their other movement, but I could also sense it. Pain has a scent, a feeling in the air. I was becoming more attuned to Darcy's body as I'd come to know them.

A visible wince and a muffled noise of discomfort when they twisted their leg the wrong way was what it took for me to finally find my voice. I released their muzzle with a wet lick and ran my hand down along their slim leg, where it rested on the bed beside us.

"You're hurt," I said with finality. "Not tonight."

They deflated, the disappointment in their eyes obvious, but alongside it, acceptance. I'd deduced by now that Darcy did better with certainty and inarguable boundaries. Unless that boundary was a locked door, and you were an inanimate object,

I suppose. But even when I'd been their prisoner, when I'd been clear on where my limits lay, they'd respected them.

I didn't want to ruin the night or let them down, but I also didn't want to hurt them. Certainty.

"I... know what I want," I said, swallowing. "I've thought on it."

Their ears perked, hope dancing back into their gaze. "Oh? Tell me." They smiled slowly. "Don't be shy."

I had trouble looking at them when I said it. I worried what they'd think of me. But I couldn't deny what I'd been imagining —what I now very much wanted to do. And Darcy wanted me to be honest with them, so....

Confession was good for the soul.

"I... w-want..." I swallowed, my gaze drifting down from where the dim lantern light in the room haloed their fur, down their torso, to the crux of their thighs where they were pressed into mine, "... I want to put my muzzle on you..." I mumbled, "... not just kiss you, I... everywhere. There."

I suppose I was hoping they'd hear me out, and then somehow, miraculously, act as though what I'd asked was not strange at all. Tell me how normal my desire was. How it was just another facet of intercourse I knew nothing about, and so I imagined my want for it to be more peculiar than it was.

But they did actually seem shocked. My heart sunk.

"You continue to be full of surprises," Darcy said, moving in to nose me in what I believed was meant to be a comforting way.

"I did not mean to offend—"

They laughed. Not mockingly, but lyrically, happily. "I'm not offended by the concept of you putting your muzzle between my legs Isidor, I'm... overjoyed," they nuzzled in against me again. "Just surprised. I thought I'd be giving that, not receiving."

"Oh, God," I let my head thud back against the bedspread, realizing what they'd just offered. "That's right, you could. I must admit, I don't know… I-I don't know how it's done, only that it… is. You could… show me how?"

"Mmhm," their smile touched their cheek ruffs now, as they laid out over top of me, their fingers walking up my sternum. "But, you offered, so you want to, first…?"

"Yes," I answered embarrassingly quickly.

They gave a sultry smile and swung a leg to dismount me, before sliding back to get comfortable in the tousled blankets, parting their beautiful thighs and gesturing at me from where they lay to come towards them.

"Disrobe, first," they said.

"F-fully?" I asked uncertainly. I'd had a very short lesson with my father about this when I'd come of age. As Templar, we were held to hygienic standards that most of civil society— Pedigree society, even—would consider excessive. But even still, Father had stressed there were areas of the body a man did not need to expose his bride to, even to consummate their union.

"You've seen all of me, I want to see all of you," Darcy reasoned, tail swishing about slowly between their thighs on the bedspread. I couldn't take my eyes off the sight, nor occupy my thoughts with anything beyond the immediate reality that they were… that all of this was… permitted. Enthusiastically. This wasn't just another dream.

If they wanted me equally nude, for whatever reason, it was only fair. I wanted to please them.

"You may find yourself disappointed," I said as I began working my smallclothes down, glancing at the candle, uncertain if I should snuff it out.

Darcy followed my gaze, and when I ventured a hand, batted it away with a light slap. "Let me be the judge of that," they said, lifting their muzzle imperiously.

Not a bland placation, an empty assurance that I would be pleasing. A promise that I would be weighed and measured, and the serval would be the final say on whether or not I pleased them. For some reason, although I knew the banter was playful, the thought that it might *not* be, that they might in fact employ those evaluating eyes to decide whether I would be worth stealing, intrigued me...

Good Lord, what was wrong with me? How my mind was rambling away on me right now, in this nervous moment?

In the light of the dim, burnt-down-to-the-wick candle, I knelt before Darcy on that uneven straw mattress, my knees sinking into it with my weight, my unmentionable parts hung low enough to brush the bedspread. I couldn't look at them, but I stood in judgment until I heard them release a long breath.

I looked at them out of the corner of my eye, then. Their expression was hard to read. Their muzzle was parted slightly, eyes fixed and sparkling in the dark.

"You're a big fellow, Isidor," they eventually said, "but I think we can make it work. Stars above, you're so handsome... I thought so from the moment I saw you practicing at the Hudson's yard, you know."

"You said," I confirmed shyly. "Your tastes are not in line with polite society, but then... I suppose mine aren't either."

"To Hell with polite society," they grinned, then scrubbed a hand over their muzzle somewhat excitedly, amusing in their momentary immaturity. "Sorry, I just still cannot believe how far we have come, sometimes. That you're here with me, like this. That I'm permitted this, with you."

I almost choked on my next breath. "I had almost exactly the same thought."

Their smile became more unbridled. "We are rather desperate for one another, aren't we? How pathetic."

I laughed. The humor was helping ease the tension I'd been feeling, being nude before them. "I have to admit, in all of my imaginings of this moment, I didn't realize there'd be so much talking."

"Don't worry, your mouth will be too busy soon," they said,

reaching forward and gripping the thick scruff around my neck, pulling me towards them.

I moved over them, falling into the kiss almost naturally. It was getting easier each time. Our muzzles found one another and joined our breath, avoiding teeth and sealing around each other in a comfortable fit. They'd been concerned at first I suppose, but earnestly, I loved the sensation of their tongue against my own. It was different, so explicitly *theirs*, but mine to play with. Their hands were so different from mine, as well. Unceasing in their roaming, delicate when they needed to be and clutching with the threat of claws when they'd found purchase they liked. Which soon became my rear, those claws kneading in between the thick, fluffy fur there as greedily as they had my shoulders. Perhaps more so.

They moaned headily into my mouth, and I found myself answering them. We were—neither of us—any good at being quiet with our desires. The small log-lined room was filled with the most despicably lustful, uncivilized sounds as I ground my body down into theirs. As they'd wanted.

Perhaps because we'd finish like this if we kept it up any longer, Darcy was the first to pull me back, hands setting back to my shoulders, clung in. They locked their hazy gaze with my own for a moment, slowly smiling... then began to push me down.

"You can use your teeth on my chest, if you like," they said, between soft pants. "Gently. But only tongue below. Move your head as you do when you kiss me. Like you're nuzzling me."

I nodded because I was beyond words. I dragged my nose down their chest, feeling their ribs expand in a deep breath, then slowly let out. They were essentially flat-chested, beyond the natural slope of muscle and flesh beneath the puff of their soft chest fur. Another part of our bodies that differed. Their fur had dried faster than the rest of them, likely from the heat and the fact that I had admittedly over-fixated on rubbing the drying cloth there.

I found one dark nipple with the tip of my nose and pressed my mouth flat to it, supping my muzzle around it and groaning again as the firmness of it changed in my mouth. Darcy sucked in a gasp, a leg kicking out against the comforters behind us. Their hand guided me from the back of my head encouragingly.

I wasn't sure why I wanted to do this, but there was no doubt I was enjoying it at least as much as they were. I ground my hips down into the bed, my cock... God, forgive me, but my mind could no longer conjure polite language... my *cock* was throbbing with my heartbeat. I could feel my knot swelling in my sheath, already.

I was nibbling at their belly when I felt their knee brush past my ear. First one, then the other, as their thighs clenched around my cheeks. I briefly lifted my head, so that I could feel the press of both of their slender, strong legs boxing me in. I lifted my palms to either side of their hips, stroking my claws up and down the expanse of them, slowly.

Their scent was muted owing to the thorough scrubbing that had been necessary to reveal their beautiful golden, spotted pelt. But it was stronger closer to their sex, and I inhaled deeply as I moved my nose down through the ridge of fur below their navel. This was my mate... or at least, may very well be, if we both found each other's company to our liking. As one of Canus's tribe, I would commit their scent to memory for the whole of my life. It would come unbidden to me when I thought of them, and I would keep it in my own fur when we were apart. It was what we called a 'remnant of one's soul'. Not a piece of it, as the soul could never be rent asunder, but a reflection of them. A remnant left behind, to track, to remember, to treasure.

I rubbed my cheek against their lower stomach and then nuzzled my nose into the crook of their thigh, just alongside their sex. I eyed my opponent, wetting my muzzle with my tongue and considering my angle of approach.

But then their hands closed around my skull on either side of my ears, and my guesswork was over. They led me instead, giving a long sigh and arching their hips as they pressed my muzzle down. I gave up control willingly, allowing them to guide me as to how they wanted my mouth on them. I curled my lip over my teeth to protect their most tender flesh, let my tongue loll out, and welcomed the rush of sensations that came.

I tried to do as they'd said and treat it like a kiss, rolling my neck into the movement they'd already struck with their hips, long, steady undulations against one another, as my tongue lathed and explored. I went slowly, trying to feel or hear how they responded to each method I tried, most only varying a little.

They were gasping and shivering intermittently from the start, especially when I curled my tongue in certain areas. I tried to commit what worked to memory, but I was certainly distracted, my mind muddled with want and overwhelmed by the whole of it. I thought I was doing well… or else Darcy was as far gone as I, and even an amateur effort would have done.

While I learned my way around this, the need in me built to the point where I could hardly stand the feel of my manhood exposed any longer. I needed… I needed it warmed, surrounded, held, *anything…* but the best I could manage was to press it down between my belly and the bed, and grunt unappealingly as I found what friction I could there.

"Ah-!" their claws tightened where they were gripping me by the scruff of the neck suddenly, and they drew a knee up, reaching down with their other hand to lace their fingers around mine, where it was still clutching them there. I felt those very same fingers drag down the length of mine, stopping at and feeling my claws.

"Thought so… before…" they said breathily. "You grind your claws? Lord have mercy."

I parted, licking my teeth, drooling most indecently. "We're... expected to if we interact with Pedigrees... it's decorum."

"I honestly don't care why," they huffed. "Slick them in your mouth."

"My... claws?"

"Fingers," they groaned, sounding just on the edge of frustrated. "Index, middle, in your mouth. Then in me."

I felt my face grow hot. I was, of course, nose-first in their most sensitive area, I'd considered this whole time that I'd... that we'd eventually, likely... but to actually *feel* them inside, first?

I suppose ground claws *would* be helpful for that.

They were all but begging me. Honestly, at this point it would be rude to turn them down, really.

I did as they said, placing two fingers on my tongue and sucking on them until I'd put some of that saliva to use. The serval watched me intently the whole while. They looked almost inebriated. I imagined I looked no better.

"One finger first, then two," they instructed softly.

I toyed at the spot gingerly first, not intending to tease, but the way the serval's toes curled and their tail thrashed beneath me, you'd think I was being cruel. When I did eventually press slowly inside, past the first bit of resistance, their body seemed to uncoil in a long, thrumming groan, with a baseline purr I could feel through every inch of my body in contact with theirs.

A noise left me as well then, like a breathless whine that bled into a growl. I felt—knew in my bones, instantly—how much more I would want this, now that I'd known what it might feel like to be inside of them. My imagination was a sensation-less void of hazy warmth and pleasure with no real visceral comparison, until now.

And the sounds they made... desperate, keening, begging me

to put my muzzle back to them, and when I did, they arched into me, their body tensing around my intruding touch, until I felt I might be squeezed out.

I groaned, muffled by their fur and my busy tongue, and trusted in the way their hips had bucked up into my mouth that it was time to up the ante. I pressed the second finger in, taking my time at it, and listened as their breath lifted into a euphoric sob.

"Please move," they pleaded.

It took me a moment to realize what they meant. Like, I surmised, in copulation...? I knew at least that much.

I tried it. Slowly at first, feeling the push and pull of their body sucking me in, and the tensing and releasing as the efforts of my mouth drove them steadily wilder.

"Isi... dor," they staggered out, clenching their claws into my neck and shoulder. I remembered my oath and drove my fingers into them with purpose, following the yearning from my own hips, as I dug my manhood down into the bed.

I did not understand the climax of this act well, yet... I had experienced it infrequently in the waking world and only once with them. I believe they had reached the same peak that night in the woods, but I would not have been certain of it until this moment. The keening cry, the way they arched their lithe back, hips straining and shaking... and of course, the change in taste.

It felt like a victory. This cunning, beautiful, fascinating person that I'd chased after in many ways for months, feeling this elation because I'd given it to them. I had spent my entire life thinking this was a gift my future mate would give me, not realizing it was something I could give in return. It's possible I never would have known, if my life hadn't changed as it had.

I found myself laying my over-large, heavy head on their stomach, catching my breath while they caught theirs. I only realized when their hands began to pry me up how uncomfortable that must have been for them.

"I'm sorry," I slurred, flexing my jaw, "I—"

"Don't you dare apologize," they chuckled in a rasp. "Get up. Over me."

I began to move to the side, but their grip—stronger than one would think for a person their size—held me firmly straddling them still. "I said over me," they corrected, pulling my hips forward, up their body. "Like this."

"Uhhh—oh—I-I don't kn—" I moved as they directed, but self-consciously. I wasn't just thick between my legs any more, I was *weeping*, my knot was nearly out….

They licked their muzzle as they lined me up with it. One paw curled around me, softly stroking the whole of my length not an inch away from their nose. I partially covered my face with a palm, staring out from one eye down at them. This was filthy, somehow more embarrassing than it had been to do this myself on them, but I couldn't look away.

"Warn me?" they asked, nosing at my tip. "I don't like the taste of it. I'd much rather it be inside me somewhere else."

"Uhhnhh…" I groaned, but nodded, fully covering my face at that.

Oh God, the first feel of that tongue on my manhood. I could have gone on to my next life contented. I whuffed a groan, which was joined a moment later by Darcy's long, satisfied, "Mmmhhh…" as they closed their warm, wet muzzle around the first few inches of it. I could feel the cool, unyielding shape of their fangs on either side. The curl of their tongue as it cupped and stroked me, Lord be praised-!

They pulled up briefly to rumble a soft, "Isidor, look at me."

"I-if I do, it will be over," I groaned.

But I pulled my hand back from my eyes and slid them open, all the same. It was a sight like I had dreamed, their muzzle stretched around my pink length, their beautiful eyes slender as crescents, their cheeks soft and full as they bobbed their head slowly. They locked eyes with me, and I swear they smiled, the black corners of their mouth turning up.

It was so much more stunning in reality than the dreams had been. The version of Darcy I dreamt of was unmarred by the world, fuzzy around the edges of memory. This version was real, with a small nick on their nose, a bent whisker, their fur still askew from being wet and tousled. Their earrings—left on throughout their capture, out of carelessness or on principle, I knew not—gave a soft clink as they swayed, catching the candlelight only occasionally.

The smile—and the fact that *so* much of it was disappearing down that beautiful muzzle, somehow—was more than I could bear. I gave a haggard breath out, and tried to form the words, "I-I am… near.…"

I'm not sure how intelligible I sounded, but the feline could take cues. They slid their muzzle fully up and down to the base of my knot once more, then let it slip free of their mouth, while balancing the tip on their tongue. Their paw tightened around me and stroked until I had to pound my palm against the wall to endure the wave of rapture that washed over me. My whole body came unspooled, muscles seizing, a shudder passing through me like a ground quake. The moan I gave was unbecoming and loud—much too loud. The wall was all that kept me from toppling over, but that might have been a mercy for poor Darcy.

I could hardly look at the mess I made of them, of our bed, some of my spend unavoidably even staining their nose and muzzle. They blinked and snuffed, licking at their lips instinctively.

I winced, knowing that was expressly what they'd asked me to avoid. But they didn't seem repulsed. More quizzical.

"Oh," they chuckled a bit, wiping an eyelid. "You taste different. I really wasn't certain, the first time."

"What?" I asked between panting breaths, baffled.

"Some of it got on my hands then, but I wasn't sure until now…" they sort of led off, abashed. "You taste different. Sort of better? Blander, anyway." They chuckled, ghosting their palm down over my whole length and briefly squeezing my knot. "Maybe the lack of seafood."

"A-ah…haahh…" I almost wanted to move away, but it still felt… good? Too much? Odd. I'd settle on odd. And just on the side of too much. "I-I don't know… wh-why that would…."

"Something the Courtesans whisper about," they smirked, running small circles around the current object of their fascination with the tips of their fingers.

"I'm going to take that bloody thing away from you now," I warned them before moving. "S'not a toy, you know. Ahhh… fuck…." I swore under my breath as they got a last lick in, before I swung a leg and moved to their side, collapsing on the bed like a dying man.

They pouted. Then rolled over and just smiled at me, resting their cheek on their forearm. "Such language."

"Doesn't sound natural comin' out of me," I agreed in a mumble.

"It doesn't," they agreed, "but I like that I make you do it."

"You've always enjoyed flustering me," I said, eyes slipping closed for a moment.

"You're even more handsome when you're mad." They moved closer to me, so that my nose was full of their scent again. I opened my eyes to find them drawn in close and lazily extended an arm, which they were quick to nestle into the crook of. "Or passionate. I guess I should try to evoke your better passions now, not just rile you up."

"Oh-ho, and then they admitted it," I grumbled. "Outright."

"Is this how you are after you cum?" they teased. "Growly? Because I have to tell you, it's not a deterrent. I like growly-voiced Isidor. You don't scare me anymore, you know."

"I'm sorry I ever did," I said quietly and leaned in to kiss them. It was brief, but it made them smile all the same. When I leaned back, I looked them in the eyes and said, "I love you."

They got over their surprise faster this time. They seemed less self-conscious, too. I daresay, charmed. "A-are you just going to say that all the time, now?" they asked.

"Probably," I answered. "I am prone to brazen and unprompted confessions, and it is forefront in what I feel needs confessing, right now."

"That is a lot of words to say you have no inner monologue," they said with a light laugh.

"I can conceal what I feel," I said, glancing aside. "To Dolus, to Malachi. I think when I feel safe with a person—then—there is no keeping it in."

A pall fell over their features suddenly. It was so swift, and so dark, it sent a bolt of fear through me. I leaned up partially, wrapping my *other* arm around them. "What just happened?" I asked immediately.

"You need to know who I am," they said, their voice bleeding off to a whisper. "You deserve to know... what... I am. Before you commit yourself so fully to me."

"I know who you are," I promised them. "And I am already committed to you."

"I am not even a *person* as far as most would see it, Isidor," they said softly. "I'm a... commodity. Stolen, smuggled, taken here for resale. To be a... a curiosity, an exotic object kept for show. For entertainment."

I was silent. They seemed to want to speak, so I saved my rebuttals for when they were finished. I hoped I had not miscalculated, there.

"I am not even a citizen, because my service contract here was never entered into or released legally," they said, their features gone tense, jaw set rigidly for a moment. "I'm a ghost. That's why the Ministry could never find me. That's why Cillian could never marry me legally… not that his family would have allowed him. Not that he would have… wanted to."

"If you were bought or sold for service here, that is *illegal*," I reminded them, when a natural pause came in the conversation. "And if you've no legal status here, that might make expunging your record easier, honestly. It could be a way to start over."

"I wasn't sold for service," they said with a dry, humorless laugh. "I was *adopted*. I was sold to the Rathbornes as a companion… for Cillian. A sibling."

"Oh," I said, trying to conceal the horror from my tone.

"Sister or brother, depending on the year," they said, rolling slowly onto their back and staring at the ceiling. "We stopped calling one another our sibling when we began… what we began. It felt so very wrong. And it isn't as though I would have ever been recognized. I was just the poor, orphaned foreigner that the Rathbornes had taken in, in their infinite charity. A companion for their only surviving son." They closed their eyes. "A servant, in all but name. A pretty, exotic doll. And if he saw fit to play with me as he pleased…."

A chill crawled its way up my spine. "Darcy," I said hesitantly.

"Don't be disgusted with him," they said, barely above a whisper. "Don't blame him. We were barely seven years old when we met. He was so reticent, more afraid of me than I was him, he could hardly speak to me without stuttering. And I could barely speak his language. We just knew we were meant to keep one another company, to eat with one another and listen to music together, to have our lessons together. Sometimes they would show me how, and I would push him on his chair through the garden outside. It took us *so* long before we could even have a conversation. It wasn't his fault. It wasn't my fault. Neither of us understood what the adults wanted from us. We just found our own way through it. And that became… what it became. No one told us not to."

They turned their head, a tear gathering in the corner of one eye. "I was six years old when the flooding took our land. Barely more than that when my sisters and I lost our parents. God, I don't even remember their faces. I don't remember how we were separated. I can't even recall if they died. I just remember... it was me and the twins, and they were *so* small. We were all so hungry, and we had somehow found our way to a place with a lot of other children, where they said they'd feed us. And they did. They were foreign, but they were kind, and they let us bathe and fed us well for what seemed like months. They taught us how to talk to them and made it clear we needed to get better at it if we wanted to stay. We didn't even need to work. It seemed good. They told us they were our saviors and earnestly, it seemed that way.

"And then, one by one, people came and took us. They said we'd live so well where we were going. Better than any house we had ever seen. And they were telling the truth, Isidor... at least for me." They dragged in a wet breath. "But they didn't tell me my new family didn't want all of us."

I curled my arms tighter around them. I hardly knew what else to do.

"I don't know where my sisters went," they said, their body shaking with a few heaving breaths. "They could be in Mataa, Carvecia, some other foreign land. I thought perhaps if they were here, I might find them in another manor, some day. But I never have. So maybe that means they aren't here. Maybe they've already left? It frightened *me*, crossing the sea, coming here to a place with people I couldn't understand, and no one who looked like me. The Rathbornes hardly looked at me, except to tell me to take care of their son. The servants resented me because I was not expected to work as they did. The tutors hardly knew what to make of me until I learned to speak the language better. Cillian... Cillian was the *only* one I had who tried to understand me. We didn't have a *choice*. It was just us. We were all we had."

"But for all of that," they continued mournfully. "For all of that, I know I was lucky. This place, these people who fostered us… they only kept girls. I had to lie to stay with my sisters. And they never checked, I-I think… they were religious," they said carefully, glancing up at me.

"It sounds like a Mission," I said softly, willing to admit what felt obvious. "But I cannot be entirely sure. Many prefer to take only female orphans. It's considered less risky to import women."

"The Rathbornes thought they were… 'adopting'… a girl," they said bitterly. "I don't like to consider what other reasons a family of means might have for adopting young girls. But I am not naïve. I may have been more fortunate than my sisters."

"It sounds as though they *were* adopting you for illicit reasons," I pressed. "I am also not naïve in all ways, Darcy. There is a practice amongst Pedigree of purchasing a young maid's contract expressly for the purpose of… being a temporary companion for their sons before marriage. The Ministry has to ferry such women off, all the time."

Darcy gave a rough laugh. "You think I don't know that? The underground I trade in is littered with the bitter, unwanted women your Pedigree cast off. But it wasn't like that with us. At least… not at first. That may have been what his family assumed. They certainly did nothing to discourage what was growing between us. Not even after years of me assuming the role of his 'brother' sometimes, when his attention turned to Dressage or shooting. Cillian's never been able to enjoy the activities most men his age take part in, but he loved watching *me*… sponsoring me. And few remembered who I was or cared. Cillian and I didn't go out into society much." They sniffed. "We just stayed in that manor reading books together, once we discovered our mutual love for them. Or going walking, once he could walk. Spending months on end together at the Lodge. When he began to realize I was able to do the things he wasn't, he supported me, cheered me on, was my patron. In whatever I wanted to pursue. We couldn't go to dances together, or court one another formally, but God, Isidor," they looked up at me, eyes wet, "can you blame me for thinking we were meant to be together? I loved him. He said he loved me."

"I think he still does," I said, even though my gut fought the words. I shook my head. "But I love my sister too, Darcy. That doesn't mean we should have been married. There are... Lord, this is so awful. How did your guardians allow this?"

"They intended to be done with me once Cillian was wed," they said, as though it were obvious. "Cast aside like a childhood toy. They knew what was happening between us—it would have been impossible to ignore. We were..." they were silent a moment, the humiliation clear on their face.

I pressed my nose down into the crown of fur atop their head, whispering a quiet, "It's alright."

"We spent all of our time together once we'd gotten past that first year," they said, trembling. "Cillian had hardly been verbal before then. That's part of why the Physician had recommended he spend time around other children. The Rathbornes didn't care to take him anywhere. They were terrified he'd catch a cold and die, or they were ashamed of their crippled son. I don't know. Likely both. They thought a living doll would suffice, and I suppose... I did. But we were one another's entire *world*, and no one but our tutors and the servants watched over us. We were almost always alone in that big, cold house. I used to crawl into his bed at night, a-and..." they gestured helplessly with their free arm at nothing. "No one told us... not to. We weren't ready, we were too young, but no one told us what we were doing. It just happened."

I stroked their back slowly. My mind was full of an endless barrage of questions I wanted to ask, Darcy, Cillian, but mostly those who no longer lived. And I'm certain the same thoughts tormented the both of them to this day.

"I was not ready to feel the way that kind of relationship made me feel," Darcy said. "As we grew older, I only became more and more certain we were meant for one another. When it became clear there was no place for me in the life his family had planned for him, I... thought we would steal away together. Cillian even told me we would."

I gritted my teeth. There was the anger for the Pedigree, again. It was tangled, complex, but hard to entirely talk down.

They bit at their knuckles with one long fang. "He declared his wishes to his family, and they didn't just turn us down. They turned the Ministry on us. His mother threatened to end her life if he disgraced the family. The pressure he must have been under, I-I..." they set their jaw. "But I was deluded. I still expected he would. I made the arrangements, I waited for him... and he sent me a letter. Saying he'd wed already, and that he still loved me, but that neither of us could find our happiness with one another. Wishing me farewell. And with it a *fortune* in coin that could have lasted me several lifetimes."

They craned their neck back, pressing their nose into my throat. "He thinks I used that money to drink myself nearly to death over the ensuing months. He's only half right. I threw the whole bloody lot of it in the river. I didn't need his coin to drink myself to death."

My fingers tensed where they were resting on the back of their head. "But, you did... try..." I breathed out. "He wasn't lying when he warned me of that."

Darcy's eyes fell to my chest. "No," they said quietly, "he wasn't lying. I saw no reason to go on. I was known by no one, valued by no one, and the only family I'd ever known hadn't merely cast me out, they had tried to *dispose* of me. I sent him a letter," they chuckled wryly. "I didn't realize he would come to find me so quickly. What a state I was in... God, he was so angry with me. It's *hard* to do yourself in with drink, as it turns out. I didn't have the nerve to use a pistol."

They were silent a long time. I could tell that they were working up the nerve to look at me again. To say something to me. But at length when they did, they did not look me in the eyes.

"So. That is the worst of it." They hunched their shoulders in, turning their face further from mine. "How... does it make you feel? About me?"

"Honestly," I breathed out through my nose, "terrified."

They didn't seem to quite know how to take that. "Not," they stammered, "revolted?"

"You've suffered as only the saints and martyrs have suffered," I said, reaching down to tip their chin up to face me. "And you are equally blameless. I am only frightened because I'm worried I'll be forced apart from you, and I do not want to be your only lifeline. You need to find reason to live aside from love for another, Darcy."

Their muzzle trembled. "Devoting myself to someone else is all I know how to do. Even the thieving, I... I just thought if I could return something lost, someone somewhere who was missing it... wouldn't *feel* this way. And maybe... I'd... find my sisters...."

"I understand how it feels to live in devotion without remembering God asks us to live for ourselves, as well. That is the gift He gave us with these lives." I nuzzled them. "There *is* a balance to be found... I'm told. I'm still seeking it, myself. We can find it together."

Darcy sucked in a short, sobbing breath. "Alright," they agreed. "Please stay with me, Isidor. Whatever comes, I just don't want to be alone, anymore."

"I'm not going anywhere," I promised them. "I swear it. And I do not make oaths lightly."

I leaned our heads together and held them. Neither of us

were able to sleep for some time. We just lay there together in the quiet. It was not the way I had imagined my first night in bed with another would end, but it felt right in a way I couldn't define.

I prayed silently. For both of us. For my family. For our future.

10

BURIED BONDS OF YOUTH

I was accustomed to rising in the morning to the tolling of bells, so when I awoke that day in that warm, but unfamiliar place to the rapping hammer of a fist on wood, I thought I could hear church bells, soft as distant birdsong. But it was just a memory ingrained, wasn't it? I tried listening a little longer, and heard nothing. Echoes of a dream.

Only my nose and the top of my muzzle and ears were exposed to the cold in the drafty cabin, the rest of me bundled beneath a stack of two old quilts and my cloak, and wrapped around the slumbering lump of warm feline curled into every crease of my body. I clenched them a bit tighter for a moment, assuring myself when they stirred and an ear twitched somewhere against my chest that they were, in fact, still breathing steadily and were truly *there* at all. This scenario was too similar to so many of my dreams for me to take it on face that it was real.

I was *far* too warm where I was to risk the frigid world outside for anything other than the most pressing reason, and even a twitch of my muscles confirmed the aches I would feel when I inevitably had to move. It was therefore easy to convince myself I'd imagined the knocking fist, like I had the tolling of bells. I began to close my eyes again.

Another rap, and my body leapt from the confines of its coverings, my fur bristling on end in a long prickle down the whole of my neck and spine. Darcy made a soft, panicked noise in my arms and dizzily blinked their eyes open, facing a similar moment of confusion, before some clarity snapped into focus there, and they roved their hands over my chest, clinging at me with their claws.

"What'is—are we—" they began.

I kept one arm in front of them while shoving them first to the side, then behind me, sliding off the bed on one knee while my free hand pulled my blade from the sheath hung over the bedpost.

"Oh, shit," the feline said, not fighting me on being bodily blocked, but clearly scrambling for something of their own beneath the pillow. They, of course, didn't find it, whatever it had been.

"Can't see out the windows, they're iced over," I said to them, glancing briefly at the tiny, frosted window in the small bedroom of the two-room cabin we were in. There was a door into this room that led into the main area and no door out this way. One way in, one way out. The knocking was coming from the main door. We wouldn't be able to see whomever it was, but they were blocking our way out if we had to run.

"I'm not armed," Darcy whispered, frustrated. "Your Order took everything on my person."

"Isi!" a distant voice called from behind the two walls that separated us, and I *instantly* felt relieved.

"That's Nicholas," I said with a soft sigh, relaxing my grip on Darcy and slowly leaning over to re-sheathe my sword.

"Alright, well I hope y'decent because we're comin' in. It's bloody cold out here," the voice continued, before there was an un-wedging sound of wood groaning and a creak as the door gave way, followed by multiple sets of footsteps.

"Someone you trust?" Darcy whispered, their head pressing out from underneath the arm I'd been using to 'protect' them, ears craning forward, body still hunkered in bed. Clearly still on-edge. Understandably so.

"My Brother in the Ministry," I said, before amending, "or, well... he *was* my Brother in the Ministry. Now, I suppose, he is simply my brother. You met him under less than favorable circumstances at the Hudson Estate."

"The fool who spied on us fondling one another?" Darcy asked.

I flattened my ears "I-I wouldn't... say it... tha—but yes. Yes. Him. He left the Order with me. I trust him. You can trust him."

"Uh-huh," Darcy still looked concerned. They blinked owlishly up at me. "Do you trust him to see you thusly compromised? Because we are both nude, Isidor, and I don't think that door has a handle, let alone a lock through it—"

"Oh," I jumped, "oh, no-!"

I heard the shuffling sounds of at least two other sets of paws and the deep, aged voice of the Physician amongst them, and I sprang for the door, making it to it just in time to push it back against whoever was attempting to enter. A surprised woof of sound and the distinctive rustle of rosary beads when he bent over to stare through the open hole the doorknob had left behind confirmed it was, in fact, my brother at the fore.

Panicking, I clapped my paw over the hole in the door, barking out at him, "For decency's sake, Brother! A moment!"

A pause. Lengthier than I would have liked. And then my brother's cheeky reply of, "Forgive me, Isi. Here I was, worried one or both'f you would be at death's door. Didn'think I'd be *interruptin'* anything."

"I take it then that the patient is well and on the mend?" Another voice, most definitely the Physician.

Darcy spoke from behind me, while pulling a pair of stockings up from a large bag that seemed to have been left at the foot of the bed. I didn't recognize it, and the clothes were clean, so it must have been left by Cillian or the Physician earlier. "I am as well as can be expected, Ruun. Are you ever going to stop taking care of us? The Rathbornes stopped paying your wages long ago."

"One should not expect to be compensated for providing care to their children when they are in need," the fox replied from somewhere in the main room, around the same time the door to the outside was pulled shut again.

"Where's Isi?" another voice, young, feminine. My heart did a flip-flop between relief and then increasing panic when I glanced down and took in my state.

The pressure eased off the door, and Nick's voice drifted towards her, assuring, "Brother's fine, just… getting ready for the day. Come on and let's get the fire started, warm this place up."

"Where is the Heart Thief?" her voice, again. "I wanted to meet them. Did they go already?"

"… sister?" Darcy guessed, while sidling up beside me, hopping a little to pull up their trousers. I was hit with a wave of affection for some reason, being privy to seeing the feline dress. I wasn't even certain why, it was just a facet of life I'd never thought I would share with another—someone not my own kin —until I was married. I suppose over the years, I had spent many mornings with my Brothers preparing for the day. And it was important to me. Comforting. It harkened to a time in my life when my future had felt more certain. Not an easy time, but… everything was structured, then. I knew what to expect. There was a comfort in that.

Being unmoored from the abuses also meant not knowing my trajectory from here on out, though. And I hadn't been raised to make my own choices. It would not come easily.

"Yes," I said softly, before backing away from the door and going to retrieve my own smallclothes. "Her name is Mabel. She very much wants to meet you."

I didn't miss the bolt of nervous energy that showed in the twitching of their whiskers when I said that. "That's right, you have family. I… am not at my best right now, Isidor. I may make a bad impression upon them."

"Even if that is so, we'll have time to get it right," I assured them with a hand on their bare shoulder and a soft squeeze.

"I don't care what they say you've done. I trust my brother!" Mabel's voice called loud enough to be heard clearly through the door. "And it doesn't matter how well put-together you are right now, I'm excited to meet you, and I'm muddy from the road, too! Isidor says you're very pretty, and I'm certain I'll agree. He never lies."

Darcy froze, clearly understanding they'd been heard, and I gave them a rueful smile. "Ahhh… we Abbey canines… very nosy. Don't ever assume you can have a conversation in private unless you're several rooms apart."

"I should have known," Darcy murmured.

"Can we come in yet?" Mabel, again. I could hear her bouncing back and forth on the balls of her feet.

I grumbled a soft curse under my breath, tugging my shirt on over my head as swiftly as I was able and, of course, catching the collar on my rosary. Darcy—who was at that moment quickly tucking the hem of their blouse into their trousers—reached up to help me with a lopsided, fond smile.

"… why does it matter if they're tidied up? He's my brother," I could hear Mabel arguing quietly and petulantly with Nicholas.

"They need to *dress*, at the very least," Nick explained quietly. "Come on, help me with the fire. They'll be out in no time."

"Brother is *dressing* in the same room with someone he's courting? *Our* brother?"

328

They were whispering, but now I was beginning to understand how they'd heard Darcy so easily. The door was little barrier, least of all with a *hole* in it. I was hot in my ears by the time I had my belt tied, and Darcy was giving me the most impish of smiles.

"I think you're in trouble," they sing-songed.

"I think you're the *source* of my troubles, so let us reserve our wit for dealing with my family," I muttered, before drawing in a great heave of a breath and finally opening the door. I made sure to check Darcy's state before I did, but they had made themselves decent far before I'd managed to, even claw-combing back some of the fur on their head and tucking what looked to be a spotless new pistol into a loop on their hip holster. Courtesy of Cillian, now I was certain. The leather saddle bag on the floor still looked full, too. God knew what else he had left for us.

Mabel thumped into my chest almost as soon as the door swung open, clinging her arm around me and clutching tight into my undershirt, her bright eyes and jubilant smile immediately warming me. "Stupid! I was worried about you for good reason."

"Wh-now where is *that* coming from?" I huffed, looping an arm around her.

"Mister Mandrake said you collapsed from exhaustion!" she said, pulling back to put her hand on her hip. "We were scared the whole night, not knowing if you'd be hurt, o-or... or worse. And then we couldn't come see you until the two foreign men told us where you were, and they didn't want us coming out until we met Mister Mandrake so we could go together—"

"Better to keep it to as few trips out here as possible," Nick explained from behind her, standing near the dim fire place and moving old, smoking coals around with the poker. "The snowcat in particular seems to know how to travel without leaving much trace, he's been... *literally* covering our tracks.

Had to move slow, didn't want to risk being followed. I 'eard whistles out there, they're looking." He blew out a puff of breath into the air. "You let this cabin get *cold*, Brother...."

"We were supposed to meet another person too, but he was late," Mabel continued. "The foreign men went to go get him. So, we waited *all* morning there at the halfway point, and they assured us you were safely hidden away, but...."

Her words fell off when I stepped out of the threshold, and Darcy silently followed, emerging into the room and moving their gaze between the two people there they did not know. Since the beginning of the time I'd known them, I would certainly describe Darcy as poised. Composed. Collected. But I knew them well enough by now to detect their nervous twitches, the tightness in their jaw, the way they were standing on their toes, as though ready to spring.

When my own eyes returned to my siblings, it wasn't hard to tell why. Nick was still wearing the primary garments of an Abbey Brother. Not his Templar red and white—that would stand out too much. But both were dressed in the loose, modest robes indicative of members of the Faith. It was so ubiquitous to me, I might have missed what sort of impression that gave to someone outside the circles we'd grown up in. They wore their holy symbols proudly, as well... Nick's wrapped around his wrist, Mabel's prominently hung over her chest.

Mabel—brave, bright star that she was—was the first to break the silence after Darcy's appearance. And she did so in her usual, bold fashion.

"You are just as beautiful as my brother said!" she proclaimed. "And, it cannot merely be skin deep, because he has *no* eye for beauty or style. It seems he has no use for such frivolities."

"Mabel," I admonished.

"She speaks the truth," Nick muttered with a sidelong glance and shy smile in the direction of the serval.

"I cannot wait to learn what sort of angel you must be to have warmed his heart so," Mabel continued on, stepping past me towards Darcy, who looked upon the young girl with an expression that even I found hard to read. Perhaps bemused. "My brother is… changed. For the better. It's my understanding, you…" she stopped in front of the feline and for the first time, some hesitance crept into her tone. "… you had something to do with that, at least. I-I don't mean to say he wasn't always brave, and he's certainly always been a good man. Maybe the best man I've ever known. He and Father, I'd be hard pressed to choose."

I reached over to smooth her fur down between her ears fondly. "No need for all the fluffery," I assured her softly.

"My point is…" Mabel cleared her throat quietly, then looked back from me to Darcy, continuing, "he has told us a bit about you, but I'd like to see what he has clearly already seen in you that affected such a transformation in him. It's very…" her voice became thready for just a moment, her eyes darting to the ground, "… very hard, leaving the place that swept us up from the suffering we each once knew. When you are unfortunate enough to sit on the darkest bottom rung of life, the future the Church promised us seemed so bright in comparison. *I* was too afraid to leave that bosom. On my own."

Nick joined us and lost his glib smile. He came to stand beside me and his sister, and the three of us seemed to instinctively bow our heads for but a moment as his hand touched mine and mine touched Mabel's.

"She is right," I said. "I don't know I would have had the nerve, let alone the reasoning, to break the chain on my own." I looked to Darcy. "You *did* help me see my Faith unclouded. You helped all of us."

"This merry chase you've taken him on and the bond you've clearly formed with my brother…" Mabel was in good humor when she said as much, but her expression soon fell to one more serious, "…may have freed us all. To be honest, I've been considering what I'd say to you every night throughout our whole journey here, if Isi was able to save you, and I think that's the main point." She paused. "Oh. And thank you. Please take good care of my brother. He's a good man, but he can be very stupid. And he is *not* good at taking care of himself."

Darcy's eyes moved over the three of us slowly. Eventually, they said with a breathless laugh, "I wasn't prepared for all of that. You may need to give me a moment, miss Mabel." The serval plucked at the edge of one of their sleeves, calm on the surface save the small tic. But I could feel their self-consciousness and beneath that perhaps, their doubt.

Mabel could not have known how acutely Darcy already felt responsible for the unraveling of my life, and even I could only guess that the knowledge weighed heavily on an already-overburdened fight for self-worth. I'd felt similarly at points in time, of course—everyone did—but Darcy fought a battle most of us didn't. An inner crisis of feeling the imposter, a substitute. They had said as much to me, and unfortunately their life experience had reinforced that terrible lie.

Mabel had meant her words kindly, and I'm certain Darcy knew that. My sister saw, rightly, that my relationship with them had been one of the key forces pushing me to break from the Ministry. The fact that she'd gleaned that in so little time spoke to a deeper wisdom than someone her age should have had. But, I'd always suspected that. The young girl had lived a lifetime already before I'd even come to know her. She had suffered as Saint Belle had suffered, and she knew the nature of man. I'd long known that she understood the world and the breadth of others' feelings far more profoundly than I did.

But she was wrong on one point. We were not free yet. I would not say as much to my siblings; they did not need the doubts I struggled with. But I'm certain Darcy was thinking them as well. And of the many, many dangers that we now faced because of what we'd done.

Darcy's countenance was not easily shaken, though. I'd seen that when I'd put a blade to their chest, and they'd held my gaze and spoken truths I hadn't wanted to hear directly to my face. So, it wasn't long before they spoke again.

"I can hear your love for Isidor in every word, even those that are... less than kind to him," their muzzle turned up cheekily. "I would like to come to know one another better, as well. Not *only* so that I might unearth some fond memories and unbecoming tales you might be able to tell me about your brother—"

"Hey," I grumbled.

"—but because I suspect each of you is an integral part of one another's stories. Which are now folding into my own story," Darcy continued. "And I do *love* stories."

"I know you're no pilferer of holy relics," Mabel said, stepping forward, now a little more excited, "but you are a thief, aren't you? A master thief, if the gazettes are to be believed. Would you tell me about some of your capers?"

"Oh, you've read about me, have you?" The feline fluffed the fur up around their neck a bit, taking my sister's hand and lifting it to their muzzle politely—an exchanging of scents. It was decorum usually reserved for Pedigree society, but my sister clearly found it charming, her tail swishing at her frock.

"I've never met a real outlaw before," Mabel grinned. "Are you like the Hound Hood? Do you dispense your purloined goods to the poor?"

"I return them to the people or places they once belonged to," Darcy explained patiently. "Or rather, I do when I can. I... may have given away some of my stolen riches over the years to those I felt were more deserving, their origin aside. It depends."

"We didn't meet under the best circumstances last time," Nicholas cleared his throat, bowing slightly. "I'm, ah... I just wanted to apologize first and foremost for... that. Isi needs looking after sometimes, I was worried about him, but I regret intruding on y—ehm. I just. Uh. I'm sorry how that transpired."

"That's right, you've already met them!" Mabel declared, offended-sounding. "You've never *really* told me how that happened."

"Our brother's bad at sneaking about when he's besotted," Nick said uncomfortably.

"What does *that* mean?" Mabel asked curiously, then to me, "Isi, why were you sneaking around?"

"That's between us adults," I told her, giving Nick a severe look.

"Not for long if you're going to keep being careless." Nicholas guffawed. "Bloody hell, I'll ask again. Who are you, and what have you done with my brother?"

"If it's all the same, I need to look the patient over," the Physician said pointedly from the one lone table near the hearth, his bag already open. "Darcy, dear, if you'd mind sitting and letting me examine your lacerations?"

"You're hurt?" Mabel tried to offer an arm to the serval, who merely smiled at her and patted her hand. "At least let me help you to the chair?"

"I'm fine to walk," Darcy chuckled, "but I won't resist the company, if you'd like to join me."

I took my cue to give the Physician the space he might need to tend to the feline. He'd already have Mabel hovering nearby, and I didn't want to add my bulk to the mix. Noting the mostly-dead embers in the hearth, I nodded to my brother and went for the door, calling back, "Just getting some firewood," before opening the door and stepping out into the bleak daylight, my brother following in my wake.

It was misting slushy snow onto what proved to be an already muddy, wet, cold landscape. It had gotten warmer, just enough to melt some of the fresh downy snowfall from the week prior, but still frigid enough to freeze in the night and nip at your paw-pads when you stepped out into it. The sky was roiling and gray, the sun a distant muffled circle of light, hardly penetrating the gloom. It was high enough that I knew it was still early in the day, but that was my only indication. It could have been dusk for how dark it was.

My mind was occupied considering what possible tale of thievery Darcy might be imparting on my sister and how distressingly excited the young girl had been at the concept, when I realized Nick had gone still behind me, his ears alerting for a moment.

"Did you hear bells?" he asked, confused.

"Lord, so it's *not* just me," I laughed, relieved. "Every dream, every imagining I've had recently, has been so vivid I've begun to doubt myself. Yes, I heard them too, or at least I thought I had, when I first woke this morning. I passed them off as a memory."

"Huhh," he shook his head, "not hearing them anymore. Far off, I think, probably carried by the winds. I didn't know there was a Church this far from Redcoven."

"The path the mercenaries took to bring us here was intentionally circuitous," I grunted, stepping over a snow-covered stump on our path out back to the mostly-collapsed stable and woodshed. "We may not be as far from the city as we think we are, earnestly. I'm not certain. And I suspect that's the point—oh, good. Some already cut... not dry, but maybe if we dig...."

I bent over and began pulling aside the sodden and decaying wood on the outside of the pile, cut at some point long ago into quarters. If I could find any underneath....

"I'm happy you were able to get h—uh—them, away from the Ministry," Nick said. He bent over to begin helping me with the pile. "Are you, I mean, you seem unharmed. Did you have to fight—"

"Yes," I said. The dane's face fell when I confirmed the

unasked question. "The mercenaries tried not to mortally wound anyone, though. I think we managed."

"Do you think you'd be able to... do it... if you had to? Really hurt one of our Brothers?" he asked, mustering his expression to a neutral one, but I could tell how much the possibility disquieted him.

"I don't know," I replied—I thought—honestly. I paused with my hands buried deep in-between the logs on the stack, before slowly pulling free one mostly-dry piece, and then another.

"No," I said after a few moments. "That's not true. I—I believe I already did. I hurt one of our Brothers. Grievously."

"Oh," he said, looking uncertainly at me.

"I violated his trust," I explained softly. "I feel terribly. I regret hurting him as I did. But it would be a lie to deny I would do so again. I believe I would."

"I'm sorry," he said, clearly not understanding, but putting a hand on my shoulder all the same. "We can pray for him later, if you'd like?"

"I have already," I said, looking to him, "but I'd like it if you'd join me. Yes."

He began to smile, but a moment later the two of us nearly fell back on our rears in surprise, when there came a rumbling, snapping shuffle, and the stack before us gave way.

We recovered after a moment from the surprise, the old firewood scattered in the mud and at our feet, and Nicholas began laughing nervously.

"We're a bit jumpy, eh?"

"Sorry, I—" I began gathering what pieces I could find. "I should have taken from the top, it just would have taken longer, it was all rotted up there."

"'It's always a bit more work to do things responsibly than quickly,'" Nicholas quoted our Father at me, and I rolled my eyes. "Shit, there it is again!" He said a moment later.

"Language," I corrected him like it was second-nature.

"Brother, we're heretics on the run from our own hunters," he grunted, standing, and brushing off his knees. "What does profanity really matter anymore?"

"At least save it for when it's warranted," I said, catching the vaguest hint of those distant bells when I listened for them, too. I stared up at the sun. "Is it noon? Odd time of day."

"Perhaps a funeral?" he guessed. "Wedding? I'm not sure."

"They'd ring them for the procession, once," I muttered. "Not off and on like this. Strange."

"So," his tone was odd when he spoke again, and when I turned with the bundle of firewood in my arms, his expression was equally-so.

"So?" I narrowed my eyes.

"Oh, come now, Brother," he glanced about, then leaned in. "You've crossed the *threshold*. Walked the path of heart's communion?"

I ground my teeth, then shouldered him as I turned to head back towards the cabin. "I am not interested in being a part of this conversation, Nicholas, wherever it's headed."

"You would deny your younger brother your wisdom?" he called at my back, before jogging after me.

"It is precisely because you are my brother that I will not," I affirmed, growling. "I can't believe you'd even press me on this."

"Are you going to marry them?" he asked, far too slyly for my liking. "Or live your lives in sin?"

I nearly dropped the firewood and had some kind of poorly-thought out rant about the young man's immaturity and the impropriety of his rapid-fire questioning, but a different sound—far more immediately concerning than the odd, distant bell-tolling—alerted the both of us at once. Even Nick, for all his foolishness, dropped his good humor and went still, ears up, eyes on the wood line.

Hoofbeats. Not many, but more than one. Hurried.

"Get inside," I told him, dropping the wood and pulling my blade from its sheath.

"What would be the point?" he said, looking briefly at me. "We haven't enough horses for everyone; it's not as though we could make a running retreat. I can't hole up in there with them for long enough to matter."

He pulled his own long knife, as well, and stood at my side. "No, Brother," he said, his voice shaking, but his stance certain. "If we must fight here, we fight together."

The door to the cabin swung open suddenly, and Darcy came striding out, their large ears pert and twisting immediately in the direction of the approaching hoofbeats. They took a moment, then declared in a calm, level voice, "Three horses."

"The mercenaries left us here to go back to the meeting point to collect Master Rathborne," Nicholas said. "He was late when we were meant to meet with him there this morning, and they did not wish to wait for him long in the woods. Three horses, could be them? Perhaps no reason to worry after all."

"Why would they be rushing so?" Darcy said, checking the powder on their pistol as they murmured the question. It wasn't really a question. We all suspected the answer.

"Isidor!" my sister called out to me from the half-open door. She had been so happy just moments ago. It broke my heart to hear her once again afraid.

"Close the door, Ruun," Darcy said, turning their body to the side and extending a hand slowly towards the horizon, leveling the pistol at the hill near the edge of the woods.

I kept my eyes on the source of the sound as well, even as the door closed behind us. It would be but a few moments, now....

The horses broke into the clearing around the small cabin, and my emotions rolled through a tumult. Relief first, because the snow leopard was hard to mistake, and that confirmed it was who we had hoped it would be. But then... confusion, and mounting worry, when I noticed that one of the horses accompanying them had no rider.

They slowed their approach only enough to avoid skidding on the ice and snow as their mud-caked steeds came huffing and stomping into a slow circle in the little yard we were standing in. The beasts looked frothy and tired, suggesting they'd had a hard run, but what immediately concerned me far more was the black, wavy-maned mare that was following Ravus by a lead. He circled us a few times, and I got a good long look at that horse.

She was fully saddled and ready to ride with no signs of injury, but enough burrs and mud coating her, and ice gathered in her mane and tail, that it was clear she'd been out in the wood through at least part of the storm. Potentially overnight.

And she looked expensive. Nothing like our modest riding horses.

"Lord Rathborne is several hours late, and we couldn't afford to linger at the halfway point any longer," Ravus said, breathing heavily in steamy pants out into the cold air. He also had a lot of ice in his fur. "But, on our way back we… we found her. Reins tangled… not half a mile off the deer trail. Don't know how long she was wandering."

Darcy brushed past me towards the horse, shakily reaching a hand out for the animal's bridle. "Is she his…?" they asked around a bodily shiver that I felt in my bones, and it had little to do with the cold.

"Yes," Ravus answered gravely. He gathered his own reins, releasing the lead for Cillian's horse. "We need to move. Now. If they have him, that means they got *close*. They must have caught him when he left here at some point, on his way back to Redcoven last night. This place is tucked away, but they'll find it eventually."

"We're not going to leave him in their hands," I insisted, stepping up close to Darcy. "We'll find out where—"

"With all due respect," Sig interrupted me, "he's a Lord. He's safer than any of us. There is only so much they can do to him. We are *not* safe out here, and he hired us to get you all to a port, not to continuously raid Ministry strongholds."

"He's right," I tried to assure Darcy. "Cillian himself told me many times that he was essentially untouchable. But still, I...."

"Isidor," Nick's voice broke through the din. There was an urgency to it, a *terror* I could not account for. He looked like he'd seen a ghost.

I looked into his eyes, and he stammered a moment, before staring off into the middle distance. And I heard it, then. Clearer. Perhaps the winds were fighting it less.

The bells.

Nicholas swallowed. "Listen to the rhythm, Isi. Do you hear it? Please tell me I'm not insane."

I tried to do so, squinting into the dim sunlight and trying to focus in on the sound. If it was a melody, it was a simple one. One large bell, two smaller, sharper. A pause. A repeat, and then faster, the toll of the larger again.

"It's... a Ministry Call to Arms," I said, eyes widening slowly.

Darcy turned to me, expression haunted. "Like the way they whistled in the woods when they were hunting me?"

"They used bell tolls during the war," Nicholas said, "to recall all able-bodied men to a House of God under attack. Carries farther than birdcalls or whistles." He swallowed thickly. "Someone is calling their Brothers to arms."

"What?" I breathed out. I remembered vaguely learning about this, but it was hardly ever used in the modern age.

"Father used to make me memorize the ancient chimes, when I was learning how to work the bells," he explained. "I always liked ringing the bells. They were so loud." He shrugged weakly. "I know you never liked them."

"They would startle me when I was studying," I said, lost for a moment. "But why would someone be calling the hunters that way? I can't think of many Templar now who'd know the ancient calls or even recognize that's what they're hearing."

"You recognized it," Darcy pointed out.

"Our Father is a Scholar," I explained. "He taught us many of the ancient ways to keep the memory of them alive. Strange things most Abbeys have let slip to time. Cuneiform. Old hymns. Archaic wisdom."

"Maybe it's not for the hunters," Nick said, nose still turned up to the wind. "Maybe it's… for you. Someone who knows you."

"Could it be the other Priest you're expecting to help you, then?" Ravus asked.

I shook my head slowly. "Father would not have made it this soon. And Dolus has no use for ancient wisdom. He has been very clear about that with our Father."

Another of the series of tolls rung out, clear as day. Nick turned his ears and eyes towards the sound.

I followed his gaze.

"*Someone* wants us to find them," he said, frightened.

"No reason we should risk it," Sig said fiercely.

I felt that clenching in my heart, the presence of the Almighty, confirming the warning. But I also knew….

… I just knew….

"They're luring us because they have Cillian," I realized, closing my eyes.

The cabin became a place of chaos. Nick was in hysterics, Mabel had gone that special kind of quiet I had only seen in the past inspired by Brother Dolus, and Darcy had disappeared into the back bedroom, tearing through the rucksack Cillian had left us. I found myself in the company of Physician Mandrake, who did not seem to understand the situation, but had grasped the gravity of it.

"What makes you so certain these Templar—whomever they are—have young Cillian?" the fox asked calmly, while aiding me in affixing my gambeson. When I'd left Ebon Gables, I'd brought along my heaviest, a suit I'd sewn myself to my own tastes, mixed with quilted padding throughout and chain I'd linked into the chest, back, and arms. It would do next to nothing against a crossbow bolt, but might disperse the damage from a glancing pistol shot or short blade. Along with my arming glove, it was all the protection I had.

I had trained for much of my life to be a warrior of God, but I was woefully unprepared to face His followers. Despite being trained by other Templar, I was not outfitted nor mentally prepared to face my own. I'd thought I'd be bringing criminals and sinners to justice.

I was the quarry, now. Not the hunter.

"I cannot say for certain they've captured him," I answered the fox, "but he is missing, and the timing is coincidental. Using ancient tolls seems targeted, as well. Hardly guaranteed, but they must be desperate to find us. Besides..." I swallowed, "I just... know it in my heart."

"Ah," the fox sounded briefly uncomfortable, "so, guidance from above, then?"

"You are not a Believer," I said, while strapping my arming glove down, flicking my eyes up to his as I finished. "Are you?"

He shook his head. "I do not need to pretend to be any more, and I would rather be honest with you. I have seen no evidence in my lifetime that supports your mythology as truth, and I have educated myself thoroughly on its doctrinal teaching and origins, enough to have grave doubts as to its benefit to the world. I do not begrudge *you* your Faith, though. Part of being a man of science is accepting there is much in the world and beyond that I do not know, and likely never will. There is always room for understanding, if not tacit acceptance."

"That is a lot of words to say you do not believe in or honor God," I muttered, trying not to sound argumentative.

"I do not dishonor your god either," he gave a wry smile. "It would be pointless to insult or dishonor a being you do not believe exists at all."

"God sees and stewards you, regardless," I assured him, "but to be clear—I do not hear His voice. I am not claiming to be a Prophet. I am guided in all ways by the Almighty, at least insofar as I am able to feel His guiding hand, but this is more earthly." I stared down, withdrawing my backsword slowly, feeling the slide of the steel, effortless. A well-maintained blade and oiled sheath could mean the difference.

"There is no better explanation," I settled on, quietly. "A large part of what I did as an investigator was just... following my gut. Sniffing out leads, weighing the most obvious decisions people would make, and assuming the outcomes so that I could put together a story. You don't always land on the truth that way, but you can usually get close."

I stared out the window, still frosted over. "These are my kin," I said stonily. "They would have formed the same picture of Darcy I did in the early days. And it isn't a stretch to assume, given their constant appearances in one another's lives, that Darcy is close with Cillian. If I were hunting them, and I knew they were near, but couldn't find them, this is how I'd draw them out."

"You're walking directly into their trap, then," Ruun said sadly. "Bringing their prey to them."

"I am ashamed to admit," I hesitated only a moment, "I would rather run. If the choice were mine. Based on everything I know and everything he himself told me, Cillian is safer in Ministry hands than any of us will be. He is a Pure-Bred Pedigree. They can't risk angering the Crown by abusing or seriously harming one of their favored sons, not until all the proper channels are followed and even the Court agrees he has fallen out of favor."

"Then why do this?" the fox insisted.

I stared across the room at the serval, who was setting down the rucksack on the small, rickety dinner table. Their movements were jerky and snappish, their body quivering in the spaces in between. A dread hung in their eyes, deep and unanswered.

"Because there is a chance I'm wrong," I said, barely above a whisper. "And if we leave now, Darcy will never know. We could escape, but they might spend their entire life wondering if they abandoned the person they…" I stared down, as I fumbled to tighten my sword belt, "… still… love… to the punishment meant for them."

"I could," the fox hesitated, "try. To find out where they've taken him. To help the boy. I could send word to you, wherever you land."

I shook my head immediately. "You can't go up against the Ministry, and you shouldn't have to. You haven't the resources, you aren't even a canine, so you won't have the same legal rights he does. They'd *destroy* you. I'm certain Cillian wouldn't want that, either." I brought my rosary to my muzzle a moment, closing my eyes, then tucked it beneath my vestments. I had chosen to wear them, both because it might prevent or at least cause my fellows to hesitate in shooting at me, and because I did still truly feel I was on a mission from God. If there was a rot at the center of the Ministry, as even my Father had begun to suspect… our cause was holy. It was my brethren who were misled. God help them, they knew not what they did.

"Besides," I said, again looking to Darcy. "There would be no stopping them going to Cillian's aid, just as I would never leave my own brother or sister to suffer in my stead. I won't stand in the way of that." I took the offered cloak from the fox's hands, the last of the armor at my disposal. It was warm, if nothing else.

Malachi's cloak. Would he be there? Would Dolus? How many of my brothers would we need to fight, to outwit, this time? How many would it take to be free of the Ministry, once and for all?

"Darcy is my beloved," I said, forcing a tight smile. "Where they go, I follow."

"I'm going with you," Nicholas interjected stubbornly. He'd been standing off to the side, giving me space to ready myself, since the last row we'd had, which hadn't been long ago. And on this same subject. But it was a small room, and he'd heard all of that, I was certain.

"You're going to take care of yourself, the Physician here, and Mabel," I told him again, firmly. "As Father demanded of us."

"Father told us *all* to stay together," he objected. "Why is it even after we've left the Order, you're the only one who gets to break the rules? The mercenaries will protect them—"

"The *mercenaries*," I said, raising my voice as I turned on him and crossed the space between us with one footstep, "are not Templar, brother. They do not understand how the Ministry hunts, how you will be pursued if you are forced to flee without us. They would not have known what those bells meant," I said pointedly, and now I was speaking loudly enough that all eyes on the room were on me.

Nick stared back at me, defiantly. Angrily. "Even I did not know, it was *you*," I put a claw in his chest, feeling the thumping of his heart beneath my finger pad. "It was you," I repeated, softening my tone, "who had that revelation. I need you to protect our sister, protect the poor fellow here who's gotten caught up in this out of a desire to heal the children he raised—"

Nicholas opened his mouth to cut me off, and I bulled on, "Protect," I said, moving even closer to him, "the *truth*."

I could see him set his jaw, grind his teeth, even through his black fur. He stared down at me—he was taller than me now. His irises shook with anger, but they were wet. Red-rimmed. He was shivering with rage. The young man was fully-grown and made of corded, lean muscle, a soldier honed by the Ministry, like myself.

But he was a child, I had to remind myself. He was still... so... young. And whatever awaited Darcy and me, I *had* to spare him.

"Father entrusted me with protecting the two of you," I said, reaching forward and cupping both of my hands on either side of his cheeks. "I am following his orders... his plea to me. If he were here, you *know* he would demand the same of you. Please, however hard it is, give me the respect in this moment you would afford him."

I tugged his head forward, resting our foreheads against one another. "Trust me," I begged him. "This is what is best."

He kept his eyes on mine, locked, despite the twitches in his muzzle, the fear I could feel and *smell* buzzing just beneath his skin. It was hard to consider it, but it was possible my brother was committing this moment to memory. There was a very solid chance we'd never see one another again.

Darcy was the one to ultimately interrupt the moment, calling me over to the table. "Isidor," they said calmly, "come here. This must be for you."

Since the moment that riderless horse had come over the hill, the feline had said very little. But the few times they had, their voice had taken on that neutral tone I couldn't read, which disquieted me more than I cared to admit. It had taken me a very long time to scale those walls, and I'd only just begun to think I could see inside over the fortifications. I was worried for what they must be feeling now, but there wasn't any time to untangle it all and absolutely no chance of comforting them until Cillian was safe. Later, I told myself.

I stepped over to the table. It seemed like some great drift of snow had shaken loose above, the room blanketed in a cold, suffocating silence. All eyes were on the table and the leatherbound case there. It must have comprised half of the available space in the bag Cillian had left, and for good reason.

It was a crossbow. The lath was larger than those I'd trained on, but not by much, and collapsible. I'd worked with a collapsible bow before, but the mechanism was expensive, required more metal bracing along the stock, and given the pull strength necessary and the obvious value of a piece like this, I expected—and yes, there it was. An equally refined crank-cocking mechanism.

"God-damn, that's a fine piece of work," Nick swore from behind me. I didn't bother correcting him on his blasphemy, this time. "Look at the lath. Lethal, if you can cock it."

"That's what the crank is for," I said as I took the weapon up, and trigger-released the bow from its collapsed state. I stared down the sight.

"Lot of metal," Nick said, "looks heavy."

"It is," I agreed. "This wasn't designed for fieldwork. It was designed for defense."

"Defense of a bloody *castle*, maybe," he muttered. "That's a beast, Isi. Did Father send that for you?"

"He would never approve of a weapon like this," I shook my head. "This is new, I can smell the clean oil on it, but it's based on a model they used to send with the Navy to the Dark Continent." I set the weapon down on the table, looking to the carefully-wrapped bundle of bowstring, and the heavy, barbed bolts stowed in the case.

"It's a Dragonslayer," Ruun said, for some reason sadly. "They used them during the colonial conflict to slay the people there."

"Cillian didn't know what he was purchasing, he probably

just wanted to arm me with a weapon he knew Templar are familiar with," I said.

"Can you use it?" Darcy asked me directly, their gaze intense and demanding.

"Yes," I said with certainty, already unrolling the thick bowstring. "Even without the mechanism, I could still probably rope crank it if I had to. But this will make for faster reloading."

"Maybe he *did* know what he was purchasing," Darcy said, staring down at the weapon. "You said these were used to kill the Dragons?"

"They call themselves 'Cathazra,'" Ruun informed them. "They are a whole people, the 'dragons' are only one species."

"They are famously hard to kill," Darcy said, "because of their natural armor. I read about them once. He expected we'd be fighting our way through Templar. Armed and armored."

"He was right," I said gravely, as I tested the crank.

"I hate this," my brother said quietly.

"Lord Cillian is why we were all able to find our way to one another and free dear Darcy," Mabel spoke up for the first time since the day had turned dark. She visibly mustered herself for a moment, her eyes closing, then snapping open and fixing on mine. "You saved them and came back to us. This will be no different."

I smiled at her and instinctively stepped up to her to scoop her up, but she put her hand out, stopping me... then stepped into an embrace, instead.

"I'm not a little girl anymore, Isi," she said against my chest.

"I-I know," I said. "I'm sorry." I stroked her ears, holding her.

"That doesn't mean I don't need you, still," she said, her voice slightly muffled against my surcoat.

"I know," I said.

· · ·

The bells were not hard to follow. And they did not cease. They rung ten or so minutes apart, each time repeating the call to arms, five times. Whoever was ringing them was persistent, I would give them that. They were either certain this call would be answered or desperate enough to try.

We did not even ask the mercenaries to come with us, this time. This was beyond what they'd been hired for, and I was not about to ask the two men to accompany us to what we all fully knew and accepted was a trap. There was always the slim chance it would be Father Helstrom… but every time the bells tolled, and my heart pitched into the bleak abyss of fear, I knew that would not be so. Our Father was still too far from here, he would have found some way to send word before arriving, and the man was a bloodhound. If he had wanted to find us, I had no doubt… he could have.

And it didn't explain Cillian missing, or his riderless horse.

We eventually found confirmation of what we feared, far before we made it to whatever church or abbey was ringing the bells. We'd followed first the path the mercenaries had told us to take, and then the deer trail Cillian must have taken the night he'd left the cabin to return to Redcoven. It wasn't long before we found horse tracks.

But they weren't his. These, though partially covered by the wind whipping the snow, seemed to criss-cross through the forest, heading in the vague direction northeast, toward Redcoven. Someone had been out here in the woods, searching. On horseback, and if the weathering of the tracks was any indication, at night. They eventually broke from casual spacing into an out-and-out gallop, and it wasn't far from there that we found where the fight had taken place.

This area cut too close to the main road, within sight of distant farmhouses and fields, so it made sense the mercenaries had not found it. They'd stuck deeper into the woods, their objective was to protect my family and hide their flight, after all. Cillian's horse must have found her way to them.

The battle looked to have been a quick scuffle and little more. There was no scent of gunpowder, nor blood, and both would be strong enough that they would have withstood the elements. Horses had pawed up the earth, and amidst them were the distinctive four-clawed, deeply dug-in prints from canines. Heavy, at least two... it was hard to tell if there were more. I was not an expert tracker.

But it seemed to be only two horses that had met in this wood. Two men who'd come to blows. And it was then that we were in no further doubt of whom one of them, at least, had been.

Cillian's sword cane lay unsheathed and nearly covered in a snowdrift. It was a rare break in the clouds, a dash of sun that glinted off its mirror-like surface that alerted us. I leapt off my horse and bolted to it, reaching amidst the drift for the handle, and lifted it slowly into the light, wet snow clinging along the blade for only a moment. It was clean. Not a hint it had tasted flesh, but he'd clearly tried.

We'd been silent as the grave from the time we'd found the clearing, but it was at that point that Darcy gave... a noise. Barely audible, like a whimper, fearful in its confirmation of what we'd by now known.

I found the sheath of the cane discarded nearby and solemnly slid the two together before stowing it on my saddlebag. I mounted up and surveyed the horse tracks. It was not hard at that point to make out which was headed in the right direction, and which had likely been Cillian's horse, making its way to eventually find the mercenaries. Cillian's pursuer, whomever they were, had headed in the very direction the bells were tolling from.

"One horse," I said, the words steaming puffs in the air. "For now."

Darcy swallowed visibly and nodded, then spurred their horse on ahead of me, following the obvious trail.

There was no discussion while we rode over what we'd do. There was no reason to plan. If we were walking into an ambush, we had already sentenced ourselves to the fate that awaited us. We could remain vigilant, we could seek a better means of approach once we had more information… but the fact was, right now we knew very little. And there wasn't time to study our opponents. The bells were more than an invitation; they were a threat. As startling as it was every time they began again, louder, and closer, it wasn't hearing the call to arms that frightened me. It was the thought that they would stop.

It had been less than a day since Cillian had left, but it had still been *nearly* a day. I couldn't know when the bells had begun to toll, but the people ringing them would give up in time. And then they would leave, taking him deeper into the Ministry's grasp. Just as we'd only had a chance at freeing Darcy when they'd been moving them, before they'd arrived at a larger city, so would it be with him. And even if it would be politically damaging to try and execute a pure-bred Pedigree, they could hurt him within the acceptable standard. They could question him. They could learn a great deal from him and use it to target us and the people I loved.

What little chance we had to prevent all of that was right now. This was it.

We were getting very, very close when Darcy said what I'd been thinking the last mile. "Still only one horse," they said, staring up through the tree-line. We'd been seeing the distant steeple for at least half a mile. Partially obscured by all the gray, low clouds.

"I don't know this church," I admitted, slowing my horse now that we were drawing close. "And I studied Redcoven's maps while we were waiting to hear from Cillian, so I should. It isn't on any of the public road maps. Must be incredibly old. But it has a working belltower?" I lifted a paw over my eyes to take in the distant, stone edifice. "Why?" I asked myself aloud, softly.

The tolling stopped, and the fur on the back of my neck prickled against the inside of my cloak. I felt it the same time Darcy did.

"Someone has seen us," they said between their teeth, spurring their horse on. "Come on! It's *one* hunter!"

"There could be dozens of men waiting to the east side of the church," I called after them. "Just because there's only one set of tracks in this direction doesn't mean—"

They weren't listening to me anymore. I cursed and kicked Blackbow into a gallop as well, following the serval on their mad rush through the thinning forest. We were traveling uphill, which explained why we'd been able to see the steeple from so far off. Everything about this—this place, the situation, the single rider, felt off in a way I couldn't define. The single man could have been a lone hunter who'd gotten lucky, and this was the meeting point to reconnoiter with the rest of his unit. But if that was the case, why stay here afterwards? They should have moved the prisoner—and maybe they had. Maybe Cillian was no longer here at all, and this wasn't just a trap, but a trap with no *bait*. Which made what we were doing *abominably* stupid.

If it were Dolus, one of the few people who knew me well enough to lure me with ancient bell tolls, he'd have scores of hunters with him. He wouldn't sit back and wait for me to come to him on a lark; he'd send his men out and *find* me. Hardly difficult with that many men. The cabin was only four or so miles from here.

And why here?

The church itself came into view as I caught up to Darcy and made enough ground to circle Blackbow around them, cutting them off. The serval may have had a better seat than I, but I was no slouch, and Blackbow was a *fast* trail horse, better in the snow than theirs.

"Stop! Acting! The fool!" I snapped sharply, but quietly, at them.

"We've already been seen, what's the use?" the feline snarled. "Guns blazing, I say. If we're likely to die here anyway, I want to at least catch them by surprise."

"If they've seen us, we won't be catching them by surprise," I pointed out. "Try. *Try* to calm down, love. I am *begging* you."

"Isidor, I can smell death on the wind," they said, dragging a soft wheeze through their nose. "They are *hurting* him!"

"We don't know that. We don't even know he is still here," I said, staring once more at the ancient, decaying building across the clearing and taking it in fully. It was in fact an old, fortified, pre-war church. The small windows on the upper levels and barred, broken windows on the ground floor, as well as the uneven, natural-stone foundation that wrapped around the entranceway and nave, attested to that. Oddly, it looked like the tower was newer construction, and in fact wooden supports still clung to parts of it, and I could see portions that would have been the gallery through some of the broken windows, if it had ever been completed. The building was open to the elements and very clearly abandoned, despite whatever efforts had been made to renew it at some point. Part of the wooden construction from the gallery had either rotted or burnt away and fallen into the choir.

But the tower stood. And the bells clearly worked. Bells were generally not installed until close to the end of reconstruction, so the whole of whatever had happened here smelled rank with poor planning.

And something else.

I had thought they were manifesting their fears, but whether they'd initially been imagining it or not, Darcy's nose had caught something mine hadn't yet. Blood. Finally, blood. Whatever fight had happened in the woods had been bloodless, but here... here it was. There was little wind either, so it was close. And old enough to have begun to turn.

We dismounted and left our horses at the wood-line. I pulled my crossbow off my back and loaded a bolt, the bow long since strung. Darcy flashed their fangs and pulled their pistol from their hip, sidling in at my left. The both of us scanned the grounds as we approached, stepping softly. It may have served no purpose. We were in the open, and there was no way to avoid that. All the land surrounding this church was clear. We were walking through the tipping, weathered stones of an ancient graveyard. The dead stalks of overgrown grasses and the clutching husks of flowered weeds clung at our spats and feet, reaching up beyond the snow. In the spring, this place must have been beautiful. Reclaimed slowly by nature, but not by man. Man had failed to retake this place.

The door to the nave had been left open, propped by a fallen piece of stone from the parapets above. Closer to the building, the sinking, eroding foundation of this place was more obvious. The whole building was tipping, slowly, the wood collapsing where it strained.

This was a twisted reflection of the church I'd been imagining so long in my dreams, and I feared what that meant. It was too big, too much of a fortress, being given back to nature violently rather than beautifully. Tacked on with new artifice, abandoned in anger and frustration, if the multiple singed places and broken bottles that littered the grounds were any indication. People had known of this place and defiled it. Not a single pane of stained glass remained unbroken to illuminate whatever image they'd once held, the jagged multicolored remnants like fangs breaking up a kaleidoscope of chaotic color. Snow had blown inside so thickly, it had wedged one of the doors shut.

We slipped in through the one door that was left open, and that's when the smell hit us fully. It wasn't just blood, it was *far* too much blood. Thick enough in the air to make you gag, and I did. Coppery enough that you could feel it on your tongue, and with it a twinge of something earthier and *wrong*, like spoiled cabbage.

My eyes traveled the drifting snow inside the massive, empty space, devoid of pews or any remaining furniture, save the candelabras and shelves, the one remaining staircase into the gallery, the choir walkways, and….

… the stone altar.

To my everlasting dismay, Darcy saw it before I did, and the sound that tore from their throat will forever be emblazoned in my memory. A cry of anguish, broken by a choking sob of anger, and then the serval was bolting across the room faster than I could follow. Down the tattered, peeling remains of the red-carpeted aisle, towards the crumpled figure lain out at rest like a King of old.

I followed, but caught movement on the steps, and stopped in my tracks to train my crossbow on the towering figure thumping heavily down those creaking, unstable boards. If he were worried, he did not show it. Nor did our arrival seem to have hurried him.

Malachi drew back the hood from his cloak, drifts of snow falling to his shoulders as he did, revealing a tapestry of painfully-swollen and lacerated, broken flesh across his eyes and muzzle. It was hard to think he'd done it to himself. It looked like someone had worked him over without mercy.

I knew the handiwork. I'd spent days treating Nick's wounds and seen their ilk on so many young boys that had come and gone from the Abbey before us. The monk's signature.

I kept my crossbow trained and barked up at him, trying to keep my voice as steady as I could and failing. "That's far enough! Do not force my hand, Brother!"

Darcy had made it to the blood-soaked altar and was mumbling incessantly and desperately, their voice cracking in between their pleas. "Cillia—my Lord, please—I-I'm here. Isi, Isi I-I need... God please, he's bled so much...."

I didn't need the feline to tell me as much. The blood had stained the altar and the ground around it so thoroughly it was hard to imagine it had all come from one man. There was a second spattered pool nearby, a place of impact, the crimson dragged to the altar a few feet away where he'd bled out. I had only ever seen something like it once before when I'd witnessed a surgery to remove a baby from a doomed would-be mother. Neither mother nor child had survived.

I didn't want to take my eyes off the malamute, but I'd finally recognized the scent in the air to be that of the humors from inside a skull. When I chanced the briefest of glances at Cillian, his face clutched protectively in Darcy's paws, darkening with bad blood... he seemed to stare back at me. Lifelessly.

"Are you mad?" I asked Malachi in a voice nearly choked by my closing throat. "What have you *done?*"

The older canine's eyes were hollow and dark. He said nothing at first, only took the last few steps down to the choir, fearlessly approaching my drawn bow. At length, finally, he simply said, "I didn't mean to kill him. The blueblood had more loyalty than I anticipated. He would not lead me to you, and... that is all I asked of him. He fought me, it... I did not intend for this. He just," he stammered a moment, "would not *yield.*"

A scream that was also a shrill roar echoed through the space from behind the both of us, and Darcy raised their pistol, the shot sounding like thunder inside the empty, cold building.

I flinched, moving my finger off the trigger so as not to misfire, and at first I thought the shot had missed. Darcy was over twenty feet at least away from the man, and I was partially obstructing their shot. But Malachi had stumbled back, and there was no longer just the stench of bad, old blood in the room.

The canine stared slowly down at where the shot had

glanced off his shoulder, close to his heart, but off by a few inches. His cloak was burnt and peppered, and blood swelled slowly from the spot, but the man was still standing.

Tensing his jaw, he pushed his cloak back from his shoulder, revealing the layered chain gambeson he wore beneath. Like my own.

"Where are the others?" I demanded, my bow still trained on him. The armor may have protected him—at least partially— from a pistol shot, but it would do nothing to stop my bolt from sinking home, and we both knew it.

"No one," he said, his voice a rasp. "I brought no one else. I am here alone."

"Why?!" I asked, my voice breaking. I wasn't even certain what question I was asking him, any more. There were so many.

He stared down at the altar, eyes lost in something. A memory, perhaps. I dared not imagine.

"I had to find you before they did. I had to," he mouthed at nothing a moment, unspoken words, perhaps. Then he reached into a pouch at his side and tossed it at me.

It fell at my side, but I did not stoop to pick it up.

"Mullein," he explained weakly. "I did not betray you, Brother Isidor. I did not tell him… it was you."

I stared at him, mouth agape. *He hadn't told the Ministry what happened?* He was out here, alone. Truly.

"Then why do this?!" I cried. "Why are you here?! Why did you come after me, if not to turn me in?!"

He gave a slow, miserable smile.

"To save you, Brother," he whispered.

11

THE SIN OF DESPAIR

"You killed a First Son, Malachi," I said through my teeth, swallowing back my gorge as the rank air of the choir-turned charnel house permeated my nostrils. I could see more of the blood now, spattered on the bare, tiered benches so familiar to those I'd grown up singing hymns on. A few moldering leaves of a hymn book—somehow left here and lost to sun-bleaching and mildew—lay scattered on the ground, striped and dotted with the remnants of a vicious assault. Frayed, knotted rope was corded around a broken banister, the wood mealy and rotten inside. It told a story that was depressingly easy to follow, of a prisoner beaten and tortured, bound to a railing that eventually gave way. The altar lay not far below, one stone corner of the raised dais it sat upon inky with blood.

He'd kept him here hostage to find us. Tortured him. God knew for how long. Until one of the blows, or the struggle itself, had led to this. It's possible he'd kept him alive for most of the time he'd had him, or that he'd unleashed his rage from the very start. I prayed for Cillian's sake that he'd died as swiftly as possible. Malachi and the Pedigree had hated one another from

358

the moment they'd met. I'd long worried they'd come to blows, I'd seen the hunger in Malachi to have some chance—any reason—to lay hands on him. The man was a powder keg of barely-repressed rage, quick to devastating violence, and his training and size made him especially lethal. The Ministry had only kept him on, I was certain, *because* of how useful a weapon he was. They'd done nothing to curtail his worst impulses, save further abusing him when he stepped out of line. And now, at last, he had done something they could not sweep under the rug. This had sealed more than just Cillian's fate.

And I was certain he knew that.

The eerie calmness that fell over the malamute terrified me. It seemed a twisted serenity, not unlike a monk nearing the end of his lengthy fast. Whatever peace the man had found in this terrible place, on this terrible day, it was nihilistic, not joyous. I'm not certain which would have been worse.

"The Ministry will never forgive you for this," I said barely above a whisper. "They'll bring you before a tribunal, *hang* you, Malachi. God help you. God help all of us...."

"The Ministry?" he blinked almost drowsily. "Brother. They have *never* forgiven me. My recompense has no *end*. I will carry it through into the next life, and the next. This, they have always made clear."

"If you know that, then why continue to serve them?" I asked desperately. "Why kill for them, why mete out pain for them, let alone abuse yourself on their behalf? This is an institution of *man*, Brother. A mortal edifice. We are servants of God, first and foremost..." I looked despairingly upon the dead man he'd so carefully lain out on the altar, "...and no faithful followers of Him would want this for His own sons."

He tilted his head back, staring slowly heavenward through the bright gray cracks in the roof above. If he was frightened of the crossbow I still held on him, he did not show it.

He did not have his own, or at least nowhere on his person.

Only a blade on his hip. If I remembered correctly, he'd been repairing his bow. He hadn't even bothered reassembling it before coming looking for me. Hunting me.

"God does not forgive me either, Isidor," he said. "He torments. He punishes. He does not forgive."

"Whoever told you that was speaking Heresy!" I said passionately. "God forgives all trespasses as long as we have the heart to seek salvation. There is *no* soul so far fallen that he cannot find His grace if he recognizes his sin and wrongdoing. I *know* you, Malachi. You have a grateful spirit and a willingness to look inward and own your mistakes—I implore of you, open your eyes to the sins of our superiors, of this *corrupt* institution that has hurt us so, has bent us towards these evil acts! Be as willing to condemn them as you are yourself!"

"I did this of my own accord," he snapped, his eyes sharpening on mine. "Once I realized what you'd done, once *they* realized we'd lost our quarry, I knew I had to act. Swiftly."

"What did you tell them?" I whispered the question hoarsely.

"I told them what they would believe," he said with the barest softening of his gaze. "That I had failed. That I had once again brought shame upon the Ministry. I know you are as fallen as I, Brother. I know what you suffer. I know what you *would* suffer if they found you first. You don't...."

His eyes were empty, hollow, and dark as a knothole in a dead tree. "... you don't know," he said after a soft swallow, "what they will do to you, how they will take you apart, for this. I said nothing of what transpired save that I had fallen short in my duties. I should be locked down, now. Awaiting an Inquisitor. But I came for you. Against orders, in defiance of my Seniors... because I knew I could find you before they did. I knew...."

His gaze went glassy, his voice dropping off from its intensity. A weakness permeated, and for just a moment he sounded like he had when he'd found me again after the Lodge.

A man, a brother-in-arms, showing me his vulnerability as clear as exposing his throat to me.

"I knew you because I know myself," he said, stepping slowly towards me, down another step. He was feet from me now, reaching one wrapped hand out, blood caked through the cloth around his knuckles. "I *was* you, once. I see what I could have been, were I not awakened to the hopeless existence of a life like the one you are chasing."

"I *have* hope," I said, shaking but resolved. "It is thin in moments like this, yes, but how is what they've made of you any better, Malachi? You've given up on *God* because of what they did to you in that place! You've given up believing in His mercy!"

"I've accepted the truth, Brother," he said wearily. "I resisted it, too, for so long. Rationalized, fought back, cloaked myself in denial and ran from it, ran from it, *ran from it* !" He bellowed the last reiteration of the words through a fanged snarl. "I tried to spare you that fight, tried to teach you who and *what* you are, so you did not need to prolong your suffering as I did, and you spat that kindness back in my face!"

"I've done wrong by you," I choked on the words, swallowing heavily. "I will not claim otherwise. I'm so bloody sorry, so ashamed of myself, Malachi. Every moment is burnt in my mind like a brand, I can never undo the harm I've done you—"

"Isidor!" a voice rung down from the altar, echoing off the desiccated walls. A sidelong glance confirmed two things quickly—that it was Darcy, that they had reloaded their pistol and were now pointing it at us. "Get out of the way," they ordered through tears, trying to aim through me at the malamute.

"Darcy, no," I pleaded. "We've lost one life today, already. He's hurting, he's their victim too—"

The serval didn't respond with words, only began stepping

sideways, posture rigid and teeth bared, as they moved across the space to find a clear line of fire.

I did not blame them. How could I? But I couldn't stand by and let another soul perish in this house of God, let alone one so lost. I had spent so much of the past year in anguish and confusion over what was right, both in my own life and trying to decide for those around me—and only now, suddenly, did it occur to me how folly that struggle had been.

It had never been for me to say. I was not *meant* to pass judgment on the lives of others, and the reason it had always felt so wrong is because *I had known that*. I had always known it.

Being a warrior for God did not need to mean that I be an instrument of His retribution, let alone the vessel of the Ministry's judgment and punishment. The only task God would ask of me in this painful confrontation was to do everything I could to prevent this hatred from boiling to another deadly culmination.

His guidance was, at last, as clear as a bell toll. I could not allow these two people—both of whom I cared for—to kill one another. That was it. That was everything.

I spoke down the line of my bolt, through the sights, at the malamute, begging him, "You have no choice any more, Malachi, you *must* break the chain or they will use it to hang you in the square, the same as us. You need to leave this place, now! Before Dolus learns of what you've done here, if he hasn't already. They will slaughter you upon a sacrificial altar to spare the Ministry the Crown's wrath—"

"Isidor, are you mad?!" Darcy's voice was high, hysterical with incredulity and rage. "He doesn't get to leave here alive!"

"He didn't kill Cillian intentionally, he fell—"

"I don't give a damn!" the feline shrieked, cocking their pistol. "I held his head in my hands, you haven't seen—he *mutilated* him!"

"You don't understand," I tried to keep my voice from faltering into a sob. "This is as much my fault as his, Dar. I-I—"

"Cillian called me that," they said icily, walking around the altar, close enough that they could rest a hand on the dead man's dark, blood-soaked ear. They shuddered when they spoke to me again, "*You* do not call me that."

Every part of my body stung, their words a lash. Had I lost them? Is that what this would cost me?

"Did you ever love me at all, Isidor?" Malachi chose that moment to ask me in a numb tone, his question echoing in the stillness of the air.

The betrayal in Darcy's eyes had begun from the moment I'd stopped them from putting a bullet in my Brother's head, but now I could feel it *acutely* boring into me. I hadn't the time to explain or defend myself, however strong the impulse. That wasn't what mattered now.

I breathed out in a long shudder, looking to Malachi. "I love you *now*, Brother," I insisted vehemently. "I deceived you most cruelly. I led you to believe something you wanted to believe… that part wasn't true… but I *do* love you as a Brother. You believed me when no one else would. You bolstered me. You were kind to me, smart, fearless, willing to *teach* me, not just discipline or reprimand. You are what a Brother *should* be, what a man should be, and you are *so* much more deserving of love than they've told you…."

"If you truly loved me or respected me, you would have been honest with me," he said, sadness in every word.

I bent my head for a moment, a tear running down into my nostril, pain welling in my gums from how hard I was clenching my teeth. "You're right," I said in a wheeze. "I'm sorry—I'm so sorry, Malachi. I was so… frightened of you in that moment. I-I tried to tell you. Considered, again and again, telling you. But every time I pushed you, it was like you buckled down even harder. The things you were saying… the rhetoric, I *know* it isn't you. But you recite it like scripture *so* emphatically. I was scared if I were honest with you then, you would have turned me over. I was terrified I would lose my chance to save *both* of our lives and *escape*. I was a coward. I did what I thought I had to. I violated your trust."

I coughed out a wet sob, asking when I'd gathered my voice enough to do so, "Was I wrong? Would you have come with us then... if I'd asked? Begged you? To join us in freedom?"

He was silent for far too long. An immediate denial would have soothed the way I felt. But when he did at last reply, there would be no satisfying my guilt. What he said was, "I don't know. No one has asked me to leave... since Eli. I don't know what I would have done."

"You didn't leave with Eli," I said desperately. I could barely see straight my eyes were so full of tears. The malamute was a blur, as he stood there staring at me, as cold as any man ever has. When he reached for his scabbard, he did so in no hurry.

"No, I did not," he confirmed. "Maybe you were right, then. To fear me."

"Isidor..." Darcy warned worriedly.

"Do you have the nerve to pay for your sins, Brother?" he asked me as the steel slid from its sheath. "As I have, all these long years? Or will you take my life?"

"My sins are between myself and God," I said. "I have asked you for forgiveness—you do not need to give it. But *nothing* that happened between us needs to be dealt with by the Ministry or end in bloodshed. People hurt one another sometimes, Malachi..." I swallowed, "... intentionally or because of circumstances beyond their control. You and I have both made mistakes. I won't kill you over *any* of those, and I will *not* let you kill me. Or Darcy. Or *anyone else*."

"I hold to my oaths," he said. The shadows inside the church were tipping slowly further into dim blue. An early night. "I promised you I would protect you, Isidor," he explained quietly.

"What *they* will do to you if they capture you, interrogate you… re-educate you… will exceed any brief pain you feel now. Please believe me. This is a mercy."

"You aren't well, Malachi," I said, trembling. "Please. Let me take you to someone who can help you."

His eyelids sunk until the dark blue were crescents in the dim light. "That," he sighed softly, "is what they told me at the camp."

When he moved next, it was faster than I'd ever imagined the large man capable of. I'd seen him on the hunt but once, and never when he had wielded his blade with killing intent. I had the blink of an eye to decide whether I would release the shot I had pointed at his throat or redirect, and as I had throughout so much of my chase with Darcy, I followed my gut reaction first, logic later.

I'd been leaning my weight on my back foot, readied at least to pivot step, and I did, just barely missing his first most obvious underhand arc. I fought one-handed and preferred underhand swings and overhand parries, so it was not hard to follow the line his body was likely to take. But he'd given that one away for free, taking his time positioning both hands on his blade. His form was obvious, and there was but one trajectory that grip could carry him into.

It gave me enough time to loose the bolt. I had to make this count, so I aimed for his knee. His gambeson was not long enough to cover it, and he had little protection other than his leathers there. A maiming shot. He might suffer for it all his life. But he'd live.

The bolt sunk nearly a quarter of its length into his thigh, just above my mark. It should still have been a debilitating shot, but to my horror, other than a grunt and a flash of suppressed pain across his wild features, he kept coming.

He followed the movement of his first swing, leaping the final step of the staircase he was on with an easy twist of his grip into a downward thrust. The man was wielding a longsword, hardly a weapon fine-tuned for impaling neatly in close quarters, but impale it would.

I backpedaled and—in a near panic—waved my arming glove into the weak of his blade, forcing the tip aside with a brief clatter of metal against metal.

The canine gave a pained growl and for a moment I wasn't even sure how I'd hurt him, until I realized he'd landed at least partially on his injured leg. The bolt was still protruding from it.

He reached down to pluck the metal shaft out, and I tried to warn him even as I pulled my own blade, but it was too late. The barbed tip tore his flesh as he pulled it out with a chilling roar, dropping the bolt wreathed in fur, meat, and blood with a clatter on the ground in front of us.

Darcy hadn't fired again, and I could easily guess why. The man was nearly on-top of me within moments. I managed to brace with my backsword just in time to parry his first pummeling swing, but the blow still twisted my wrist back with the impact, and I soon lost control, yielding my footing.

Dolus, of all people, had taught me this maneuver. Parry center, allow your opponent to overpower you—not hard, because he very easily was—fool their mind into believing they are being blocked by any normal combatant, and leave your right guard open. Most will forget—

I saw him move his body weight into a terribly fast, overhand swing down, and there it was. An opening at his midsection, his attention focused on my right as he leaned into the swing, forgetting—

I was left-handed.

I hit him at his core where he was most armored, but I was no slouch in a swing either, and even without cleaving flesh, I heard a rib crack.

The man was accustomed to pain—to a frankly astonishing degree I hadn't anticipated, *no* one should have been able to stand on a leg that injured—and I wasn't fighting to kill. He was. It didn't so much as stagger him. In fact, he didn't even stop the swing, and I'd have no luck deflecting such a sure strike with my arming glove, this time. I made a paltry attempt to shield my head, and the longsword connected with my wrist, the sheer force of the blow shattering something inside me that I felt as well as heard, before the edge slid down along my forearm to my elbow, slicing clean through the straps of my glove, leather, and cloth, and leaving a searing line through my flesh.

My arm fell limp at my side, I sucked in a breath of rotten, ice-cold air and unsteadily found my footing, pulling my blade up to eye level to guard against a follow-up attack. My vision briefly spun from the pain, and I tried not to look anywhere but my opponent, fighting through a wave of nausea.

I'd lost my guard. The man was simply too strong, too fast, and even the hits I'd scored were not slowing him down enough. I heard Darcy calling for me, I think.

Malachi stumbled for a moment on his bad leg, then drew his blade to the side, and readied to charge me again.

"You can still die clean, Brother," he promised me, as though that were a comfort. "They know nothing of what you've done. You can be consecrated and mourned, pass on into the next life…."

"Neither of us needs to die here," I said, trying not to follow the serval's silent movements behind him with my eyes. Give them the best possible chance. Either I'd gotten through to them, or they didn't want to risk shooting into combat, but either way, they'd turned their pistol in their hand to use the heavy metal grip as a sap. They'd be on him soon, and then we might stand a chance.

"And neither of us needs to die to cleanse ourselves," I pressed. "Our souls are not *tainted*, either because of who we are, or because they deem us so. Who determines our worthiness, Malachi? Man? The men who happen to be our elders in the Ministry? Who invested that power in them? That is God's sole right, and they have claimed it! Look at what they have done. Look at what they command their *children* to do." I swung my blade and my good arm in a wild arc, denoting the blood spilled between us, the dead young man on the altar, and all the world around us. "How could the love you have felt—the love I have felt—be more worthy of punishment than this?!"

His muzzle quivered, the tips of his fangs flashing. Something traveled across his eyes like a memory, a bolt of nostalgia for a bygone past I would now likely never be privy to. "I don't know," he confessed at length voice thick, "I have *never* understood. But it is what tarnished me. What broke me, forever. And it is why no one will mourn *my* passing. All that is left to me is to spare you the same."

"I would mourn you, Malachi," I promised the man softly. "Please spare me that pain, as well."

"If you see God," he said, advancing slowly, "ask Him why. What sins you and I committed to deserve this... *one* of us should learn the answer." He raised his sword. "You're good at finding the truth."

Darcy leapt up to clap an arm around his thick, maned neck, swinging the barrel of the pistol down with their main hand, and as they did, I charged in, dropping my blade to grapple the man with a gut check and my one good hand.

His jaw yawned open to howl into the frigid air, fangs flashing in the muted strips of light barely illuminating the dark chapel. I'd managed to lock my arm around his elbow joint, and he wasn't letting go of his sword yet, but he also couldn't use it well with me bearing down on his back and locking his legs together. I tried to bring him down with my weight alone, but he planted his legs—even his injured one—and stood his ground.

Darcy pistol-whipped him in the back of the head but failed to concuss or stun him on the first blow. I tightened my bicep around his arm, yanking it further down, and he finally released his sword with a clatter on the ground. I was confident then that it would only be a matter of time, that we'd bear him down soon, or one of Darcy's blows would knock the man out.

To my shock, the canine suddenly fell away from me, all at once. Backwards, pulling me partially down with him and intentionally flinging himself back a step or two into the altar. Darcy tried to scramble free in time but was as unprepared as I and was crushed between the malamute and the stone, collapsing off him with a dizzied, pained look on their face. Their head hadn't struck anything, but with the force he'd flung himself at, it was impossible they hadn't broken something.

I fell to my side on my hip, catching myself on my bad wrist and crying out, agonized. I struggled to right myself, but I was still dizzy, the pain coming in waves so intense now that I could hardly think through them. I lifted my gaze in time to see the malamute reaching over to scoop the pistol from Darcy's grip and standing like a tortured, blood-drenched saint from one of the paintings on the walls at Ebon Gables.

He lifted the pistol in my direction, staggering forward on his bad leg.

I stared down the barrel of my own death and tried in my final moments to make peace with it. I had done everything I could. Had I doomed all of us because I had not wanted to kill my wayward Brother? Would it have mattered?

Darcy had shot him. I had shot him. We had fought and lost, two-on-one, nonetheless.

Once again, I was forced to ask the same question of myself I had asked throughout this whole ordeal and been so certain I had found the answer to. So many times.

Had I done the right thing? Had I lived a good life? Had I done... all I could?

If Malachi was right, and I stood before God, I might finally have the ultimate answers. But if I was reborn, I would not remember them.

The curse and gift God had given us. We could only ever look to this life for answers.

I bowed my head, tasting blood in my teeth. And I prayed aloud. Not for God to hear me… that was not in doubt… but in hopes that Malachi would.

"Please do not end our love as they ended yours," I begged.

"What?" he whuffed out hoarsely.

"Eli," I said softly. "You said I reminded you of him. Was he… foolish like me?"

His breath shuddered. At length, he replied, "We both were. That's why he's gone."

"They took him and all of the love you may have shared together," I said, my tears falling dark on the stained stone floor, between my spread palms. "Your *future* with him. They stole that part of you away, and I'm certain they thought they were saving you, too."

I looked up slowly, relieved to find I wasn't the only one crying. The malamute wasn't even looking down at me anymore. He was staring again at the bits of sky he could see through the cracks in the roof, a hurt deeper than any lash could bestow in his eyes.

"Please, Malachi," I begged, "I've only just realized I'm in love. I've only just begun to understand how it feels and what life can be now that I know it. If any part of you remembers, please… *please* do not take that from us."

He continued to stare at the ceiling and the vague outline of the crescent moon, appearing in the sky, diffused by gray clouds.

Darcy was conscious, if barely, and had pulled themselves up to a sitting position, curled in on their ribs. They stared first at him, then to me, terrified. The gun was still held at the ready in Malachi's hand.

The malamute wouldn't look at me. His eyes were on the moon. But in time, he said, his voice a ghost of the deep timbre I knew it to be, "Isidor. Do you think it's all real?"

I swallowed. "I have faith in God. But our book... our Ministry... is authored and led by mortal men. I—I do not know. I do not know how much of it is real. I don't think we will ever truly know."

"I'm not certain which would be worse," he admitted quietly. "If... the men who raised me are right, then God... hates us, Isidor. He *hates* us, He hates me, and He has allowed all of this to happen. Despite possessing the power to stop it. To stop all of the pain. The needless... endless suffering. He could end it all. And He doesn't."

He finally tipped his muzzle back down towards mine, his eyes catching moonlight in the coming dark. "... but if it isn't real, then... I have done these monstrous things... I have lived a monstrous life... for nothing." He gave that broad smile of his, twisted, humorless, empty. "Either way, it has all been for nothing, hasn't it? Worthless. All of it."

I opened my mouth, no words coming at first. I finally insisted, "No. No, you... you helped me. You've helped others. You are worthy of life and love, Malachi. It's just that no one's told you that enough."

I extended a hand slowly towards him. He did not reach back for me.

"All this hurt, it's meant to be a sacrifice," he murmured. "Martyrdom. And here I'm... I've taken another life, again. It's all I seem capable of." His eyes widened for a moment as if in realization, and then just as quickly... dimmed.

"They'll have what's in my skull," he said, the words making no sense at first. "They'll find you."

"We'll run," I promised him breathlessly. "Don't worry about us."

"They'll hunt you to the ends of the earth," he said softly.

"You and I alike. God, I'm just so tired of being afraid. Tired of the pain... the isolation. I've driven every warmth in my life away, been forsaken by every soul who I once called Brother, crushed every surviving ember of light. All that answers my prayers is that cold, lonely silence."

He looked to me once more. "I'm just so tired, Isi."

He lifted the gun. I squeezed my eyes shut instinctively, but when it went off, it was his body that dropped to the ground.

12

IN DEFIANCE

I t could have been any other day in the Redcoven Square, outside of Saint Rhine's. The flags were hung high, bold crimson and gold against a pristine blue sky. The symbol of the Faith of the One True God flared proudly at the crest of the cathedral, people going about their lives on the streets below in the literal shadow of the tallest building in this country city. *Lono cara aulacriste,* 'to reach heavenward,' an elder monk once told me when I'd asked why our Churches were always so tall compared to every other structure. Saint Rhine's was no exception and stood out particularly in an otherwise modest, rural city like this. When I'd first come here to Redcoven, I'd been relieved to see it. I'd seen a bastion. Hope and home.

Now, gazing upon it, all I could think of was whether I was signing my own execution warrant in coming here.

One could be forgiven for not realizing there was a funeral here today. There were no signs of grieving, no mourners or march present in the streets, the flags were not hung at half-staff. If the Church desired in any way to honor their fallen son, they were not doing so openly. The only clergy I saw around the grounds at all were the *verminae decitus,* the rat monks who tended the grounds of the church in exchange for the right to worship in the cathedral hall with the canines. Several of them were finishing clearing the steps of ice and snow, suggesting they'd been the only ones here this morning when they'd brought in the body.

These rats were the only worshippers here who were dedicated enough, or the least afraid that the dead man's ceremony would stain their soul, to be here today. To literally clear the way for the funeral to proceed.

Their faith was stronger than so many others. Canines, the One True God's chosen people. The sons and daughters of Canus....

How were they less worthy than us?

The simple answer, I knew, and the knowing sunk into my chest like a blade, was that they weren't. They weren't less worthy. The scripture was wrong.

The book that sat like a lead weight, clasped tightly to my belt on my hip, was not the Word. It was *words* written by fallible men, and they had made mistakes interpreting the will of God. Biases, bigotry, and power had corrupted those words, and determining what was truth and what was concocted for their own ends would be nothing short of a lifelong agony to untangle.

I'd never have all the answers. It would be easy enough to give up. Discard the whole of it. Remake myself. But it was hard —impossible—to imagine my life without my faith.

I sat for a time in the small carriage I'd taken into town, staring out the yellowed, cloudy window. The other occupant of the box sat at my side, his tail twitching where it rested partially at our feet. The only sign of his nerves. The fox was composed, forcibly calm, and had been the whole ride. He was being so for my benefit, I was certain.

Physician Mandrake had shown incredible bravery throughout this whole ordeal. For a faithless man who did not believe he would be reborn, he possessed remarkable nerve. He was, I suppose, proof positive that a person—a well-read person who knew the Word but had nonetheless chosen to discard it—could live an atheistic existence and retain their empathy, their purpose, and their courage. Men like him were not supposed to exist, or so I'd been led to believe.

And right now, he was the only familiar face, the only 'family' I could bring with me on this terrible day. If my Father Helstrom's recent message was accurate, the Ministry still had not accounted for Nicholas and Mabel's absence. Father had made some variety of excuse for the both of them—that Nicholas was spending several months performing penal labor before he'd be returned for training, and that Mabel was being readied by her Godmother for her upcoming marriage. We had a small window before they were ever truly missed.

Darcy could not accompany me, for obvious reasons. And the mercenaries had to continue to escort the feline and my siblings to safety. Which left me to undertake this task alone.

Or so I'd thought.

"You should be on your way to Amurfolk," I said sympathetically to the fox without turning my head. "Mourning your patient... your son."

"I am long since disavowed by the Rathborne family," the fox confessed quietly. "They suspected—correctly so—that I aided and abetted Darcy's flight and concealment from the prying eyes of the first Inquisition into the family, and that made a lot of trouble for them. His mother never forgave me. She felt I had stoked her son's rebellious spirit and led him astray. She believed I would be the ruin of him."

His whiskers twitched once pensively. "Perhaps I was," he whispered. "Given what it has all led to."

I stared down at my bound and splinted hand for a moment. "I do not agree with that sentiment, to be clear," I said. "I think you led both to pursue their own truth, and that is what a good father *should* do. But, as you are an atheist, I must ask you," I looked back up at him and found his eyes on mine now, "how do you soothe your guilt without someone to confess to?"

He gave me an understanding look. "How do you confess your sins to your god, generally?"

"With help from another," I answered, even though I knew he must have known that. "A Priest."

"Exactly," he reached for my good hand. "I talk to someone. Someone..." I could sense that he was trying to find a way around saying something like 'real', for my benefit, "... someone I trust. Someone whose counsel has helped me in the past."

"I don't know who to confess to anymore," I admitted, abandoning all pretense that we were still talking about him. "I hope I'll see my Father soon, but that is not certain. Darcy has hardly spoken to me since..." I sucked in a short breath, pressing through the wall of fatigue that was always there—had been there since the church on the hill—but chose moments like this to truly suffocate me, "... and it is too much... it is too much to lay on Nicholas. He's so frightened. I need to be strong for my siblings, or at least appear that way."

I stared out the window again, the dread clawing at my heart. "Dolus suspects I was involved in Darcy's escape and what transpired afterwards."

"Did your Father say as much in one of his letters?" he guessed.

"No. He can only tell me what he knows from home. But I don't need insight from my Father to tell me that," I said with certainty. "The monk is cunning. He deduced what happened at the Lodge, and he *will* put the pieces together on what happened here in Redcoven soon, if he hasn't already."

"Then you should not risk this," he said seriously. He pulled up his cane, readying to tap the front of the carriage box to alert the driver. "Let's just go. You can step outside a moment if you like, or at the gate. If you're right and they're watching for you, they'll follow regardless."

"No," I shook my head, reaching across with my good hand to turn the handle on the carriage door, pushing it open into the chilly midday air. Amongst the sounds and smells of the city was one distinctive scent, etched into nearly every memory of my childhood. Inextricable from the complicated tapestry of my faith. Rosewood and myrrh with an undercurrent of citrus for potency.

The citrus was the only sign of what was being conducted inside. A uniquely-powerful mix for funerals. His body had been reclaimed nearly three days ago from the shrine we had left him in. Even with careful preservation and washing of the fur with water and oil, the scent of death would be on him. I wanted so badly to remember him as he'd been… but….

"I promised him," I said, my voice failing me, the words coming out weak and quiet as I stepped onto the cobblestones.

I shut the carriage door quickly behind me, before pulling back the hood of my cloak. I could feel eyes on me the moment I stepped out—or I was imagining it—but it hardly mattered, because they'd be on me soon enough. I didn't want them seeing the man I'd come here with. We'd intentionally hired a very small carriage, so it would appear I might be alone. While Ruun had been insistent upon accompanying me for this, there was no reason to personally implicate him.

I was not doing anything illegal by coming here, I had to remind myself yet again. The Ministry would know, Brother Dolus would know, that this was my last break with the Templar Order. A final link in the chain, cut. Of course they would. But I was not breaking any laws, strictly speaking. I strode across the square with that in mind.

I'd come dressed down and unarmed. The chance I was arrested or taken into custody, either by the Ministry or on some falsified charge we couldn't anticipate by the local constable, wasn't zero. Just my being here was suspicious. I was meant to be in Amurfolk by now. If I was arrested on suspicion alone, better they not take me in with the very weapons I'd used against the Order. I was walking into their waiting arms. If they decided to act against me, I would not be able to fight my way out, regardless.

I tugged my sleeve down again over my brace, flexing my fingers as well as I could inside one of the gloves I was wearing. I didn't wear gloves often—most canines didn't. But it was necessary to conceal the injury.

I walked unhurriedly across the street, and then up the steps to those two large wooden doors, all the while waiting for the hammer to drop. It never did.

I paused to set my paw on the full moon emblazoned between the two doors, bowing my head in prayer for but a moment.

God, give me the strength to stand unashamed amongst your followers and protect me from their wrath.

I pushed open the right door and entered.

Two rats greeted me with bowed heads. They were lighting the incense and wearing black robes instead of brown. Mourning clothing.

People he himself would have called lesser, strangers, tended his ceremony and mourned his death. Perhaps not the souls he had hoped would pray for him, but I was glad to know he'd been wrong. These men would have prayed for the soul of any person because they truly believed in the value of life. Even the life of a heretic, a murderer, a lost member of the flock.

Every pew was empty, save one. The bowed head sat at the very front of the room, nearest to the closed coffin. No eulogy nor last rites came from the empty pulpit, although as I began slowly walking the aisle, the reason for that became clear.

The only soul in attendance here was Father Whitehall. The

old retriever I'd met only briefly when I'd first arrived at Saint Rhine's.

Malachi's Father.

He likely would have been responsible for sending his own Son to his next life… but he could do so just as easily in silence for an audience of one.

Malachi's coffin was simple, a pauper's. If they had decided to do his service here, that meant he would at least be buried in consecrated earth. I had feared worse, but I suppose his fall from grace was another uncomfortable truth the Ministry would need to conceal for their own benefit. They would literally bury his misdeeds rather than follow their own traditions because that would force them to publicly admit them.

In this case I was glad for the hypocrisy.

I had expected the empty grief. The intermittent waves of guilt and frustration, pulling back then rolling forward again ever stronger as I walked down that aisle and smelled the incense and somewhere far beneath it, the scent of him. His fur, his presence. I'd known it would return here, perhaps stronger than it had even in those final few moments, when I'd opened my eyes in time to see the life leave his.

I had never seen someone's visage destroyed so utterly, let alone someone I'd known. Someone I'd come to care deeply for. It was horrifying in a primeval way that made you question what you were, what little you mattered. Was that all we were? A skull, flesh, blood, and teeth? Features I'd seen twist up in a smile and snarl at me in rage. Aquamarine eyes and the soft, short fur on his muzzle, as close to me as any person had ever been.

A person. Reduced to viscera before my eyes.

Defiance, finally, in the end. They would have nothing from his skull. He had denied them that last pound of flesh in the most terrible way he could have.

I let out a breath I hadn't realized I'd been holding, not fighting the stutter, the sob that came. I'd known... I'd known it would all come back to me here.

What I hadn't expected was the anger. Boiling, churning rage. At myself for failing to do the one thing I'd aimed for in that damn church—prevent anyone else from dying. I had run over everything I could remember saying, supplanting what I *should* have said, changing my mind, imagining what responses I may have gotten. Over, and over, and over again.

Anger at the Church, the Ministry, at Brother Dolus, and every other Templar who had allowed this farce to go on as long as it had. Whoever had begun it all, from the initial murders on.

And yes, shamefully, even Malachi himself. That one hurt the most to realize. It seemed cruel and pointless to be angry at someone for taking their own life because it had hurt the people he'd left behind. But I couldn't deny I felt it.

Any regret I might have felt at coming here boiled away when the only other mourner in the church turned to see who'd entered. And the relief, the gratitude, the sympathetic *agony* I saw etched in the old canine's face... it told me I was in the right place.

He struggled to his feet, not simply because of his age or a weakness of body, but because of evident exhaustion, and I crossed the space towards him at a jog, heedless of any etiquette, so he would not need to.

I came to his side, supporting him by the elbow. The retriever took but a moment to look up at me with a trembling smile, his one remaining good eye red-rimmed and shadowed. When he spoke, his voice was thin and weak.

"I hoped you would come, son," he said, before wrapping his arms around me.

I did not know the man well. But right now, we were Brothers in mourning, sharing the pain of loss. And that did not require familiarity. Only decency.

I held the old man to my breast and stood with him, pushing aside my discomfort to allow him the freedom to grieve. And to myself.

I clutched tighter to the old priest as his body began to shake and firmed up my own resolve to speak, weakly at first, then gradually with more conviction. "Bless... blessed be the fallen, blessed be the mourning, that we shall know His everlasting love in this life and the next...."

The Father lifted his head marginally and began to murmur, to speak the prayer aloud with me. First in rough whispers, then steadily finding his voice, as I had.

"Lord, give us the strength to gaze beyond our sorrow and embrace our memories joyfully and with gratitude for the gifts we have already been given."

"Help us, we children of Canus," I continued, "to find peace even in the throes of pain, to love and forgive our kin, and hold no animus for our enemies. We pray for the renewal of those we've lost. Lord, your love heals the brokenhearted and comforts the suffering. May your shepherd's crook guide the departed toward better days of comfort and friendship."

"Amen," the Father said, his voice breaking.

The incense burned. The church was quiet save birdsong from the rafters and the distant sounds of the city outside. The windows here were more elaborate than those at Ebon Gables and not shattered as they had been in the church on the hill. They cast their myriad depictions of saints and holy stories in a flickering cascade across the white marble, the two of us, and the coffin. Rainbows of light. God's love made manifest.

What a world we lived in... that feared love.

"I did not want to send him off to God alone," the old canine said, finally pulling back enough that he could look me in the eyes again. "Thank you for having the courage to come here."

I forced the slightest smile for his benefit. "Of course."

He kept a hand on my arm for support, then turned slowly

towards the coffin. It was laid in one simple wreath of holly leaves and dried lavender. I did not know the significance, but I could imagine them being a flower he would have liked. His Father knew him better than I ever would.

As if following the direction of my eyes, he said, "Purple. He liked the color."

I only ever remembered the man wearing vestments, and drab, regular cotton, and leathers. "It's a powerful color," I said, not knowing what else to say. "A color for kings and great men."

"In the language of flowers..." he murmured, "... a study generally left to women, but I have always thought the study of their significance far too interesting to limit to one gender, it is the color of devotion."

His face broke, jaw trembling. "I have never known a more devoted boy. Inquisitive, studious, obsessive, empathetic." He took a trembling breath before saying, "Sensitive. He understood people in a way few do. He would have been a scholar or a teacher in another life."

I could hardly find my voice. "He was to me," I assured him in a shaky whisper.

"I had him from his third day of life," he confessed into the empty, echoing hall. "From the time he was a babe. Everything he was... everything he could have been... I was responsible for." His head fell until his long ears covered his face. "I have raised dozens of boys. I have made mistakes. I have *never* failed a child as I failed this one."

I set my jaw, trying to find whatever words I could to comfort him. That was what I needed to do here. That is what *needed* doing.

But I wasn't certain how to refute the man. This was Malachi's Father. His guilt may have been—at least partially—accurate. And if that was the case, false platitudes would not help. Not now. Not when it was too late to course-correct.

If I were in any further doubt, he explained in a tone thick with regret, "I thought I was doing what was right for him. For the both of them. I didn't see it—I-I wasn't sure what was happening. I had never had one boy, let alone two... *like* that. I knew of it, of course. I'd heard stories of Lords with peculiarities, of male courtesans, and the Huudari practices that permit such... such...."

I kept my attention on him, not moving my gaze. I did not mean to stare the man down, but I needed to hear what he said. I needed to understand him.

"But I," he choked back a sob, placing a hand over his muzzle, "I am a Lay Priest. I—I think I have spent my life too isolated from the world. I did not understand what was happening to my child. My boys, stealing off to consort with one another, that way. They were grown then, and I knew they would contend with what most young men contend with. I knew what to say to most of my sons. I knew what the doctrines taught. I had experienced it myself in my youth. But with Malachi and Eli, I..." he swallowed, "... I had to consult for help. I reported my own sons to the Ministry. I didn't know what else to do."

His voice was haunted when he said, "I didn't think they'd send an Inquisitor."

My eyes widened. "Malachi endured an Inquisition when he was young?"

"That wasn't the darkest chapter," he said, "but it heralded it. You don't know, do you?"

I shook my head. "He told me a bit about Eli, but that was it. The rest, I've mainly inferred."

"He couldn't stop talking about you," he said. "Especially after you went missing for a time, and you were reclaimed. You know he was frantic trying to find you, all that time? He came to me for Confession, more than once. Spoke on his fears. He thought he had failed to protect another of his Brothers."

"Malachi was always protective of me," I said, meaning every word even as my wrist throbbed. "Right up to the end."

He looked towards the coffin, his features a misery. "All these years, and I saw the signs, again. I knew what was in my boy's heart and this time, I did nothing. It brought only tragedy the first time, asking for help from the Ministry. I thought... I thought if I let it be, just *this* time... God would forgive."

He swept a sleeve across both eyes, good and bad. "But this has nothing to do with God. Does it? God could not save Malachi. My boy died over a decade ago. In that camp. The man they sent back to me was a broken remnant of the child I'd known. They tell them all that, you know. He would repeat it like a prayer whenever he gave Confession. That he was broken."

The graying edges of his shivering muzzle pulled back to reveal his yellowed teeth for just a moment, as he cried desperately, "*They* are the ones who *broke* him! And I *sent* him there! A lamb to the slaughter."

"Why?" I found myself forced to ask. "Were you ordered to?"

"Not at first," he admitted. "They said conversion was possible, that this sin could be purged, redirected... it seemed wrong to me, even then. I cannot forgive myself. I knew then in my *gut* it was wrong." He brought in a slow breath, then released it even slower.

"They recommended," he continued, "shaming the two boys, first. Publicly. For their trespasses. Their sinful nature. I thought it best that such things be kept between us and God in Confession. But the Inquisitor said that would give them lease to pursue their heresy with no accountability. So, I relented."

He had kept his hand on my arm. And I realized in that moment that this might have been his own Confession. We'd not performed any rites, but nothing about this was doctrinal.

"The two boys were stripped and made to labor in the yard," he said, shame in every word. "Their Brothers were told of their heresy at that morning's service, and they were permitted to punish them with words. *Only* words."

I knew what came next. Because I, too, understood people. And I honestly could not imagine how Father Whitehall had not seen the obvious outcome of allowing a public punishment, sanctioned by a *sermon*, at the *pulpit*, no less.

"When did it escalate to violence?" I asked, stone-faced.

"That night," he said, shoulders falling. "Some of the boys— we never learned who—assaulted Eli while he was sleeping. Eli was not a big lad. I would not say he was frail, but he was not capable of defending himself against such an attack. No defense he was capable of warranted such brutality as… the state we found him in suggested. It wasn't a fight. It was a beating." He blinked rapidly, sniffing through his wet nose. "Eli died the next day of his injuries. Malachi was only spared because he had been isolated in confinement for retaliating at one of the boys in the yard."

"I thought Malachi killed someone," I said before I could consider my words.

His head snapped to look up at mine. "How could you know that? You dug into him, didn't you?"

I opened my mouth, but he cut me off. "It doesn't matter. Don't answer that."

I felt myself compelled to look to the choir and the rafters. Only birds that I could see. But the fact that Whitehall's gaze following mine told me all I needed to know. We were not alone.

"Malachi attacked one of the boys he thought was responsible a week later," the old canine said tiredly. "I tried to defuse the anger in my flock, but you cannot tell someone the sky is clear when they feel the rain on their muzzle. Malachi was grief-stricken, humiliated, guilty, and had to watch as we failed to find justice for the boy he'd loved. We could never isolate any one of them that had been responsible. But ultimately… the guilt was mine. My boys were all children then. Even he and Eli, even whoever dealt the blow that killed Eli. I was their Father."

He lifted his muzzle slowly, tracing the bloodlines of the Faith up towards the moons emblazoned high above the pulpit. "I was their shepherd, and I led them to ruin. To hate one another, to kill one another. And then, I sent my boy away. The Ministry did not give me a choice. Prison or re-education. He would only ever have a chance at freedom if I sent him to the camp. So… it is what I chose."

His gaze was turned to God and God alone when he said, "I do not want forgiveness. I will seek that in the next life. But please, forgive my son. I *beg* of you. He has suffered enough."

I turned my chin down to my chest and shifted his hand from my arm to my good hand instead, gripping it tightly.

"You were there, when he…" he guessed softly, after a few moments spent in silent prayer. "The bolt wound. Disabling. We have tried to put the pieces together, but you could tell me…." Then, "No. Don't answer that either. Just… did he suffer?"

I stared down at the shifting hues of the spectrum dancing on the white marble floor. "His entire life," I answered finally.

There was respect for the dead, and then there was placation. I would not lie about the tragedy this man's life had been, even to comfort his Father. We learned nothing from burying our mistakes.

He gave a hitch of breath and turned his own head down, squeezing my hand. "Please grant my son peace, at last," he begged again, but not to me.

"Let him know joy in his next life," I said, squeezing my eyes shut tightly. "Let him know love. I pray he is born into a kinder world than this one, where hate is not empowered by ideology, but cast aside as a relic of a bygone age."

The old canine gave a fragile smile. "What a wonderful sentiment. I shall have to work that into my next sermon."

"Spare your congregation the blasphemy, Whitehall," the voice I had been dreading—the voice that had terrorized me in soft, false kindness my entire childhood—echoed from across the chamber.

I did not release the Father's hand, but turned a cold stare towards the tall, simply-dressed man standing above us on the choir steps. He was walking down them slowly after emerging from the shadows—perhaps Hell itself—but what mattered was that if he was here, so were others.

"I hoped you wouldn't come, Son," he said, shaking his head in a mockery of the real sadness in the room, "but unfortunately, you are as predictably dull as you've always been." He stomped a foot down suddenly, the sound reverberating through the chamber. "Shame upon you!"

Use your body to speak louder than your words can. You can damage resolve far before it becomes necessary to damage flesh.

"Only children stomp their feet when they don't get what they want," I said to him, ignoring his outburst otherwise. Last year, I would have flinched.

"I had such *hopes* for you!" he proclaimed. "Certainty you could rise above your weak making. After all the years of effort we put into your raising and training, when the rest of the world would have left you to starve on those steps you were left on—even your own mother would not have you! *Why* must you put your family through this?!"

"You aren't my family," I said, finally helping Father Whitehall to sit back down, before turning towards the monk.

"Snobbish, turning your nose up at one of the only righteous men to ever care for you," the lurcher said as he approached me, arms folded neatly behind his back. He was, as ever, underwhelming in person. Even now, even knowing the harm he'd done me and my siblings and so many others, he was an unimpressive man. His shadow loomed long and dark, I'd been terrified of him for so long… but face to face, he was just a man.

If nothing else, the last year had freed me of that ingrained fear he had reared into every one of us. I saw him for what he was, now.

He looked briefly and dismissively towards the coffin, before curling his lip, "You know, you sodomites might stand a better chance of making it past your thirtieth year if you could just keep your disgusting proclivities beneath the notice of decent society. But you can't, can you? You're all whores at heart. It's not enough for you to fuck courtesans and criminals, you can't even keep your hands off your own *Brothers* —"

"Dolus!" Whitehall growled out. "This is a *wake* in our House of *God.*"

"He's trying to incite me to violence," I said calmly. "Which means he has no cause to arrest me otherwise." I narrowed my eyes at the lurcher. "Isn't that so, Monk Cuthbert?"

Use their name. Use it as an accusation.

It wasn't just to throw his own tactics back in his face. I wanted to remind him where he came from. I wanted him to face his roots, no different than mine or Malachi's. And I wanted him to know I did not see him as a Brother any longer.

He was nearly nose-to-nose with me now, expression placid on the surface, but I could see the tics. The rage I knew resided there under the deceptively calm waters.

"How did I never see it before?" I wondered aloud.

He arched an eyebrow. "What?"

"How small you are," I answered simply. I pressed in closer, fearlessly crossing the threshold between where grown men would consider 'intimate.' I didn't care any more. Another thing the last year had absolved me of.

Discomfort them, force them to take a submissive posture.

His features twisted and he stepped back as though burned by my very presence. Disgust, wielded as a weapon. If I'd used it on another, I think he might have been proud.

"I thought of you as this… *force*… within our little world," I

389

went on. "We were—all of us—living our lives around your wake. Fearing your tantrums. But you're no storm, no monolith, you have no real *power*." I glared at him. "If I didn't detest you so much, I would pity you. You're so insecure in your place in the world, you have to take out your frustrations at your own impotence and unimportance on *children*."

He snarled at me, and I saw his elbows unlock, the moment Father Whitehall tried to warn me.

I stood my ground as he struck me, hard across the jaw. I did not retaliate.

But I also did not cower.

The pew behind us rattled as Father Whitehall forced himself clumsily to his feet, stammering out a harried, "I am getting the Temple Guards and reporting this affront! This is *hallowed* earth—"

"This," Dolus said calmly between a sneer of his fangs, "is discipline, Father. If you had exercised your palm more freely during the raising of your own boys, perhaps you would have raised a more righteous flock."

I didn't turn, but I heard the gasp of the old man clenching back a sob. And then, shockingly, he rallied and bellowed back angrily, "Your *discipline* does not seem to have had the effect you intended, Brother. That boy is not afraid of you, nor obedient. And perhaps that is well for him."

Dolus tipped his head vaguely in the old man's direction and said wryly, "Well, we can only work with what we are given. If the soil is foul, I can't be expected to turn a good crop from it. At least my disobedient son is *alive*. Some ghost of a chance remains yet to bring him back into the light," he said while leveling his gaze back at me. He was staring through the back of my head. "How many of your boys have you lost to this whole messy affair, now, Whitehall? Three?"

"Enough," I growled, the rumble of my voice, the venom that permeated the air between us, so unlike me as to be almost unrecognizable, even to myself. I knew I felt my emotions—however rational—with my whole chest. I had long fought against my bouts of temper. But I wasn't accustomed to *this* level of anger. It had never made sense to me before... the desire to kill another man, simply for the sake of it.

It was beginning to.

Dolus merely arched an eyebrow at me, unimpressed. "So bold, child. You feel empowered to make demands of me now, do you? I'm curious where that confidence stems from."

He was searching me for signs of any weapons. I felt that pinning stare, as surely as I had every time he'd looked me over at the Abbey, plucking at my flaws, looking for contraband. A book I shouldn't have. Extra food.

Except now, he was looking for an angle. Proof of something he could bring me in for. Perhaps evidence of where I'd been or where I intended to go. If he could not see what he wanted on my person, he would instead drive me to slip up. Say something I didn't intend.

I answered his question, even though it had not been in good faith. Because the answer would give a man like him... nothing.

"God gives me strength," I said, the words feeling somehow truer now than they had in the past, when my belief in the doctrine had been stronger. It wasn't God I doubted.

Dolus laughed at me. He *laughed* at the concept of a Templar empowered by his faith, by his God.

"Your arrogance is... stunning," he huffed. "I do not claim to be the holiest of holy men, Isidor. At least I am honest about that. But you have fallen so far from God's purpose for you, I am shocked your Tome has not combusted. You are openly embracing heresy, and you dare to invoke His name?" He swept an arm in the direction of the coffin. "Where was God's power in your life when you made the series of ill choices that led to *this?*"

"Malachi made his own choices," I said softly, sadly. "And

God has been with me since birth. My Father told me that. And you, but I don't think you believe half the things you say. Through piety and sin, through every mistake and every victory, God is with us. His hand has *always* been offered to me, but He empowers us only when we have the will to do the right thing ourselves. I could not find my footing when I was under your sway. I was bound by doctrine I did not feel in my heart. I was uneasy, unsteady, searching. And it was easier for you to frighten, coerce, and control me then. *That* is what has changed. God is steady. Faith may waver, but God does not."

"You'll be Excommunicated, Isidor," he said coldly. "I know what you've done. We'll find the evidence of it in time, and then, you won't simply be shunned, you will be *hunted*. By men more skilled than you, or I, or that dead fellow over there. Will you kill all of *them*, too?"

"I didn't kill Malachi," I said, my gums aching with how clenched my teeth were.

"He took his own life," Father Whitehall spoke up—nay, cut me off. Perhaps fearing I was about to reveal I knew how the malamute had died. That would have given me away. And I very nearly had. "Because of what the Order did to him," the old man continued miserably. "Because of what I… did to him. Sending away my boy to be… to be 'changed,'" his voice broke on the last word.

"We cannot change God's design for us," I said to Dolus. "Didn't you used to say that? You would say it to deride the worth of beggars, prostitutes, the starving people the Abbey could not take in. 'It is all part of God's design.' We are as we are meant to be." I felt my eyes burn. "Why wasn't that justification wielded in Malachi's case? Why wasn't he enough as he was?"

"Sin," the lurcher hissed, "is not part of God's design for us. It is a temptation from Ciraberos. A deviation. An affront! To God's design." He gestured down at his threadbare, inexpensive, plain clothing. "This modest life was enough for me, despite being precisely one generation, *one* affair with a harlot of a housekeeper—my *whore* of a mother—from inheritance and nobility. I've suffered for the sins of those who came before me. I have lived my life within the bounds of my limitations." He lifted his nose. "Why should his life, or yours, be any different? What arrogance compels you to think you are entitled to more?"

"They should all suffer because you've suffered?" I asked him flatly. Something was yawning open before me in that moment. Enlightenment. Understanding.

"Of course," he said with a curl of his lip. "We are born to suffer, Isidor. Every one of us."

My shoulders fell, and I softened my tone. I felt a bolt of genuine empathy for the man I hated.

"I don't know what shaped you into the man you are," I said, "but your beliefs, the way you think, must be a misery to endure. You should never have been a preacher. I don't know what would have made you happy, but not this."

"What 'beliefs' led *you* to cast aside your entire life, everything we painstakingly ingrained in you?" he demanded, again pushing, prodding, trying to find out what I knew. "The sheer *ingratitude*. Tell me I've not lost a son merely to the wiles and seduction of a criminal. What is it between you and this thief? Have you been promised a fortune, as well?"

"I do not know where the Heart Thief is, any longer," I said, narrowing my eyes. "And I'll point out—when I did, when I was *imploring* the Ministry for aid in tracking them down, when I was hot on their trail and pursuing the investigation with all my heart—no Inquisitors, yourself included, wanted me to continue the hunt." I brought in a breath slowly. "Except Malachi."

Father Whitehall had made his way to the steps leading up to where the malamute was laid at rest, and laboriously lowered himself to his knees to pray. I spared a glance for him, reminding myself to help him up before I left.

I lowered my voice, continuing. "You did not believe in me. None did, save that man there. It's almost as *if*," I tilted my head just-so, "the Ministry did not *want* the Heart Thief found. Perhaps because it would raise more questions than anyone wanted answered. *Perhaps* because the Ministry is afraid of unearthing the answers to those questions."

Dolus gave a humorless smile. "Earnestly, boy... I cannot fathom what you mean by any of this. And I don't care to," he cut me off before I could snap back a reply. "But that feline is a *criminal*. That much is inarguable, and all you or I should need to know. Whatever conspiracy you've dreamed up in that hollow head of yours, self-aggrandizing I'm sure, the Ministry has no fear of whatever a murderer might have to say when they are facing the noose. Let alone a feline of foreign descent."

"The Crown might care what a First in the Line Son of a high Pedigree house has to say," I pointed out. "And given their connection—which I reported up the chain—I think it's safe to say he would have spoken out."

"Difficult task for a dead man though, wouldn't you say?" he asked with a cruel smile.

I didn't bother falsifying surprise. He knew. I knew. All that mattered was what I said for any onlookers.

"Cillian Rathborne is dead?" I asked.

"Regardless of what you're claiming, Isidor," he said in a level tone, "you must know with that overactive conscience of yours that you are directly responsible for both of these men's deaths. And you will answer for that in time, in this life or the next."

I felt the sting of his lash this time. I bit down on the inside of my mouth to force my expression to a neutral one and to staunch any agreement I might have expressed.

Instead, I said, "Not before you answer for it."

He gave me an uncertain glare.

"Does it bother you, to have lost twofold over?" I asked. "You failed to bring in the criminal at the root of all of this, despite having them briefly in your grasp. Which is worse, as far as I see it. You lost the Ministry its asset, and embarrassed us. Not to mention yourself. You'll have no grand trial in Amurfolk. No scapegoat, no blood offering."

I was keeping my voice and my disposition forcibly calm, but I could see the flickers of that fire raging behind the man's eyes. The fury I knew to be there, tempered only by the realization that we were both being watched.

This man was used to being permitted to vent his anger on those the Ministry didn't deem worth protecting. At least not enough to stop him. Watching him boil in his own broth while helpless, as we had been when at his mercy so many times... God help me, but it soothed something.

"You are a dead man walking," he promised me in a hiss.

"I know not who commanded you or what your orders were, but it's safe to say you failed them," I said, narrowing my eyes. "But you'll still have the Crown bearing down on your neck, demanding to know why one of their favored sons turned up dead while under Inquisition. You'll *still* face a Royal Inquiry. You've avoided nothing."

"*I* am not the Ministry," he scoffed.

"You lost the target," I said. "Do you really think this won't be seen as *your* failure?"

"The man who lost that scum is dead in a box to my right," he said, and now he was beginning to sound defensive. Good.

"This case is poison," I said. "Walk away from it, as I have, before *you* are the one in a box."

I felt the weight of the words in my flesh, bones, and sinew. Nothing of the optimism, the naïve yearning for travel and solving this puzzle, remained. I'd seen now the people involved, watched several of them die, and gotten enough of a glimpse of the moving parts behind all of this to be terrified at what the implications were. I could not surrender myself to being as incurious as Dolus was, but I feared what we would learn as equally as I wanted answers.

It *was* poisonous, this conspiracy. Once it got into your veins, it did just enough damage to compel you to find a cure, if you survived it at all.

Dolus gave a laugh that showed his fangs. "Are you attempting to preach to me, son?"

"You're still a Templar," I said, "and you are not unskilled. You could put your talents to better use, even within the Ministry."

"Do not talk to me as though we are equals—"

"If you continue to work this case," I said, narrowing my eyes, "I fear we will inevitably be at cross-purposes. And I don't want that."

"I'd imagine that idea frightens you, yes," he said, "given that I am still the steward of your much-beloved siblings. What stories I shall have to tell them, now."

I was ill-equipped to hide my feelings normally. But right now, on this subject at least, I felt no need. The *lack* of a response from me, of anger or concern, must have tipped him off, because his face fell slowly as I said calmly, "They have their own minds, and will make their own decisions. I know they will be well."

"What have you done?" he barked suddenly, lunging at me.

I let him grab my surcoat, only leaning back fractionally when his spittle hit my cheek.

"You are crossing the five-paw distance, Brother," I said, barely above a whisper, "best take your paces before my sin rubs off on you."

"Brother Dolus," Father Whitehall said in a warning tone, from where he was still kneeling. The threat was implied and apparently real enough that even Dolus was forced to take him seriously. This was Father Whitehall's church, after all. He *could* call on the guard to evict someone off the grounds. Even a Senior member of the Ministry.

"You will shame us all," the lurcher said as he slowly withdrew back. Not far. "Ebon Gables, your siblings, your Father Helstrom. Someone will pay penance for all of this, Isidor. Your cowardice ensures only that it will be your family that suffers *first*. You will bring us all down with you. Your betrayal of the Ministry will be a *stain* we must all wear."

"If I'm to be Excommunicated," I said, "and, in earnest, I am still not sure *why*, as even my involvement in this case and using my connection with the Heart Thief was at *your* direction—"

"I was trying to *cover* for you, ingrate," he growled.

"—I invite you to explain to them what I've done wrong. What we've *both* done," I said, lifting my eyebrows, "as part of this pursuit of a criminal. Or are you just going to conceal the whole of it, so that whoever takes over this next has no good information to work off? One hand not knowing what the other is doing is what got us here, after all."

"What evidence do you even have for your theories?" he spat. "I've heard an awful lot of accusations and no proof."

I paused a moment, considering my words. "What I have are doubts," I answered at length, "and that should be enough to withhold conviction, especially when the penalty for a crime is death. I have heard *multiple* first-hand accounts from people who had little to no reason to lie, and information keeps coming to light that makes the Ministry's story make less sense by the day. The picture I've formed is incomplete, but it is… wholly different from what I was told. And I spent more time with the thief themselves than any other Inquisitors have. I questioned them at length and," I stared upward a moment, feeling the sun warming my face through the multi-hued glass, "I believe them," I finished, resolutely.

"You believe them," he repeated, dubiously. "*That* is all the justification you ultimately have?"

"I plan to continue investigating the case on my own," I said, turning. "When I have more answers, *I'll* not hide them. The country and her people deserve to know what happened to a relic that mattered to so many. I will make sure that whatever I learn, I share."

I walked over to Father Whitehall, helping him up with an elbow he could grip. He accepted my offer, casting one last mournful look at the coffin before lowering his head.

I reached up to unbutton my cloak. Malachi's cloak. It was a bitter reminder of everything that had transpired, and Darcy despised it and my reasoning for keeping it. But I felt I needed it. The reminder it would always embody.

We needed to remember those of us who had not made it. Darcy and I had survived this, somehow. Malachi had not. In another life, born ten years earlier, raised by different Fathers, our positions may have been reversed. I needed to remember him. His tragedy, his mistakes... and my own.

"Belief," I said after a moment, "is what the Ministry was founded on. It is *all* we base our convictions on, ultimately. The Tome of the Faith is a collection of accounts and stories we are meant to believe because the men who penned it were wise and learned or claimed to have guidance from the Almighty Himself. I was taught to *believe* that."

I stared across the space at Dolus. "I think trusting my own eyes, ears, and heart... as well as studying the teachings... is reasonable. Faith should be able to stand up to scrutiny... and so should my beliefs."

I lifted my good hand up to my jaw, rolling and flexing it, the blow from Dolus beginning to smart and swell in a familiar way. I hoped rather than believed it would be the last time I felt his sting.

"Malachi," I spoke softly, my whispers meant only for him. I reached beneath my cloak and unwound my scarf, woven in rare violet yarn by my sister Mabel, dyed at our very Abbey. I had worn it throughout the whole of this terrible ordeal without ever regarding the color with any importance.

I smiled, in agony. "Your Father says you loved this color. I'm sorry you did not feel you could wear it, or… weren't permitted to. I-I don't know."

My face broke. "There is so much about you I will never know. An entire story, an entire life, lost. I would have liked to help you find your way. I failed in my part in that…" I blinked, chasing the blurriness in my eyes, "… *so* many people failed you. I… will grieve you, all my days. I will pray for your soul, every night, until I am tilled under and join the same cycle you have."

I clenched my teeth, settling the scarf over his simple coffin lid, alongside the flowers his Father had left.

"I love you, Brother," I said, bowing my head, "and I forgive you. I will *not* forget you," I promised.

I released Father Whitehall, turned, and began to leave. As I did, I called back, "The case of the Heart Thief is yours alone now, Dolus. Search for *truth*. I will do the same on my own terms."

The man did not reply to that. But he let me leave, and that was all I desired from him at this point.

I tried not to actively check over my shoulder or even swivel my ears, but I was on alert. I expected to be followed. Even if I didn't catch sight or scent of anyone, I had to assume I would be. I'd come here knowing that, and at this point if we'd been wrong, it would honestly frustrate our plans.

This church had a large narthex seating area for penitents who were not permitted inside during a service but wished to listen to the sermon. It was a separate room, the doors only kept open during a service, and in the winters, they kept them closed on either end to serve as an antechamber to keep the cold out. I closed the first door behind me, intending to head straight for the entrance in a hurry since time was of the essence, when someone's hand wrapped around my wrist. Suddenly, I was no longer alone, a robed figure sliding in beside me and keeping pace with me.

"Don't slow down," a familiar, aged voice said from beneath his winter cowl, his scarred ears dangling past the edge of the hood, "just keep walking. And don't act surprised to see me once we are out of this chamber. They have eyes above."

"Father," I said, nearly choking on the lump in my throat. I could not *imagine* someone else I wanted to see more, right now.

"I'm proud of you," he said without lifting his head. "You held your ground in there and gave him nothing. I'm very glad I did not need to intervene, but I was prepared to if need be."

"How…" I stammered, gathering myself before we made it outside, "…I mean… how did you know to find me here?"

"I have my ways," he said, and I caught the vaguest hint of a jowly smile.

"Thank you," I said quietly, "for trusting me to handle him. Better your presence here not be known. You're still… in."

He only nodded at that.

"I'm glad you had faith in me," I said, "but why risk coming to listen in at all, then? We could have met at the coordinates."

"You've decrypted them, then?" he asked.

"Yes," I said, admitting abashedly, "it took over a day, and I had help. This was a hard one."

"I'm sorry for the difficulty, but it was necessary," he said. "You keep throwing yourself into the clutches of the Ministry. I couldn't have them finding the letter and discerning a location out of it. This place is known to them, but they have *no* cause to believe we'd be going there, and if they did, we'd be endangering more than just ourselves. I've made promises to be careful."

"*They've* already taken to the road, headed for this place," I said, glancing down worriedly at him. "The others. It was a real leap of faith, given we know nothing of where they're headed, but I trust you."

"I trust you as well, Isidor," he said, and I briefly caught a hint of his dark green eyes. "I had faith that my brave, brilliant son could handle himself against that man, against the Ministry, even. But faith is a compass needle, not a map. It can only point us in the right direction. At some point you must exercise caution and reason, as well."

His hand squeezed my arm once more, before slipping back to his side. "I was worried about you."

I gave an unsteady breath out as we neared the door. I saw him glance briefly at me, gathering his cloak around his ears more before we headed out. "I have my ways," he repeated his sentiment from earlier, "but they have their limits. What is your plan?"

"We lead our pursuers on a merry chase for a few weeks," I said. "Until we are certain we've shaken the tail. We lead them nowhere near the map coordinates you gave me. I have a friend of," I swallowed, "the... late Cillian... Rathborne... with me."

His brows crinkled as his eyes went wide, and he gasped out a quiet, "God rest his soul. They've slain a Pedigree. A First Son?"

I nodded grimly.

"Lord help us all," he said through his teeth. "Now the Crown will be involved in this. The Council of Lords will demand blood. Who is this friend?"

"A local who knows the area. He is intent on accompanying us and treating this as a business trip, attending to patients of his across the countryside. This is not outside his usual behavior this time of year. In the cold, most of them prefer house-calls. I'll accompany him as a guard, we'll stay at roadside Inns as he travels his route."

"And the others have already gone," he said, understanding. "Are you certain they can travel beneath notice?"

"Nothing is certain right now," I confessed, "but they have help. Two guides who know the roads. They'll travel quietly and outside of public view. They won't even pass through towns. The guides know a few scattered cabins and houses along the way they can take their rest at, and the stretches in-between, they said they'll 'improvise.'"

My Father made a brief face of worry, but then nodded. "Your siblings have both known hardship, Isidor. They'll survive a few rough weeks on the road."

"Is this place they're headed for truly safe?" I asked fervently. "And even if it is, what then? We can't hide forever."

"It is, insofar as the Ministry is concerned, neutral ground," he said. "The man who keeps a residence there is known to them and is considered a grave threat to the Ministry, but he has the protection of a *very* powerful coalition of Pedigree families, merchants, and capital backing that up. He's a real thorn in their side, preaching his Heresy, but not one they can afford to anger. The hope as I understand it is that he'll simply... die... before his movement gains any traction with the populace. He's very old."

"And you know him," I surmised, "and trust him."

"Yes," he said, although the sentiment he expressed was... mixed. "I won't lie to you, I don't understand his radicalism, and I think it's very dangerous for our country and our faith, but I do believe his heart is in the right place, and he is most certainly still a man of God. A good man." He began to push open the door. "We worked together several times when I was younger. He is no Inquisitor, but he is the reason I have the utmost respect for House Templar."

"The Heresiarch is a *Templar* ?" I whispered fiercely, shocked. But by then we were outside, and it was time to make for the carriage.

"No longer," he said quietly. "Now, come. Let us lead these Brothers in circles like our tail is on fire."

. . .

Every week we spent on that seemingly endless diversion was a week spent not knowing what had become of my siblings and Darcy. It was agony.

Thankfully, I had my Father to speak with, pray with, and find comfort in. That was a blessing I hadn't expected and one I found I badly needed. The guilt came overflowing now that I had an ear willing to listen.

My Father did not demand nor ask that I make Confession, and when I finally got up the nerve to ask for myself, he only said he would be willing to perform the rites, but that God had certainly heard my earnest pleas for salvation. He would have been willing, but... I think he was inferring that this time, I should peer more deeply inward and work through my feelings with him as much as possible before giving it all up to God.

I might have felt better if we'd said the words, performed the rites, gone through the cleansing ritual I'd relied on throughout my whole life so far for closure. But he was right. Confession right now would have felt hollow. I had not yet begun to make sense of what had happened, what possible purpose it all might have served, or come to terms with my own mistakes and stumbling as I'd walked this rocky path. I had to be willing to forgive myself first, before asking God to. Or it would all be in vain.

Talking to my Father helped.

But more than anything, I wanted to talk to Darcy.

We'd said so little to one another in the days following what had happened at the church on the hill. Watching them recede into themselves, becoming unknown to me again, was heartbreaking. They hadn't chosen to leave my side... but that too, I knew, was still possible. Condemnation or anger would have been *something*. Something more than stoic silence. I'd almost hoped for it, but it had never come, and then we'd had to part ways.

Did they blamed me for Cillian's death, as I blamed myself? Were they furious at me for having failed to protect the both of us from Malachi? If he hadn't ultimately done... what he'd done... we both would have died there. I can't say that committing myself to fighting lethally would have made the difference, and I knew I had fought with all my heart, but Darcy did not. They could easily have condemned me for everything that happened in that church.

God knows, I did.

Darcy had also chosen not to shoot the malamute in the end, when they could have. It might have been a decision made purely to avoid risking shooting *me*, in the midst of a melee. They had never said one way or the other why they'd chosen to hold their hand, even when I'd asked afterwards.

Darcy hadn't killed me and had stopped Cillian from killing me, when it would have benefited their survival to see me in the ground. I think some part of them saw Malachi for what he was... the worst possible outcome for someone like me. And the feline was a good person. I would forever believe that was why.

But this had all been a most terrible test of our fragile bonds with one another and I wasn't sure we'd weathered it. The serval had been in such shock in the wake of it all, culminating with the devastating decision we'd had to make to leave Cillian's body at a watch post for a Road Warden to find. At least that way, the local civil government would take custody of him, not the Church. We'd left his ring with him, to be certain he'd be identified.

It was cruelty beyond measure that Darcy could not mourn him nor leave any trace of their bond on his person. I had to search the man's body to ensure he carried nothing that could be tied to us. And distressingly, I'd found something. A journal.

Darcy had it now. I feared what lay within those pages, as I had feared no book before. It was truly forbidden reading, for me.

If they were not there waiting at the safehouse for us, if I never saw Darcy again, I would not blame them for running this time. And I would not chase them. Not again. Never again.

It was gut-wrenching to think that in one horrific hour, this person that I loved—who had led me towards what I'd thought to be damnation, but had revealed itself to be freedom—may hate me, now. I think I would always love them... but I also would not fault them if they'd lost all affection for me. And each day that passed, I became more certain that must be so. That I had lost them and any future we might have had together.

My Father tried to comfort me, but he hadn't been there. Seen what I'd seen. Cillian's death... Malachi's. When we'd spoken about that day, he'd mostly listened, more than responded. I think it had given him a lot to think on, as well.

The second time we'd talked about it, I'd gotten only a historical account of the church in question—he knew of it— and a cryptic rumination on the tale.

"The church of Final Light," he'd said, his gaze distant, steeped in memory. "Named thusly because the hill catches the very last rays of the sun in that area of the valley. I remember when they began the attempt to restore it. Redcoven is not so far from our Parish. The church was ancient and beloved in its time, but had been given away to the souls in the graves out back for so long... and when they tried to restore the structure, they soon learned the hard truth of why it had been abandoned to begin with. A faulty foundation. Sunken, cracking, surrendering to the earth. No matter what they built atop it, it would never stand the test of time."

He'd looked at me, at that. "You cannot build a new world entirely upon an ancient, decrepit foundation. Sometimes it is necessary to tear down and begin anew. We cannot always restore the old world, only tell its tales. And if you force conservation over new wisdom, especially when lives are at stake, it can end in tragedy. They abandoned that restoration when a collapse took the lives of several of the workers. They knew the risk… and disregarded it."

He'd hung his head at that, and for a moment I'd thought he intended to pray for those who'd died. But instead, he merely looked pensive. Troubled.

"I fear there is too much of that within the Ministry," he'd said. "Ignoring new knowledge at our own peril. Burying it if it is inconvenient. We are scholars, first and foremost, we monks and priests. We are meant to spend our lives in study, not ignorance. There is a poisonous line of thinking, a frailty in our ranks, where protecting our flock from sin and vice ceases to be the mission… and protecting our Order—at all costs—takes precedence."

"All of this happened because the Order did not want the Heart of Faith faithfully translated, or dated, or studied at all by modern eyes," I'd said. "They're afraid of the truth."

"It is worse than that," he'd said, "They are afraid of the mere *chance* that something unpleasant may be discovered. Knowledge should strengthen our faith, even if it is difficult to contend with. God does not want us to base our beliefs on lies. They doubt *Him* when they bury and obscure our past. It is not simply ignorant to hide from history; it is *sacrilegious*."

"This has hurt so many people," I'd whispered, running my rosary through my palm. "It's *wrong*. That's all that matters."

He'd looked me in the eyes and there, in that moment, I'd felt the final burden leave me. The last anchor that held me to Ebon Gables. My Father's faith in me, restored.

We had so much more to say. More than I could put to words—so, so many words—in Confession. But it felt possible, now. It felt like he would listen.

It was nearly a month before we were certain we'd seen the last hints of any tail, any men asking at the Inns after us, or plain-clothes fellows with blades on their hips lingering on the roads near the country homes of Ruun's patients. A further two weeks of travel following that before we'd found our way far west, closer to the sea. We were in sparse country, out here. Only rural estates and small towns, and none that we'd seen for nearly a day when, at long last, Father Helstrom slowed his horse. We were at a deer crossing on the snow-slicked cattle road we were traveling, Father pulling back his hood to glance around at the ubiquitously-dense forest surrounding us on either side.

I slowed Blackbow as well, my breath coming out labored in the cold air. We'd been going at a good clip for the last hour or so, which I'd *hoped* meant we were getting close. According to the map we'd consulted last night, we should have been arriving today.

But there was nothing. Not even fields for grazing, at least not for hours now.

"Are these the coordinates?" I asked, concerned. God, what if we'd sent Darcy and my siblings to the wrong location? Where might they have gone?

Father didn't seem worried, though. He ambled his horse towards the edge of the wood-line and pointed in the direction of something I'd missed earlier. A single lantern, unlit in the middle of the day, but hung alongside what just barely looked to be a trail, heading off into the forest. Not wide enough for a carriage. Horses or on foot only.

"It will be a mile from here," he said, spurring his horse on. "Only take heed. They don't like visitors, and we're not likely to have a warm welcome at first."

"Do they know we're coming?" I asked, following him. I glanced back briefly at Ruun, whose presence I could not account for. The man should have parted ways with us long ago, but I know he was concerned for Darcy. There had been no convincing him to leave. He wasn't handling the travel well at his age, though. My concern—and my respect—for the man had both grown.

I was certain my father was in pain, too, riding this long. But he was not letting on to his condition nearly as much. The man was a sphinx, even to me.

"Did they know to expect the others?" I pressed my Father.

"I do not know for certain," he answered truthfully. "I sent word, but they intercept his letters sometimes."

My worries mounted. Surely there must have been a better location, a better safehouse, to have used. Why were we here? What could this man offer us that was so critical?

My Father put out a hand suddenly. I slowed my horse to a stop and watched him scent the wind.

"What—" I began.

"Keep your hands away from any of your weapons," he said. "Make it clear we mean them no harm and do not invoke the Ministry for *any* reason, do you understand?"

"I understand," I said, but if I'd been anxious before, now I was terrified. I did not know what sort of man we'd be facing, *who* might be coming over the patchy, forested hill ahead of us. I began to hear a horse soon, but my nose was nowhere near as refined as my Father's. As to its rider….

Whatever my imagination had conjured up, it would likely never have been the pretty, well-appointed canine woman who rode unhurriedly down the lane. Alone.

She, like Darcy, did not ride side-saddle. She looked expensively-clothed, but oddly so. Practical. Despite the bold, deep red of her winter dress—an expensive color—she also wore a long, brown leather duster over it and britches beneath her dress, the trellises of her maiden's wear drawn up to the hip on one side with a gold cord. She wore riding spats, steeped in the same mud all of ours were, suggesting she'd been out in the field for a time. A hunting rifle hung over her shoulder, and two dead grouse were slung across one side of her saddle.

She looked to be of the Spaniel line, her spots attractively spaced across her face, suggesting high breeding. Her fur was well-groomed, but windswept, and she had a maturity and seriousness to her bearing that belied her young age.

She brought her dapple-gray horse to a stop not ten feet from us and looked us over appraisingly. When she spoke, her tone was calm, civil… but commanding. I don't think I'd ever been spoken to like that by a woman before.

"They just shoved that young lad there out an Abbey door last week, by the look of him," she surmised, brown eyes briefly on me, before moving to my Father. "The Ministry's not sending their best these days."

"I am Father Germain Helstrom," the bloodhound said, bowing to the woman. "I've been in correspondence with your guardian. I sent word that we'd be arriving, although I hadn't time to confirm my message got through."

"And I'll give no such confirmation now," she said coolly. "You will follow me, wait until such time as I can confirm your identity, and until then, I'm not particularly interested in conversing."

"Thank you, Lady," my father said, again bowing.

"Who are you?" I demanded, unable to stop myself. I didn't think it was rude to ask, at this point. My Father seemed to know her, and if we were going to throw ourselves into her care, I wanted to, as well.

She turned her horse slowly, before answering, eyeing me over her shoulder. "Bold, young Templar. I just told you how I'd prefer things; will you not honor my request?"

"I… shall of course," I said after a moment, tipping my nose down.

I believe I might have seen the barest hint of a smile from her. "Respectful. Very good. You may call me Miss Cross until we are on a first-name basis. Now, follow me. Up here, there is a sightline to the main house, where they can confirm if you say who you say you are. Follow me, or leave."

I followed. What choice did I have?

13

DREAMS MADE MANIFEST

We waited in what was likely a verdant glen in the warmer months, but for now was a damp, cold hollow, nestled between several old oak trees. The only marker as to where we were was the house in the distance, barely a silhouette from so far away, and a well nearby that had been boarded up, by the look of it very recently. I felt there was a story there, but I dared not ask our hostess.

The Pedigree woman—or at least, I assumed as much based on her dress and bearing—busied herself while we waited, dressing the grouse. Other than Darcy, I'd never seen someone so monied preparing their own food, let alone so efficiently. It was baffling. I wanted to ask her how or why she'd learned... I wanted to ask her a great many things, but she'd stayed stalwartly silent while we waited, and I was honor-bound to hold to my word and do the same.

She'd said nothing about us talking amongst ourselves, though. And Ruun seemed eager to speak, while we took our rest.

"All very cloak and dagger," he said with a tired huff as he settled himself down with a pop of his knees and a wince as he rubbed his gloved hands over his trousers, specifically his thighs. I was almost a third his age, and I felt his pain. So much time in the saddle.

"He's *my* Father, and he hasn't revealed exactly who we're throwing ourselves in with," I agreed ruefully. "Other than the man himself… this Heresiarch, if he is indeed here."

"Ah, the reformation leader," the fox arched an eyebrow. "I've heard tell. What a wicked name for an editor."

"He's 'editing' our holy book," I explained as patiently as I could. "Thus, heresy."

"If so, why hasn't your Order, ah…" he swished his tail awkwardly. Once a fox, always a fox, regardless of age. The mannerisms stayed the same, I suppose. "Well, you know," he cleared his throat. "I don't mean to cast aspersions, it's just—"

"As a target for Inquisition and summary execution, he'd be inconvenient," I said simply. "He was a respected Templar in his day, I hear. I don't know his name or history, but my Father has inferred as much. That means he had connections, not only within our Ministry, but in Pedigree circles. I wasn't in the room when the decision was made, but I'd wager they decided killing the man would make a martyr of him. Not worth the risk. And he's very old, apparently. The movement is more likely to die out on its own… or with a little help."

"Hmm," he hummed thoughtfully. "I've read different editions of the Tome of the Faith, based on the different eras of Jarls and Kings."

"… right," I agreed uncertainly, since he'd paused long enough to let me know it was a declarative statement. "As the Sons of Canus became Clans, which became Tribes, which became Lords, and the last few successions led to the Council of Pedigree, Amuresca's founding itself, obviously the text would be…" I sighed, suddenly realizing. "Oh. That's your point."

"What does this particular revisionist preach that is so heretical and antithetical to your values?" Ruun asked.

I didn't immediately have an answer. I knew whispers of what the protest movement on the fringes of our faith spoke about—primarily, it had caught fire with other races that occupied our country, who likely wanted a more equitable relationship with God and better social standing. But as to the particulars….

"I don't know," I admitted. I didn't hide the frustration in my tone. "It's forbidden reading."

"Now *that*," he shook his head, "is heresy. At least, to a scholar like myself. Forbidden knowledge? No such thing."

"Not everything written in a book is true," I countered, "or written in good faith. The written word can be many things, and I thank God every day—quite explicitly, it's part of my morning *and* evening prayer—that I'm literate and educated. I think everyone should be, regardless of who they are or where they were born. But it can also be misleading, propaganda, or outright lies."

"I believe what is 'true' is too often dictated by the powerful," he said. "And I spent my life working for them. Long enough to know how often they are wrong."

I pursed my muzzle, unable to rebuke him. "This is dangerous territory," I warned him instead, softly.

"It is," he agreed immediately. But he didn't sound afraid. "But innovation, advancement, and learning always are. I have seen such changes in my own lifetime concerning health and medicine, the practice of surgery, our knowledge of anatomy… I think we are on the very cliff edge of a massive canyon of knowledge, only now opening to us. I find it exhilarating, even if I only get to see the very beginning of it."

"A 'cliff edge,' hmh?" I asked dubiously. "Pride goeth before a fall."

"I won't claim I'm bereft of pride," he admitted, "but isn't it also pride that compels us to cling to our preconceptions rather than challenge them when new information is presented? You're a smart fellow, Isidor. A discerning head on your shoulders," he tapped my muzzle with a claw, rendering me briefly cross-eyed for a moment. "I trust that you'll be able to uncover for yourself what is propaganda, what is misinformation. 'Truth' is elusive. I won't claim to have it. Even most holy men admit they are forever seeking it."

He exhaled a moment, then unslung his shoulder bag and began untying the flap. "If I had to answer, say, an understudy, when they were to ask me what is true? I would say nothing, until someone has proven it."

"That leaves no room for faith," I said. "Not everything that exists is observable."

"Right you are," he agreed, chuckling. "Our Darcy for instance, perhaps? They believe in who they are... they know their truth... and it seems to me at this point, you do as well. That is both observable and a matter of taking them on faith." He pulled a neatly-bound, well-worn book from his satchel. Black, mostly bare cover, with stamped, blocky lettering.

"But," he continued, offering the book to me, "who they are is nowhere in that book of yours. The rules established therein do not allow for people like Darcy to exist... and yet, they do." He smiled. "As does your love for them."

I took his book slowly, glancing once down at the cover. I knew the humbly-printed text immediately for what it was once I saw the author's name. And it suddenly made sense to me why the book was so nondescript.

"Transitional Evolution of the Modern Canid," I said, unsurprised, but also somehow terribly, wonderfully *excited* by what I held in my hand. "The vulpine who wrote this is considered an enemy of the *state*, you know." I rubbed a thumb pad over the cover, feeling the weight of the blasphemous book in my paws. "This is banned even in Pedigree households. Is the author a friend of yours?"

"No," he laughed. "No, alas, afraid not *all* of us foxes know one another. Not even those of us who call ourselves academics. That fellow travels the world to conduct his studies, and I've never left Amuresca. Quite content to practice as I do, with the families I do. But I've a wandering mind, you see."

"Is this the book that pushed you from the faith?" I asked pointedly.

"That was a long journey, and I was quite far along it by the time I'd read this particular book," he assured me. "But it did change how I thought of the world, and how we might have all come to be here."

"And now you think I should read it," I surmised.

He only inclined his head towards me and said, "Do you wish to?"

I stared down at it. Internally warring with two parts of myself—the innate retaliatory urge to rebuke something so unabashedly blasphemous, something I would need make Confession for even opening, something *corrupting*... and my curiosity. Moreover, the very stark realization that the fear of learning something uncomfortable is precisely why every terrible thing concerning the Heart of Faith's disappearance had happened. If I was going to uncover information the Church wanted hidden away, risk their ire, and the foundations of the very faith I loved, how could I be afraid of a *book?*

"I propose a trade while we shelter here," Ruun said, clearly sensing I was considering it. "Your Tome, your favorite passages."

My eyes widened. "You want to read the Tome of the Faith? But you're—"

"I want to understand your faith through *your* eyes," he

explained. "I want to talk to you about it. We can talk about both books if you like."

"If you're reconsidering the Word," I said, reaching to my belt to unclasp my book and offer it to him, "I cannot turn you down, on principle."

"And I'd wager that makes this easier for you," he said with a brief wink, taking the book. "But earnestly, while I can't say my beliefs will be shaken, I recall many stories I found… inspiring. Fascinating. The men who penned these led very different lives to ours, and I think several of them had what would now be considered revolutionary ideas, ironically. Love for all beings, mercy for one's enemies, a hope for a world in which poverty and starvation were not a necessity for building nations. Beliefs our Lords seem to have forgotten."

He put my tome away into his satchel and continued, "I'll return it to you before we part ways here, obviously. But… you may keep that book if you like it. I've a first edition at home, and I think in the hands of such an inspiring fellow as yourself, it will do more good."

I looked at him quizzically. "You shouldn't find me inspiring. I've stumbled through the last few months in a confused haze, I've let my passions rule over reason, I've been dishonest, a coward…"

"What you're doing is unbelievably hard, young man," he assured me softly. "That you are doing it at all… is inspiring."

"There's the signal," the Lady's voice suddenly came from her side of the clearing. She was standing with a grouse held in one hand by the feet, staring up at the distant hill. I wasn't certain what she'd seen, but there was briefly movement in one of the windows, I think.

She turned to regard us, and even as composed as she was, I picked out the relief in her features. "You are who you say you are," she confirmed, "but I still do not know you particularly well, so you'll forgive me some discretion until we are all better acquainted."

I stood, nodding. My Father came from where he'd been tending the horses, and the Lady looked us all over.

"Proper introductions, then," she said with a smile. "I am Lady Brook Denholme-Cross, here representing my family guardian's interests and caring for him. As you might imagine, given… who he is… we are rather protective of him. Apologies for the thorny reception."

"'We'?" my father immediately asked.

"My brother is here with me as well," she said. "You'll meet him at the house, I'll let him introduce himself."

"It's a common enough name," I murmured, "so I thought… but you're the heirs of the Cross estate, then? The late Richard Cross?"

"You know our stepfather," she said with a blooming smile.

"There are books about his exploits in the Kadrush," I explained shyly. "Not family gossip, not Ministry knowledge, just… I liked high-seas adventures, growing up. There are quite a few he features in."

Her smile waned for just a moment. "Just him?"

"Well, other Captains, Admirals…" I stammered, not certain what she was looking for. "But he was very renowned."

"My own family, the Denholmes, had many navy men as well," she said neutrally. It was hard to discern what emotion lay there beneath the veneer.

"Right," I nodded. "That's how I knew. Your mother's remarriage was mentioned in an old gazette I read. Quite the merger of families."

What I didn't say is that I remembered why the heiress had remarried. The Denholmes were disgraced, fallen from esteem. Nothing that mattered anymore, given how long ago it was, but… no, best not to bring it up.

Sometimes—more often than not, in fact—Pedigree marriages were arranged for economic or social reasons. The Denholme and Cross families were not compatible for producing pure heirs, but both had fleets, maritime connections, and now as one they'd become a formidable trading family. There was even talk they'd allied with a Carvecian Cartel, something I'd heard Lord Hudson discussing in the cigar room on one of the occasions I'd been invited to sit in. I'd only remembered it because of my fascination with the late Richard Cross, but my impression was that the Cross family's standing was falling, again. Becoming bedfellows with Carvecian traders, while likely lucrative, didn't make you many friends in Pedigree circles.

It certainly explained why we were here, though.

"You're going to send us away," I said to my father sadly.

"That was always the plan," he sighed. "You aren't safe here."

"I'm not opposed to leaving the country," I insisted, "but I thought... the Kadrush, perhaps Mataa. You're sending us to Carvecia?"

Lord, it was half the world away. Depending on which passage we took, months at sea. Would we ever return?

"Since you've not seen fit to introduce yourself," the young woman cleared her throat, "might I assume you are the fellow Darcy has been waiting for? Ah.. Isidor, yes?"

I whipped my head around so fast towards her that it hurt my neck. "Darcy? Darcy's spoken to you? Are they..."

She laughed. "Yes, they're here. We're quite overwhelmed with guests at the moment—almost more than our little cabin can handle—but Darcy and I have struck a particular accord over the last few weeks. I enjoy speaking with them," her eyes sparkled when she said, "and they speak about you... often. I knew you immediately by sight, truth be told, but I promised my guardian I would be certain."

God, what had they said about me? We'd been on uncertain ground when we'd parted ways. Honestly, in the whole of the months I had known Darcy, I had spent precious little time *with* them. It seemed every time fate brought us together, we were soon ripped apart.

Maybe this time, it had been for the best. Everything had felt so raw and bleeding when we'd last been together. Perhaps time to clot, to heal, to think on what had happened... perhaps it had helped.

I was no more certain now of what I'd say to them than I had been then. Except to apologize. To beg their forgiveness.

But I was afraid. *So* afraid, even more so now that seeing them again was imminent.

"Ruun Mandrake, family Physician," the fox was introducing himself, while I was internally spinning. Lady Cross gave him a polite curtsy, before turning once more to me as she made her way to her horse.

"You should take the lane up ahead," she said, "on the left. Darcy takes their rest in the ruins this time of afternoon, usually. Reading. I think I saw them headed that way before I went hunting."

"'The ruins'?" I repeated uncertainly.

"Old stone building," she explained, hiking up onto her horse. "Think it may have been part of a church. The cabin was a rectory at some point and the only part of the grounds that were kept up. My uncle, well my guardian, still goes to the ruins to pray sometimes. Darcy seems to like it there as well, although you're here in the wrong season. It's more scenic out that way in the spring when the flowers come up."

She must have noticed my shock and mistaken it for worry, because she quickly assured me, "They will wish to see you as soon as possible, I assure you. You should go. It isn't far."

I looked to my Father and he nodded, taking the reins of my

horse. "Go," he echoed. "I'll get your siblings. We'll join you soon, but you should…" he fell short for just a moment, before sighing softly and pressing on, "… this is the person you are courting, son. Regardless of my feelings on the matter, you are a grown man. You are permitted some measure of privacy. We'll give you time to speak alone."

I turned to go, thought the better of it, then undid the clasp on my cloak. I bundled it then lashed it over my saddle.

"You're warm?" Ruun asked disbelievingly, closing his own coat around him tighter.

I shook my head as I left. "It was Malachi's," I explained quietly.

I would not come to them now, after such an absence, cloaked in the mantle of Cillian's murderer. While keeping a remnant of him mattered to me, it would be there when I needed it.

The wood seemed to grow lighter and warmer as I walked the lane, tucked in on all sides by evergreen tree cover and the bare limbs of brush and poplar. The sun had decided to greet my approach, peeking through the canopy in dancing flashes of light. I smelled the usual scents of the forest, earth and leaf decay, pine, the smell of water from somewhere distant, perhaps a stream. This deep in the forest the snow cover was broken and cracking around the land, little islands of white amidst the mud. It smelled like winter at the woods around Ebon Gables. It smelled more like home than anywhere I'd been in a while.

The sun blinded me ever more as the trees began to thin, and by the time I caught the first hint of Darcy's scent on the wind, I found myself in a small, wild garden surrounding the remnants of a stone building I could not yet see very well. Several overgrown rosebushes blocked my path, and my eyes had yet to adjust.

But the rose window was unmistakable. Rising into the glare

of the sun, a humble height for the tallest part of a religious building, barely two stories... but the adjacent supports and roof were gone, so the sun shone through those unbroken windows and lit the moons and the flower they surrounded in stunning color. Gold, red, and rose pink, a beautiful yet simple design for the small circle of stained glass. I could imagine how worshippers must have walked this very lane long ago and seen this window just as I was seeing it now, welcoming and warm, promising renewal and life.

I blinked into the stark daylight of the clearing I'd stepped into, moving around one of the tangling growths of rosebush—dead now, but I could only imagine how verdant it would be in the spring—and I saw the ruins at last.

I nearly fell to my knees.

I had stepped into the landscape of my own dreams.

So overcome was I, so lost in this exultant and breathtakingly conflicted moment, somewhere between reality and prophecy, that I didn't hear their footsteps. I didn't see their silhouette. I felt them coming, I knew they would appear, only because *they had been here* so many times before.

And so had I.

"Isidor."

I lifted my muzzle, swallowing heavily, fighting tears. The silhouette stood in the threshold of the old ruins. A church, an abbey, a school of some kind, it was hard to say. There were no doors, just rusted hinges. No roof, nor belltower. No attempts at restoration. This building had been left to the wild for nature to reclaim. And reclaim it she had, vines growing over most of the available stonework. A rosebush jutted through a window and several trees grew from inside, their branches creating a roof all their own. Moss had spread between the cracks of every paving stone.

And there, amidst the somehow impossibly real, pieced-together fragments of my dreams, was Darcy. Wearing a long petticoat, a flower-print dress, and a man's coat over it all. The pistol was still slung at their side, and they half-held a book in their other hand.

When they saw me, they dropped it on the ground.

They were here. They had waited for me. Hope sprung anew in my heart.

"*Peridetius alcan graccenae*," I whispered fervently. "You are my grace and my salvation, stood before me like the first glimpse of daylight in a long and dark winter. You are the guide for my wandering heart."

Darcy was pinned to the spot they stood in, indecision flickering across their features, but I saw the way their toes flexed and their body shook slightly. I strode towards them, crossing the space.

"Isidor," they said again, relief washing over them.

"In love, be bold." I said, the words erupting from me for no reason other than they were what immediately came. "Listen and take heed of your intended. But do not shy from offering all your heart. At worst, you shall know what it is to give of yourself fully. A feeling all men should know."

Darcy made a sound somewhere between a gasp and a choke, smiling at me like I was a man to be pitied. "That isn't from your holy tome, is it? It's—"

"'The Admiral's White Claw'," I admitted shamelessly. "I read that damned book so many times, Darcy… trying to understand what you see in it. I still can't. I'm sorry, but it's rubbish."

They gave a sobbing laugh, before I gathered them into my arms. I pulled them in tight until their warmth crushed against mine, and they wrapped their arms up around my neck, their cold nose pushing into my throat.

"It took you so long to make it back to me," they murmured, frustrated, even angry-sounding. "I thought they had you."

I went lightheaded in the euphoria of the dream made flesh,

forgetting all else. Not the Ministry, not Darcy's past or their looming sentence, not even God had space here between us. This place was for us, for but this moment in time, and none else.

God would understand. He'd shown me the way here, after all. He would want us to be happy.

That's the God I chose to believe in.

We'd both begun to snuffle and make piteous noises in the cramped and fur-muffled space between us. At some point, I managed to speak past the rock in my throat and ask, "H-how are you doing?"

They were silent a few beats, before answering uncertainly, "I don't know."

I nodded.

"… you?" they asked, sniffing.

"… I don't know," I said in one long exhale.

They pulled back just enough to lean forward again and tug me down by the collar. At first, I thought they were going to kiss me, but it didn't feel like the time for that. Instead, they pressed their forehead to mine and simply rested it there.

"I missed you," they said, voice soft and reedy.

"I missed you too," I replied, closing my eyes.

"There's, ah…" they gestured vaguely with one hand. "There's a place to sit inside that's dry. If you want to… it's… it's beautiful in there."

"I know," I said, before I could think about it.

They blinked their big eyes up at me. "How… you've been here before?"

"It's very, very hard to explain," I said, shaking my head. "Maybe later. Let's go sit."

We had barely begun to walk inside the walls of the crumbled edifice when we both caught the sounds of hurried paws on brittle snow down the lane. Darcy turned with a hand on their pistol, and I with a hand on my blade, and I felt the last vestiges of my childhood's assurance of safety fall away. Perhaps they should have before now. The both of us were so paranoid of pursuit now, we were on guard at the snap of a twig. We likely always would be. And that was a daunting, exhausting thought.

"It's my family," I said, releasing my palm from the hilt of my blade and giving a long, shuddering sigh. "I recognize the way Mabel's paws sound on paving stones."

"That's rather endearing," Darcy admitted, taking my hand in theirs.

This was it. This was Eden, the garden from which all love bloomed, or the closest I'd ever know. It was no sermon that awaited me, nor a wedding, nor was it the veil between life and death. Some part of me feared, all this while, that I'd only experience this reunion when I met God.

But this was real. Darcy stood beside me, my brother and sister were bounding through the center of the ancient building, while my Father ambled behind and stopped in the threshold, his aged gaze sweeping over the place before settling on me warmly.

"I tried to delay them," he apologized, "instead of coming *directly* out to see you, but they could not be persuaded to wait."

"Isi!" Mabel shouted jubilantly, leaping into me and wrapping her arm around my midsection, turning to look up at me with a wide, puppy-like smile on her face... that faltered somewhat when she saw—

"Isi, are you crying?" she asked, worried. "What's wrong?"

Nicholas joined her, soon followed more slowly by my Father. It wasn't long before I was surrounded by my family, standing there on the cracked stone dais, cast in multicolored hues by the rose window and the leaves above.

It was not my dream. I'd had it so many times, and it had shifted, changed... there couldn't help but be inconsistencies. It was no vision. I was no prophet.

But it was... my *dream*. And somehow, despite the odds, we had manifested it. We had made it real.

"I love you all," I declared, blinking back the tears and staring heavenward. "Thank you for coming this far with me."

"You told me of the dream once before," my father said as we took the lane back to the rectory home. This place which, I had to remind myself, was *not* the promised land of our journey. A tiny cabin tucked into the Amurescan countryside seemingly forgotten by most of the world might have seemed a good place to hide. This man had enough friends left even within the organization that had branded him a heretic that he'd been left largely alone here in his safehouse. Seclusion, neutral ground... but also, ultimately, a prison.

The Ministry knew he was here. They probably had to be careful about keeping vigil over him. A Templar would catch on, after all. But they'd find us in time if we stayed here long.

"Son?"

I nodded at my father. "The dream. Yes. Sorry. I still don't think it's a vision, but it is perhaps a sign?"

"I don't believe in visions," my Father confessed, shocking me. When he noticed my wide-eyed stare, he gave a humorless huff. "Yes, I know. It renders the words of many a prophet and several tales concerning Canus himself suspect. But Canus was uniquely-cursed. Any mortal forced to bear the knowledge of all the world, of every generation and every life come before, would know unspeakable suffering. Canus was humble. Tormented. He resisted taking the reins of power, all his short life." He shook his head. "God does not speak through the powerful. These men who claim to be prophets are almost always Patriarchs or Jarls, Generals or Kings. Convenient," he snuffed. "God speaks through the lowly. Through those who understand suffering and pain. In their words, unbeknownst to them... we find His wisdom. No Isidor... I do not believe in visions...."

I stared at him, transfixed. He was so certain in his words. So resolved. I knew then that this was not a new understanding he had come to. My father did not jump to wild conclusions. He was methodical. He thought things through for great lengths of time. Especially as they concerned faith.

He had felt this way, I think, for a very long time. And if he'd spoken a word of it from the pulpit, he would have been defrocked. How long had he believed in reformation?

"What I believe," he pressed on, "is that God gives *all* of us a chance at some point in our lives when we are laid low... to see the world as He does. With empathy. With compassion. It takes *feeling pain*, Isidor," he looked to me, that pain evident in his eyes, "to understand pain. We do not dress humbly, or eat humbly, or live humble lives to impress Him. He does not care for how we soothe our egos. We do so—we live our lives in the margins between—so that we may understand and spread hope to the marginalized. If you have a closer relationship with God now, if you feel Him working through you, speaking to you by way of dreams, or guiding you... I believe *that* is why. Because you have learned—earlier than I would have liked—how to feel the pain of the oppressed. And you are simply too good to ignore it. You love the world too much to turn a blind eye. As I did for many decades."

"You think too well of me," I murmured.

"I'm your father. It's my job," he tutted at me, tapping me with his cane. "But don't take that to mean you can't still better yourself. Straighten your posture. You're slouching."

I had to laugh. "Is now really the time? I've been in the saddle for *days*. My back hurts." I could allow myself the chance to whine, just this once.

"I may not have had much luck with married life," he dropped his voice slightly, despite the fact that Darcy would

426

definitely hear him, "but even I know a slump like that is not likely to impress your beloved. Do not stop putting in the effort simply because you believe you've secured their affections. I didn't raise slobs."

I sighed and straightened my back, grunting, "You know, honestly? I'm glad for this. You've begun to sound less and less like the Father I know. I was worried."

"The modern world is more nuanced and terrible than scripture can possibly prepare you for," he said. "Now that you're an adult, I can be more open with you and know you'll understand me. And perhaps, I should have done so long ago." He sighed, staring up at the sky and the waxing crescent moon just beginning to form in the deepening blues. "To prepare you earlier for all of this."

"Can I say something? I'm… confused on where you stand on Darcy," I admitted after a reprieve trying to find my words. "You were devastated when I told you I'd become enamored of my quarry. Understandably. And that wasn't so very long ago."

"I am still," he assured me. "I'd wager most fathers would be, given my position."

I couldn't deny he was right. Darcy's gender—or lack thereof, as my culture understood it—aside, they were an admitted thief. A suspect I'd been pursuing, which made this whole situation strange from multiple angles. And then there was our difference in kind. We would never have children. We would never be permitted in respectable society nor be allowed to purchase land together. Interspecies couples were not desirable for landlords to rent to, either. The future we faced was bleak whether we escaped the Ministry or not.

Perhaps the laws were different in Carvecia. I wasn't sure.

"But I know how stubborn you are," he continued, "how stubborn all young men your age are when they're in love. I'm not willing to make an enemy of you—"

"You will never be my enemy," I promised him.

"—nor am I willing to lose you," he said, softer. His gaze moved away from mine and got lost in the trees for a moment, and I knew he was thinking of Malachi. Of Father Whitehall. He'd been there at Saint Rhine's, watching. He'd heard everything the old Father had said. He had beheld the very darkest outcome of a story like ours. I'd seen it in his eyes since the funeral.

He was afraid of what could become of us.

"I have seen too many children die," he said in a hoarse whisper. "In my care, on the streets, even in the hallowed halls of the Pedigree. I would give *anything* to bring those young souls back." He shook his head, his long ears brushing past his cloak hood. "God would not ask me to sacrifice my children upon the altar of tradition, however hallowed those traditions. I do not agree with some of the choices you've made, Isidor. I do not *like* that feline; I will not lie to you about that. But the dawn of your courtship is young, and in time either you shall come to agree with me, or I with you. Either way, we *must* come to find a middle-ground on this, somehow. I will not bend you into a mold you cannot fit until the strain of trying to do so *kills* you."

I gave a fragile smile. We were close to finding a state of grace, he and I. We were so close.

"My only worry in the short term is that you pass as—at the very least—a husband and wife," he said, glancing briefly back at Darcy, "and that is purely for your safety while you travel. But your feline—"

"Darcy."

"Darcy," he sighed, "seems very adept at costuming and blending in. Follow their lead, for now. It will come in handy when you've had a chance to genuinely wed, as well. They'll need to assume the role of your wife, you know, regardless of how they feel on the matter."

I nearly choked on my spit. "I haven't—" I stammered, "—we

aren't… engaged, Father. I never assumed you'd *want* us to wed. We're not planning for marriage, right now."

"The hell you aren't," he growled. "You think I'd be permitting this behavior outside of wedlock under *any* other circumstances? Accepting that unless I allow this young love, I might lose my son, doesn't mean I've given up on you living as moral and righteous a life as I expected before. You are living in *sin*, Isidor, do not mistake that. Beyond the impropriety of the shameless affections you two share in front of your young sister, Nicholas has let on that you've been *sharing a bed*?"

"Damn it," I slumped over again.

Nicholas mouthed 'sorry' at me from behind us, and I glared at him. "You were together with Father for ten minutes before we reunited. How did you even have the time?"

"Lord, it's true," my father growled, briefly gripping his rosary and murmuring a prayer for patience. "Alright, enough glaring at one another," he snapped at us. "You—don't blame your brother for your own lapses in moral fortitude or your incompetence at being covert. Nicholas—deception, my boy. Learn to school your features better when you harbor illicit knowledge that can endanger your siblings and lower the volume of your voice when a man with ears like mine is about."

Nick's own ears perked. "You mean you want me to learn to lie better?"

Father intentionally ignored him and turned back to me. "You *will* do the right thing here, Isidor. I do not care that there is no threat of pups, and God does not parse that difference, either. You will step up and keep whatever promises you made to the—to young… Darcy. I didn't raise a rake, either."

"The house is just up ahead!" Brook called from the distant front of our procession, spurring her horse into a trot. When I lifted my head, I saw the clay-shingled roof and the eves just beyond the treeline, and a stocky male figure standing at the gates that ended the lane. He had a rifle balanced over his shoulder, but seemed to be at ease, despite keeping the weapon on his person.

That must have been the brother, I realized. He was dressed more humbly than his sister, with a dirty apron over a simple shirt and trousers, and long, mud-stained gloves, suggesting he'd been digging, for some reason.

Ominous.

He had the same seriousness and wariness to his features that his sister had upon first meeting strangers. They looked very alike as well, possible litter-mates. He regarded us coolly as we approached, saying nothing until his sister leaned down from her horse to put a hand on his shoulder. "Uncle confirmed from the house—they are who they say they are. And Darcy knows them, as well."

His brows lifted slightly, and in a slightly less confident tone than his sister, he greeted us with, "Hail. My name is Klaus, ah... we've been waiting for you. Pray, feel free to take your rest inside. I need to wash up, first."

The door to the cabin opened suddenly, albeit not quickly, with a creak of wood. And then came the final occupant, I had to imagine. The man himself.

I'll admit, I'd been massively curious about the Heresiarch the whole journey. Who he was, what he'd look like, what sort of presence he'd have about him. In retrospect, given that I knew of his providence, I should have been better prepared. But I wasn't.

I took a step back and felt Darcy move up behind me to clutch my elbow and steady me. "It shocked me, too," they assured me quietly. "You get used to it eventually."

The old wolfhound standing in the doorway of the cabin, tall despite the slight stoop age had given him and physically frail for the same reason, bore a shocking resemblance to the lurcher who had raised and tormented me. His coat: the same steely gray. His expression: the same calm, placid demeanor, but with a certain sharpness to his eyes that indicated the deadly life he'd led. Even in advanced age, he had that Templar bearing. As straight-backed as he could be, one arm folded behind him. His fur neatly-groomed but not styled. He even walked with a cane in a manner similar to Father's: Like he was more comfortable considering it a weapon.

He did not dress like a Templar, any longer. He wore a long, dark gray coat, over simple rural attire, much like young Master Klaus was wearing. Clean, tidy, but inexpensive. A rosary, tied at his waist around a red sash, indicating his continued loyalty to our armed men. Navy or home guard, I couldn't say.

The only thing that was out of place was a bit of old, gold cording, tied in a knot alongside his rosary. A personal memento out of step with the Templar standard of attire. We were not supposed to adorn or add to our rosaries.

"Germain," he said, in a rough, deep voice. Not just naturally baritone, but thick with age and possibly something else. An affliction, an ailment. It was hard to say.

"Johannes," my Father replied. They were both speaking neutrally to one another, but I knew my Father well enough to detect the hint of affection. He, at least, was glad to see the man.

"Good to see you still live," the Heresiarch said with a slight upturn of a mustached smile.

"You as well," my Father replied, stepping forward with a few taps of his cane on the paving stone. "Thank you for having such faith as to take in complete strangers for me. It was not an ask I made lightly. And I am cognizant of the risks you've taken on along with them."

The wolfhound made a dismissive sound in his nose. "Save your concern for my charges, here. Germain, this cancer—this affliction, whatever it may be—will consume me and send me to my next life any day now. I know each night I lay my head down that I may not wake. There is no risk to my personal safety that fears me, any longer."

My Father's ears drooped, and I saw the dawning sadness in his features. "You're dying."

The wolfhound only nodded, peacefully. "For some time now. This body clings, stubbornly, as it always has. But it will not be long."

"It isn't cancer," the young man, Klaus, said suddenly. Angrily. "The Ministry has been poisoning him."

"You cannot prove that," the wolfhound sighed.

"I might be of some assistance," Ruun spoke up, after clearing his throat. "Have you seen a Physician?"

"Several," he confirmed. "I've had a different diagnosis, every time. Cancer, an affliction of the bowel, simply age...."

"And every bloody one of them paid off by the Ministry not to say it is what it is, I'd wager," Klaus said again, frustrated.

"The well," I realized aloud.

"If the young buck there picked out the likely cause that quickly," Klaus snapped a finger, "that's relevant, ain't it? He thinks like they do, I'd wager."

Brook clucked her tongue as she stepped up beside her brother. "Aye, he's got an insight into those rotting cunts' heads we haven't had for decades, now. Knows how they operate."

"Enough," the wolfhound said calmly, authoritatively, and discussion ceased just like that. "There is no point in debating this right now. And stop clapping your maws like privateers when you're in my home. Lord help you if your mother heard that language."

"We should get inside," Brook said suddenly, staring out towards the vista in the direction of the road. I could see now how they might have spied on us from up here. It looked like at some point, someone had cleared just enough trees that you could probably see horses, lanterns, or carriages from the road.

Every head turned towards the same direction, ears perked, noses to the wind. I saw and smelled nothing but the woods... but that didn't mean anything.

"Just deer on the trails, I think," this man Johannes said, "but all the same. Come inside. Let's start dinner."

It was impossible not to catch the parallels there, between my own father's well-meaning but strict way with his children, and this family I'd never known. It felt familiar, if strange. So much here seemed unspoken and secretive, like they were several steps ahead of where we were. Caught in the same or similar circumstances, but better equipped.

I knew little of what had befallen this family, save what most people knew. Pedigree families fell to scandal all the time. Theirs had been particularly tragic, but not remarkable in its impact. The fact that they'd stayed together through it, at least somewhat, struck me as what mattered.

There was hope.

"It's uncanny, isn't it?" Darcy whispered softly from my side. Their claws were clinging through the fabric of my sleeve, a little more tightly than they needed to be. It comforted me, honestly. To come here and find them still enamored enough of me, trusting in me, to clutch to me when they were uncomfortable.

After everything that had happened, a part of me earnestly worried it was over between us. Being rejected by them now would have stung worse than any lash, but... I would not have blamed them.

I looked up and watched as the old wolfhound spoke quietly with my father, the two of them falling into step as they walked back towards the house.

"It is," I agreed, "he looks so much like Dolus... older, more fragile. His fur's longer. They had the same father, apparently. That sort of thing happens with Abbeys, sometimes. Taking in bastards. Some Lords are particularly prone to indiscretion with their hired help, or prostitutes. I believe Cuthbert's took in two such boys from that estate, a generation apart. Different mothers. Both servants."

Darcy gave me a scalding stare. "It's rich, you know. Your Order going on about purity of body and spirit when they willingly allow rich men to sire bastards left and right and then ferry them off to abbeys or workhouses to get rid of them."

"They don't just allow it," I sighed, "they *enable* it."

"How is that right, Isidor?"

"It isn't," I said softly. I turned to look down at them, at their beautiful, angry eyes, and I felt a *good* kind of shame. It was odd to think of it that way, but it felt healing. Painful still, but as though it were scarring over. "What happened to you, this man Johannes, the women who were taken advantage of... even Dolus... it *isn't* right. And to be honest, I'm not certain how I ever justified that it was. They give you reasons. Some of them *sound* like they could be justifiable. I think the reason I went out searching for something everyone told me was unattainable, impossible, a fool's errand... was because I was grappling with taking the real steps to becoming what I'd been brought up to be. I knew what I was supposed to do, but something about it all felt so *off*. I hunted you because... because I was looking to find answers. To learn why my heart felt so out of step with my life."

They gave a mirthless laugh. "So, you tried to find the Heart Thief. Return your Heart of Faith, and... what? Fix how you felt?"

"That might have been my intention, I can't say," I sighed.

"I'm sorry I couldn't help you, then," they said. "I never stole it in the first place, so...."

"You *did* help me," I assured them, moving my hand down to wrap around theirs. My wrist still ached from the injury, but... not as much, these days.

Darcy gave a ghost of an impish smile, like they might have in happier times. "If you say something like 'you stole *my* heart instead'…"

"I wouldn't dare," I scoffed. "Even *my* melodrama has its limits."

"I like your melodrama," they said softly. And they leaned against me as we followed my family inside the cabin. My brother and sister headed immediately towards a table where a loaf of marbled bread and a butter dish sat and began pulling out chairs for my Father and Ruun. Nick said something about getting some tea going while Mabel began cutting the two old men some of the fresh bread. The Heresiarch—or I should say, Johannes—sat stiffly alongside my Father, and the two of them rested their canes against one another in the space in between the chairs. The camaraderie there was clear, and I was happy for my Father. Despite his reservations about the man, he seemed very glad to see him.

"Isidor," Darcy spoke again, their presence at my side a constant warmth now I hoped I'd have a chance to get very used to. I instinctively leaned down and pressed my nose into the crown of their head, kissing them between the ears.

"I'd like to give Confession," the serval said, the whispered words freezing me on the spot. I looked them in the eyes, just to be certain. There was no humor there, no uncertainty either. Just stoicism.

"With you," they said seriously.

"I'm… not a priest," I said. "If you just mean you want to talk, then we can—"

"No," they shook their head. "I need… I need to confess something. I want you to hear it. If you'd like your Father present for it, I'll confess to him, too. And… maybe I should, earnestly."

They slowly slipped their hand from mine and took one

tentative step towards the table, but no closer. Looking back at me afterwards, they said, "If I'm to be a part of your family... we both ought to decide whether or not that's what we want."

"Darcy, I-I..." I was at a loss. "I want you in my life. That isn't a question, at least not for my part. All that matters now is that you want it, too."

"You might change your mind when you hear what I have to say," they whispered.

I went silent and frightened. But eventually, I relented with a nod.

"I'll speak to my Father after dinner," I said resignedly.

"We'll do it together," Darcy promised.

I nodded tightly. "Together," I agreed.

"By the Grace of God this day, I compel thee—speak the truth, answer all questions asked in as detailed a recounting as your faculties are capable of, make no excuses for sin or misbehavior, and know that deception of any kind under His eyes is grounds for retribution upon the flesh in this mortal world and descension of your soul in the next."

I'd never heard the Inquisitor's Prayer in my father's firm timbre before. How many times had he sat with a criminal or a sinner, or an innocent for that matter, and said these words?

"Now," my Father continued calmly and neutrally. "You've never done this before, have you?"

"Once," Darcy admitted haltingly. They chose their next words carefully. "When... the family who adopted me—"

"You can say it was the Rathbornes, child," Father said. "I know."

"Alright, well," they cleared their throat quietly. "When they first learned my relationship with..." here they paused, swallowing thickly, "... with Cillian... had turned physical. They brought in an Inquisitor to put the fear of God in the two of us. I don't remember what he asked, but I don't think that was the point. They just wanted us to know we couldn't speak on what was happening between us, or they'd see to it the Church did something about it. It worked. We didn't... stop... but we hid what we had. We got really *good* at hiding it, in fact. So, I'm not sure it had its intended effect."

"You're insisting that this be a proper Inquisition Confession," the bloodhound reminded them. "I could instead take your Confession as merely a Priest and keep what we say between us and God, instead."

"No," they said firmly. Then they tapped the table with a claw. "I want you to be able to record this within your Ministry's Archives. I want the truth recorded *somewhere* in between all the lies, even if no one ever reads it."

"As you wish, then," Father said, offering his hands. One to Darcy, one to me. "God, hear through mine ears the willing testimony of sin from this, your child. Relieve them of the burden of bearing it alone and show them the way to redemption." He looked between us. "Repeat this part after me: So He has said, and so I swear upon His name."

The both of us spoke the final, personal verse of the Inquisitor's prayer, and I felt my father's hand close around mine tightly for a moment. His eyes moved to me, concern there, questioning without words if this was truly a wise idea.

But we'd given ourselves to God, already. And Darcy seemed to need this relief of burdens. I did, too.

Darcy opened their eyes slowly. I hadn't even realized they'd been closed. I wasn't sure if they prayed, but if they did, it seemed they must have been sending their own hopes heavenward before beginning.

"So... are we...?"

"Yes," my Father said, his tone empathetic despite his

discomfort with the feline. He took his oath here to heart. I had no doubt of the man's desire to do good in his role as Priest, and I hoped Darcy felt the same, but it was hard to say. "You can speak now," he said, without urgency.

"Well, first off, I never stole your Heart of Faith," Darcy said. "I looked into it when I realized I'd been accused of the crime, but that's the extent of what I know of it. I've never taken the pilgrimage, nor seen anything but a rough rendering of it; I'm not even certain I'd know it if I saw it."

My father nodded but said nothing. This was not the time for interjection or questioning.

"I am a thief," they said, lifting their chin. Owning it with little evident shame. "My entire life was stolen from me. That's not an excuse. I'm trying to explain my reasoning. How I became what I became."

My father nodded again for them to continue, so they did. "I couldn't return what I lost, but I thought... I thought I could return what others had lost if I was careful and cunning. It started with a few simple capers at households I traveled to Cillian with, and it grew as I grew apart from him. With no further need to protect his name and no name of my own on any legal documents, I was a ghost. I was good at it. And I only got better at it as I grew bolder and less concerned about risk."

I frowned, my teeth worrying at my lower jaw. I didn't like how unapologetic they were being about their crimes when my Father already had little reason to trust them... but... this was a Confession. And it was important they be honest, even if that honesty was inconvenient for me.

"I don't regret taking... things," they said, their nose twitching. "I've beheld so much willful and neglectful cruelty in my lifetime from the very people whose riches, art, and curios I pilfered... most of it directed at those whose livelihoods and chance at happiness they *owned*. I'm not a child. I know it's like this the world over. I know the moneyed, the powerful, and the vicious aren't punished for invasion if it's seen as conquest. Or murder, if it's part of making war. But theft...."

They set their jaw. "Theft is the great equalizer. It's not equal in the *law*, don't misunderstand me. The rich don't hang for it—of course they don't—because to them, it's spoils. It's gifts given at the point of a sword or taken when they 'civilize' the lesser races. It's a mission from God. To send poor, unfortunate children away from their dirty little village to a big, foreign house, in a big, foreign country, to bless them with the more righteous, more educated, more civilized life... of a servant. If they're lucky, *only* a servant."

My father's expression softened to sadness slowly, and I watched in real time as he learned what I'd learned months ago, when Darcy had revealed their past to me. Except in his case, I had to believe he'd known of the practice before, and Darcy was not the first he'd met of these displaced, used, and abused people. Would it help him understand them better? Or was this worse?

"So, I don't regret taking things from them," they said. "Nay, I refuse to apologize. They steal *lives*, as *well* as things. I cannot do much for people like me, but I can restore connections. Artifacts, not unlike your Heart, but taken from other countries. Other people, who I assure you, are as bereft as you are to be missing your pilgrimage. It wasn't always a piece of art taken by colonizers or pilfered from afar for some Pedigree's private collection. Sometimes it was a family heirloom, seized for a debt. A coffer or purse from a Lordling denying his staff their proper pay. Whatever struck my fancy that I could get away with. None of the people I took from were worse off for the lack of the *thing*," they emphasized that part.

And then stopped.

"There is," they pressed on with some difficulty, "one part on which I do not reflect well. One terrible night that gave me pause. Not enough to stop, clearly. And I cannot tell you why that is so. I cannot say what compelled me past this other than the inability to find any other purpose in my life. I was simultaneously trying to get caught, I think… and terrified of the penalty I would pay when I was. I'm a coward."

Whatever this was, it had them terrified to speak. They were shaking, almost imperceptibly, but I was close enough to them to feel it. I was certain my Father felt it through his hand. As he had so many times in the past when he'd held my hand, he did not berate or shame them to continue, or remind them of the punishments they would face if they did not. He waited. He gave them silence to fill on their own, when they were ready. This was no interrogation, after all. Darcy wanted to do this. To unburden themselves.

My Father was very, very good at his vocation. And he was able to do so without the violence, intimidation, and coercion Dolus and Malachi had employed. No accusation, no intimidating body language, no domination nor threats of bodily harm, none of that mantra was in practice here. I would never be a Templar, let alone an Inquisitor, again. But if I had been, I hoped I would have been like Germain Helstrom. For all his self-admitted failures, he'd tried to do more good than harm.

And if anyone could take this Confession—the account of the supposed Heart Thief themselves—and do some good with it, it would be him.

Darcy was silent for a long while. Finding the words. When they did speak again, their voice was frail, thin, and sad.

"Someone died," they said, trembling. Then, forcefully, "I *caused* someone to die. I think. I—I don't know…."

My Father kept his voice steady. "What do you mean? You aren't certain they died, or…?"

I could not hide the expression of betrayal on my features.

They'd told me on more than one occasion that they'd never killed anyone in the course of their crimes. In fact, they'd said they'd never killed anyone *at all*. Multiple times. And I had believed them. It was a certainty I hadn't doubted for a long while now.

"She died," Darcy said, their voice wavering. "She stopped breathing, she... went cold. But, I... I didn't intend to kill her. I didn't even used to carry a weapon, back then. I only kept a pistol after the bounty hunter kidnapped me, and I knew the Church was hunting me. I didn't have one that night."

"How did she die?" my Father persisted, and I felt his grip on my palm squeeze again. Reminding me of his presence. His support. Knowing I might need it. I did. I was so confused.

"I think I... startled her," they admitted miserably. I could see the memories dancing across their eyes. "It was a small estate, and I couldn't blend in with the staff or even in town. I had to steal into the place in my dye in the middle of the night. It was raining, I had my cloak hood up, the dye was running in my fur... I must have looked a fright in the pitch dark of that old manor. She'd heard something, I suppose, and came with a lantern. I was near the grand staircase when she saw me. I don't know if she had an attack of the heart right there on the spot, or if... if she was just so startled, she... she fell."

"The housekeeper," I realized aloud, wincing as it all fell into place. The death had never really fit into the conspiracy. I'd assumed it was a crime by another thief, pinned on Darcy. Or someone the Ministry had decided didn't need to speak on what they knew.

"The house was small for an estate, but still so big that no one heard," Darcy said, eyes squinting shut as tears boiled out the corners. The feline swiped an arm past them, their voice growing choked. "I didn't mean... I didn't intend it. I wasn't even *trying* to scare her; I was just caught unawares, and she was an old woman. She lost her footing, or her heart gave out and then she lost her footing... I've never been sure. I sat there with her at the landing of that staircase for over an hour. I thought about calling for help, but she was... she was *dead*. Not breathing, limp as a ragdoll. I was frozen."

"I... stayed there," they said, haunted, "expecting someone would eventually find us. I was certain I'd be caught that night. That it had all come to an end finally, and... I was ready. I was ready then." They sniffed wetly. "But no one ever came. Honestly, I'm not even certain the family was home. She might have been alone in that house. Eventually, I-I just... left. I crawled into a bottle for a month, I wrote to Cillian; he never wrote back. I realized how *alone* I was, and I almost gave it all up."

They hung their head slowly. "But it was how I justified my existence by then. I was the Heart Thief. They were going to catch me and hang me for the one I *didn't* do. Inevitably. So why not go down in infamy? Maybe I'd make a few people happy before I did. Return what was lost."

They tipped their head marginally to chance a glimpse at me. I wasn't sure what my face looked like, but 'torn' would probably be apt. They said, "Cillian never knew. I didn't tell him in the letter I sent. And I'm glad. I'm glad he believed I was better than I am, right to the end. I know I'm meant to be asking God here, but Isidor...." They were desperate when they asked, "Will you forgive me?"

I wanted to. So badly. And I knew I could. But....

"I will," I promised them, "but Darcy. Please. Swear to me you'll never put yourself—or any other innocent person—at risk, breaking into houses, again. I *know* how strongly you feel about all of this, and I understand *why* better now than before. But it's dangerous. It's so bloody dangerous, and there has to be another way. A better way. Even if it's the most important relic imaginable… it's a *thing*. It isn't worth a single life. Not taken intentionally, not by accident. No matter what it is."

"No matter what it is?" they asked pointedly.

"No matter," I agreed sagely with a nod. "Whatever happened to the Heart, it is my firm belief God would not expect us to sacrifice one of His children for a metal plate. These objects only have the power and importance *we* attach to them. God does not imbue the mundane. And He does not want us to suffer or kill for material things. That's how all of this started. And I won't do it anymore. I won't be a part of it. I can't abide you being a part of it, either. I won't knowingly risk the lives of others, then stand before God and say I did the best I could. That just isn't so. We can *both* do better than this. *Be* better than we are. I think you must know that, or you would have taken this to your grave."

"I swear," Darcy said softly. "I'm done. I'm not certain there *is* another way, but… it all has to end at some point, doesn't it? I never wanted to hurt people. I never wanted to scare people. I just wanted to do something that made me feel like… I *was* someone. But this isn't who I wanted to be."

Their words made me ache. I wanted to say something, to help them somehow, but that wasn't my role, here. I was a Confessor, as well.

"I must pray on this, before I give you my own thoughts on how to make repentance," my Father spoke up. "And I think you should consider how you regard this serious misstep more carefully. I heard many excuses made, just now. The fact is, this is a death you must own, not for my son's sake, but your own. You are chasing after ghosts if you think this guilt will fade today. Take my advice at least in this, child. You will *never* be completely at peace with being responsible for the loss of another's life, however indirectly. Not if you are a decent person. It will haunt you until the day you die."

They nodded stiffly and depressively.

"And it should," he said with conviction. "That is the weight of it, and it is a gift from the Divine, so that we know the value of life and seek to preserve it. To be less reckless, to curb our anger and our desire for vengeance. It is that burden that ends wars and forces those of us who've led violent lives to reconsider our choices. To, as Isidor said... be better than we are. You'll feel it forever, and that is a *good* thing. It may not seem it now. But trust me."

He looked to me, for some reason. "Laying down one's sword is hard. Especially when you believe in what you fight for. But there are battles won without violence, brazenness, or violation. The next phase of your life may see you battling injustice with a pen. Or leading by example. Or simply... caring for the vulnerable. Helping them heal. Perhaps helping yourself heal, in the process."

He held my gaze then and smiled just enough that I saw it. He'd never smiled at me during Confession before. It was warm, if fleeting.

"I don't know that I believe in the God your religion teaches of," Darcy said softly, "but, insofar as you know them, do you think they'd forgive me?"

"They already have," he assured them solidly. "Tell me. Do you not feel slightly better, having told someone you trust what was weighing heavy on your heart?"

"I'm telling you because I know you'll faithfully transcribe what would have been my confession at the gallows," they clarified seriously. "I don't know if I trust you, yet. But..." they looked to me, "... I didn't like keeping this from you, Isidor. It hurt every time you bared your soul to me. Being unable to do the same. I don't trust easily. I'm sorry."

"That feeling inside that you are experiencing now is what we call the Relief of Burdens," my Father said. "The sensation of weight, slowly lifting from you? That is God's grace. A relief for... Their... children, given because you had the strength and courage to share your truth here today."

"Hah," Darcy huffed quietly. "You dropped the 'He' for me. Don't think I missed that, old man."

"There is but One True God," my father declared kindly but firmly, without any pretense, "but what care He for how He is addressed? If it helps you find your way to God to think of Them more like yourself... I have ministered well. Sharing the Word means understanding people are different and will have different views of Him. Of Her, of Them. God is God."

"If the rest of your Church felt the same, I might consider it," Darcy said, stoically, "but your Institution denies the existence of people like me. They revoke the right to live or exist as they are for people like Isidor, Cillian... even the bloody malamute. Look what it all led to. What that zealotry has wrought."

"Malachi's torture was at the hands of mortal men misunderstanding the Word in ways that suited them," he said. "Their 'doctrine' was designed to mold him into a soldier, whose loyalty was promised through guilt... not protect his soul. And certainly not to honor God."

"You know, your Inquisitors demonized me, literally, when they assumed me a temptress who was 'poisoning the mind' of one of their chosen sons," Darcy said. "What *that man* did to Cillian was the act of a demon. If such a creature exists, we met him that day."

"Malachi was not born angry and violent," my Father said. "We, not God, made him that way. Misled men of faith, making horrific mistakes. Some made out of hatred, some... misunderstanding. Malachi's Father loved him. He just did not understand him."

"Your 'mistakes' have gotten a lot of people killed," the serval said venomously.

The bloodhound didn't deny it. He was an honest man, after all.

"They make their own demons," Darcy said. "They would have done the same to *your* son, you know."

My Father hesitated only a few pained seconds before replying, "Yes. I know. The Ministry is not a safe place for him anym-"

"Not just the Ministry of Templar," Darcy said fiercely. "Your *Church*. The Institution itself. I appreciate you trying to reach out. It's more consideration than I've warranted in the past. But your religion..." their gaze lingered for a moment on where my hand clutched my Father's. I realized, suddenly, that they were eyeing our rosaries. The both of us held them wrapped around our hands when we gave Confession.

"... your religion hates me. It hates... us." Darcy said, their eyes downcast, voice betraying how battered down and exhausted they were by that reality.

The words and the pain imbued in them rolled over me like a wave, pulling me under and stealing my breath. Because the fact was, Darcy was *right*. Overwhelmingly. I'd spent months now deconstructing all the separate parts of my faith that didn't ring true to my experiences, or the God I knew in my heart. But it wasn't just incorrect scripture, men preaching lies, or atrocities being committed in God's name. It was *all of* those things, but more importantly...

It was the Church.

Not just the Ministry. The whole bloody Institution was corrupt. And beyond the corruption, they were just... wrong. A lay Priest would still tell me my feelings for Darcy were lies whispered by Ciraberos, sins I would need to repent for, and that was *never* going to change as things were.

Darcy had sat with me and listened to me speak on my faith, on the organization I had such doubts in, had stood at my side while I wore the vestments and my rosary, and now they were even partaking in Confession with me. For my sake, I had to assume. They had never been dishonest with me about their own beliefs being different, but they had always sought to respect mine.

And my Church denied their very existence.

I felt the beads of my rosary in my palm, squeezed between my grip and my Father's. The weight of them stood out to me like a thorn in my paw, suddenly.

"*I* do not hate you," the bloodhound said, as if settling the matter for himself out loud. "My son has chosen you as his beloved. He is part of the family I made for myself in the walls of that Abbey, and I will not cast aside family because I don't understand every choice they've made in their life. Earnestly…" he leaned in just a bit closer to the feline, crossing a hairsbreadth into the five-paw distance. Darcy would not know the significance, but I did. Father only allowed kin so close.

"Whether or not you intended it, speaking to you tonight means a great deal to me, personally. Not just because it may help us find the truth of this case, but because I can see how the guilt of this misstep weighs on you, and that means you have a healthy heart. You yearn for redemption. Not in the religious sense, but… in the personal. And that sets my soul at ease more than you can know. You will be with my son when I cannot. You will be a larger part of his future than I."

His deep-set green eyes moved to mine again, passionate as I had ever known. "I love my boy. Please take care of him."

Darcy inhaled with a staggered breath and nodded, wiping their eyes once more.

"You aren't alone," I nearly whispered. Both of them turned to look at me. "We may have killed a man when we were breaking you out," I went on. "One of the secular agents, but a member of our Order nonetheless. I think he must have survived, or Dolus would have leveled his death against me at Saint Rhine's, but...."

Darcy looked crestfallen. "Isidor, I'm so sorry, that's on me t—"

"No," I felt bad interrupting them, but I didn't want another pain like that on their conscience. "You were being tortured by a depraved man who uses God as a cudgel to take his frustrations out on the vulnerable. I don't regret that we did what we had to get you out. We had no choice. But Malachi... I regret everything about what I did to Malachi."

My Father's expression had softened, but Darcy's had soured to anger at the mention of the malamute. It didn't seem directed at me, but the heat of their eyes, of their pain, scalded me all the same.

"I killed Malachi," I rasped. "I'm the reason he died."

"*No*," Darcy said vehemently and furiously. "That monster ended his life because he couldn't bear what he'd done. The world is a better place with him gone, Isidor. I only wish he'd done it sooner."

"I seduced him, Darcy," I said, looking up at them. They flinched as if lashed, but not in shock. They seem to have anticipated the admission. Hardly strange, given what had passed between us in that church. My Father clearly hadn't expected it and seemed woefully confused, although trying to maintain his composure.

"I let him kiss me," I explained, closing my eyes a moment. "At the apartment, when I was meant to be distracting him. While the mercenaries retrieved you. I... I didn't realize I'd been luring him that way, leading him on, but I must have been." I was rambling now, as I was wont to in Confession, but if there were any time to let this all out, it was now. "I'd intended just to... to talk to him. But he kissed me, and I let him, and then it kept happening, a-and... all I could think of was that I had to allow it, to not rebuff him, or I'd have to fight him, instead. And I was frightened I would lose. I had opportunities to catch him unawares, I-I probably could have, but given what happened at the church on the hill, I'm not even sure that would have been enough. The man bested me handily even gravely wounded."

I opened my eyes, scared of what I'd see. Darcy looked horrified, my father verging on angry. But his gaze wasn't directed at me, which meant he was angry at someone else. When that man was angry at you, he looked you square in the eyes.

Both were holding my hand tighter now, my father across the table, Darcy under it. I felt assured to go on.

"I played the part of Incubus to misdirect him," I confessed, swallowing thickly. "But I did try to talk to him about my misgivings, about the case, about how men like us were treated within the church, and... he just buckled down. Repeating the same things he'd always said, and... it was like he'd fortified himself in those beliefs. I wasn't sure how to show him there might be another way. A way out for him. But I... I considered telling him, anyway. Everything." I swallowed, remembering the scent of his blood from the lash, the fervor in his eyes, the manic way he'd spoken, desperately clinging to his self-inflicted pain as an anchor to justify his existence. "Considered it," I said in a whisper. "But in the end, I was just too frightened."

"If you had, he would have killed you," my Father said without hesitation.

I blinked at him, shocked. "How can you be sure?"

"Because he tried to kill us in the church," Darcy said with a growl in their voice. "He *murdered* Cillian."

"I'm not defending him," I began to say—

"Then don't," Darcy cut me off. "Whether he meant for him to die or not, he tortured him to within an inch of his life, Isidor. He used him to get to me, to *us*, and now Cillian is gone, and I will never get him back. I barely remember the last moments we spent together... any reconciliation we might have had in the future is gone *with* him. He was... is... a piece of me. That man killed my oldest friend." Their eyes burned. "And he hurt *you*. He twisted you up so badly, you're blaming *yourself*. He nearly killed you for daring to have what he wanted with you with someone else, and you're making *excuses* for him."

Their words were sharp but measured. Not so raw as they had been in the days following. They were choosing what they said carefully with the restraint only time could bestow. I was glad for it. Glad that we'd both had time to think on what had happened, before either of us said something we regretted. I wanted Darcy to pour their heart out, but I knew how cutting they could be, when pressed. Any accusation from them now would have rent through me like a knife because I felt that's what I deserved.

But I was so tired of hurting.

My father brought in a long breath, slowly, before asking, "Did he force himself on you, son? If you'd rather not say—"

"No," I answered simply. "Not... there was a lot of touching, but...."

Darcy turned their eyes from me, biting at their lower jaw with barely withheld rage. They were clearly struggling with their feelings, but their grip on my hand had tightened, not pulled away. For some reason, it felt like none of the anger in the room was directed at *me*, like I'd been anticipating.

"... but if he had," I said roughly, my voice strained, "it would have been my own fault. I'm not the best actor, I... don't know how he didn't feel my discomfort, but he didn't, and I let it all continue. I even kissed him back once when a sound from outside nearly gave the mercenaries away. I was scared of what might happen if I rejected him. To me, to *you*, Darcy. I led him to believe his feelings were reciprocated, and the deception ultimately broke his heart. Broke *him*. I caused everything that happened."

"That poor boy was damaged long before you came into his life, Isidor," my Father said gravely. "You aren't responsible for what the Ministry did to him. There are corners of our Order so dark as to be unimaginable." His face twitched a moment, as though contending with a dreadful memory. "Malachi endured a terrible loss when he was young, reacted violently—perhaps understandably so—to that pain, and was taught to loathe the sin inside him with such vitriol that he turned that violence on himself."

"He didn't just abuse himself, though," Darcy countered. "He was always aggressive with Cillian. He told me. Antagonized him, browbeat him, threatened him. He stood by while the monk tortured me, for no reason—he wasn't even asking me questions—and said *nothing*," they snapped the words out. "He wasn't just some lost, confused, good-hearted person, Isidor. He might have hated himself, but he turned that hate *outwards* when that wasn't enough to satisfy him. He took his pain out on *us*." Their fangs glinted in the candlelight as their voice rose. "I hate that you're agonizing over that man. He wasn't worth all of this."

"I cared for him," I confessed weakly. "Not in the way he yearned for, but I felt for him, as a Brother. He helped me understand things about myself, and he was *trying* to help me avoid the troubles he endured. I think it's why he... killed himself." I sucked in a breath, my words coming out in a tumult. "He knew they'd interrogate him. He *was* in pain, he *was* struggling with what he'd done, but he also knew they'd use him to find us. His death robbed them of that option."

"I won't consider that man a martyr," Darcy said icily. "And I will never forgive him for what he did to us. What he cost us... and what he nearly cost us."

I nodded, unwilling to fight them on their assertions. I understood their anger, even if I didn't entirely share it.

"Cillian's children will never know their father now. The cycle continues," Darcy said bitterly. "And no, I don't like that he laid hands on you. But—" they pressed on before I could argue my part in it again, "I like even less that you're *blaming* yourself for it. Our lives were at stake, Isidor. I'm glad it didn't come to it, but I would've understood... whatever you'd had to do... to leave that apartment alive. The shame isn't yours. You did what you had to."

"Father?" I asked trepidatiously. The man had been silent a long time.

"I'm just so sorry you've had to endure all of this," he said. "But son, regardless of what you may have said or done with that man that gave him the impression he could... do that to you... he was your Senior Brother. He was meant to be serving as your veteran, experienced agent in the investigation, as a *guardian* to you. I was worried when I first looked into the man that he might teach you what was taught to him. Teachings I knew to be poisonous. *That* was my concern."

"He tried," I confirmed quietly. "It all sounded so wrong."

"You are a *good* man, Isidor," my Father said emphatically. "Your heart guides you true, and I am *so* proud of you. But you are also—for another month at least—nineteen. Malachi taught you arms when you were a young boy, and he an adult. He held as much power over you as Brother Dolus, or any other older man in our Order. He should *never* have had designs on you, let alone acted on them. For a *bevy* of reasons, but what matters here is *you are not to blame.* On this, there is no need for forgiveness. From anyone here, or God. I hope in time you can come to see that."

"I'm... struggling to, now," I admitted hesitantly. "It's confusing. It's so confusing. I wish I could talk to him again. There are so many things I would ask."

"I wish I could talk to Cillian again," Darcy said, hanging their head. "Even just write him a letter."

"You should," my father said, and both of us looked up. He nodded, smiling through the obvious tension in his jaw. "It may help. I wrote in my journals for years, sometimes to people who yet lived, whom I could not bear to argue with, and sometimes to colleagues who had passed. It… helped. To put it all to the page, it felt a bit like Confession. Prayer as well, but there is no harm in doing both. Consider it. No assurances of forgiveness I give you here will fully set you at ease. These are terrible losses the both of you have suffered. Talk to one another, as well. But ultimately, wounds this deep take time."

He released our hands gingerly, lingering on mine a bit longer before he laced his fingers in front of him on the table.

"There is a stark line most of those with a beating heart draw, before and after they've taken a life," he said. "That you are struggling is right, and you will struggle with it forever. Trust me."

At length, I asked the obvious question, even though I felt I'd known the answer for a long time now. "Father. Have you—"

"Yes," he answered immediately. "During the very last mission I took before my retirement from active duty as an Inquisitor, I killed a man. I killed many men and women during my time serving as a soldier for God and Amuresca. Those faces haunt my dreams and always shall. But this man… this man was Mabel's blood father."

I think I'd known. But to have it confirmed….

"I wasn't sanctioned to kill him. It was a problem for the Ministry that he died, in fact," he admitted. "Not so much that they weren't willing to sweep it under the rug for a Senior Inquisitor, but… that isn't the point. I killed him because I was angry. It was murder." He lifted his gaze to us, the shadows beneath and the folds above his brows hiding so much of what he must have been feeling. I would never know the depths of an

Inquisitor's trauma. And that was a blessing I would not soon forget.

"I regret it less than I should," he admitted. "I knew it meant I had fallen from grace and lost any right to serve as a blade for the Lord. I wasn't sure what my life would be from that point on... but I knew one thing with certainty. I owed it to the girl I'd found chained in that man's cellar to be her safe harbor. To do everything in my power to be a bridge to a happier life for her."

He looked between us. "You two, and your brother and sister, need to be that for one another, now. You must take up the mantle. The pain, the grief, the guilt of what you've experienced... will not fade easily. But we cannot spend our whole lives looking behind us, or we will miss what matters in the present. Ciraberos taught us that, and it is a wisdom I have struggled to embrace, myself."

He reached forward, tipping my chin up, and I felt myself straighten my posture instinctively. He smiled once more at me, this time his jowls touching his cheeks. His eyes were glossy, but proud.

"Nose to the wind, son. Ears up. Ever vigilant. You'll persevere. You always have. God is with you. You will be in my prayers and my heart, no matter how far apart we are."

Darcy and I left the cabin that night, walking the short distance to the ruins, led by little more than moonlight and one another. Their presence was close at my side, their hand brushing past mine as we traveled in silence.

There was too much to discuss in that house. More than we could stomach tonight. Planning, goodbyes, new allies. It could all wait until tomorrow. One thing remained unsettled between us, and I think we'd both sensed we needed to be alone to do so.

The rose window was purplish-blue, lit from behind by the

crescent moon. Darcy looked ethereal beneath it, reaching a hand up to tap emptily at the design in the air, like they could pluck the flower.

I sat on the altar, watching them. My body was exhausted, and my mind felt hazy with how overwhelming the day had been. My thoughts were erratic, replaying what I knew, what I'd learned, and what had been said.

The untethered new reality of my life stretched before me like an empty map. It was… so much. I hardly knew how to feel.

"What do you wish us to be?" I finally asked them, the words having been on the tip of my tongue since the Confession.

It was the obvious—and only—question that mattered right now, between us.

"Are we… friends?" I ventured. "Are we lovers? Are you uncertain what you wish for us to be?"

I didn't want to entertain the final possibility. That we were enemies, again. It didn't feel like that's what they wanted, but it could be that all the tenderness and closeness was some form of goodbye. Darcy was, even now, a mystery to me in many ways. I don't think the feline was ever going to be fully known to me. And that was fine.

I liked mysteries. I liked untangling them, I liked being challenged by them. I wanted Darcy to challenge me, forever. If they'd still have me.

But I had hesitated when it had mattered most. I'd failed to protect them. We disagreed on the subject of Malachi, and that was a heavy burden for a relationship to bear. They might feel we were better off not growing any closer than we were. Or even stepping backwards.

I would have to accept it, if that were the case.

"Do you no longer wish to be with me?" Darcy asked, without turning around. I don't think it was indifference. I think they were hiding their expression from me.

They hid so many things. It's how they'd protected themselves all this time.

I got up and walked across the broken stone floor towards them, stepping over upturned roots and mossy fragments of the fallen roof. I didn't look heavenward once. I had to have my own courage here, so that I could show it to them. I couldn't rely on God for everything. Least of all what Darcy deserved to have *from me.*

I stepped around in front of them and slowly reached for their chin with a claw, to tip their eyes into the moonlight if they'd allow it. They did.

"I love you now more than I ever have," I assured them, my heart in my throat. "I'll belong to you, body and soul... if you'll have me."

Their whiskers shook with a shiver so subtle, you'd only see it inches apart. "I'll have you," they whispered.

I let out the breath I'd been holding, my body uncoiling as it never had before. In all that had befallen me throughout my chaotic life, I had never known such fear as I knew in those intermittent moments.

"But," they said, and my chest tightened, "not without a promise. You asked me to give up thieving."

"Because it's dangerous," I insisted. "Because of what can and has happened-"

"You don't need to justify it," they said, shaking their head. "I'd already made the decision, I just didn't have the nerve to say it. I should have walked away from it all a long time ago, even though it's a deeply-held conviction." They looked up at me. "It was hurting the people I care for."

"Darcy," I said, my voice threadbare. I squeezed my rosary in my palm, again. I don't think I'd stopped holding it since the Confession.

"Your Church," they said, obviously knowing the gravity of

their demand, because I saw the tenseness in their every feature. "Not your faith," they amended more softly. "Not your beliefs. But your Church, Isidor... the Order, the Ministry, the institution itself. I can't share in your life if you're still pledged in your heart to them. They don't believe that I exist. They preach from the pulpit that people like me should be shamed, jailed, mutilated...."

"I am a person like you now, too," I said, unashamedly.

"That frightens me, too," they said. "To consider that you might try to return to the fold. To be with your Father or reclaim the purpose you felt as a Templar. I'm not just scared for myself. I'm scared for *you*. I'll support you however you wish to practice your faith; I will listen and try to understand. But your religion teaches that anyone non-canid is a lesser person. It empowers families like the Rathbornes who make this country a less safe and prosperous place to live for anyone except people who look *exactly like them*. Even Cillian suffered because of them."

They reached a hand up to gently cup the fringe of fur along my jaw. "I know how much that book matters to you, and the experiences you had in your Abbey. I'm certain many of them were... inspiring. Joyous."

I nodded, leaning into their hand with my cheek. I found myself walking the halls of Ebon Gables in memories, realizing then that I'd never see the sun set through the stained glass again. Never feel the paving stones of the cloisters on my paw pads. Never again smell the library... except perhaps in dreams. I'd been doing so much crying today, but it was impossible not to stain Darcy's hand as the realization of what I'd lost hit me like a wave.

"I'm *so* sorry to ask this of you," they said again. "But I've never been an equal of anyone who claimed to love me, Isidor. I've never known what it is to feel my dedication repaid in kind.

And I will *never* be your partner, your priority, your equal, if we live under the banner of your Church. I can't do it again. I can't know I matter... less... to you... than what they'll ask you to do. How they'll ask you to live. Wondering if the day will come when you'll decide I don't *fit* into your life. That I've become... inconvenient. It will drive me to madness, being frightened it will all happen again."

They leaned up and kissed me briefly, their expression pained as they pulled away. "Love your God, and pray, worship... keep your faith, for as long as you still believe. I've seen what it means to you and how it bolsters you. I don't want you to lose that. But the Church itself..." they leaned into me, their breath warm against my clavicle.

"I'm sorry, Isidor. I'll be your friend if you must remain a part of it. But you need to choose."

Even excommunicated, I could still sit down in a church in Carvecia, or wherever we were going, if I was not known there. I had assumed that I would, eventually. The idea of never stepping into a house of worship again had honestly never occurred to me.

But I could never walk amongst the clergy again, never take Confession again, unless I was willing to be dishonest about who I was. Never wear my rosary without risking being asked which Parish I hailed from. I would have to use a false name for safety's sake. Even a continent away. I had effectively lost my surname. I would not be buried in consecrated soil, when I died. I would never marry. Not unless I lied about my birthplace, my past, Darcy's very identity... and I was not willing to lie to a Priest.

I knew this should have been more difficult for me. It should have.

But it wasn't.

"I choose you," I said simply.

Darcy began to smile slowly. It was the most beautiful they had ever looked to me. The quiet joy, the happiness I was able to bestow, finally… upon someone who'd been waiting their entire life to be loved.

"I already made my decision, as well," I said. "I've just clung all this while, because I thought it… defined me."

I slowly unwound the rosary and held it in my palm, staring down at it for a long time. It was Darcy's palm moving under my own, closing my fingers back around it, that snapped me out of it.

"Your Father gave you that, right?" they asked.

I nodded.

"I did a lot of good over the years through thievery," they said with fearless certainty. "It's still a part of who I am and it always will be. I can't even say I won't find good cause to do so again, if our survival is at stake. *Most* thieves steal to live."

"I relied on the Ministry to survive, when I was young," I said quietly. "They saved my life."

They nodded. "Nothing's so neat and easy as washing your hands of your past. The Church did a lot of good for you, meant a lot to you, and that's simply a truth. Even if you're at cross-purposes in life now. A lot of the relics, the art, the jewelry I've reclaimed for people over the years have complicated histories. Keep it. Hold on to it and remember."

I wrapped the rosary back around my wrist and the bracelet left to me by my blood family. An heirloom that apparently had a spiritual significance to northern peoples that I'd never even known.

Complicated. That was the truth, if ever I'd heard it. Life had been simpler when I'd lived within the rigid restrictions and confining routines of Ebon Gables. I was becoming a patched tapestry of experiences and beliefs at odds with one another. But I was questioning. I was learning. I was in love. I was loved.

If it didn't all fit together just yet, that meant I had more to learn, before I was whole. And I liked learning.

"God is with me," I pressed a closed palm to my heart. "He is everywhere, not just in houses of worship, sermons, and ceremonies. I'll find my faith somewhere. There is too much I wish to know, to understand, that they will not allow me to experience. I love my God, and I can feel His love, I have not lost that. But I love you too, Darcy. And until the Church I grew up in can love you, can open their arms to people like you... like myself... I won't risk our health and happiness clinging to what I once had there."

Darcy leaned up and pressed our noses together, whispering a soft, "Thank you."

"I am an open book," I said, brushing our muzzles alongside one another. "I cannot curtail my feelings or offer myself halfway. Whatever there is for us out there, together... I promise, I will give you nothing less than all of me."

Their laugh, breathy and sweet, like the one that had taunted me outside my coach house door a lifetime ago, lit me up inside like spring had blossomed in my chest. "Then I guess I'll take you, Isidor of Ebon Gables. How does that sound?"

"You stole me away long ago," I promised them.

They kissed me again, and I them. When they leaned back after several long, breathless moments, they said, "You are a fine prize for my final heist."

I laughed. "You were my first *and* final quarry." I wrapped my arms around their waist, tugging them in closer, and leaned down to whisper against their ear. "Caught you."

End

SPECIAL THANKS TO

Special thanks to all of my Editors, Sensitivity Readers, Beta Readers, and supporters from streams and Patreon. This world and the denizens of it would never see the page if not for all of you.

From the bottom of my heart, thank you.

Kyell Gold - **Bryan Ozawa** - **Cassie** - **Chris** - **Alastair** - **Brandon RavusFur** - **Randall** - **Rolf Piercey** - **Snøw** - **Glassan** - **Scandhoovian**

Colin Leighton - Marcwolf - BlackDawg - Petrov Neutrino - Commander Wolf - Soulwolven - Trejaan - Lucian Greywolf - Marmalade - AJ Nemeth - Edef - Ferlynx - RaiderWolf - AeroWolfDeer - SILVERWOLF380 - Dyxxander - RF Red Fox - Roarschach - Sylleath - Seth Cherwell - Doug K. - Alteo - Wulfgar Marrock (RGFuzzwolf) - ScionOfSkoll - J. N. Squire from Baguetteland - Flann - Clint Marsh - Madi - Jhey Wolffe - Windwolf55x5 - Lillian Rafter - Y-Fox - Tiderace Jenkins -

SPECIAL THANKS TO

Verager - PhyerPhox - Zachs - Yuuryuu - AiraActual -
Mvh. Mads Damgaard Mortensen - Kiska Beaust -
Skunkbomb - Andrea Jae - Sunkawaken - Thomas Proffitt

ABOUT THE AUTHOR

Rukis is a freelance illustrator/writer who lives in South Carolina, USA.She has a BFA in Animation from the Rochester Institute of Technology, with a focus in Conceptual Design for Animation and Film. Early in life, she knew she wanted to work in either the animation or comics industry, and struck out on her own after college to do just that. After many years spent working a 9-5 and building her portfolio, she published her first comic *Cruelty* with FurPlanet in 2010. Since then, she has published two other comic titles, various short comics in anthropomorphic anthologies, and written and illustrated ten novels, as well as done a number of illustrations and covers for other writers in the Anthropomorphic community. Her comic *Red Lantern*, novel *Off the Beaten Path* and her cover for Kyell Gold's *Green Fairy* won Ursa Major Awards.

Other than illustration and writing, Rukis spends almost all of her free time hiking, mountain biking, gardening, and working on her small farm in South Carolina.

Her desire for her books is that they entertain, educate, make you feel something, stoke a curiosity for history, and a hope for a more loving and diverse world.

𝕏 x.com/rukiscroax
🅟 patreon.com/rukis

ABOUT THE PUBLISHER

FurPlanet productions is a small press publisher serving the niche market that is furry fiction. They sell furry-themed books and comics published by themselves and most major publishers in the community. If you can't get to a furry convention where they are selling in the dealers room, visit their online stores: FurPlanet.com for print books and BadDogBooks.com for eBooks.

facebook.com/furplanet

x.com/furplanet

animal.business/@furplanet

Milton Keynes UK
Ingram Content Group UK Ltd.
UKHW022006211124
451438UK00009B/233

9 781614 506232